Twisted City

THE COMPLETE DUET
RIA WILDE

Copyright © 2022 Ria Wilde
All rights reserved

The characters and events portrayed in this book are fictitious. Any similarity to real persons, living or dead, is coincidental and not intended by the author.

No part of this book may be reproduced, or stored in a retrieval system, or transmitted in any form or by any means, electronic, mechanical, photocopying, recording, or otherwise, without express written permission of the publisher.

ISBN: 9798842554997

Author Note

This is a dark romance meaning there are themes commonly found in dark romance, this includes a captor/captive romance, kidnap, murder, violence, drug & alcohol use, heavy sexual content & strong language.
There are mentions of SA, Human Trafficking, Self Harm and Suicide.
It is advised not to be read by those under the age of 18.

PART ONE
LITTLE BIRD

She kissed me.
She kissed the devil.
Only a beautiful soul like hers would kiss the damned.

- Daniel Saint

Prologue

Lex

"Get down!" The order comes from Ryker, a beast of a man with an even beastlier temper. He drops like a lead weight, his body hitting the floor with a loud thud, and I follow, a little dazed, my ears ringing and pulsing, the blood pumping like a drum inside my head. The blast that happened only moments ago was, to say the least, unexpected.

I feel blood, warm and sticky, slowly trickling down the side of my face, rolling over my skin until it seeps into the stubble lining my jaw. The smell of ash, blood and death saturates the air. Dust makes it almost impossible to see, huge clouds of white smog disturbed only by the wind blowing in through the smashed windows at the front of the house, curling like snakes as it is illuminated from the flood lights outside.

What the fuck is happening!?

On my front, my elbows to the ground, I begin to crawl across the debris, pushing passed the dead bodies and the puddles of crimson blooming in the rubble. Death wasn't a new sight for me and seeing these people, people I know, staring wide eyed at the ceiling with blood leaking from various wounds does nothing to me. It brings no emotion, no pain or guilt or sadness.

Death, after all, was inevitable. One of the only things in life that is guaranteed. I learned long ago that you'd never be able to run from it, you cannot hide but sometimes, and it's rare, you *could* control how it ended.

There was no way, with the life I lead that I would be granted a peaceful exit. You enter this world violently; I see it only fitting that be the way you leave it too. And that's how I hoped it would be. I wanted bloody, destructive, a ruin that flattens buildings and is remembered for years to come. But that time is yet to arrive, this won't be the end for me.

I grip my gun, pulling it from where I had stashed it earlier this evening and move towards the smashed windows. The device had been launched through the glass where it landed and promptly exploded. There was no warning, no tell, one moment we were enjoying a small gathering with some of the city officials, an event set up by my father, the next, the window shattered, and a small round object hit the mahogany floor, a little red light flashing rapidly. It must have only been a few seconds at most and then *boom*! The device detonated, sending bodies flying. Some were hit with shrapnel, others slammed into the walls or other objects close by.

"Alexander!" I hear Ryker call out, but it's muffled, like I'm listening while I'm under water. "Lex!"

The man was only doing his job, protecting me but at the end of the day, he may be a beast, a monster to anyone looking in from the outside, but I was the motherfucking devil. And the devil wouldn't take this laying down. No fucking way would that shit fly, he'll be standing amongst the carnage with a smile on his face.

Whoever had just hit us has broken the one rule that separates us men from beasts.

There's no hiding the fact that, as the Silver family, we had made countless enemies, but in that list of foes, who would be stupid enough to hit us like this?

No one is innocent, they never have been but there are unwritten laws that are woven into the fabric of who we are. We run this city and have done for generations, those around us abide by it if they want to remain within the city limits and capitalize on what we have created.

With my Glock gripped in my hands, slicked with blood, I rise to survey the gardens through the broken window. The flood lights blare a white light onto the lawns of the city centre house, and within it, I see shapes moving through the grounds.

It's a fucking small army.

"Who the fuck is it?" I demand.

"The Valentine's!" Ryker answers immediately.

The fucking Valentine's.

I growl but don't respond as I watch the small band of armed men approach. Of course it's the fucking Valentine's.

Those sick motherfuckers had been threatening us since their last shipment got intercepted. If they had listened to the fucking instructions, we wouldn't have gotten involved, but clearly they were too dumb to catch on.

The Silver's rule Brookeshill and while it's big, there's no room for the two of us, not when Valentine wants to take the crown.

"Lex!" My father's voice rings through the chaos, through the shadows and bloodshed, I hear the grief tearing him apart. My heart sinks, my gut churns. I don't feel the physical pain of my injuries, years of conditioning and training makes that a dull ache in the background, but this, this is something I haven't been trained for.

I may be ruthless. Brutal. The fucking King but no amount of warning or preparation would have made me ready for what I see walking through the ruin towards me.

My father, dirty, battered, bleeding, carrying a lifeless body in his arms. Her hair dangles limply, her arms and legs swinging with each step he takes towards my prone body at the window.

"Mr Silver," Ryker panics, "Mr Silver, they're preparing to fire, you need to get down!"

The men take aim out the windows, if I look both left and right, I could see them all, hidden for the event but now available and ready to be used.

The Silver's are royalty in this city. We are Kings. Queens. Fucking Gods. And these guys, the ones preparing to rage war on the intruders are loyal and they always would be.

My father doesn't heed Ryker's warning, instead his legs numbly carry him forward, towards me.

"Cover me," I demand from Ryker who immediately takes my position. The fucker is huge and takes up the entire window, using his mass to shield me as I move towards my father.

As feared, the woman in his arms is dead. Her eyes are open, her smooth skin covered in blood, the white dress no longer white and instead stained in crimson and black.

I hold it back. The emotion that begs to be released gets lodged in the back of my throat becoming acidic and poisonous. It makes my windpipe close, my lungs constrict.

"Son," my father's voice cracks.

Cracks.

We're talking about a man who never questions his morals when he raises the barrel of a gun to someone's head, never bats an eyelid when the blade of his knife slices across someone's throat and will stand upon his enemies with his chin lifted and madness in his eyes, breaking – fucking *breaking* – in front of his men.

We don't do that.

We don't show weakness.

"I'll kill them all," I declare. "Slowly. Painfully. If it's war the Valentine's want, then it's war I'll give them."

ONE
Wren

Six months later

"Again," Griff orders, breathing in heavily with his body still prone to fight, watching from his position in the middle of the mat.

The rims of my nostrils flare, my skin wet with sweat and probably a little bit of blood too. The motherfucker got in a cheap shot earlier and it's been bleeding a steady stream ever since, a stream which mingles with my perspiration to make it watery enough to drip from my chin and onto the blue foam beneath my bare feet.

I grunt and cross the mat in a sprint, my legs carrying me stealthily. When I'm close, instead of running right into the guy like he expects, I leap to the side, spinning around and hooking my arm around his throat, throwing my body down. I quickly release and land in a crouch to the side as Griff hits the mat hard. His back thuds and his head bounces, and for a moment, just a brief second, I worry I went in too hard.

Twisted City

RIA WILDE

Unexpectedly, a rough laugh vibrates from his chest, "Good. That was good."

"Are we done?" I breathe in deep, trying to steady the chaotic thump of my heart. I wipe the blood with the back of my hand, no doubt spreading it over my cheek but at this point, I don't care. I have places to be, people to see.

"Yeah, Wren, we're done." Griff levels himself up onto his elbows, quirking one dark brow my way, "You're distracted today." I liked Griff, I've been training with him for a couple of years now and he's taught me everything I know but because of that, he knew me well enough to be able to pick up when my head wasn't in the session.

"I'm busy," I snap back, grabbing my towel and rubbing it across my brow and then down my face before swiping up my water bottle and taking a couple of healthy gulps.

"Too busy for your family?"

And there it is. Regardless of whether I liked Griff, I knew any and all information he got from me during these sessions would end up back with my father. He had become a middle man, a messenger of sorts.

I roll my eyes, "More like they're too busy for me."

"Your father asked me to request your presence at dinner tonight."

"Of course, he did," it's like the man has a link to my diary – if I had one of course – and purposely steps in when he thinks I'm about to go out and have fun. God forbid I do anything where I actually enjoy myself. "Tell him no."

"We all know, 'no', isn't in the vocabulary that your father understands."

"Well give him a dictionary at the same time, you can find it under the letter N."

Griff chuckles, "I'll tell him, but I'd turn your phone off if I were you, you'll have a thousand voicemails by morning."

I nod. That would be likely, "Later Griff, take some aspirin for the headache."

He shakes his head and climbs up from the mat as I push through the doors that'll lead back to the changing rooms. The gym is quiet this evening, only a few other people work out on the equipment in the main room, the steady thump of sneakers on the treadmill mingling with the heavy bass music that crackles from a sound system that has seen better days.

Whenever we train, we use one of the back rooms, a private area that's usually reserved for lessons, but Griff owns the gym himself and personally sees to my training. Training my father demands I take, along with the gun training, knife training and any other means of self-defense. The man is paranoid, that much is obvious.

I supposed I had him to thank for the ease in which I'm able to defend and protect myself, in this day and age, being a woman who can hold her own is everything. I shower quickly and then change into the dress I had stashed in the bag, pulling out my makeup and hair brush at the same time. It wasn't ideal having to hit the bar straight from training, but with time against me, I had no choice.

I knew better than to believe my dad was simply just paranoid. I'd heard the late-night calls and witnessed the guys coming and going in hours not meant to be seen by civilization. Not guys like him, dressed in tailored suits and Italian loathers, but big guys, in leather and ripped jeans. It wasn't their clothes that set them apart from the men my dad usually associates with, but the ruthless glint they all held in their eyes. Hard, rough…not much scared me but those fuckers were *terrifying*.

Now you tell me, what would a man, who sits as a CEO of a multi-million-dollar company, have need for guys who carried guns concealed and tucked away on their body, the same men that carry knives placed into boots and holsters at their thighs.

It's not the behavior of a man who lives life within the carefully set boundaries.

The conversations I've overheard suggest something much darker, dirtier in fact, drugs, guns…

I had no doubt my father was involved in something way bigger than the company he is determined to give to me when he retires. Something much seedier and dangerous.

The paranoia is one reason he forces me to train like this but it's his lifestyle that has determined that fact and made it a necessity.

I apply a small layer of makeup to my face, hiding the flush in my cheeks still present from training, trying my best to conceal the split in my lip, and run my fingers through my still wet hair, the strands curling already. By the end of the night it'll be wild, the curls tight and unruly, but I don't have time to tend to it now.

Rory – Aurora, my best friend – was meeting me in twenty minutes at a cocktail bar down the street and if I were late, she'd have my head. We made sure to plan far in advance,

Twisted City

RIA WILDE

like six weeks in advance and she's been reminding me every other day for the past three weeks. My schedule was always manic, thanks to my family but I made sure my father knew and understood tonight was blocked out. His request I join him for dinner isn't his want for a nice family meal, it is, in fact, a try at controlling my life, just like it always is.

The dress clings to my frame, the neckline low, dipping well below my cleavage, almost to my naval and the hem sits just above my knee, the swirls of black ink on my thigh only just peeking out from the bottom. It's late summer so the nights are still warm enough to forego a jacket which means my sleeve tattoo is on full show tonight. I stare at my reflection, at the copper hair already kinking and curling atop my head and my wide green eyes that seem almost too big for my face.

It'll do, I guess. My feet slip into the black strappy sandals I had packed to go with the dress and then I walk from the locker rooms and out into the evening. The light of day clings to the skyline, the sky a dusty indigo colour with slashes of pink and orange. My Audi lights blink when I press the button and then I climb into the drivers seat, shoving my gym bag into the back where it'll likely stay for a week. Music blasts from the stereo when I turn the key in the ignition and press on the gas, peeling out of the near empty lot of the gym, heading towards the bar. It's where we're starting but not where we're finishing according to Aurora. It's been far too long since I hit the clubs with my best friend, after the last time it had become almost impossible to plan anything with her, until I put my foot down with my father.

I was twenty-three, far too young to spend every weekend locked up in the apartment I rented downtown, but with the security personnel my father hired it had become impossible to escape.

I had managed, somehow, to convince my dad to let it go. What happened a few months back was something that could have happened to anyone. The guys that cornered me after a night out were thugs, criminals and while I had tried to handle them myself, I still ended up in the hospital with several broken ribs and a face that looked like I had gone ten rounds in the ring with a professional MMA fighter. I took out at least three of them, a point my dad overlooks. Ever since then he's hired bodyguards to see me everywhere. Not tonight though. Tonight I'm free.

A little bubble of excitement works its way through my system, and I press on the gas, heading down the street to my apartment building where I'm planning on leaving my car. I park in the underground garage and then take the elevator up to street level. There are still enough people and traffic out that I don't have to worry about being in trouble and wander down the sidewalk towards the glowing blue sign for the cocktail bar I was meeting Rory at.

I find her perched at a high-top table, her black dress tight and revealing, her blonde hair dead straight and hanging around her face like a curtain. She's not like me in the sense of the word, where I grew up in a huge mansion at the edge of the city, she grew up down at the trailer park with an alcoholic father and a mother who walked out on her when she was only three.

Not that you would know it by looking at her now. She was finishing up college and will go on to become a teacher at Brookeshill Elementary School.

She waves enthusiastically and I cross the room, the clip of my heels loud in the quiet space. The music is on low, a gentle hum rather than blasting, and groups of people laugh and converse all around me.

Fuck, I hadn't realized how long it had been since I felt normal.

I try to ignore all the shit with my family, the dodgy dealings, the late-night phone calls and the odd blood stains on my father's sleeves but that shit isn't easy to forget. I know, *I know*, that my family is far from clean, I just hope he didn't expect me to follow in his footsteps.

I had no idea what exactly he was involved in, and I don't want to know.

"Damn," Rory grins, "you look great."

I flick my hair and flutter my lashes dramatically, with a laugh I say, "Thanks."

With her manicured fingers, she pushes the pornstar martini towards me and takes a sip of her own, "To freedom!"

I chuckle, tipping my head back, "To freedom!"

The first sip of the cocktail goes down far too smoothly, "So where to after this?"

She wiggles her brow, "Club Silver."

I quirk a brow, "Wow, how'd you secure that?"

Club Silver opened in downtown a little over four months ago and has been in popular demand ever since. The city was alive at night, with hundreds of clubs thriving, but since that one opened, it's where everyone wants to go, to the point you now have to book in advance and pay a premium booking fee to secure a space.

She purses her lips with a frown, "I'm not really sure, actually," she laughs, "I ran into some guy the other day, a bit scary looking but he was handing out personal invites to the club and I just so happened to be in the right place at the right time."

I shrug, "Seems like fate to me."

Rory giggles and tips back the remaining dregs of her cocktail before she hops from the stool and heads to the bar to order a few more. I sit there, the alcohol I've consumed warming my veins, settling into my empty stomach. Shit I didn't have time to eat after training and by the end of the night I'm sure I'll be feeling it. I glance towards the front of the bar, looking behind the servers running back and forth to accompany the heaving crowd to see if they do food or even small appetizers, just to line my stomach and yet what I find, is anything but food.

Well I mean, I suppose he could be classed as a snack, I guess.

A tailored suit, the fit not too tight yet tight enough to tease at the muscles he has concealed underneath. The white shirt is tucked into black pants, the buckle of his belt gleaming in the dim lighting. Silver cufflinks, no tie, the top two buttons undone to reveal tanned, olive toned skin. Dark stubble lines the sharp edge of his jaw, high, defined cheek bones and low set brows, low enough to cast shadows over his steel eyes. A mop of dark hair falls over his forehead, too long to be deemed professional and I should know having been around the stuffy suits working at my father's offices every day, none of them would dare let their hair grow that long. Always short, always tamed, like the good little robots they are.

He's staring right at me. I've never been one to flirt or

even hook up, I'm no virgin but the look he's levelling me with can only be classed as *hot*.

Though it's not quite there, like something is missing but I just can't figure out what.

Sure, from the way his eyes travel over my body, his gaze moving over my bare legs, stopping a little at the black ink peeking out from the hem of my dress but then moving on quickly over my hips, to the curve of my waist and then further up, following the deep V of my dress where my breasts push together – thank you body tape – and then down my right arm where the ink is etched into my skin. Flowers and mandalas, intricate and delicate, feminine, though my family hate them. It's probably why I did it. I knew they wouldn't like the art, just like the nose ring, just like the piercing in my naval. I was young when I did them, a little naïve and yet I don't regret it at all.

A frown mars his brow, as if confused but it happens so quickly I wonder if I imagined it and then his eyes travel the rest of the way up my body, over my collar and neck before finally levelling his stare with my own.

He tips a short crystal glass to his lips, a small amount of amber liquid pouring into his mouth, keeping his eyes on me over the rim of the glass.

When I finally allow myself to concentrate my eyes on his and truly look, all I find is heat, an intense burn but it's mingled with a ruthlessness I'm sad to recognize. A coldness, a brutality I've seen in the guys that visit my father. His is harder, deeper, colder, like that side of him isn't something that comes out every now and then, it is what makes him the man he is. A shiver runs its way down my spine, a warning signal and natural survival instinct to let me know I'm in the company of a predator.

Twisted City   RIA WILDE

My father made damn sure I'd never be a damsel, even the attack a few months back I stood my ground, but I can't help feeling less than and weaker here. He isn't the type of guy I'd want to encounter in the dark. Though you'll be damn sure I'd give it a good go.

There are monsters everywhere, Wren, my fathers voice echoes inside my head, a phantom whisper ensuring I stay alert at all times, *it isn't the monster under your bed or in your closet that you need to watch out for, it's the ones that look like me and you that you should fear. It's the ones that seem completely normal and yet they hide an evil in their eyes. That's where you'll find it, Wren, in their eyes. When you see that, make sure you run. Run as far and as fast as you can.*

I didn't want to run though. I wanted to show the world I could handle myself. I didn't need bodyguards and security. My father saw it fit to train me to the absolute best of my ability, he honed my skill, taught me how to use my size and speed to my advantage, all because of his shady side business and while I may *disagree* with it, I wanted to prove I could handle myself.

I square my shoulders and narrow my eyes, a pretty face and a body made of sin wouldn't be enough to deceive me. He can believe he's found an easy target in me, but I'm prepared to prove him wrong.

Aurora saunters back with two glasses filled with a sparkling pink liquid laced with small pieces of cut strawberries and hops up onto the stool. Her brows draw down as she follows my eyes and slides my drink towards me.

"Well hello tall, dark, and handsome," Rory sucks her teeth.

Twisted City RIA WILDE

I force my eyes away and turn back to my friend, giving the guy my back which seems like a mistake. You never turn your back on a predator. I'm not prey though and if he chooses to strike, I'll be ready.

"What's this?" I ask, sliding my glass the final few inches towards me and wrap my lips around the straw, drawing from the glass.

Fizz and sugar hit my tongue, the drink is so sweet it makes my jaw ache. Rory just shrugs, "Last one and then we're heading to Silver."

I nod, taking another sip. The alcohol buzz from earlier has dissipated, leaving only awareness in its wake. I'm alert, ready, my senses homing in on my surroundings, listening for approaching footsteps. If there is one thing I have learned from all the self defense classes I have partaken in, it's that the human instinct to danger is very rarely wrong, but as humans evolved we started to ignore that basic nature, choosing to blindly trust and naively believe we were all safe.

We drink our drinks and I act my part, laughing, talking, joking and it's only when I'm halfway to finished, that the heat in my back finally subsides. I subtly glance behind me to find the stool at the bar vacant, the space where he was occupying completely empty.

I relax. Hopefully, he's gone on to find some other helpless girl to terrorize.

I don't know who he is, or what he could ever want with a girl like me but I sensed that danger and when I saw him, the man with eyes so pale they rivaled the moon, I could tell that his breed of brutality wasn't one I'd easily survive.

TWO
Lex

I've studied the images. I've followed the lines of her bountiful curves, the dips and flares of her thighs, her hips. I've watched videos. I've witnessed her beauty through those, seen it already with my own two eyes, and even then, I thought she was a beautiful woman, but seeing her here, in a dress that barely covers her sinfully delectable body, with her delicately painted tattoos and wild red hair, I was caught off guard, unprepared for what she could look like face to face.

The legs, the body, the face with the mass of copper curls and the innocent eyes.

The innocent eyes. No one is innocent, there is always something they are guilty for, we are all sinners here but there's something about the way the innocence looks on her that almost makes me feel guilty.

Almost.

I laugh at myself. Emotion. I lost that a long time ago. The guilt tugs at the corners of my mind, trying to push in but I shut that shit out. Just like I was taught. The girl is a means to an end. The need for vengeance far outweighs a crisis of conscience. I am not a man of morality, and it wasn't physically possible for a woman like her to suddenly arouse any sense of right and wrong. We didn't get to be where we were with integrity or decency.

She's gorgeous, I can appreciate that, but in this walk of life I encounter beautiful women all the time, I have them on my arm, in my bed, impaled on my cock and screaming my name. There was nothing special about her apart from the purpose in which I needed her for.

I glance down at my phone, looking at the image on the screen.

Wren.

Twenty-three, recent graduate with honors.

Smart girl.

And *exactly* who it is I need.

The plan has been in the works for six months now, and we're finally in the last stretch.

My father hasn't been the same since the night my mother was murdered, and it's been on me to keep going. I stepped up. It's *my* fucking time and I'm going to start it by sending a message.

A message to show no mercy, no pity. There will be no question from here on out who rules this city. I am King.

And they're all going to fucking know it.

I push off the stool, my eyes still trained on her back,

following the curve of her waist, the flare of her hips, the swell of her ass and allow myself, just for a moment, to picture how her plump lips would look wrapped around my dick. It's a shame such potential will end up buried in a six foot ditch.

Marcus Valentine was smart, I'd give him that, *if* I could give him anything.

I knew exactly where she would end up tonight, after all, it was my plan this entire time, and there was no way I was letting her slip from my fingers.

Leaving her in the cocktail bar with her friend, I head down the street to Club Silver. Music thumps from the building, filling the street in both directions and I head right for the front doors, slipping in past Matthew who nods at me and continues checking ID's at the door.

The dim lighting of the club casts me in shadows and instead of weaving the crowd that grinds and gyrates to the nineties music that blasts from the speakers I cut left and head through a door, camouflaged to look like it's part of the wall, one that is marked Storage but drops to a steep stairwell that will take me beneath the club. There were only two doors that will get me down here, this one and another outside. The concrete is thick, the music above only a steady thump as I descend, vibrating the walls.

A second club opens up before me, one not known to the people above, to the simple mundane citizens of this city, one where deals go ahead, gambling, girls in scantily clad gear that rub up against men in suits with lines of coke dusting the tables and offered on silver platters. A place where blood is as common as the soil lining a flower bed and corruption is what fills the pockets of this city's most influential people.

A girl wearing red lace lingerie struts towards me, her skin almost glowing beneath the lighting, a smirk lifting the corners of her red painted mouth as she offers out a tray. Right alongside the scotch are two lines of the white shit and I debate, I really do, but with the need to have my head in the plan I bypass it for this evening.

I take a glass and throw it back, draining the amber liquid inside before taking the second and leaving the drugs.

"Anything else?" She asks in a low sultry voice, her eyes hooded, the long lashes she's applied casting shadows over her cheeks. She thrusts her chest out, the half-moons of her breasts spilling out of the cups that hold the rest of her in. "Does the boss need a little relaxation perhaps?"

I couldn't have any distractions tonight, I wasn't risking my plan.

"Another time," I tell her, leaning in to whisper the words in her ear, "make sure to find me when I'm next here."

"Yes sir," she breathes and I step back, eyeing the athletically toned body, slim, long legs and narrow hips.

"What's your name?" I ask.

"Josie," she answers.

"Have a good night, Josie," I say, extracting a wad of cash from my pocket and tucking it into the waist band of her tight, red lace panties.

A flush of pink rises to her cheeks, even under this dim light I see it, but I leave her still and head towards the elevators on the other side that'll take me up to the balcony that overlooks the revelers in the club.

My key card opens the door and muffled noise greets me inside the metal cart. A mixture of the low, erotic music of the underground club and the heavy bass of Club Silver above. The elevator is slow, but I don't mind as it takes me back up.

In the time it takes to move up levels, I remember the faces I saw, the Mayor and police chief were here tonight, that's good, buried in the lines of coke offered to them and the girls perched in their laps. The hidden cameras will be enough should they ever step out of line. A couple of high-ranking corporate bodies were there too, a few government officials.

Of course these people would never enter through the main doors, they would slip in behind, down a back alley that would take them through the back entrance and then further down to the club below. Club Silver offered them anonymity, something they'd never get anywhere else. Everyone had a darkness to them though they were never given the opportunity for it to come out. That's where I come in. I give them what they crave and in return, I get what I need.

When I set up the club this was exactly what I had in mind.

My father was a ruthless leader, but he didn't have it all planned out.

He went forward on brutality and bloodshed, fear that would stop even the fiercest of men, but I would be smarter. I will *stay* king, because of my reputation people knew, like a deep-rooted instinct that in this city, they were the prey and me, I was the predator. I didn't fear that these men would cross me and even if they did, I had plenty of back up to ensure they stayed in line. Images.

Transactions. Videos. All of which could be shared to the entire city, to the entire world in fact in a matter of seconds. It is that knowledge that keeps them in my pocket and me on top.

Blackmail.

Every man in this city was riding on power and if you threatened to take that away you could guarantee they'd be on their knees begging. Every damn time.

It makes life a whole lot easier when the cops aren't breathing down your neck and the mayor is backing your every move without a single question.

And if that didn't work, well there are other methods of keeping people quiet and in line. Something a lot bloodier. There wasn't much I wouldn't do, blood to me was as normal as turning on a tap. A little messier but a whole lot more fun.

The elevator doors slide open though now the clock has struck eleven, the music and atmosphere of the club has changed. The playlist is now blasting out more modern music, hip hop, garage, and the bodies on the dance floor continue to grind. There is no need to grab a drink, one is waiting for me as I exit the elevator and I lift it from the tray, continuing my way forward until I'm at the glass railing and looking down at the floor below.

Ry steps up beside me, "it's all set, boss."

He'd started calling me boss about a month after my mother's death and coming from my closest and longest friend, it took some getting used to. In closed quarters, we were still that, but here, in the open, he was nothing more than a loyal dog, he knew it, I knew it.

I dip my chin in acknowledgment and sip at the scotch in my hand. Behind me a few guys take the affection a couple of the wait staff give them and for now, I allow it. Until *she* shows, they can do whatever the fuck they want.

They've earned it after all.

It's a little past midnight when a security guard steps into my space, "She's here, Mr Silver," he whispers close to my ear so only I can hear.

I nod and continue to watch.

She's a presence to be known. A goddess amongst the mundane. Her unruly copper hair and tight curves draw attention but it's the look in her eyes that has people stepping away to create a path. Her friend tags along behind, following the tempest that is Wren Valentine.

"Damn," Ryker chuckles.

I risk a glance his way, taking my eyes off her for a second, "What?"

"I mean, Wren is," he presses his fingers to his lips and blows a kiss, "but her friend, I'd drop to my knees and promise her the world if I could."

"You always did like the blondes," I grumble, turning my attention back to the girl in question.

She makes it to the bar and leans forward, no doubt showing the deep cut of her dress to draw attention. She was beautiful and she knew exactly how to use it. I liked a woman unafraid of using her strengths to her advantage, but I also wasn't stupid enough to believe that it was only her body she could use to win over the enemy. Her smarts were impressive and if I were any other man, I may even congratulate her on her achievements. But I am not any other man and that girl, leaning over the bar to get what she wanted, was exactly where I needed her to be because I deemed it so.

It's a matter of moments before she's served and then she's passing back a cocktail of some sort to her friend and a simple drink for herself, a beverage with cola I assume judging from the dark colour of it.

With a grin they weave back through the crowd to the dance floor.

I need information from the girl and yet my mind can't help but snag on the way she moves to the music, the hypnotic way her hips sway and her body curls. She brings her arms up, her hands tucking into the under layers of her hair as she sensually sways to the beat. I'd call it magic if didn't know any better. She was a fucking siren.

"Fuck," I hear a guy say behind me, "I'd fucking destroy that."

I follow his gaze and, low and behold, it's Wren he's talking about.

She is fucking *glorious*.

She'll look even better when she is strapped to a bed, legs spread, curls wild around her face, at my mercy, the fucking king.

I twist my head to him, my eyes narrowed, jaw tight, "What did you just say?"

His eyes meet mine and he visually cowers, "Nothing," a stutter, "nothing boss."

"Keep your fucking eyes in your head," I tell him, my voice warning enough as I turn back to Wren.

A couple of guys have descended on her and her friend, one has slipped behind her, his hips moving forward to grind into her ass.

Her brows draw low and she spins on him, fists balling. I can't hear what she says but he backs off, raising his hands in surrender.

Wren resumes dancing but it's not long before another guy steps up to try and claim what is rightfully mine.

My nostrils flare.

"Keep your eye out," I tell Ryker.

He nods once, knowing my entire plan as I take the first step down to the dance floor. I feel his gaze follow me until I find my mark in the middle of the dance floor.

Wren smells as good as she looks, sweet and yet deadly, it assaults my senses as I step up close behind her.

She spins on me, her little fists balled up real tight, her brows pulled down low and violence shining in her eyes.

"You," She accuses.

"Me," I answer back, knowing she already clocked me back at the cocktail bar.

Her eyes narrow as she brings her hands up, unfurling her fingers almost absentmindedly to grip my biceps, her nails digging in just enough to allow a bite against my skin, "You found me."

I laugh though it holds no humour as I lean in and whisper

in her ear, "I own this place. It appears *you* found *me*."

Her breath comes out in a gasp that teases my hair and brushes against the shell of my ear.

"Who are you?"

"You want to know?" I ask.

Her hands slide from my biceps to the lapels of my suit jacket. She seems to be at war with herself, wanting to know more but telling herself she shouldn't. Good, it means the book smart leaches into the street smart. Her eyes narrow further as my arms slip around her waist, holding her flush to my body. Seeing and feeling are two very different things, you can imagine what something may feel like but until it's in your grasp, it will only ever be make believe. Feeling the way her waist dips and curves is so much more than what I could have imagined. The urge, the primal need to simply take her, have her, *own* her almost has me wishing to throw her over my shoulder and lock her up for completely different reasons.

"Yes, I want to know."

"You can call me Alexander. Or Lex."

"Surname?"

"Silver."

I wait and then wait some more for the realization to come but it never hits.

"I'm Wren," she continues, sliding her hands to my shoulders, "Wren Lawson."

"Want to know me a little more, Wren Lawson?"

A grin tugs at her plump mouth, her lips stained with a deep burgundy colour, "I don't think so."

My brows shoot up. Was there ever a day I had been denied?

"No?"

"No."

My fingers trail down the curve of her waist until I find her hip where my fingers then grip, biting into her flesh. Her eyes flash something dark, seductive, dirty but she quickly conceals it all. "Goodnight, Mr Silver."

I let her weave back through the crowd towards the bar, watching her, if she knew who I was she would have bolted for the door. A sheep in the lion's den was a dead fucking sheep and yet here she still is.

Suspicion and curiosity war with each other in my head.

But at the end of the day, this was a war and she was the next step to winning.

THREE
Lex

Fuck knows why, but I let her continue thinking she's nice and safe here, while I question everything from my perch on the balcony.

"She's playing dumb," Ryker shrugs, "perhaps she's here to do the exact same thing you are."

She sways mesmerizingly to the music, her hips moving in that tight little dress. Surely her father wouldn't have sent his precious little girl here. No that man is a lot, and he makes stupid choices, but I know his weakness.

Her. Wren Valentine.

And he wouldn't send her to me if she were of value to him.

She told me her surname was Lawson but that isn't true.

Not even a little and even if I didn't know exactly who she was, I'd spot the Valentine looks in her from a mile away.

My molars grind, what the fuck is going on?

Her friend wobbles unsteadily, almost toppling over but Wren grabs her quickly, her reflexes sharp. With a shake of a head and a few words I'll never even hope of catching, she guides her towards the exit.

Shit.

"Move," I order, abruptly standing and heading back to the elevator. We're on the street in less than a few minutes but when I round the corner the girl is nowhere to be seen.

"Fuck."

"Why did you stall?"

I turn my anger to my second hand, my eyes narrowing. "Excuse me?"

Ryker's eyes flick to the men behind me and he realizes quickly how he just fucked up. I don't get questioned. Not here, not at home and especially not in front of my men.

Getting her to the club was the easiest way to lure her into my trap but now she's gone which means it's going to be considerably harder. And bloodier.

I've scouted her apartment, armed guards are on call twenty-four seven, there were probably even a few in the club tonight but with the amount of people in there they never would have seen it. Not that it mattered. I wanted Valentine to know who had the little princess and the few to the many wouldn't have stood a chance.

Cooling the anger, I turn to the two that followed us out,

"Get back inside, Ryker with me."

I head in the opposite direction of the club and cut through a back alley across the street, turning at the end through a door that will lead me down to the underground parking garage. The beep of my Maserati is loud in the silence of the night, echoing off the concrete walls. My shoes tap furiously across the ground.

Ryker is silent behind me and when I get to the car, I throw open the door and slide inside. The entire ride across the city is quiet, the tension making the air in the car tight and coiled, ready to snap.

I don't address the question he asked before because I didn't have the answer. And right now I don't have time to fuck up. I just didn't expect her to up and leave so suddenly. I do not make mistakes but there's always a first for everything. Her apartment building is dark, all but one. The lights inside are on, lighting up the windows like a damn Christmas tree in the darkness.

"How many?"

"Five," Ryker answers, "Probably two inside."

I nod, reaching into my jacket to check my ammo. Ryker does the same.

"You sure you want to do this?" Ryker asks, "We can send a couple of the guys. It'll be just as effective."

"We leave one alive, I want him to send a message."

Ryker nods.

There was a limited window in which we could take this opportunity so while the guard, trying to pretend to be a normal citizen wandering the streets at night, is turned, I climb silently from the car, heading in that direction.

I hear two distinctive pops immediately, not as loud as they should be thanks to the silencer on the gun as Ryker takes out the two guards posted on the other side of the street.

I level my Glock, take aim, and pull the trigger.

The bullet hits my target in the back of the skull, splattering blood up the wall. He hits the ground with a thud, a puddle of crimson pooling around his head.

I swipe a card at the door and head inside, pausing to listen for footsteps.

Just when I think they aren't coming, heavy boots hit the stairs to my left. I press against the wall, my body hidden from view until I see the legs of the first guard. I shoot out his knee and he tumbles down the remaining steps, hitting the floor with a grunt. Before he can even look at my face, I put a bullet between his eyes and take the stairs up two at a time. I find Ryker in the hall, his arm cuffed around the last guard's neck in a choke hold. The man thrashes for a final time but then goes out like a light.

Ryker just simply drops him, raising his hand to wipe a trickle of blood from his face. "Fucker got in a cheap shot." He grumbles, kicking the guy.

I roll my eyes and head to the door. She's still awake inside so as soon as I boot this door down, she'll likely scream and bolt, so I need to be prepared.

I count in my head, lift my foot and hit the door right at the weak spot. It flies open and slams into the wall with a loud crash, causing ornaments and picture frames to fall from their shelves and shatter against the floor.

When I step inside, gun levelled in front of me I almost laugh at the scene waiting for me.

Wren stands on the other side of her living room, her own gun pointed right at my head. Ryker steps in behind me, his own weapon aimed at her. We've got ourselves a good old-fashioned stand-off.

"I can take you out before he shoots me," she threatens, jerking her chin towards Ryker. There's no fear in her voice, no tremble or worry.

Hmm, that's interesting.

"How good is your aim?" I ask, cocking my head, "because if you're going to shoot me, you're going to want to make sure it kills me."

"Oh it'll kill you," her lips curl back, showing her white teeth, "What do you want?"

The fact that she hasn't shot me already is telling enough, all bark, no bite. Not like me, my bark is just as vicious as my bite.

"Put the gun down," Ryker snarls, "put it down!"

"Get the fuck out!" She screams back.

Girl's got balls.

Ryker takes a menacing step forward and she moves her aim away from me, levelling it on Ryker. There's still no fear though. She's calculating her escape. Her eyes dart between the two of us and then to the exit behind us, it's done so quickly I'm sure she thinks I haven't seen it. But I see everything.

I allow myself a look at her for the first time since finding a gun pointed at my head. She's in sleep shorts, tiny cotton ones and a tank that reveals a slither of pale skin around her hips. Her copper hair is pulled into a pony tail and she doesn't have an ounce of makeup on her face. Her green eyes narrow and her jaw clamps tight. I can appreciate beauty and this girl has it in spades. It always was the psychotic ones that got me off the most.

"What did my father do?" She suddenly asks, "Does he owe you money or something?"

I laugh, "Oh he owes me something. And I'm here to take payment."

"The cash is in the safe," she tells me.

I lick my teeth, shaking my head, "Do I look like I need your money?"

Her brows twitch as if she wants to frown but she is good at hiding most of her emotions.

We're at a stand-off right now and time is ticking. I have no doubt someone is going to stumble on those bodies soon, if not already and Valentine's men likely check in with a central point every thirty minutes or so, when that check doesn't come, questions are going to be asked and I'll have a whole new problem to deal with.

Death didn't scare me, little did, but it would complicate the matter.

"Wren, lower the gun and we'll do the same," I try to reason.

"How about you get the fuck out of my apartment before I shoot you."

"You're not going to shoot me," I growl, "if you were, you would have done it already."

Suddenly she pulls the trigger and a vase behind me smashes into thousands of pieces.

"And here I thought your aim was good," I taunt.

"I was aiming for the vase," she spits, "That was your last warning."

I have no doubt that shot would have woken half the building.

"You're pissing me off, little girl. Put the gun down."

She laughs, "You think you scare me?"

"I should," I rush her, zigzagging in hopes of avoiding any bullets she does send my way.

A loud pop sounds and pain slices through my arm.

Bitch shot me. She fucking *shot* me.

My shoulder rams into her stomach and we tumble, her back slamming into the wall behind her hard enough that the frames fall from the hooks and smash on the floor. She must have dropped the gun with the impact so now she's using any tool she can get her hands on. A hard object collides with the side of my head and I feel the skin split near my hairline, followed by a warm trickle of blood.

My patience shatters. In a move too quick for her to counter my hands go around her throat, squeezing.

I press up, straddling her hips, my fingers squeezing around her windpipe, the heels of my hands pressing down hard enough it could crush her neck. Fear flashes in her eyes as her fingers claw at my skin, her nails drawing blood as they drag through the thin flesh on the top of my hands.

Fuck this girl likes to make me bleed. I feel a steady stream of hot liquid rolling down my arm and face though the pain has been dulled by the adrenaline that is pumping my system like a drug.

Ryker stands behind me, silent, simmering…

I press harder on her throat, her eyes become saucers, the blood vessels begin to pop as she tries and fails to draw oxygen into her lungs. I feel the strength starting to seep away from her body.

I'm going to kill her. I *was* killing her.

Her hands fall away from my wrists and to the sides, the limp limbs hitting the hard wood floors beneath us with a dull thud.

"Lex!" Ryker suddenly yells, breaking the trance of taking another life and he bolts forward though he is too late. I make out the shape of a long silver blade, but I quickly recognize the object to simply be a letter opener though it's as sharp as a knife as it slices through my thigh, cutting through the skin like butter and penetrating deep into the muscle.

"Fuck!" I bellow, my hands releasing her throat to stem the bleed.

She chokes but the fight has left her, leaving her weak beneath me. With a quick jerk, the butt of the gun slams into her temple and finally – *fucking finally* – she closes her eyes.

FOUR
Wren

Pain thumps through my skull and my throat feels as if I've swallowed a thousand razor blades. Groggily, I force my eyes to open, my lashes are stuck together, only when I lift my hand to rub them I can't. I pull my arm again, the sound of metal-on-metal scraping against my eardrums. What the fuck?

My ankles are in much the same state. Shackled.

Okay, don't panic. This could be a dream, a sleep paralysis perhaps but I know I need to figure it out. The feel of the metal against my skin seems too real to be just a dream and even as I will it not to come, the dread of what this means settles into the pit of my stomach.

It all comes back in a reel of images.

Alexander Silver.

His gun pointed at my head, my own at his.

Twisted City

RIA WILDE

The fight.

His hands around my throat, the press of his weight against my own as he attempted to steal away the breath in my lungs.

Shit. What the fuck have I gotten myself into and how do I get out of it?

I try to peer around the room but there's no light and no windows at all. It's cold, the air tinged with damp and dust but there's something else, something old and rotten that makes me choke. Pushing down the need to gag I breathe through my mouth and settle my head back. The pain is a constant pulse, both inside my head and in various points in my body. The fucker hit me.

I don't know how long I lay there in the dark but eventually a door opens, allowing light to spill into the room. Instinctively, I narrow my eyes to stop the sting and allow them to adjust. A huge figure fills the door frame, so large it almost blocks out the light, the shoulder width alone almost touching each side of the frame.

"She's awake," his voice is rough, husky in a way that suggests he's a smoker or a man who doesn't use his voice all that often.

He steps to the side to allow another man in, with the light at his back I can't see his features, shrouded in shadow but he's big too, probably the same size as the first man but this one has an air of violence that surrounds him. An aura of menace that rings as a warning to anyone who bears witness to his presence. There's something in the set of his shoulders, the way his hands dangle loosely at his sides, so very relaxed in a sea of chaos and violence.

I immediately know who I'm staring at, even if I can't see

his face.

When he came up to me in the club my hackles instantly went up. My instincts were very rarely wrong, and they certainly didn't fail me on this occasion.

This man was dangerous.

No, he was more than dangerous, he's the monster under your bed, the villain in your stories. He's the motherfucking devil in the flesh.

I grit my teeth, was he here to finish the job? I uselessly pull at the shackles restraining me, feeling the metal biting into my skin, grazing and cutting away at my flesh.

I had no idea what they even wanted with me, the only connection I can think of is my father. I knew he was dodgy, but this… fuck, what even is this?

"Hello, Wren," his bourbon smooth baritone rolls over me, both a caress and a slap.

"Let me go, you asshole!"

He chuckles, "I like the fire in you."

"Come here," I hiss, "let me show you just how much fire I have."

"We've already danced this dance, little bird," he steps closer, an edge of steel to his tone, "it didn't work out so well for you."

I avert my eyes, allowing a smirk to tilt up my lips, pushing as much condescending snide into my voice as I say, "how's the arm? Or was it the leg?" My eyes flick back to where he stands above me, allowing them to roll over his tall, muscular frame.

He growls, a noise neither belonging to man nor beast.

A tinkle of laughter leaves my throat but a wince cuts it off short as the pain there radiates through my neck, stifling me.

"Once we're done here," he steps forward and I notice the limp, how he holds himself and favors his left leg. Good, I hope it fucking hurts, "there won't be even an ember of life left in you. You can keep your fire now, Wren, but just know, I'll snuff those flames out quicker than you can even blink."

I had no doubt about it. I won't be leaving here alive. It was a given considering *who* I was dealing with.

That should terrify me. It should shake me down to my core, but all I feel is a fury building inside of me that makes me want to rip out of these cuffs and watch the life drain from his eyes.

He steps to the side of the bed I'm restrained to and reaches forward, brushing hair away from my face in a move too soft for a man who holds this much malevolence. "Touch me again," I breathe through the anger, "and I'll bite your finger off."

"Aren't you quite the savage, little bird," he comments, "Such a shame you're on the wrong side."

What?

I don't have time to answer when he turns and stalks out the room, shutting the door behind him, plunging me into a darkness so deep I wouldn't even be able to see my hand in front of my face.

The next visitor to come to my room is neither Lex nor the other man, instead it's a woman. She's lithe, tall with long blonde hair that's been pulled back from her face tightly. She's dressed in tight black pants and a tight top that follows the shape of her body like a second skin. I spot the gun tucked into the back of her trousers.

Ocean blue eyes meet mine and she quirks a brow, "Not that you could, but I wouldn't even think about it."

Her voice is melodic, but I quickly realize it doesn't match the owner. Her face remains impassive as she pushes my head roughly to the side and when she presses her red manicured fingers to my temple with no sense of empathy, a burst of pain has me hissing through my teeth.

"Did a number on you, huh?" She reaches into a box I hadn't noticed she'd bought in with her and presses something to my head, more pain, the pulse of it throbbing through my skull.

"Get the fuck off me," I growl.

"Quite the mouth you have there," she comments, amusement lacing her tone and tipping up her lips.

My nostrils flare.

I needed to get the fuck out of here. I had no idea what these guys wanted or who they were, but I knew a predator when I saw one. If I don't get out now, I doubt I'll be breathing for much longer. My death wouldn't be quick, it would be a torturous event dragged out over days. When the girl is done, she stands and exits the room but comes back a moment later holding a tray of food and a bottle of water with a straw in the top.

I quirk a brow, "What are you, their little pet?"

"Ha," she laughs, "by the way, you want to *not* give me all the attitude, I'm the reason you're even getting to eat."

"I'm not hungry."

"Fine," she thrusts the bottle at me, the straw hitting my bottom lip, "Drink."

I turn my head away.

She tuts loudly and stands from the bed, "Very well."

But those weren't parting words, instead she proceeds to stand and pour the entire bottle of water over my face.

I inhale automatically and then choke as the water hits my throat.

With no more words, she leaves the room and shuts the damn door again, plunging me into that void of darkness.

The silence and the dark will surely drive me crazy way before they get around to doing whatever it is they want to do.

I needed to get out.

The sudden burst of determination has me thrashing on the bed, tugging at my restraints. I'm pretty sure they're handcuffs, though I can't be sure without seeing them, and every time that door opens, I'm too distracted to get a good look.

Come on. Focus Wren.

I think back to all the training I've done with Griffin. All the hours I've been forced to endure learning self-defense, trying to remember if I was taught how to get out of different types of restraints.

I remember being taught how to pick the locks or even shimming but that won't work here, I can't get to them, even with my fingers. I tug my hands down hard, the metal of the cuff biting into my skin. Pain slices through my wrists as the metal carves at my flesh, bruising, pinching, but unless I can break my own hand, I'm not getting out.

I thrash my head down, wincing with the pain that fires through the back of my skull and blow out a frustrated breath. I suppose I should be thankful for the training. I wonder if my father knew something like this would happen, and that's why he forced it for all these years so I could protect myself in this kind of event. Not a lot of good it does now, mind you.

If that were the case, it really begs the question as to what it is he does in his spare time. Me and my dad didn't exactly have a loving relationship and my mother was long gone. The training taught me to remain calm, fight but also raise hell if I must. And I wanted to raise hell. Who said dying had to be peaceful?

I scream. My throat pulls tight, turning from a wail to a croak too quick for my liking, but I don't stop.

"Hey!" I yell. "Oi, you fuckers!"

I thrash my arms and legs, clanging the metal of my restraints against the metal posts so the noise echoes through the empty room.

"Hey!"

I scream and yell for what feels like hours and finally the door slams open, "What!?" It's the same rough husky voice from before.

"I have to pee."

"Are you serious right now?"

"Oh I'm sorry," I snap, "I didn't realize that the normal bodily function would just stop because you guys said so."

The guy stomps across the room, "Why are you wet?"

"Oh, I have the bitch you sent in before to thank for that."

He growls something I don't quite catch but fishes into his pockets for keys. Okay, good. He's going to let me out and if I can get out, I can run.

He slides the key into the left lock and frees my hand but before I can do anything, he twists my body and promptly cuffs it to the arm still restrained on the other side.

"This is a little much don't ya think?" I push sweetness into my voice, "Little old me can't do much harm."

"Ha," he shakes his head as he removes the other cuff, forcing my arms down. I peer down to see the gleaming silver around both wrists, secured together.

"Nice cuffs," I say, "is there something you're not telling me? Are you guys secretly some weird bondage society?"

He doesn't answer as he removes the cuffs from my legs and forces me to stand by yanking on my elbow. I get up, swaying a little as the blood rushes around my body from where I've been in the prone position for too long.

I stumble forward but he catches me quickly, keeping me

upright as I'm dragged from the small dark room. We step out into a narrow hall with only a set of steps that lead upwards. He makes me go first, pressing into the small of my back.

"No funny business," he tells me.

I roll my eyes, "Jesus Christ."

The door at the top suddenly opens and the chick from before comes into view. She smirks and lets me pass before falling into step beside the guy who let me out.

They're silent and eventually I come to a junction at the end of the hall. I realize I'm in a house, a big one, one that screams money and power. Expensive art hangs from the walls, Persian rugs line the mahogany floors and crystal chandeliers dangle from the high ceilings, prisms of colour dancing across the white walls as a breeze teases the little diamonds. I've been around wealth my entire life but this is a whole other level.

"Left," Gruff orders.

I turn left, my bare feet squeaking on the polished floor.

"That door there."

I stop in front of it, waiting for them to open it. When neither of them does I turn my attention to them, "What do you expect me to do? Open it with my teeth?"

"I like her," the girl suddenly declares, stepping forward and opening it for me. I step inside, using my heel to kick it shut but it's stopped before it can click closed.

"Oh I don't think so," the girl says, stepping in with me.

"I can't pee with you in here."

She rolls her eyes, "Do your business, this isn't a luxury we give to most *guests*."

"Oh, I suppose being cuffed to the bed is also five star treatment."

"Would you prefer we dangle you from the ceiling? It can be arranged."

"You're all fucking crazy."

"No, we're fucking Silvers and it's about time you learned your place."

FIVE
Lex

"Valentine," I drawl, kicking my legs up onto the desk, swirling the whiskey in my glass so the ice clinks against the edges.

"Give her back."

No greeting, how very rude.

"I see you got my message."

"Oh, I got your message, you sick son of a bitch, Wren has nothing to do with this."

And this is where he's going to fail. There's his weakness, like a beacon for my eyes. Little Wren Valentine is his absolute weakness, one that'll destroy him. Just as I planned. It's like exposing a jugular to a predator and in this game of predators it is always going to be me who comes out on top.

"Oh, I think she has everything to do with this, though I'm confused."

Twisted City

RIA WILDE

Heavy breathing on the other end of line puffs in my ear but he doesn't say anything else, so I continue.

"I will give it to you, you kept her a secret for a long time, I'm impressed actually, not a lot escapes me." I tip the whiskey to my lips before bringing it back down to dangle between my fingers.

"Give her back." I don't miss the way his voice lilts at the end, a barely restrained anger though I don't hear concern, just rage and that piques my interest. He doesn't seem concerned with her well being, he hasn't asked how she is or if she is even still alive, only that he wants her back. I keep this all to myself, I'll get to the bottom of it, one way or another.

"It wasn't until a little piggy squealed that I figured it out. At first, I thought she was staying with you, that she knew exactly who you were, but I've come to realize she's completely and utterly innocent."

Innocent wouldn't have been the word I would have used to describe her, not when the little she devil shot me and continues to fight me at every turn, but he doesn't need to know that. She may come across as the perfect little doll, smart, composed but I see beneath all of that. I see the fight, the fire, the lust for vengeance. It's one hell of an aphrodisiac, watching a strong woman fight and not bow down, witnessing the unadulterated fury in her stare as she watches you, calculating all the ways she may hurt you should she break free from her restraints. Just the thought of her fighting me has my cock hardening. In this life, you don't get anywhere by rolling onto your back, had she been on the right side of the line she would have made one hell of a companion.

"How does that feel, Valentine?" I didn't usually toy with

my victims, but Marcus Valentine was a different breed. This fucker is going to pay for everything he's done to the Silver family and its interests. I'll make the asshole pay with more than just his blood.

He probably didn't realize it when he walked into this city all those years ago just who he was playing with, but he's soon going to find out he's swimming with sharks.

"What do you want?" Negotiation is his first point of call.

"Nothing."

"Money? The trade? My suppliers?"

I roll my eyes even though he can't see me, "I know each and every one of your transactions, Valentine, but don't you worry, I have that handled along with your little princess."

"Silver!" He growls. "You're fucking with something bigger than you."

I wonder how far he'll go to free the little bird. Not that I have any intention of letting the girl go but playing with him is appealing.

"Goodbye now, Valentine. You have yourself a nice night."

Is this really how we deal with shit in this family? No. It is not, my father would be furious but I'm in charge now and it's my city to rule as I see fit.

Innocent blood is going to be spilt, it's inevitable and I've quickly learned how to push pass that guilt, it doesn't affect me.

I do what I need to do for the success of this family, for

these men and women working for me.

I hang up the phone and drain the rest of my glass, savoring the sweet burn as it rolls down my throat. My first taste of revenge against the Valentine's leaves me salivating for more. Standing from the chair in my office, I stretch out my muscles and cross the room, swinging the door open only to find echoes of a fight meeting my ears. Grunts and thuds travel down the long narrow halls of the house, meeting me where I stand in the threshold of my office.

For fucks sake, what now?

I follow the sound and stop short when I see Ainsley on her back, eyes closed, unconscious and Ryker and Wren going at it in the hallway outside the bathroom.

I leave them for five fucking minutes.

Ryker should know better.

"Enough!" I boom.

Ryker's back goes ramrod straight and even Wren has stopped, turning her attention to me. Her eyes narrow and her lips curl back enough to show me her teeth, and just to spite me no doubt, she raises her knee, hard, and hits my second in command in the dick. When he's hunched over, she jumps onto his back and pulls the chain securing her cuffs to his throat.

Seriously.

This chick is batshit crazy.

Ryker huffs impatiently but she tugs back, cutting off his air supply. He looks to me for approval and a slight nod of my chin gives him everything he needs to finish this off.

With his bulky frame, he throws himself back and slams her into the wall. It startles her enough for the grip on his throat to loosen, and as she tries to readjust Ryker uses the distraction to bend at the waist with enough momentum to throw her over his shoulders and head and onto the hard wood flooring.

She lands flat on her back in the middle of the hall, hair splayed around her head.

Winded, she stays there, sucking in a breath as I start towards her, leg twinging with pain from where she stabbed me.

I peer down at her, "I believe we're due a chat, little bird."

"You don't say," she wheezes. "You know people are going to miss me, the cops are probably already on it."

"I know they are," I nod, "but I've dealt with that, no one's coming to look for you."

Her eyes widen but she doesn't fight, it's almost like she's just realized she's got no hope here.

I reach down and haul her up. She's weak right now, dazed and injured which makes this a whole lot easier. I pick her up, cradling her to my chest. It would almost be intimate if we were anywhere else and I was *anyone* else. I ignore the pain in my arm and leg as I carry her, letting it fuel this need.

"I'm tired," she complains.

"It's not nap time, little bird."

"Stop calling me that," her words are slurred and I dare a

glance down, her face is pale, lids hooded. She's slipping into unconsciousness. The hit to the end when she went down must have been harder than I thought.

Her head rolls back as her eyes slip closed.

I know Ryker will be tending to Ainsley so realizing I have no eyes on me, I detour and take her to a guest room on the top floor.

Why? I have no fucking idea.

When I lay her down on the bed I just stand and stare. Taking in her delicate features, the bow of her top lip, the plush bottom one and how her lashes cast long shadows over the apples of her cheeks. Her copper hair has since fallen out of the hold she had it in and it falls around her head like a halo. Long toned legs, skin milky and smooth. My eyes follow the lines of the tattoo on her thigh and then the one on her arm, intricately etched into her skin, delicate and feminine, a complete contrast to their owner.

There's something about her that interests me. Piques my curiosity and flames a well of heat inside my body that's completely inappropriate given the circumstances.

I hook my fingers beneath her chin and tilt her head, inspecting the bruise that has bloomed on her temple and the gash from where I hit her with the gun and then following the deep purple bruises around her throat.

Fuck.

I almost killed her.

Almost.

That wouldn't have been good, not when I needed her to

see this through.

Still out cold, I shackle her to the bed so she can't get any ideas for when she finally wakes. And then I leave her there, heading back down.

Ryker is tending to Ainsley who is now awake and sat on the couch, leaning forward with her elbows resting on her knees.

"You underestimated her," I accuse.

"She's so small!" Ainsley grumbles and Ry laughs.

"I thought the same," he nods, frowning when his phone buzzes in his pocket. Pulling it out he checks the screen and then heads out the room, answering it.

I cock my head at Ainsley, the side of her face is red, turning purple as the bruising starts to take shape, "Not like you to pull down your guard, what happened?"

She shakes her head, "Won't happen again."

"Make sure of it."

She grumbles something and then stands, exiting the same way Ryker did and then I'm alone again.

Why the hell did I set her up in the bedroom?

This isn't a fucking hotel and she definitely is not a guest. She's the means to an end. Not even a bargaining chip.

She's revenge.

Cold hard revenge.

My words taunt me.

Twisted City   RIA WILDE

She's completely and utterly innocent.

They're not wrong.

It wasn't hard to figure out that he had sent her away when she was young, young enough for her not to remember who he was and put her with another guy in his inner circle so he could keep an eye on her and pull whatever strings necessary to ensure her life turned out the way he wanted it to.

I wasn't interested in the little guys. It was Marcus Valentine I wanted.

The only reason I even found out he had a daughter was because his men are weak as fuck and turned the moment I pressed a barrel to his temple. No loyalty. No integrity. That canary sang until he was blue in the face.

And I found Marcus' weakness.

Though I should have dug deeper. Pushed harder. I would have figured out quick enough she wasn't close with him. It struck me odd that she was staying at the Lawson house, he wasn't high up in Valentine's command which meant I wouldn't have looked at him twice unless I needed to. The intel I picked up didn't show the link to Lawson, only Valentine. I didn't dig deep enough.

That was a mistake I would never make again.

My impatience to finish this far outweighed all else.

I needed to move her back down to the room below, she's the enemy and I needed to treat her as such.

I head towards the door.

"Lex!" Ryker storms into the room, "We have a problem."

"What?" I bark.

"The warehouse is on fire, Valentine torched it."

"Fuck!"

Wren will have to wait, I grab my keys and the jacket discarded over the back of the chair and head out, Ryker falling into step behind me as I dial the fire chief.

"You better get that blaze under control," I growl down the line.

"Silver," Chief Donald Arthur was an old git and a grumpy bastard, and he made sure every damn time I called I knew he was unhappy to hear from me. I didn't care, he was a pawn as much as every other fucker in this city, sitting pretty in my pocket and to be called upon whenever I needed it, there wasn't a choice in the matter, "Who'd you piss off now?"

"I don't think you heard me, Arthur," I throw myself behind the wheel, Ryker climbing into the Range Rover next to me.

"My best guys are down there but it doesn't look good."

"Then you best make it look fucking good Arthur, I'm not fucking around here. You want to keep that job I suggest you fix this."

I have a million dollars' worth of drugs in that fucking warehouse damn it, and a shit ton of business will literally go up in smoke if it is not contained. With the next shipment not due in till next week, I can't afford the mess this will make.

Twenty minutes later I park the car in the lot outside the

warehouse. The whole building is on fire, the sky around it lit up in an orange hue as the flames lick at the night sky. The blaze roars wildly and furiously, and there's no damn hope that the stock inside is still there.

The firefighters tackle the fire but it's no use.

Ryker steps up next to me, "A couple of guys saw Valentine's men come in with explosives and gasoline. They killed the guards and then torched the place."

"He wants his daughter back," I grumble.

"There's something else," he says.

I huff, "Of course there is."

He unlocks his phone and shows me a picture. It's one of my guys, head blown open but it's not that that has my attention. In the centre of his chest, held there with a blade buried into his flesh is a note.

Three days, Silver.

Give Wren back or I'll burn your entire world to the ground.

A cruel smile curls at my lips, if he wants Wren back, he'll have to come get her himself. By the time he grows the balls to do so, she'll be dead.

SIX
Wren

Perhaps it was all a dream, a fucked up dream but a dream because this bed isn't the same one I've been in for the past God knows how long and this room is lit up with the moonlight streaming in through the window, casting shadows over the white painted walls and lighting up the paintings hanging there. I shift, feeling the silky sheets beneath my back and legs and almost groan at the luxury, even if my arms and legs have been restrained again and are slightly numb from being in this position for too long.

I wonder how many times I can take a hit to the head before I should start to worry about the lasting damage it's going to have.

Taking out the girl was easy, she had severely underestimated me and all it took was a swift elbow to stun her and then a knee to her temple and she went down. Gruff however was another matter. That fucker was big.

Twisted City   RIA WILDE

I gave it a good shot though, but there isn't going to be a next time for a while, I know that for sure. That was my only attempt at escaping, they won't make the same mistake twice.

My throat is as dry as a desert and my stomach rumbles, cramping with hunger.

How long have I been here now?

It's got to be days, three maybe but I have no idea, everything has blurred into one, making it impossible to tell one day apart from the next.

I lean back on the soft pillow under my head and take a deep breath.

The house around me is quiet, too quiet which is unnerving, and I still have no idea what they want with me.

Somewhere downstairs the door opens, and slams closed immediately before feet pound on the stairs, and then across the hall, loud and angry, heading right for me.

Great.

The door to the room smashes open, hard enough to vibrate the paintings hanging on the walls, and there he is.

There is something disturbingly beautiful about the man, he was lethal, unhinged and clearly batshit, but he was as brutal as he was beautiful. All sharp angles and hard lines. The scent of smoke and ash fills the room, getting stronger the closer he comes to the bed.

"Didn't peg you to be a smoker," I comment. That's the truth, his teeth are too white, too clean but then he clearly has money so the effects of smoking can just be wiped away.

"We're going to send a message, little bird," He growls down to me. Oh he's pissed.

"Okay, cool, why don't you hand me my phone and I'll get right on that."

Pushing him now seems like the wrong thing to do but I just can't help it. I've never been one to just take shit lying down, if there's a fight, I'm going to fight.

He withdraws a blade, turning it over in his hand, the steel catching in the light as he rolls it, pressing the sharpened edge against his palm hard enough to slice the skin and allow beads of crimson to bloom on the surface.

He smirks down at me, a cruel tilt of his lips that strikes fear right down to the pit of my soul. "You're funny."

"Thanks," I force the word from my lips as he leans forward and runs the very tip of that blade down the centre of my chest, the razor edge snagging and tearing the material of my clothes and further down to slice at my skin. The pain is almost a phantom, a sting barely present but it's there, nonetheless, making you uncomfortable, making you want to kick it away if only to ease the frustration of having it irritate you.

He follows the blade with his eyes as he moves it down my abdomen and then back up, all the way up until the tip sits right atop my pulse point, with every thump my wild heart gives, the blade pushes in further, drawing blood that wells and then rolls down my throat.

He appears to be hypnotized by the trail of blood, his silver eyes following it down as it rolls over my skin before his eyes bounce up and land on my mouth.

My lips are parted, my breathing shallow and fast, the warming between my thighs worrying and yet welcoming.

He brings the blade away from my neck, the silver now laced with red ribbons, a mixture of my blood and his and reaches forward, placing the very tip of it against my bottom lip. I'm frozen, unable to move as he watches me intently, not blinking, not moving except for the hand that holds the blade. Slowly, he pushes the blade down, the tip biting into my bottom lip and I have no choice but to open my mouth. There's a sting on the sensitive flesh where he's cut me, and I feel more blood rolling slowly over my lip and onto my chin.

His shoulders square and his spine straightens as the pupils of his eyes seem to devour his irises.

I'm prepared for him to cut me, to stab me, ready for whatever wound he's about to inflict. I see it there, a warning inside his eyes, a promise of violence and I only feel it sinking deeper into my body as he draws closer, taking the blade away from my mouth quickly, the edge slicing through my lip before he places it back at my throat, pressing it against the windpipe. There should be pain, but the threat of death simply numbs everything and knowing that a simple jerk of his hand will end it for me keeps the panic and fear behind a barrier. His eyes bounce between my eyes, my mouth and the blade pressing into my flesh. All the air leaves my lungs, a tightening in my stomach that really didn't belong in this situation. Instinctively, I swallow, the move making the blade scratch against my skin and just when I think this is it, he's going to slice that blade through my neck his mouth slams against mine with a ferocity that I am not prepared for.

Twisted City

RIA WILDE

I should fight.

I need to fight, bite him, headbutt him but I don't do that. Of course I don't because my body has turned against me, and I tilt my head to let his tongue stroke deeper.

One hand still holds that damn blade to my throat but the other grips my hair and tugs, pulling painfully but instead of lashing out like I should, I whimper and purr like a damn cat.

My arms pull at the restraints, my legs curl and heels dig into the mattress, my back arching towards him. The threat of injury from the knife and the way his tongue lashes at mine creates a mixture deadlier than any weapon he could use against me.

He yanks away from me, abruptly, withdrawing both himself and the blade and simply stares down at where I'm a mess on the bed, restrained and confused. The metallic taste of blood sits on my tongue. His jaw pulses as he clenches his teeth and without a single word, he sheaths the knife, keeping his eyes holding mine, and withdraws his phone, snapping a picture before spinning on the heel of his shoe and exiting the room.

My lips tingle from the kiss, my body coiled up tight as heat continues to pulse low in my belly. I try to press my thighs together but the damn ankle cuffs stop me from being able to squash the sensations.

This is not normal. Clearly the knocks I've had to my head in the last few days have already taken hold.

Lex

I stare down at the image, the blood smeared across her throat, her chin and mouth, eyes wide and confused, staring right at me while I stand above her. I hit the send button.

He wants to play fucking games, we'll play games.

But what the fuck did I do?

Kissing her.

Shit.

I still taste her on my tongue, taste her blood, feel the soft pillowy mouth yielding beneath mine with my blade pressed to her throat. The soft little mews and whimpers fueled me to go harder, hoping, like the sick son of a bitch that I am, that she would fight a little, let the blood roll and the violence add fuel to whatever fucked fire is burning between us.

I shake my head to dislodge the thoughts and fall down onto the couch, resting my glass in the centre of my chest.

I inhale the smoky scent surrounding me, a mixture of the fire and the whiskey in my glass.

I went into that room prepared to break her. I was ready to crush her, crush her pretty little wings and any fire she may still have burning. Use it to send a better message but I kissed her instead. Fuck.

I throw the remaining liquid in the glass down my throat and then proceed to launch the glass at the wall. It smashes, raining shards of crystal all over the fur rug that sits in front of the fireplace.

Twisted City

RIA WILDE

I didn't live here. Fuck that. This was the compound, a safe house, set far away from the city with no prying eyes or nosy neighbors. It was guarded to high heaven with cameras all over the ground, a security system at the gate and sensors to alert me of any unwanted visitors trying to break through the perimeters. It seemed the best option to bring Wren to, but I want my penthouse.

I want to look down at the city below through the floor to ceiling windows that stretch the entire way around the suite, I want to feel the power in my veins, see my empire at my feet.

I feel weak right now. Fucking weak and that's not a feeling I want to have for long.

I had hoped to drag this out a little, really make Marcus beg before I put both him and *her* out of their misery but I'm not sure I can last much longer.

I knew Valentine would try to make good on his threat which is why I've doubled the man power across the city at every location the Silver family own plus on the streets.

Marcus Valentine had been a cockroach from the very start, a dirty little snake that thought he would take the South side of the City. He was small at first and my father chose to negotiate rather than take out the problem. For a few years that was fine, they put their business through us, we controlled their connections, the supplies, dealings and negotiation but at some point Marcus slipped through the net.

He found allies in our enemies, grew his circle, his connections. I still have no idea which of the fuckers it is that supported him and funded his desire to take over the city but once he was dealt with, I'd find them, and I'd end them.

When my father found out Marcus was going behind our back he paid him a visit.

The thing about my father was, he truly was ruthless, brutal even but he wanted some semblance of peace in the city, so he tried to renegotiate.

Men died.

War started.

It was a year after that, six months ago that Marcus hit my fathers house while they were throwing a party.

We didn't involve the citizens, especially not the ones that kept the businesses running and the cops looking the other way but that's what he did.

The Police chief died that night and the resulting pain of having to renegotiate with the new guy that filled his place was long and frustrating.

Everyone has secrets, you just had to find the ones worth using.

Threats and violence only worked sometimes. It didn't matter if they hated me or what I stood for, it didn't matter if they loathed the fact that I held the true power in this city, despite their titles and appearance of authority, long as they stayed in line.

Everyone has a place and me, along with the Silver name and the ones closest stand on fucking top.

SEVEN
Wren

What I wouldn't give right now for a nice stroll in the park. My legs ache from being still for so long and with my arms pinned above my head the blood can't circulate properly meaning my fingers tingle every time I move them.

I'm starving too. My stomach cramps painfully and I blow out a frustrated breath. The sun is blaring through the window, the sky a perfect cloudless blue. Every now and then a bird will fly passed the window but other than that, it's completely silent and still. I tilt my head and sniff.

Jesus. A shower would be nice.

The need to get out of here was still as strong as ever but I had no idea how I was going to manage it. I've been alone more than I've had company and still no idea why I'm here.

It all leads back to my dad, of course it does but whatever it is he did, it doesn't look like their willing to negotiate with me or even share the information.

I wonder if he's fighting for me at all. I wonder if he knows it's Alexander Silver who has me.

When the door opens to the room I don't bother looking up. I just lay there staring at the ceiling, waiting for whoever it is to step into view.

Alexander stands at the side of the bed, looking down at me. He's dressed in a pristine charcoal grey suit, his unruly hair falling over his forehead. His hands are buried into the pockets of his trousers, causing the jacket he has on to open a little, showing the handle of his Glock. There's no tie to finish the look, just the two top buttons of his white shirt open, showing off bronzed skin. My tongue traces the cut in my bottom lip, the sting of it making me wince as I remember the way his mouth felt when it was on mine, hard, unforgiving and all consuming. Even if I don't want to remember how it made me feel, the thought of it still warms me through, how dangerous it was, how fucking dirty…

"It appears we've hit a bit of an impasse, Little bird," he says quietly, crouching until his eyes are level with mine. Lazily I roll my head to the side, sucking in a breath to prepare myself for his ruthless beauty.

It really isn't fair that a man like him has been graced with such looks. He's a wolf, beautiful and yet deadly, one snap of his teeth and you'll lose a hand, or he'll simply rip your throat out. He isn't a man to be underestimated. There's this calm storm that seems to always blow around him, it doesn't appear to be harmful but then if you step into it, it'll sweep you away.

The man is the devil, in all his glory.

I knew it in the club, I knew it when I was staring down the end of his barrel, my own pointed at him, and I certainly knew it when his hands wrapped around my throat. He was fully prepared to kill me there and then, with his bare hands on my living room floor. Had I not stabbed him when I did, I had no doubt I'd be buried in an unmarked grave somewhere out in the sticks for the scavengers to dig up.

I swallow, but I refuse to fear him. I won't give him that power over me. I may be on the bottom here, but I'll never show it to him. He can keep me here all he likes, he can tie me up, he can even hurt me if he wants but I'll never give him my vulnerability.

Showing a weakness in front of this man would be like showing your jugular to a lion.

Foolish.

"Oh yeah?" My voice is croaky and hoarse from lack of use and hydration, and I swallow painfully, eyes watering with the pain, "how so?"

"It appears daddy wants to send a message," he rubs a hand across his scruff, his eyes rolling slowly over my body. I squirm under the heat of it.

I have to be all kinds of fucked up to get turned on by him.

But the clenching in my belly and the ache between my thighs tells me all I need to know.

He may be a monster but I'm the depraved little girl too curious to heed the warnings ringing in my head, wanting to know exactly how it would feel to be fucked by a man like Alexander Silver.

"What message?"

So he was looking for me and negotiating perhaps?

"Well he set one of my warehouses on fire." Alexander rolls his head, cracking his neck.

I can't hide my shock at that news. I couldn't imagine the man I knew as my dad to set anything on fire. He looked too tidy to get dirty himself, I'm sure he had men to do that for him.

"Interesting."

Alexander quirks a brow, "I lost a lot of money you know."

"I'm sure you have more to spare a few thousand."

"Try a few million."

"What did he want to say?" I change the subject.

"I have three days," he smirks.

"To do what?"

"Return you."

"Or what?"

"He'll burn my whole world to the ground."

Silence settles between us. I don't have anything to say to him. He continues to stare at me, eyes holding my own and I don't want to break it, I don't, but the look seers me to the soul, it has my brain scrambling and my body trying to keep up.

I drop my eyes. He laughs.

Asshole.

"I don't take threats all that lightly, little bird."

"Aw," I snap, "Did someone hurt your feelings?"

"There it is," he grins so suddenly it catches me off guard but is gone in a second.

"Fuck you, Alexander Silver."

"Maybe if you're lucky."

He unfolds his body, "Seeing as I only have you for three more days little bird, it's time to start planning."

"You're going to let me go?" I feel idiotic to allow so much hope into my voice but it's there, a lilt in my tone that wasn't there moments ago.

"Oh no, little bird. I'm sending my own message."

I watch him cross the room and stop in the door, his massive body filling the frame. He tilts his head, looking at me from over his shoulder, "Someone will be up shortly with food and then I'll allow a shower. Don't bite their fingers off."

"How chivalrous of you."

He leaves then, with the echo of his soft laughter bouncing down the hall.

Sure enough, a woman enters the room carrying a bowl of soup and bread. The smell of tomato and basil hits my nose and I practically drool, salivating at the thought of food.

"Can you release my hands so I can sit?" I ask the woman.

She looks about forty but not hard like the others, she doesn't respond to me, instead she takes the spoon and dips it into the red liquid.

"How am I supposed to eat if I'm led down?"

Again no answer. She pushes the tip of the spoon against my lip and begins to pour it into my mouth.

With a huff I open and hot soup hits my tongue. I groan as the taste bursts against my tastebuds, sliding down my parched throat far too effortlessly.

It goes down easily and quickly and when the woman breaks off a bit of bread to feed me, I shake my head, turning slightly so she can't force it.

"I've had enough, thank you."

She nods once and grabs the bottle of water and straw, holding it to my mouth.

I take it gratefully this time, sucking down half the bottle before she pulls it away and quirks a brow.

I shrug, as best I can in the current position and then she pushes it back to my mouth, allowing me to finish it off. It's ice cold and refreshing, quenching the thirst instantly.

After that's finished, she gets up and leaves. "Hey! Alexander told me I could shower!"

"You think we're going to let a housekeeper shower you?" It's Gruff's voice. I still haven't heard his name so he's still Gruff to me. It suits him, he's a beast of a man, one you'd likely find chopping wood somewhere far in the mountains. His beard is groomed, his hair long but slicked back. He's dressed similarly to Alexander, his suit black rather than grey and I have no doubt he's packing too.

"Well you're not showering me," Gruff flashes me a grin.

"Don't knock it till you try it."

"I'd like to maintain at least a little dignity, dickhead."

"Come on," he makes quick work of the cuffs, and instead of putting them in front of me when he restrains me again, he puts them behind my back, so tight it pulls my shoulders, my muscles protesting at the unnatural angle.

"I can still use my feet you know," I tell him smugly, "I could break your neck just as easily."

His warm chest presses into my back, "Lex might be stalling to put a bullet in your head, but I won't hesitate little girl."

I tuck that little bit of information down about the stalling and snicker, "But you won't."

"Why's that?"

I was baiting him but if I was going to die anyway, what did it matter?

"You're too scared to disobey your master."

He growls menacingly behind me.

"Am I wrong?"

I'm shoved hard, losing balance I hit the hard wood floor on my knees, pain vibrating up my thighs and hips.

"How someone hasn't cut your tongue out already is

beyond me." Gruff grumbles, tugging me back to my feet. The quick glance I get of his face I swear I see a smile but that can't be right.

The bathroom we stop at is on the same floor as the room I'm being held in and it's huge, a clawfoot tub sits in the centre with brass taps, and off to the left, up against the far wall is a marble vanity, the mirror above it taking up the entire wall, the gold frame intricately weaving over the sides and edges with vines and flowers. There's a shower big enough to fit four on the other side and a toilet. It smells floral in here, clean and I take a deep breath. Despite the situation, a shower is going to be delightful.

"You can leave now." I tell Gruff.

"I don't think so."

"I'm not showering in here with you!"

"You can always go without."

"No!"

Gruff laughs, crosses his arms and leans against the counter, watching me, daring me.

Is he serious right now?

I want to hit him but with these damn cuffs I can't do shit.

Frustration makes my eyes sting. Damn it, I'm not going to cry.

"I can't wait until I can wipe that damn smile off your face."

"You can try," he growls.

"Now, now," Alexander steps into the bathroom, amusement tilting up his delectable mouth. "Carry on Ryker, I might just let her take a shot at you. Now what's the problem this time?"

EIGHT

Lex

Wren stares at me like she would love nothing more than to rip my throat out with her bare hands. I believe she'd do it too.

What kind of man does it make me if that shit turns me on?

"Are you going to be good, little bird?" I ask, waiting to hear the tell-tale sound of the door clicking behind me. Ryker wasn't really going to stand in here with her, no, no, no one else gets to see her like this.

I try to think back to all the prisoners I've held in my keep and allowed them the comfort I've given her, but I think of none. The people I bring here are here for one reason. To die.

They've fucked up somehow and are being punished or they're simply a means to an end, just like Wren here is. Only I shouldn't be allowing her to shower, I shouldn't be feeding her and making sure she has comfort beneath her back and yet here I am, allowing her just that.

She glares at me, the rims of her nostrils flaring as she takes steady breaths.

"I'm going to uncuff you now," I tell her, "You'll be wise to behave yourself."

I cross the space between us and go behind her back, slotting the key into the cuffs, waiting for the click of the locking mechanism to release and then I pull them away. Red welts mark her flawless skin and she rubs at her wrists, fingers pushing against the marks.

My chest twinges.

What the fuck?

"Strip."

"Are you serious? You're not going to allow me some dignity?"

I quirk a brow. "No."

"Turn around."

"No."

A puff of air huffs from her mouth. "Why don't you just kill me now, huh?" She hollers, "You're gonna do it anyway, just get it over with!"

"All in time, little bird."

She visibly swallows, the first show of fear she's given me since I took her all those days ago. I don't like it.

But I don't like this feeling anymore either. There's

something wrong with me, there has to be. The sickness that rolls in my gut, the twinges in my chest, I must be coming down with something. Just what I need.

I step forward.

"Touch a single finger on my body, Silver and I'll break every single bone in your hand."

"Don't kid yourself little bird," my hand cups her chin, fingers pressing into the soft tissue on her cheeks, "If I were to press these hands to any part of your body it's because you've begged me for it. You've pleaded."

Despite the hand that holds her face she still manages to lift her chin defiantly, showing me that pretty face.

"By the time a single finger runs through your pussy, you'll be slick and wet and wanting for what I'd have to give you."

Her eyes widen and her throat works on a swallow. I don't miss the way her thighs tremble, begging to be pressed together, if only to ease the ache between her legs. I can practically smell her arousal and that shit ain't good.

My cock jerks, fully prepared to slide balls deep inside of her and have her screaming my name.

"You want that little bird?" I tease through gritted teeth, my fingers pressing harder.

"Stop calling me that," She breathes, no heat to her words. She secretly likes it and hates that she does.

It's no doubt confusing being attracted to me. The man that almost killed her only a few days ago, the same man that kidnapped her and strapped her to a bed in a strange house, giving little to no information as to why.

Completely and utterly innocent.

Those words taunt me.

I've made it my own personal mission to push all that shit away. There's no way to make it in the world with your humanity still in place. You take what you need, what you want, and you don't care who gets hurt in the process. You steal and you kill because that's what gives you the power. You drive fear into the people around you to maintain your authority.

But this. This *guilt*, it'll kill me well before I get a chance to harm her.

I'm standing so close I see the tones of red in her hair, the light dusting of freckles on her skin. I drag her towards me, dropping my head so my lips whisper against her skin.

Her chin is still tilted up defiantly inside my grip, her hands balled into fists at her sides.

"You can say it," I tell her on a whisper, running my tongue up the shell of her ear, "your secret is safe with me. You want me and you hate yourself for it."

She lashes out, swinging wide, on course for her fist to hit me square in the jaw. I catch it last minute, gripping her entire fist in my hand. I snatch my hand away from her face, pushing slightly so she stumbles away from me but don't release the fist inside my palm.

Ainsley was right, she's so small, this tiny fragile thing, easy to crush and yet she stands tall. She roars loudly, and holds herself as if she were the biggest person in the world. It's not hard to see why most people would underestimate her and she uses that to her advantage.

I squeeze her hand, not hard enough to break anything but it's going to hurt as her knuckles roll together and her fingers curl in too tightly. The edges of her eyes crease but other than that she gives no sign that she's in pain.

"You're such a brave girl," I tell her.

"And you're a pig."

I suck my bottom lip into my mouth, scraping my teeth across it before releasing it again. I let her go abruptly and take a step back before I do something stupid like kiss her again.

"Strip now, little bird, shower," I tell her, "I'm allowing you some semblance of normality before I take that away."

"That's cruel you know," she tells me, seeming to give up the fight for me to leave the room.

She tugs her shirt over her head, revealing tight and toned abdominal muscles. A silver bar glints in her naval, and there's another tattoo etched in her side over her ribs.

I realize my error immediately.

Her curves, all of them are on show to me right now, the dip in her waist, the flare of her hips. Her breasts are covered with a lace type of cropped top, resembling a bra but not quite as supportive. I don't know what they call it, but it hides nothing. I see the shapes of her breasts, her nipples showing through the translucent material. Her chest moves rapidly, her breath coming fast.

She moves to her little shorts next and tugs them down her toned legs, stepping out of them until she's left in just that tiny little bra and her panties.

Holy fuck.

I thought I'd felt pain before but staring at a woman like Wren and not being able to even touch her wasn't just damn painful. It was *torture.*

I tilt my chin towards the ceiling, staring down at the little bird in front of me, the fiery desire burning so hot and powerful in my veins it takes everything in me not to snap and rip the rest of those clothes from her body. I feel my nails biting into my palms, the sharp edges cutting through the skin to allow beads of blood to sink beneath the nailbeds.

Fuck.

I've witnessed nails being pulled from fingers, brains being splattered over the wall and yet I can't see a grown woman naked without reacting like an adolescent boy!?

It truly fucks me in the ass to watch her and want her and not touch her.

She keeps her green stare on my face, never once turning her back on the monster in the room and switches the shower on, allowing a few seconds for the water to heat before her bare feet squeak against the tile on the bathroom floor and she climbs under the spray, still in her underwear.

The glass steams up immediately and it's only then, when she has some protection from the fog on the glass that she removes the rest of her clothing, throwing the damp lace to the corner of the shower basin.

She stands under the spray, the water coming down

powerfully and soaking her naked body. The glass has already steamed up, but I can see it all, the curve of her breasts, the way they push out as she arches her back and tips her face to the water.

Damn siren.

The water soaks her red hair, straightening out the curls and plastering them to her back. Her ass is curved and tight, perky, perfect for a hand to squeeze and caress and slap. She keeps her face tilted to the water, allowing it to wet her skin and roll over the surface, droplets rolling between her lips, clinging to her eyelashes.

Turning away, I cross to the vanity and grip the marble counter.

I can't just leave her in here on her own, fuck knows what kind of trouble she'd cause but if I stay in here any longer, I believe I might just join her in that shower. Have I ever been so tempted before?

No, there was never any need to be tempted, I could just have what I wanted.

But her, she's the damn enemy's daughter. The opposition. The fucker threatening my city.

Even the reminders aren't enough to push down the compulsion.

She doesn't even know *who* she is. Why she is here.

I keep myself firmly planted at the counter, hands gripping the marble tight enough I'm sure I'm able to crack it but, even I know I'm not super human and this shit won't crack under the pressure unlike me right now.

Finally the shower turns off and the glass door opens.

I catch her reflection in the mirror above the vanity, and if I thought seeing her before was bad, seeing her like this is agony.

Wet skinned, droplets of water running over the curves, following all the lines of her body I wish my tongue could trace, red hair clinging to her back. Pink skinned, wide eyed.

So very innocent.

Shit.

Shit.

NINE
Wren

There's something empowering about a man brought to his knees – figuratively of course – by your body. I see it as clear as day, he wants me, and it fucking kills him.

Good.

I hope seeing me tears him apart inside. I hope it turns his gut and forces his heart to pound uncomfortably.

What I'm not prepared for is my own desire burning hot as hell in the pit of my stomach. It's sick, it's twisted and yet no matter how hard I try to control it I want him just as badly.

If he's the monster, what kind of sick fuck does that make me?

The man kidnapped me for heaven's sake, I *stabbed* him and yet my pussy clenches, I grow wet, the lust making my head hazy and the lines between us become blurred.

One little taste wouldn't hurt, surely. Just a touch, a slight caress.

No.

I won't do it. He can continue to want me, he can continue to war with himself, but I won't give him the satisfaction, only for him to put a bullet between my eyes. Because that's how this is going to end. He hasn't said the words but I'm not stupid. There's no way I'm walking out of here with my heart still beating.

It's sad that my life will end at only twenty-three years old, but I don't fear the end.

I pluck a towel from the folded pile near the shower and secure it around my body before picking up another to knot around my hair, holding the wet tresses atop my head in a turban. Now covered, his eyes go back to that blank yet slightly amused stare.

"Are you finished?"

"Yes."

"Good."

Clipped, short and icy.

As I follow him back to my room a plan forms in my mind. The man wants me, that much is obvious and if I can get him close enough, maybe I can use it to my advantage. He carries a gun on him, probably other weapons too I just needed to find them.

I watch his formidable body, the way the muscles move in his back and shoulders, how quickly his legs eat up the space before him. His wicked beauty is unfair, the brutal lines that make up his body means that this little war between us is unbalanced. A monster shouldn't look that good.

Back in the room, I look towards the bed, the sheets pristine and not the rumpled mess they were before. His housekeeper must have changed them since we had been gone.

"Can I trust you won't jump out the window if I leave the handcuffs off?"

"That depends," I shrug, heading towards the window to peer down. Three floors and a straight edge with absolute zero way of climbing down, no guttering or trellises in sight. If I jumped, I'd break both legs if not more.

When I turn back to Alexander he's grinning, a condescending and smug tilt of his lips. I roll my eyes.

"I won't be escaping out the window," I tell him.

"Good."

He says no more as he turns and heads towards the door, "There's some clean clothes in the drawers. Help yourself."

"You know this isn't how it's supposed to be," I call after him, "All this kindness is going to make me believe you have a heart after all."

"Don't be fooled, little bird, this isn't kindness, this is me simply," he purses his lips and rolls his head side to side as he chews over what words he wants to use, "offering you a little comfort before I have to take that away."

"So it will end that way then?" I say, keeping him in the

room a little longer. When I don't elaborate, he places his hands in his pockets, arching a brow while he waits for me to continue.

I head to the drawers, pulling the top one open to find simple tank tops stashed within. I pluck a black one out and then move to the next drawer, grabbing a pair of sweats that are going to be too large for my frame. I'm short, only five foot three and a hundred and thirty pounds which makes buying clothes that fit me perfectly a hardship.

I get to the bed and then drop my towel.

"Fuck!" Alexander roars, eyes widening. I hold in my chuckle, slowly easing my legs into the sweats. As expected, they are too big so I tie them as much as I can and then roll both the waist band and the legs so I can move without tripping or the things falling to the floor. I slip the tank over my head, covering myself.

I continue to watch him, seeing how tightly his neck is strained as if barely withholding his restraint.

I sit at the edge of the bed, cocking my head as I watch him.

"I'd like to believe you're not the monster you come across as, but I also learned long ago what you see is usually what you get."

"You'd be wise to listen to your instincts, little bird, this kindness is from pity and nothing else. Do you think I'll feel guilty when I eventually have to do what I set out to do?"

"You know," I tap my finger to my lips, "in all of this, the threats, the conversations, not once have you stated the words 'I'm going to kill you.' Why is that?"

His eyes narrow, "You want me to lay it out?"

"Yes."

He crosses the room and stands in front of me, looking down at where I'm sat on the bed. I was already much smaller than him but in this position my eyes are level with his crotch.

A little thrill shoots through me.

My hormones clearly aren't getting the memo.

"You want me to say it?" He growls.

"Yes."

Suddenly his hand comes around my throat and he shoves me onto the bed, flat on my back with his weight pressing into me. My thighs cradle his hips and I don't miss the hardness pressing into my clit through the material of the sweats. Arousal floods me and my hips grind against the sensation, needy and wanton despite knowing how dangerous this is.

Damn it.

His pupils are blown, eyes that were once silver appear black with only a neon rim, haloing his pupils. His nostrils flare and his fingers twitch, but he isn't pressing hard on my windpipe, I can still breathe perfectly fine. The pain of the bruising there already makes my eyes water but it doesn't take away from the sensation going on down there, especially not when I feel his own hips roll to mimic the movements of my own.

"Why say it when I can show you exactly what I plan to

do?" His voice is all animal, a growl, husky, rough, the vibrations of it travelling from his chest into mine.

I tip my chin back defiantly and his eyes drop to my lips.

"Then do it," I tell him on a whisper.

I press my hips up harder eliciting a moan, whether it's from him or me I don't know.

His lips crash down on mine, with his hand still placed around my throat, and right in this moment I'm his willing captive, the delusional little girl begging to be touched.

Escape. Live.

The words push in at the corners of my mind, through the fog of lust running wild inside of me, I realize how much of an idiot I am being. His tongue duels with mine, heavy with shameless need and desire and I match the pace, pushing back. I dust my fingers up his side, feeling the muscles jump under my fingertips beneath his shirt and I follow them around to his back. The hard butt of his gun hits the heel of my hand, but I don't linger long enough for him to realize I've felt it. I just need to get it. I pull the bottom of his shirt from his pants, digging in my nails. He nips my bottom lip and I almost lose it. His teeth sink into the plump, sensitive flesh and a very real moan leaves me.

Fuck, I've never been so damn hot for a guy. It just so happens that the guy I'm suddenly fucking batshit for is the same guy destined to end me.

Quickly, before I allow this to go any further, my hand curls around the gun and I yank it from its place, finding the safety catch easily. I press it into his side, pushing hard enough to leave a mark.

He kisses me one last time before he chuckles, lifting his face away from me.

His eyes bore down into me and a dark smudge of a brow lifts.

"Up," I order. "Now."

Slowly, he eases off of me, adjusting himself but I see the stiff rigid length of him pressing angrily against his zipper. I know exactly how hard he is for me right now.

Yeah buddy, I think to myself as I push up off the bed, *I'm just as hot for you too.* In all the crazy shit I've done in this life, this has to take the cake. Not the gun levelled in his direction, the indecision on whether this is the right thing to do.

Crazy bitch.

I push the thoughts aside, standing from the bed with the gun still pointed in his direction, I try to steady my breathing.

"House is awfully quiet," I comment.

"I sent them away," he nods.

"That was silly, whatever will you do now without your trusty sidekick?"

"Ryker is my second, not my sidekick," he corrects, "and if he finds me dead there isn't a place in this world you can hide where he won't find you."

"Oh I believe that," I nod, "but that's okay."

"You're brave," he nods, "a little stupid but brave."

I narrow my eyes, "How am I stupid, Alexander?"

He chuckles, "Damn, when you say my name like that it gets me real hot." As if to prove himself he palms his cock through the material of his pants.

I'm staring. I know I am, but I can't fucking stop.

"Answer the question," I grit out, "how am I stupid?"

"Are you going to shoot me, little bird?"

"Yes."

"And that there is where your foolishness is," he rubs a hand across his kiss swollen lips, "because if you had really thought about this, do you honestly believe that I would have kept a loaded gun within reach of your greedy little hands?"

My eyes widen, he's bluffing.

My finger twitches on the trigger and he just grins wider, the sick bastard. He's taunting me, has to be, to save his own skin.

"Go ahead," he nods, "shoot me."

Do it, Wren. Shoot him.

The muscles in my hands cramp up, why the hell can't I do this!? Damn it!

"Pull the trigger."

My heart thumps wildly in my chest, my stomach churns.

"Do it, Wren, pull the trigger! Shoot me!"

He steps forward and I press the trigger.

TEN

Lex

The click is loud, deafening really, second to the sound of her heavy breaths. Her eyes are wide, swollen lips parted.

My cock is harder than it has ever been before, pressing painfully on the zipper of my pants.

The girl pulled the trigger with the gun aimed at my head. She was prepared to do it so, why the fuck am I hotter than hell for her?

I take calm steps towards her when really, all I want to do is rush her and strip her from the clothes she's only just pulled on. I'm not thinking straight and right now I don't want to be. All I want is to be balls deep inside this fucking crazy woman.

She presses the trigger again and again, frantically, so much so that the gun isn't even pointed at me anymore.

I wasn't stupid to leave my own gun on me loaded. There

was always a chance this could happen, even if the kiss didn't occur, and I have so many weapons stashed around the house I wouldn't be unarmed for long. Right now I am weaponless. Did I need a weapon to take her out? No, of course not, doesn't mean I wouldn't come out of it bleeding though. I'm sure the girl will put up a hell of a fight.

In fact, I hope she does. When it eventually happens, and it will, she better fucking fight. She deserves to give herself that much.

I step into the gun, the barrel pressed to my sternum as I reach forward and tilt her chin up so she can see my face. Her eyes are wide, swimming with panic but not fear. This was her plan. Seduce and take out.

The little siren.

"Brave girl," I murmur, leaning forward to whisper my lips across hers. She allows it, her lashes fluttering closed. Her copper hair, darker now it's wet, is pushed away from her angelic face, falling down her back with little droplets of water rolling over the strands and dripping off the ends to soak into the fresh sheets below. "But very misbehaved."

I pry the gun from her hands, but she doesn't let go so easily. When it finally comes away, she whimpers against my mouth.

"Do you want to feel good, little bird?" I mumble, dipping my head to her throat.

She doesn't answer me, but she doesn't pull away either.

"I need words," I tell her.

"Y-yes."

"Good girl."

I tuck my fingers under the hem of her tank and push it up, feeling her silky smooth skin under my hands. She's burning hot, her skin feverish and soft. I discard the tank behind me, leaving her top half bare to my eyes. She's so fucking perfect. Curves in all the right places, a taut belly and her breasts sit perky and round on her chest. My fingers feather on the underside, a swarm of goose bumps pimpling her skin. Her nipples are hard pebbles, begging for my touch. I follow the curve of her breasts, watching and reveling in the way she arches her spine and pushes them forward for me.

"So very pretty," I mumble.

Her breathing comes out faster as I roll a nipple between my thumb and forefinger, pinching hard enough to straddle the line between pleasure and pain.

She might not realize it yet, but this girl likes a fight with her pleasure. I just know it.

I'll push and she'll push just as hard back.

"Stay still," I order, dipping my head to capture a nipple between my teeth. When her body jerks I bite down harder.

"Ow!" She curses.

"Stay still," I order again.

Her nostrils flare but she holds still this time as my tongue laps at the hardened peaks.

"Shit," she mumbles, "shit. This is wrong. So fucking

wrong."

I grin against her skin, she's right about that at least.

This is where lines get blurred, goal posts get moved.

Her father is out, set to destroy my entire world and here I am, getting myself a sweet taste of his daughter.

Like the good girl I know she can be, she stays dead still, the only give away that she wants this as much as I do is the way her breathing comes out heavy, the way her eyes are hooded and pupils blown.

I run a hand up between the valley of her breasts, nails biting into the skin at her collarbones until I find her throat, still injured from the fight she put up in the apartment.

An unexpected pang of guilt tightens my chest and I find myself feathering my touch over the delicate areas, somehow wishing that the bruises would go away if I just loved them enough.

Replacing my hand with my mouth I trail kisses up her chest, scraping my teeth across her collar and she tilts her head back, allowing me access to her throat. I bite and nip at her skin, pressing hard into her flesh.

My cock presses into her lower belly, wanting in on the action.

I shove her back on the bed and she glares up at me, her eyes narrowed.

I cock my head, watching her, top half naked, breasts heaving with each chaotic breath.

I've never seen anything more beautiful. I see the war

within herself, the one in which she battles on whether she wants to kill me or kiss me and I live for this shit.

"Take them off," I refer to the sweats.

"No."

"Are you going to deprive yourself of this?" I ask.

"Are you?" She taunts.

I grin.

"Take them off, little bird."

Grumbling, she hooks her fingers into the waist band and tugs them down her thighs, shoving them with zero grace.

"Happy?"

"Very."

With her bare pussy on show to me, glistening with her arousal I almost snap. Seeing her naked is one thing, seeing her naked, needy and so very ripe for the taking is a whole other story.

"Touch yourself."

"Fuck you."

She does as she is told though, her delicate fingers working over her flat stomach and then dipping between her legs, smearing her wetness over the folds until she finds the little bundle of nerves at the top. Her head rolls back as she rubs her clit, eyes fluttering closed.

"Look at me." I bark, palming my cock through the material of my pants.

Her eyes ping open and she levels me with a look that would flail a weaker man.

Her jaw twitches as her body tenses up, ready for her orgasm.

"Stop." I order.

"What?"

"Stop!"

Her hand stops moving but she doesn't come away from her core. I press forward, snatching her hand away.

"You're a fucking asshole," she grumbles.

I bury my face between her legs, licking her from her hole all the way to the top and she crashes down on the bed, her hips lifting, wanting more. I flick my tongue against her clit, sliding a hand up until it presses against the entrance.

"Your pussy is so fucking sweet," I growl against her flesh, lapping at her, tasting her arousal on my tongue.

I slide a second finger in.

"So tight, little bird."

"Shut up."

I pump her with my fingers while I toy with her clit, sucking it into my mouth, nipping at it with my teeth.

"Oh fuck!" She moans.

"Come for me," I demand.

I curl my fingers inside, finding the rough patch on her

internal walls and she comes undone. "That's it, little bird, all over my tongue, I want to taste it." Her thighs clamp around my head, her hips grind on my face and I continue to lick her, tasting it, feeling it with every spasm and roll of her hips.

"Yes, oh fuck, yes!" She screams.

When her pussy calms I pry her thighs apart and come up for air, leaving her arousal all over my face. Her eyes narrow when I go to the first button of my shirt.

She watches with intense focus as I flick through each one and then slide the shirt off my shoulders. Her eyes roam over every inch of me, eyes snagging on the scars that litter my abdomen. The stab wound beneath the ribs, the lacerations across my stomach, the bullet hole in my shoulder. Let's not forget about the fresh one in my arm, courtesy of this little siren.

I flick the button on my pants and shove them and my boxers down to the floor. My cock bobs in front of me, hard and ready.

She swallows.

I jerk my hand up the shaft, smearing the precum over the crown.

"Are you ready, little bird?"

ELEVEN
Wren

This is insanity.

This is going to kill me.

And yet, I'm shameless as I peruse his entire body. All the hard lines, the ruthless edges, the sharp corners. He's as hard as stone, all his muscles defined, peaks and ridges, rolling muscles and valleys. His defined abdomen is riddled with scars, some easily identified as bullets, others not so much but it doesn't take away from the appeal of the man. His waist tapers into a V, forming an arrow down to his hard, proud cock that juts out from his hips. Muscular thighs, one still bandaged with a white gauze where I stabbed him.

I grin a little at that.

He steps towards me, his jaw clamped tight.

"Open your legs."

I comply but scowl in his direction, making sure he knows I'm not happy obliging to his demands. I just want him. I need him to settle this ache in me, the one that has been present since I first laid eyes on him. This man is both poison and antidote.

Once won't hurt then I can go back to hating him and plotting my escape.

He kneels on the bed, coming towards me.

"This isn't going to be sweet," he warns. "I *am* going to *fuck* you."

"Then do it already," I snap.

He quirks a brow and grabs an ankle, pulling me towards him where he then settles between my legs.

"You have quite the mouth on you," he growls, pushing his thumb between my lips. I bite him.

He hisses out a breath but doesn't withdraw his thumb, instead he pushes down on my tongue which only forces my teeth to withdraw from his flesh so he can remove his finger.

"Maybe we should put it to good use," he contemplates.

"You put your dick in my mouth and I'll bite it off." I warn.

"No returning the favor?" He smirks.

"Not to those who don't deserve it."

He nods his head back and forth and without warning, he shoves his hips forward, impaling me on his cock. He's so big and I'm well, not, that the pain of it makes my eyes water. The invasion is all consuming, my pussy frantically pulses, a mixture of pleasure and pain as it tries to accommodate the size of him.

"Shit!" I groan.

His hand comes up to grip my throat, just below the jaw, pressing hard against the pressure points at the joint.

"Maybe I should teach you some manners," he warns, his voice all growl.

"Fuck you!"

He pistons his hips, pulling out almost all the way before slamming back in so far I'm sure he's touching something deep inside me that should never be touched.

The pain has evaporated. Gone.

He fucks me hard and relentlessly, his cock pounding me, our skin slapping together.

The grip on my throat becomes tight as he lifts himself to pound harder, pushing me further into the mattress.

"Shit," I moan.

He keeps going, pulsing his cock in and out of me, my body reacting with each wave of pleasure that shoots through me. This isn't sex. This is anger. Frustration. Rage. He fucks me with his emotions. Punishing me for crimes I did not commit. And I let him and then some.

"Such a good girl," he comments through gritted teeth.

"I hate you!"

He growls, releasing my throat as he lifts himself onto his

knees and yanks my hips up. In this position he goes deeper, rubbing up against that sweet spot inside me that has me seeing stars.

"Are you going to come for me?" He asks through gritted teeth.

"I'm going to come for *me.*"

He chuckles. Taking away one hand from my hip to press his thumb against my clit.

"Yes!" I scream. He presses harder and I'm gone. My walls clamp around him as the orgasm grips me with everything it has. My muscles coil tight, my spine straightens and I cry out. I fall off the edge with no parachute and fall into the darkness below. And I allow it. I take it. I want it.

His own release comes seconds later and I watch him, through hooded eyes I see when it happens. His jaw clamps tight, the corded muscle in his neck becomes unbelievably taut, like it'll snap at any moment and his hips still, his cock jerking wildly inside me as he empties himself.

"Fuck!" He roars.

Spent and breathing heavy he falls on top of me, holding his weight on his elbows. My eyes close as regret churns almost instantly, making my stomach roll. There's no denying how much I wanted him, how much I still want him but the guilt of doing it, having it, it wars with the desire. I feel ashamed. Stupid.

I shove him off me, using my hands to cover myself. I feel his eyes watching me, it burns everywhere they touch but I can't face him.

Twisted City

RIA WILDE

For the first time since being here I feel uncontrollable tears sting my eyes, emotion clogging my throat and making my nose sting. I tilt my face away, trying to regain composure but I can't stop it this time.

The first tear slips down my cheek but clearly, I haven't been successful in my attempt to hide from him.

He pinches my chin and turns my face towards him before the rough pad of his thumb swipes away the fat tear. Shock has my eyes bouncing to his face but he's not watching me, he's looking at the droplet of water on his thumb as if he's never seen tears before, never witnessed sadness, regret or pain.

The tear rolls down his thumb and eventually he drags his eyes away from that to look at my face. His silver eyes bounce between mine, a frown dragging at his brows then simply sucks his thumb into his mouth, tasting my regret on his tongue. Without another word, he collects his belongings and struts, naked from the room, closing the door loudly on the way out.

I break.

For the first time since he kidnapped me at gunpoint, I fucking break hard.

I've always been good at keeping my emotions in check, deep breathing exercises, yoga, meditation but this unrelenting turmoil makes me want to scream.

I snatch my clothes from where they've been discarded and shove them on, wincing when I feel him seeping onto the insides of my thighs. Just fucking perfect that is. He didn't even wear a condom. Jesus Christ.

Granted I was on birth control, but I hadn't taken it in

days, not since they took me, and I doubted he had any diseases, but I wasn't the girl who got so worked up she forgot to use protection. I doubted this one time will cause a pregnancy, but this shit happens all the time.

Who am I kidding? I'm not going to live long enough to worry about being knocked up.

I walk towards one of the doors in the room and open it, finding a huge walk in closet but it's empty, not even a single box here. Closing that I head to the next and sigh in relief, finding a small en-suite. No shower or tub but there is a toilet with a basin over a small white cupboard. I quickly clean myself up, discarding the sweats I'd only just put on for a pair of fresh leggings I spotted in the drawers earlier. No underwear but beggars can't be choosers.

My eyes sting as I head over to the one window in the room. The sun is setting now, the sky turning a fiery orange as the sun lowers in the sky, sitting on the horizon. Shadows stretch across the pristine lawn. The entire house is surrounded by a ten foot wall and from this room I can't see where you enter or leave. Beyond the wall, trees surround the compound, thick and dark, the canopies lush and full. Birds dart between the branches, disappearing into the woods. We must be a decent way out the city, as far as I know there are no thick wooded areas until you start hitting the outskirts of the city centre. If we're even in the city at all.

I rejudge the drop from the window. There's absolutely zero way I'd walk away from a jump this high without some serious damage and he knows it, which is probably why I'm in this particular room.

I head to the door and pull the handle but of course it's

locked, why wouldn't it be?

What else is there to do but go to sleep? Fatigue makes my limbs sluggish and lazy so I crawl up the bed, burying myself into the downy pillows. A nap will do me some good. It'll help clear the sex haze Alexander left me in and then I can figure my shit out.

My lids close heavily and it's not long before the claws of sleep drag me under.

TWELVE
Lex

I fill the glass for the third time, not bothering to stop at just a couple of fingers like I had the first two times. What's the point? I'm just going to drink it too quick and have to repeat this process in a few moments anyway.

The house is eerily quiet, too quiet though I'm far from alone.

A couple of men are stationed through the house, they know better than to make their presence known, especially when I'm in this particular mood.

I stare at the smashed mirror on the other side of the room and then down at my split knuckles. There are still shards of glass inside the wounds, I couldn't get them all out so I may as well let them fester.

That was a stupid mistake. Fucking her, feeling her… seeing her cry.

Twisted City

RIA WILDE

I can still smell her on my skin, taste her on my tongue. Sweet, sweet little bird.

I take a healthy sip of the whiskey, feeling it burn down my throat, warming that desolate place inside of me.

But it's not so desolate now, is it? No, that would be simple. That would make this whole thing easy but when has my life ever been easy?

Never is the answer to that.

I was young, too young really when my father introduced me to the evil of this world and this life. At ten, I witnessed him kill a man. At twelve, I stood by as his men tortured and beat the living shit out of another. At sixteen, he put the gun in my hand.

"If you want power, son, you have to take it. This life is cruel and dark and the only way men like us make it is if we become just as cruel and just as dark."

"What did he do?" I asked, looking at the grown man on his knees in front of me. His face was covered in dirt and blood, one eye was swollen shut, his bottom lip split and still seeping fresh blood over his wet chin. The blood and the tears mingled together, causing it to run faster and drip from the tip of his chin. He looked broken. So very broken.

I knew what my father was. I was *proud* of him. I vowed to be just like him. I would take the power. I would hold this city in the palm of my hand and I would control it all. He was right, in this life nothing comes easy. Nothing is given and if you let it, it'll all slip away, and you'll be left to rot in a ditch of your own making.

There will be those who will want what you have, those

who will use force to take it from you, the enemies will be vast and plentiful, each one worse than the last but you had to be bigger, better.

"He stole from us." My father said, *"He tried to take something that did not belong to him. He was given trust and he used it. For that, we do not forgive. We show no mercy."*

"When do we show mercy?" I had asked.

My father stepped towards me, he gripped my wrist and forced me to level the gun with the man's head.

"Mercy is something no one can tell you to give. Despite what many believe, we are not evil. We feel and we hurt like everyone else, we may straddle the line between right and wrong but what is power without consequence? When you rule this city you will understand that mercy will come to those who deserve it."

"And this man doesn't deserve it," I concluded. Because he didn't. He may have worked for the family for a few years, he was even trusted but he broke that trust and every action, good or bad has a consequence. To keep power you have to prove your worth. If I didn't pull that trigger and I gave him mercy, people could see me as weak. As the Silver too compassionate to do a damn thing about a thief.

I still remember the way the trigger compressed under my finger, the loud bang that echoed around the small room. It made my ears ring. Blood splattered up the wall as the bullet pierced through his skin and then his skull.

I threw up after that. My father patted me on the back and told me he was proud. It was only few weeks after that that I did it again and then again until killing became something of a chore. When I ended a life now, I felt nothing because the people dying deserved it in one way or another.

This life isn't for the faint of heart, you come into it knowing that your life could be cut short in a matter of seconds but we continue anyway because the rewards are just as great.

The Silver's have run the City of Brookeshill for generations and for generations to come it'll only be the Silver name that rule these streets.

Killing Wren Valentine gives everyone the same lesson. Try to take what's mine and you'll feel my wrath. And I would do anything and use anyone to make sure they knew it.

When Wren is dead, when her father has felt the pain, then I'll do what is needed. I'll kill the man. Slowly. Painfully. Unforgiving.

This is *my* city and I'll be dead before it goes anywhere else.

I know what I have to do. I know it and yet here I am, a busted hand, half way to drunk because the girl has got in my head.

This shit doesn't happen to me.

I'm Alexander fucking Silver. I'm fucking king!

Valentine kept his promise. It's been three days and Wren

has not been safely deposited back in his hands. He burned down two more of my locations. Luckily, I had everything moved into new warehouses and buildings that only a few on my payroll know about meaning his arson was pointless.

He thinks he can hurt me but he clearly doesn't know me. I'm three steps ahead of him.

I sit on the plush sofa on the balcony overlooking the dance floor of the club. Revelers grind and pulse to the fast beat of the music. The scent of sex and sweat permeates the air. A girl, dressed scantily in a red dress slides onto my lap. My hand goes to her hip and I roll my head to the side to look at her.

"Hi," she smiles. Plump red painted lips pull back to show pearly white teeth and her eyes flash with desire. Blonde hair spills over one shoulder, the ends tickling her breasts that threaten to spill from the satin of her dress.

I cock my head and narrow my eyes. If only her hair was darker, redder, her eyes green, mouth pink…

Shit.

I push the girl from my lap and lean forward on a growl. With a scathing look the girl prances away to find another man willing to play her games. I've avoided going into Wren's room since I fucked her, unsure if I'd be able to control myself now that I'd had a taste.

"Why haven't you done it yet?" Ryker asks next to me as if sensing where my thoughts have taken me, tipping his whiskey back. His voice is low so the other guys around us don't hear but I still shoot him a look. If he were anyone else, I'd have rammed a blade straight into his throat for questioning me.

"It isn't time."

It's a lie. I should have killed her days ago and dumped her body for daddy to find and yet she's still sitting pretty in my compound.

I needed to send him the message that I wasn't to be fucked with but then how am I to do that if I'm avoiding the girl like a fucking pussy.

I could send someone else to do it, I almost did on a couple of occasions but then I changed my mind, telling myself I had to be the one. I had to be the one to level that gun to her head and pull the trigger, I had to be the one to witness the life draining from her. She was a Valentine, and they were fucking parasites. They had come into my city and tried to take over, but this host wasn't willing. No, it would be me to take out the Valentine's. Only me.

He took away the only woman that ever mattered to me, my mother and for that I would take away the only woman that matters to him, his daughter.

It made sense.

So why the fuck wasn't she rotting in a grave by now?

My fingers tighten on the glass in my hand, so hard that the cuts over my knuckles split back open. I feel the warm blood trickle over my fingers, snaking around the digits like a crimson snake.

Ryker chuckles next to me and I swing my glare on him. I've always had a short temper but this short? No. I feel like I might explode.

"What's funny, asshole?"

He shakes his head, "Someone has a soft spot."

"Fuck you."

"Is that what she said?"

I roll my eyes, "Grow up."

He quirks a brow, "Fuck her and get it out of your system. The quicker you end this the quicker we can all move forward. There are deals on the table that you're ignoring."

"What deals?"

"Sanchez has been with the Mexicans, they want to move Coke into the city, real good shit according to him but the Mexicans know they need to come to you."

"Dawson won't like it," I comment.

"Dawson can grow a pair."

I shake my head. The Dawson family has been working with the Silver's almost as long as we've had this city. It would be wrong of me to consider a new drug route without going to the man himself. He's always managed that side of the business so it begs the question as to why Sanchez didn't go to him directly.

My brow tugs down at that train of thought. There's been a lot of shady shit going on recently that I haven't had the brain capacity to think of but now, with this on the table it's all coming to light.

"Shit," Ryker hisses, jumping to his feet as he peers down at the dance floor below.

I follow his eye line to see what's snagged his attention.

"That's Valentine's right hand," Ryker says.

"I see him."

"He's brave," Ryker growls, pulling his gun from the holster.

I grab his arm, "Really? In a crowded club? Use your fucking brain."

He rolls his eyes, "As if the cops will do shit about it."

I curl my finger to a couple of my guys and jerk my head to the guy sat at the bar. Samuel Jameson is as much a pain in my ass as his boss but why the fuck is he here?

I guess I'm about to find out.

THIRTEEN
Lex

    Samuel jerks out of my guys hold and smooths his hands over the lapels of his suit jacket. His dark hair is speckled with silver, and he looks years older than when I last saw him a mere few months ago.

"Times hard?" I kick my leg up, resting my ankle on my knee as I tip my whiskey back, "You look like shit."

"Fuck you, Silver."

I chuckle, "Touchy."

His eyes dart around, not at my men even though it should be them he's worried about. No he looks everywhere else, at the cameras installed all around the club, at the dancers below, the bar. He doesn't seem to care much for the guns trained on him at all. I don't comment, instead choosing to keep that information to myself.

He looks nervous as all hell, jumpy, paranoid and something tells me it isn't because he's just entered the lion's den all by himself.

"Valentine send you?"

He nods once.

"Interesting," I say, "couldn't get the balls to do it himself?"

"He knows you'd put a bullet in his head quicker than he could speak, or am I wrong?"

"You're not wrong," the man is in hiding. Has been since the day he murdered my mother because he knows how this will end and he's only delaying the inevitable.

Ryker squeezes his shoulder and lowers him forcefully into the sofa opposite me. He was stripped of his weapons the moment my guys got a hold of him, but he didn't try to run which is how I know he's here to relay a message.

Brave. Neither Valentine nor Jameson could know whether I would let him leave here alive.

I'm still debating it myself. I pull the gun from its holster and hold it in my lap, carelessly stroking my fingers over the smooth surface, caressing the trigger like one might a lover.

His eyes glance down at the weapon and then back up to me, "You don't want to hear what he has to say?"

"Not particularly but humor me anyway."

"He wants to set up a meeting." Jameson swallows, "a trade."

"A trade?" I'm not even remotely interested. There isn't a single thing Valentine has that I could want.

"He'll leave the city in exchange for his daughter."

I laugh, "You honestly expect me to believe that?"

"Believe what you want, he's just a father who wants his girl back."

"Wren isn't his girl," I growl, "in fact, has she ever been? He sent her off to live with Benjamin Lawson, pretended that he wasn't even her father."

"That was for her own protection."

"No, if it were for her protection then he would have sent her far, far away. To a family not even linked to this city or this life, he kept her close for one reason."

"What reason is that?"

"He wants her in eventually, to take over from him one day."

Samuel doesn't answer but he grimaces which tells me he doesn't believe that to be true. But what else could he want Wren for?

"You're making a mistake, Silver."

"Am I?"

"Yes," Samuel growls, "You have no idea what you're playing with."

"Oh I think I do," I say to him, "this is my city, it's you who have tried to come in and take it, and it's you who's going to fucking lose it all, starting with the girl."

"So you'll kill a completely innocent woman in the name of revenge?"

"Yes."

"You're making a mistake, this is bigger than you. You'd be wise to surrender."

"I'll be dead before I give up this City."

"Trust me," Samuel stands, "it won't be long before you join all those you've buried yourself."

I level the gun with his chest, "You can send a message back to Valentine that his daughter will be dead in less than twenty-four hours. He best make his peace because he's next."

Samuel shakes his head and then turns his back on me, heading to the elevators to take him back down.

"Oh and Jameson?" I call out.

He stops, back stiffening, "If I see you in my club again, I'll decorate the walls with your brain."

A couple of my guys see him down and Ryker takes the empty chair.

"What do you think he meant this shit is bigger than us?"

I shrug, "It's a bluff. Valentine knows he can't win so he'll use anything."

"I don't know," Ryker shakes his head, "Something doesn't feel right."

"Just keep an ear to the ground, report back if anything raises your suspicions."

"So this is it then?" Ryker asks as I stand and tip back the remainder of my drink, "You're gonna finally say farewell to your little house guest?"

Twisted City

I nod once and head out.

As much as my cock liked the girl it's time I wring that little birdy's neck.

As always, the downstairs section of the club is rammed, familiar faces swim in the chaos of people, naked girls grind on laps and dance on the poles, and I watch as people who pretend to have the authority in this city lean down and snort their money up their noses. There's white dust on damn near every surface and more money than sense being stuffed into the panties of the girls I employ here.

I tip my head to the chief of police, noting the security camera trained right on him as he snorts a line of coke off the stomach of one of my girls.

That'll be a nice little bribe should I need it.

Outside, the air is humid, the promise of a storm pressing in. Angry dark clouds roll through the sky, suffocating the moon and stars.

My driver waits for me at the curb and I slide into the back, finally taking a breath.

It'll be twenty minutes before I hit the compound, so I settle back and close my eyes.

This will be the only time I get peace, here in the back of the Mercedes. The windows are heavily tinted, the engine smooth and quiet as it rolls through the streets of Brookeshill.

The partition between the back and front seats is up and I can pretend, just for a moment that all this shit isn't happening.

Twisted City

RIA WILDE

I don't remember a time in my life where anything was easy. Don't get me wrong, my transactions were smooth, my business dealings successful but there's always something. Like a shadow, you can't get rid of the shit that comes with running this city, it'll always follow, even in the darkness, you're never quite alone.

We're turning down Commercial Avenue when the back windscreen shatters.

"Fuck!"

I duck low, pulling my gun but the fire is heavy and quick. A bullet pierces the partition ahead of me, right where my drivers head would be and the car careens to the side before slamming into a streetlight. My body slams forward, hitting the seats in front of me, my head colliding with the side of the car. The fire continues, pouring shards of glass down on me. It feels as if it's from all sides, but I know it's only on the left, so I use that to my advantage and slide out the right, keeping my head low and ignoring the way my body protests at the movements.

I peer around the edge of the car finding two motorcycles, their riders pointing machine guns at the car. The smell of gas hits my nose. Shit, they've pierced the tank, any minute now it's going to go up in flames.

I realize quickly the guys are low lives, belonging no doubt to one of the small gangs that keep popping up on the south side of the city. Valentine probably has them on his payroll.

I check the ammo in my gun and figure out the best way to take them out without having my own head blown off in the process. If they were my guys they would have stationed themselves on both sides of the vehicle to ensure nobody could escape but that's what you get for hiring idiots. Valentine isn't a smart man after all.

Eventually the bullets stop flying and I peer around the corner, finding the riders jerking the handle bars of their bikes to the left before twisting the throttle and speeding away.

Fuck.

With a sigh, I stand from my position and check through the window. My driver stares lifelessly towards me, the front windscreen red with his blood.

Again, if they were part of my crew, they would have checked the target was dead before hitting the road.

The only way they could have figured out I was alone was intel. Samuel saw me leave and called it in.

The fucker. That's why he was here. Not to relay some bullshit message but to check my whereabouts, my movements. I should have known.

I should have figured that shit out! I didn't get as far as I have got by being stupid and there's only one person to blame for this distraction.

Wren fucking Valentine.

FOURTEEN

Wren

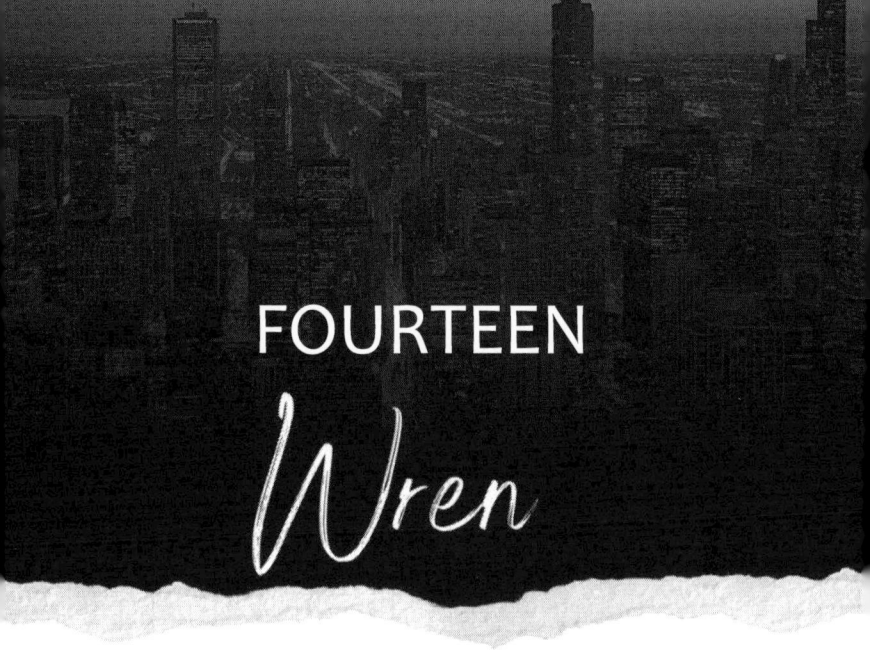

I hear the door slam loudly. Considering how quiet the house is, and has been for the past three days I can only assume who ever just entered is pissed or is, in fact, a bear.

I climb from the bed, I don't know how I know but I know that whoever it is, they are coming for me. My nerves light up, adrenaline pumps through my system, coiling my muscles. I might die here but there is no damn way in hell I'm going out without a fight. I'll be sure to do damage where I can.

I'm ready when the lock on my bedroom door disengages and the mammoth of the man that is Alexander, storms into the room.

He is covered in blood, there's a cut on his brow that is leaking red liquid down the side of his face, bruising has already started to shadow his jawline and partially down the side of his neck. Damn, he looks like he got hit by a truck.

Twisted City

RIA WILDE

I spot the gun he has levelled at me, not at my head though, my chest but he isn't pulling the trigger despite the murderous glint in his steely eyes.

I rush him, if he were going to shoot me, he would have done it by now, either that or I have death wish. The gun doesn't go off as my shoulder slams into his abdomen. I won't lie, it feels like I just charged into a brick wall though he does stagger a bit from the impact. A grunt leaves his mouth but he's quick to wrap his arms around my middle, pushing back with his own weight which is considerably more than mine. The man is a tank, a broad-shouldered wall of pure muscle and violence though size isn't everything in a fight. I'm lithe, elegant even, I move quickly and don't think for a minute that my size gives me a weak punch.

I slide out of his grip and wrap my fingers around his wrist, twisting it until his elbow threatens to snap.

The gun clatters to the floor and I kick it away, watching where is slides so I can grab it for later use.

I'm using his weakness right now, the fact that he's clearly taken a beating before coming here is my advantage even if a tiny piece of me is worried about his injuries. I mean how fucked up is that? The guy kidnaps me, fucks me and then leaves for three days. Whenever I asked where he was, I got grunts and growls in response, that seems to be the native language amongst the fuckers Alexander employs.

He snatches out of my grip and shoves me hard enough that I stumble back onto the bed. He advances like a lion stalking a gazelle, eyes watching every movement, every flinch and twitch. I roll from the bed until it's the only thing that separates us.

His shoulders heave and his eyes narrow.

"Should have pulled the trigger," I taunt.

His brow twitches, "You're right, I should have."

"Why'd you hesitate, huh?"

"Perhaps I wanted to give you a head start. Maybe I wanted to watch you run. Wanted to see how far you could get before I eventually caught you."

I scoff, "Of course you did."

I don't miss the heated gaze he throws my way, I don't miss the way his pupils dilate and his jaw clenches as his eyes roam down my body. I'm back in my sleep shorts now that they've been washed and a small sports bra after getting too warm in here the night before. I wouldn't sleep naked, but this was enough to keep me cool.

He wants me. Even when he wants to kill me, he lusts after me, I just don't know which one he wants more.

It's terrifying and exhilarating all the same.

I should probably get my head checked.

My eyes track to the door, he's left it wide open, probably not expecting such a push back. He grins, with his bloodied face and the violence shining in his eyes, he looks manic and sexy as fuck.

Just get out, I tell myself, we can admire him from afar. Preferably far, far away.

I have speed on my side, but did I really think I could make it? Only one way to find out. I sprint for the exit, weaving past the furniture and it's right there, freedom so close I can taste it, but a thick arm bands around my waist and I'm tugged back hard enough the wind is knocked out my lungs as I collide with his chest. His breath comes out heavy as he pants next to my ear, causing the curls around my face to tickle against my skin. The warm scent of whiskey clings to him but there's other smells on him too, gasoline, smoke though I can't focus on that too much as he presses me up against the wall, his chest to my back. I feel his hardness resting on my spine and memories of the last time we were here flash in my mind.

Warmth floods me.

"What is it about you, hm?" He growls, pushing his cock harder into me, "that gets me harder than a fucking rock every time."

I don't mean to, but I moan, a slight whimper that puffs from my lips.

"You're fucking batshit, that's why," I breathe.

"I fear you like this kind of crazy little bird."

Yes, "No."

His hand comes up to cup the back of my neck, holding me against the wall while his other slips away from my body, coming back a moment later. Something sharp is pressed against my rib cage, enough that it bites into my skin but doesn't cut.

The mix of adrenaline, fear and desire causes my sex to clench, a wash of lust and heat running wild through my body. I can't think straight, only feel. And I feel everything. Every puff of breath, every twitch of his finger on my neck, the way his hard shaft digs into my back.

"What will you do?" I ask.

"What I want and what I need are two very different things."

He slides the blade down my body, stopping at the waistband of my shorts.

"So which one will win?"

I'm helpless right now, he has the upper hand with this position and the knife and I'm glad my logical sense is still working, even if it is sluggish and constricted beneath the haze.

"I don't know," he admits and for the first time I sense his reluctance here. Something or someone is telling him he has to end me but that's not what he wants.

I push back against him and he groans, the tip of the blade presses a little harder into my skin. It'll cut if I'm not careful.

His lips find my throat and presses a gentle kiss there before his teeth sink into my flesh hard. He licks the sting immediately before doing it again and again, with each scrape of his teeth comes the soothing caress of his tongue and it works like a damn charm. My insides have knotted so tight I'm not sure I'll ever come undone on my own. It needs to be him. With each pass of his mouth that blade digs in just a little more.

"Fuck," I growl, pushing back, "touch me damn it."

He spins me suddenly and presses me back against the wall, the blade poised in front of him. My chest heaves as I watch him step forward, positioning the sharp edge at the hem of one leg. A quick slice and the fabric opens, he does the same on the other side and I feel rather than watch the thin cotton fall to the floor at my feet. I'm bare to him completely, in just my sports bra which he gets rid of just a moment later in the same fashion.

"You're so perfect, little bird," he coos, eyes roaming over every inch of exposed skin. "So pretty."

His heated stare burns me from the inside out and in the silence the regret of giving him this, this power, starts to churn my insides. With him distracted, I lunge for the blade held loosely in his hand and snatch it away.

I hold it out in front of me, pressing the tip into his abdomen enough that I see blood begin to bloom on his white shirt.

His eyes finally drop from my naked body down to the blade as if only just realizing I have it now.

"Do it, little bird," he breathes, daring to lift his hands to trace the outline of my body, fingers spread, his palms a whisper away from my skin. Even his phantom touch makes goose bumps chase across my skin.

"Stop calling me that."

Hearing that name, the one he's been calling me for days now gives me a fluttery sort of feeling in my stomach and I hate it. I don't want to feel anything for this man. I want nothing from him.

But I want everything.

"Do it," he presses, leaning into the blade, dropping his hands.

Shit.

Twisted City — RIA WILDE

This is it. I could stab him and make a run for it, granted I'd be as naked as the day I was born but I'd be free.

And yet, I can't fucking do it.

I can't do it!

His nostrils flare as his eyes level with mine, there is no fear of death in his eyes, just a sense of acceptance. I fucking hate it. I hate it all!

A loud cry leaves me as my fingers open, dropping the knife to the hardwood floor. It clatters loudly in the deafening silence.

And then he's on me, his tongue pushing between my lips, his cock grinding into my pussy as if he's starved and the only thing that will sustain him is my body. He lifts me, slamming my back into the wall as my legs go around his hips. In this position the bulge in his pants presses to my swollen clit. Blood and dirt smears against my skin, the grit on him scratching against my skin, rubbing off onto me from him but I don't care. His kiss claims me, it kills me and brings me back all in the same breath and I let it because I'm weak. Fucking weak.

Pleasure builds in my core with the grind of his hips against my centre and my nails claw at his back, drawing even more blood from him.

"I can't do it," he pants against my skin, "I can't hurt you."

"*Please*," I whimper when he pulls away.

Hands and fingers pull at his belt and buttons and then he's entering me in one swift movement. His cock fills me until all I can feel is him, pressing into me hard and everything else, all that I was before melts away.

FIFTEEN

Lex

She is my weakness. *Mine*.

Despite all that is fucked in this world, this woman belongs to me.

I piston my hips, fucking her hard against the wall. Her cries and pleas like damn music to my ears. She feels so damn good, her tight pussy like a vice around my cock, taking everything from me, all that I have to give, she takes and gives back. The loud slap of our skin echoes in the room, her nails dig into my shoulders as my tongue punches between her lips, mimicking what my cock is doing.

Her legs tighten around my hips, a sign she's almost there so I stop.

"What are you doing!?" She screeches.

I can't help it, I grin as I pull her from the wall, my dick still buried in her core and walk her to the bed, dropping her ungraciously to the mattress. The ache of the car crash is long gone, replaced with the burning need to lose myself in the girl in front of me. The enemy no less and yet I'm addicted. I need her as badly as I need air to breathe.

I kick out the rest of my clothes, taking great pleasure in the way her eyes follow the lines of my body.

"You're hurt," she breathes, watching me kneel between her legs and line myself up with her entrance.

"Do you care, little bird?"

Her eyes narrow but then widen as I slam back inside of her, gripping her hips until her ass levitates off the bed. A tingle rushes down my spine as my climax builds and I drop her hips, leaning forward until I have her throat in my hands.

"Are you going to come, little bird?" I growl, my hips jerking chaotically. Her whole body moves when I slam into her and her back arches off the bed, her breasts heaving. Her climax comes quickly, her core spasming and tightening around my cock, forcing my own orgasm to barrel through me.

I come with a roar, collapsing down onto her slim frame but managing to hold most of my weight off her. Her breath comes out in quick rough puffs against the shell of my ear, and I don't know if she realizes she's doing it, but her fingers feather lightly up my rib cage, a touch so gentle and soft I wonder if it's actually there. It's a complete contrast to the way we are, the push and the pull, the fight and the violence, this is something in between that, something dangerous.

I have had every opportunity, every chance to do what is needed but I can't. I've never hesitated, never questioned it, regardless of situation, if it needs to be done, I've done it and yet I can't hurt her. I can't destroy her.

"So what now?" She breathes softly.

"You're mine," I pull out of her, wincing at the loss of the tightness around me, "Just because I'm showing you mercy doesn't mean you're free."

Her brow arches, "You don't own me."

"That's where you're wrong little bird," I tug my pants back on, wincing with the pain in my body now that the adrenaline and the lust has seeped from my veins, "You belong to me now. All that you were and all that you are is *mine.*"

I come down just as Ryker is storming into the house, a frantic look on his face.

"What the fuck happened!?" He hollers, no doubt referring to the car and the shit I left behind. I called it in of course but then I grabbed one of my guys to bring me here. I don't even know where the guy went after I came in here like a raging bull ready to destroy everything in its path.

"Valentine put out a hit," I say calmly.

"You need to get rid of the girl," Ryker growls, "this is becoming more hassle than it's worth."

"I've made a decision," my voice is calm, steady, the anger roaring in my veins only an hour or so ago gone now. I'll have my vengeance, but it'll be in a different form. "I'm keeping her."

"She's not a pet," Ryker huffs, "put her out her damn misery."

"I don't pay you to have an opinion," I warn.

"I'll fucking do it myself."

"Touch her and I'll fucking kill you," I snarl.

He stops in his tracks, his body stiffening.

"Friend or not Ryker, you answer to me!" I bellow, "and I will cut you down just as quickly as I put you up. Touch the girl and I will not hesitate to put a bullet in your fucking skull. Do you hear me?"

He shakes his head, "Loud and clear."

"Get the fuck out," I roar, "get out!"

Ryker turns to me, his eyes searching my face but then he sighs, stepping up to me. I resist the urge to pound into his face when his hand slaps down onto my shoulder, "Let me know your next move."

With that, he takes his leave. Ryker would do it, he would do what I haven't been able to and if it were anyone else, if it wasn't her, I would have let him. But she, she's like a drug, addictive and dangerous. You know you shouldn't take a hit, but you do it anyway because the euphoria is too damn good to resist.

I hear her shuffling around upstairs, her steps hesitant. I left the door open, gave her free rein but she no doubt thinks it's a trick. The girl isn't stupid. Far from it.

With her lingering upstairs, I ensure the security system is engaged and give the heads up to the guys I have stationed around the place. An eye is to be kept on her at all points except when she is in the room with me, she's not to leave the house but can go anywhere within these walls.

I shake my head at myself, running a hand down the front of my white shirt. I'm fucking filthy. Bloody. Bruised.

Valentine had some nerve sending those fuckers after me but the way it was handled just proves how right I've been about him this entire time. He's a little fish in a big pond, barely able to tread the water it's so deep.

A creak of a floorboard being compressed has my head turning towards the stairs. Wren moves like a scared cat, no, cat is the wrong word, she's more lioness if I were to compare her to a feline only, she's a little nervous, thrown off by the sudden freedom from her cage.

"Well hello, little bird," I grin, watching her watching me with narrowed eyes and pursed lips. She's dressed but not showered meaning my scent and my essence is still on her skin, in her body. I've never been a possessive man when it came to women, they were mere bodies used for convenience when I needed to let out some tension but with her, there was no doubt in my mind that I had to have her, mind, body, and soul. There was a tether between us now and no matter how hard she pulled there was no way I was letting it go.

She was mine.

Her eyes drift from me to where the front door is and I see it work through her head, the calculation of getting out, of getting away but before she can even step foot in that direction, one of my guys, a big fucker really, steps in front of the door, blocking the way.

"You can't run away from me," I tell her, settling onto the couch.

"So, what? You'll just keep me here?"

I shrug, "It depends."

"On what?" She snaps.

"Whether or not we can come to some kind of understanding. If I let you go your daddy is just going to get you and I can't be having that."

"What did Lawson do that was so bad that kidnapping his daughter was your only option?"

I laugh, "Lawson isn't your father."

Her eyes go wide, "You're lying."

"Unfortunately, I am not, little bird."

"I have nothing to do with whatever fucked up shit you get involved with."

"You're right but that was before, now, you've just become my most valuable possession."

"I want to hurt you," she admits on a breath.

"I know but you won't."

I tap the couch, inviting her to come sit with me. I'd entertain the thought of her hurting me, not because I thought she couldn't do it, she most definitely could, I have a bullet and stab wound still healing from her to prove that but because she won't. She can't. She's as obsessed with me as I am with her. It's unhealthy but then nothing in my life can be deemed healthy.

What's another unhealthy habit to add to the mix?

"You're so sure of that," she comments but sits like a good girl, as far as possible away from me mind you, with her elegant legs tucked beneath her and her hands clasped in her lap. She takes a deep breath and then meets my eyes, holding her chin up defiantly. "This situation isn't going to work for me."

I laugh, "There's a lot shit that isn't working for me," I shrug, "I'm learning to accept it."

She rolls her eyes.

"Shit like that will have you over my knee."

"Try it," she growls, rising to her knees, "see how that goes for you."

Damn, I love her temper.

"One day," I tell her, readjusting my hard cock, "and you'll love it."

"Fuck you."

"Perhaps another time," I stand from the couch, rolling my shoulders, "I have things to do."

"So what, you're just going to leave me here? What about giving me some damn answers!?"

"Another time."

She stares after me as I head towards the stairs, I stop at the bottom and turn back to her.

"Welcome to my Twisted City, little bird, together we can be formidable."

SIXTEEN

Wren

I take my time in the shower.

I lather my hair with the expensive shampoo that smells like honey and smooth the foamy bubbles over my skin, careful over the bruises still healing plus the fresh ones Alexander so kindly gifted me after our last little tussle.

When I reach between my legs flashes of his body flexing atop of mine has my core pulsing. He had well and truly wormed his way under my skin. It was an itch I couldn't scratch, a damn ache that wouldn't go away no matter how hard I tried to remedy.

I suck in a breath as the pad of my finger rubs across my swollen bud, eyes fluttering closed as my mind conjures images of his thick body moving, his muscles flexing, the murderous glint in his eyes shining bright in the darkness.

Come for me, little bird.

Twisted City

RIA WILDE

My teeth bite into my bottom lip as the deep baritone of his voice rumbles through my body as if he's just said the words in my ear. My thighs shake as an orgasm hits me hard and unexpectedly.

This is what it has come to. Sleeping with my fucking kidnapper and masturbating in the shower over him.

I have a sickness and I fear there is no cure.

The shackles may be off for now, but I am no where near free. He's made sure of that with his goons stationed at every door, on every corner and every room. There's no way I can get past all of them though I'm sure it could be fun to try.

I dry off using one of the thick fluffy towels in the bathroom and step up to the mirror, rubbing the condensation on the glass with my hand.

A girl I hardly recognize stares back at me.

I look the same, they're my eyes and my lips, my freckles and wild copper hair but I don't feel like me.

Is it odd that I feel powerful?

The bruising on my throat is a mere shadow now, the one on my temple practically gone and my skin looks healthy considering the circumstances. I haven't seen myself in the mirror since he took me and I expected harsh shadows under my eyes, sunken skin, but I see none of that.

I dress in fresh clothes put out on the bed for me and go in search of the man himself. I ignore the men stationed throughout the large house which I now realize is a mansion, likely big enough to be a hotel should they wish to convert it.

Something tells me however, Alexander isn't into the hospitality business.

No, the type of business Mr Silver deals is dark, and gritty, violent and bloody. He's the man your mother warns you about, the one that looks like an angel but sins like the devil. He'll corrupt your soul, tempt you and tease you before ripping out your heart and feeding it to the wolves.

He didn't scare me though. Even though he should, I didn't feel an ounce of fear when I stood head to head with him. I felt equal, even if everything between the two of us was never in my favor.

I find him in a bathroom further down the hall, one on the other side of a large master bedroom but because the door is open and the mirror inside stretches from one side to the other I can see him in the reflection.

He's shirtless, his bronzed skin stained with dried blood the color of rust and cuts mar his back, chest and arms. There's still a bandage wrapped around his arm where I shot him and it's likely his leg is still wrapped but if they hurt him, he was a pro at hiding it. Even now, with the bruises and the cuts that look angry and raw, he doesn't wince or flinch, just does his business like it's a normal day.

And it probably is.

He's probably been through worse more times than he can remember, and these wounds are nothing but an inconvenience.

I step onto the plush carpet, my feet sinking into the fibers as I make my way across the room. The air in this space smells like him, dangerous, spicy, intoxicating and when I get to the bathroom, I notice the shower is running, steam bellowing out from the top of the glass cubicle.

His eyes flash silver as they meet mine in the mirror.

"I'm surprised you don't have a personal nurse service," I grumble.

His teeth flash as he smiles, "Care to volunteer?"

I shrug and head over to the counter, stepping in front of him and scanning over his body. His pants hang low on his narrow hips, the firm muscles of his abdomen tapering off into a V that disappears beneath the waist line. A fine dusting of hair travels from his naval and disappears under the belt but he's hairless everywhere else. The wounds on his body are superficial, grazes more than anything else but they are dirty, covered in grit or mud though the deepest and cleanest wound is on his stomach, just below his ribcage. It's clotted and the blood that had run from it has dried so I start there, taking the cotton pad from his fingers and tipping some fresh antiseptic onto the pad. I slide it over his skin, wiping away the blood before getting to the cut itself.

I didn't go deep, just enough to cause a small incision and the skin has already started to knit together. When that's clean I move to the other grazes, cleaning them up, changing the pad and reapplying the antiseptic with each new cut I find.

He stands perfectly still, the only way I can tell he's even alive is by the steady rise and fall of his broad chest. I move around his body, cleaning up as I go and start on his back. There's new and old scars all over him, some aged and silver, others still angry, raw and pink. These scars tell a story of a life lived violently.

"I should check that," I tell him, referring to the bandage

on his arm.

"Want to check out your handiwork?"

"Something like that."

He holds his arm out to me and I begin to unravel the white gauze. When I pull it away I inspect the injury I caused. It wasn't a through and through, just hit him at the edge though it's deep. It looks healed enough and someone had given him stitches, they were clean too.

"You should leave this off for a while," I tell him.

He dips his chin in a nod, eyes looking down on me.

I take a fresh pad and jump up onto the counter, leaning forward so I can do the cut on his forehead and cheek. When I struggle to reach, he forces my legs apart and steps between them, his hands coming down to rest on top of my thighs. Almost absentmindedly his large hands squeeze into the soft flesh of my thighs, his fingers indenting into my skin.

A few hours ago he wanted to kill me – again – and now he's looking at me like he wants to devour me – *again*.

I ignore the heat in his gaze, I ignore the rampant desire to shove his pants down and let him take me right here on the bathroom counter. That last time was the last time. It can't happen again.

The lines have already been blurred and crossed two too many times, I can't let it continue to destroy me.

"You're good now," I whisper.

"I've never been good, Wren." He sighs, stepping from between my legs and turning to the shower.

I don't look away when he shoves out of his clothes and pulls on the door to step inside. I don't even look away when he turns to me, his cock clearly on show through the glass. Watching is different than doing, right? Right. So while I might not allow myself to sleep with him again, I can watch.

And there's no denying I'll enjoy it too.

I watch him work the soap into a lather, smoothing the foam across his muscles, rubbing away any remaining dried blood on his skin. There're bruises now forming from whatever happened earlier.

"So are you going to fill me in on anything or is my presence here always going to remain a mystery?"

"Anyone ever tell you how very sharp your tongue is?"

"My trainer," I shrug, "answer the question."

"You're really quite demanding for someone who isn't calling the shots."

"Don't test me, Alexander."

His smirk is smug and infuriating, "Unfortunately Little bird, you're just a pawn."

"For what?"

"Your father crossed the wrong family, it's time he learned his lesson."

"So why draw it out?" I growl, jumping off the counter to stand in front of him. The glass separates us, but I still feel the power radiating off him, the way he stares, fixated on my face. His confidence is paramount to anything I've ever felt, the promise of pain and retribution is as clear as my own reflection. He wants to make my father hurt and he's using me to do it.

"I told you I wouldn't hurt you."

"And you expect me to believe a man like you?"

The shower shuts off and he steps out, leaning across to grab a towel. His muscles roll and flex with the movements as he hooks the white cotton around his hips. Water droplets roll through the crevices between his abdominal muscles, licking at his skin, clinging there as if they couldn't bear to be parted. Water clings to the long dark lashes framing his silver eyes and the muscle in his jaw jumps.

"I am a lot of things, Wren but a liar isn't one of them. What could I gain from lying to you?"

I think about that. The air in the bathroom is hot and stifling, perspiration dots across the nape of my neck so I turn and head into what I am now assuming is his bedroom. I take a seat on his bed, crossing my legs, trying like hell to ignore the scent of him that wafted up from the sheets when I sat down. The mattress is plush, soft, yielding to my weight and welcoming me, so snug and tight I could roll up and sleep.

"Well, you've made it clear that my family has somehow wronged yours and now you're using me to get your revenge, right?"

Just saying that out loud makes me feel like I've just stepped into some sort of thriller movie or book but whatever, I've always known the world is a cruel dark place, whether I expected to witness it myself however is a different matter.

"How do I know you won't just make me trust you and then pull the rug out from under me?"

Alexander saunters to his drawers, pulling the top one open and sliding out a pair of sweats. Huh. I'd pegged him as a guy who only donned designer and perfectly tailored suits.

Before he utters a single word, he drops the towel that conceals what he has beneath. I avert my eyes before my brain short circuits while he tugs on his sweats.

"You'll be wise to follow your instincts little bird, I'm not to be trusted but right now, we both win."

"How so?"

"You get to live…" He shrugs as if that's no big deal.

"Well gee, thanks, I hadn't realized my life was so easy to throw around."

"In this world, little bird, your life is nothing."

I swallow.

"As I was saying," his voice is bordering on impatient now, "You get to live, and I get the pleasure of seeing the pain it causes your father knowing you're on my side in this war. That pain will follow him until I put the bullet with his name on between his eyes and bury him in the ground."

"You told me Lawson wasn't my dad, say I believed you," I wasn't sure what I believed truthfully, "then who is it?"

The rims of his nostrils flare as he stares at me, "Your father is Marcus Valentine."

SEVENTEEN
Lex

There's been a part of me that has been expecting a lie.

It's what people do. We lie. We protect ourselves. Our loved ones. Sometimes we don't even mean to do it, it just simply happens because at the time it's what we think is best.

A part of me has been expecting this whole thing to be a ruse. A thing Marcus and Wren have thought up to ensure her safety, her innocence but as I stare at her face, at the big green eyes, filled with an innocence I'll never recognize in anyone else in this world I realize I've made the right choice.

My father always told me mercy is given to those who deserve it and there is no one more deserving than Wren, despite her last name.

She has no idea who her father truly is. Having been raised by Lawson, he's been the only man she's known and while he's far from innocent he isn't who I am after.

After deciding her death would not come by my hand I started to think of another plan.

Regardless of the situation and my incapability to do what I need to; I knew there was another way to hurt Valentine.

He's kept his daughter safely tucked away but never too far. He's watched her, doted on her from afar, ensured her future, all in preparation to bring her into the family fold.

Granted, the family fold is built on lies and thievery but to him I'm sure it's very precious.

She was being groomed to take over from him. I was almost certain of it. But that *almost* was giving me doubts, what if I was wrong here? What if that wasn't the plan at all? If that's the case, what the fuck could he want her so badly for?

They taught her how to fight, how to hold her own, that much was clear.

I had no doubt she could take down a man twice her size, hell she could have taken me down had I eased just a little, let my guard down just enough for her to slip in. She had no problems protecting herself and with the right motivations and incentives it wouldn't have taken her long to get into the swing of things.

But really, what will it look like if Valentine's daughter started fighting for their enemy?

People will question his authority, his command and power, if, after all, his own daughter could turn against him then why shouldn't they?

And once he starts to feel it slip, when he realizes he's losing it all I'll ensure he knows, in those last final moments, he has most certainly *lost it all*.

I'll keep the city, I'll keep the power, I'll have his daughter and what will he be? A rotting corpse buried six feet under.

Watching her face now, after I've given her his name, I see nothing but a blank expression.

The girl is fearless.

She simply doesn't give a fuck who I am or what I can do, she'll stand in front of me and she'll give me shit and I won't deny it, I fucking love it. I live for it.

Her push when I pull, her fight, her fucking everything…

I stalk towards her and grasp her chin, tilting her face up so she's staring me directly in the face. There's so much hate in her gaze, it burns hot but not nearly as fiery as the desire that swirls in the mix. She hates that she wants me, loathes it but there's no denying this basic instinct.

Like a moth drawn to a flame, she wants to touch, to see, to feel, despite the very real threat of pain. Of death.

She fights it. Tooth and nail but she'll learn.

She'll be the good girl I know she can be and until then, I'll keep her here. With me.

"Together, little bird, we'll bring your daddy to his knees."

"I think you're mistaken," she breathes.

"Oh no," I shake my head, leaning down to brush my lips across hers. It's soft, unlike the last kisses I gave her. This one is a promise.

A promise that she'll always belong to me now that she is in my grasp.

She seems taken aback at the gentleness. She doesn't reciprocate the kiss, her lips stay still, slightly parted and her eyes open but there's a mass of emotion there I can't wait to dissect.

"I'm very rarely wrong," I tell her, "you'll learn soon enough now, sleep, we have a busy few days."

She frowns, "You think I'll bend to you, but I won't. You don't and will never own me."

"We'll see."

She scoffs, "Asshole."

"Sleep little bird," I jerk my head to the pillows, "tomorrow is a new day."

"I'm not sleeping here."

She says this as I gently coax her down onto the bed, pushing gently until her back hits the mattress.

"I'll follow," I promise. "Wherever you go, I'll be one step right behind you."

Fatigue clings to her fibers, pulling her under. I've put her through the ringer, it's bound to have caught up by now and the promise of a plush mattress and a warm body is singing to that deep seated desire for comfort. Her body curls in on itself, in the centre of the bed, she tucks her knees to her chest and wraps her arms around them before her eyes fall closed, too heavy to fight.

"I won't let you win," she mumbles, half asleep.

Leaning over her, I tuck a single copper curl behind her ear, "Oh but little bird, I've already won."

Leaving her sleeping in my bed, I head down to my office. I've been detached from the business for too long and it's time to get back on track.

I text Ryker to meet me here in an hour, he's been on the ground while I've been busy with Wren so he's the perfect person to get me up to speed with what's happening out there.

I'm sat in the chair behind the desk, swirling amber liquid around a glass when my right hand walks in. He still looks pissed but he's loyal. I wasn't bluffing when I told him I'd put him down and he knows it. We may have been friends since we were kids but no one questions me. Not even him. And no one, I mean fucking no one, not even the devil himself, will threaten what belongs to me.

"Boss," He greets, lowering himself in the chair opposite me.

"I want a report," I tell him, leaning forward.

"Two shipments hit the dock tonight, our guys are on it, moving the cargo to the new warehouses. The dealers were getting a little mouthy since the last lot they were due to get went up in smoke but they've settled now."

"Which dealers?"

People are forgetting their place. Not being out and in the masses is clearly giving them the wrong idea that I won't get involved should I have to.

"Dawson is dealing with it," Ryker grumbles.

"Is he now."

Ryker nods, shoulders stiff.

"What else?"

His eyes dart to the left and that's not a good sign. He's hiding something.

"What is it?" I demand.

"Valentine's men showed up at the dock tonight, throwing threats to our guys, nothing happened but one of them mentioned something that I think we need to keep an eye on."

"Go on."

"We all know how much of a pain in the ass Valentine is, he wants his daughter back and I'm sure he'll go to whatever measure he needs to, to get her back but I don't actually think Valentine is calling the shots anymore."

I lean forward, "What do you mean?"

"The guys weren't happy to be there, they found it pointless coming after a girl and whether they meant to or not, they mentioned how the boss wouldn't be happy deviating from the plan."

"What boss?"

"They called them the Syndicate."

"So Valentine has teamed up with this organization?"

Ryker shrugs, "I think it might be wise to give her back.

Settle this down for a while."

"Good job I don't pay you to think." I growl. There was no way I was giving her back. Not only is that weak as fuck and goes against everything this family has built, the girl stays by my side at all times from here on out. There was no question about it.

"Well you're not going to kill her, there's no reason to keep her."

"She's mine!"

"I feel a war coming, Lex, one that I'm not sure we're prepared for. Giving her back is the smart move here."

"Valentine is tiny, you're worried he'll destroy this?" I stretch out my arms, "this is an empire Ryker, and our army is bigger, better and stronger. We have the power. He has nothing."

"Except this Syndicate, we don't know who they are and what strings they can pull."

I roll my eyes, "Well then, let's set up a little meeting shall we? Get some information."

"When?"

I scrub a hand across my mouth, "Tomorrow night. Take him to the club."

Ryker nods and stands, "Is that all?"

"Set up a meeting with Dawson," I tell him, "for Sunday, he needs to handle his dealers better."

With another nod, Ryker steps from the room. Silence settles around me once more and my mind drifts to the girl asleep in my bed.

My legs carry me from the room quietly, up the stairs until I'm hovering above her. To look at her now you would never assume the girl is feisty as hell, it's easy to forget when she sleeps so peacefully.

Without thinking too much about it, I slip into the bed beside her, pulling the blanket up to cover us both. A soft sigh escapes her lips as she rolls towards me, tucking her face against my chest. I stiffen when her arm comes around to hold my waist, her leg thrown over both of mine like she's ivy clinging to a pole. Her breath fans against my bare chest.

This was a terrible idea. I didn't sleep with women. We don't share beds other than for fucking, we certainly don't fucking cuddle. When I try to move, her body tightens against mine to the point where I truly believe if I stood, she'd still be hanging off me.

"Fuck," I grumble as she settles in further, as if trying to climb inside of me and now I can't move.

It would be easy to throw her off, wake her and kick her out of bed but now I'm here and she's curled into me like she needs me, I can't bring myself to do it.

I'm clearly going fucking soft.

That'll change tomorrow night.

When I woke this morning Wren was gone, I had searched for her, but she had made herself scarce, if I didn't know better, I would have assumed she'd made her escape. But my men have been posted throughout the house and I had confirmation Wren had been seen last in the kitchen a little over twenty minutes ago.

I hold the fabric in my hands as I continue my search for her. The house is big but not that big, she's either literally hiding likes she's a six year old playing hide and seek or she's purposely avoiding me. I'm not the quietest of people, my size doesn't allow me to be stealthy and silent but hers does. She's likely keeping an eye out and darting off without a peep before I can catch up to her.

It's pissing me off.

As I storm down one of the halls, a rhythmic thud has my ears perking. It's coming from the gym I had installed a few months back and contains every piece of equipment you could ever need. The door is cracked and through it I see her. Her copper hair is pulled up into a pony tail, it swings like a pendulum side to side as she jabs at the bag suspended from the ceiling. Her small body moves quickly, the power she packs in her punch surprising. Sweat makes her skin shine under the lights and her eyes are laser focused on her task.

"Unless you're offering to replace the bag, I don't want to talk to you," she grunts, slamming another fist into the leather. I notice then she isn't wearing any gloves or tape, her knuckles are split, trickles of blood snaking around her fingers and dripping onto the mats under her bare feet.

"That's enough," I order.

She ignores me, slamming another fist into the bag, harder this time. Blood smears across the bag.

"Enough!" I roar. "Don't fucking push me."

Her body comes to an abrupt stop, spine stiffening but then she whips her head to me, "Or what?" she taunts.

"I'm warning you, little bird, you won't like what happens next."

"You and your idle threats," she rolls her eyes.

I snap, my temper bursts and I storm across the mat towards her. The game of cat and mouse this morning, her attitude, her taunting, I've had enough today. She growls when I grab her around the waist and throw her over my shoulder. Her skin is slick with sweat but she smells fucking amazing. She slams her fists into my back, squirming and fidgeting wildly as she tries to escape. I hold her tighter, pinning her legs to stop her from kicking me. I ignore the quizzical looks my men are giving me as I take the stairs two at a time, her body bouncing roughly on my shoulder, hard enough no doubt to wind her. When I make it to my bedroom, I throw her down onto the bed.

"You'll be wise to remember who fucking owns you!" I bellow. She gets up onto her knees and glares at me.

"You don't fucking own me, Alexander Silver," she says through gritted teeth.

Her defiance should not be a turn on, but it is. I pounce on her, pinning her beneath my much larger frame and grind my hard cock into her pussy. The warmth of her penetrates her leggings and my own trousers, wrapping around my cock as if it's her delicate little palm. Her lips part, eyes rolling back as the friction presses on her clit.

"Get off me!" She breathes though it's said with zero conviction.

"This is mine," I nip the lobe of her ear, my hands slide

up her slim waist, cupping her breasts, "mine." My hands travel over every inch of her, whispering against her feverish skin, committing her every dip, curve and edge to memory. "All of you is *mine*."

"Lex," my name whispers from her lips, her back arching as I grind against her through our clothes.

"Say it, little bird."

"Fuck you!"

I chuckle, "You'll learn, until then," I climb from her, swallowing down the urge to fuck her hard. When I'm sure I can control myself, I throw the fabric I've been carrying around for the better part of an hour at her. It lands on the bed next to where she is still laying, her chest heaving with her breaths.

"Put that on."

"No."

"Little bird, you'll do as you're told. There is no negotiation here."

Her eyes narrow but she takes the dress and slides it into her lap. At least she know what's good for her. "We leave in an hour."

I don't give her time to argue further, instead I spin and head to my walk-in, closing the doors behind me. I've been relegated to a fucking closet. By a woman.

Damn it.

EIGHTEEN

Wren

The dress slides over my skin, satin material that sits around mid thigh but has a split all the way up to the hip on one side. Basically it's a wardrobe malfunction waiting to happen. It's too tight and the split too high to get away with wearing underwear but I debate for a little while wondering how much I care about that. The real question is, how vulnerable do I want to be around Alexander?

I've left my hair down, it falls wildly around my face, silky and soft from the wash I gave it an hour ago. I'm still debating when Alexander strolls back through the door.

He had hidden himself in the walk-in for twenty minutes and once he was dressed he left me in the room alone.

He's in a pristine suit, black in colour with a white shirt tucked into his pants. The top three buttons have been left undone, showing the hard expanse of bronzed skin. He's trimmed the hair around his mouth and slicked his dark hair back though a tendril still falls forward across his forehead.

His eyes devour me, taking in the high slit in the skirt and the way the material hugs my curves.

"You look beautiful."

My brows shoot up. I wasn't expecting a compliment, so much so I can't control the blush that steals its way up my cheeks. Fuck.

I hate that he affects me in anyway but mostly, I hate that I can't control my body's reaction to him. It wants him, despite my better judgement, I react and I lose control.

"I had someone collect your belongings from your apartment," he tells me a moment later, "it's all up in the attic room. You can select some shoes and then we need to go."

"You broke into my apartment?"

"I had a key," he smirks.

"You are an absolute psycho" I seethe.

"Off you go, little bird, times ticking."

Just like he said, all my clothes and shoes have been bought here, they have been unpacked and folded away, my shoes lined up in the closet, my toiletries in the small bathroom. Well at least he's not expecting me to share his room. Waking up with him was terrifying to say the least, especially since I had curled up like a fucking cat right up against him. His arm was around me, holding me close. I got the fuck out of that situation quickly. It didn't even occur to me at the time I could have probably offed him in his sleep, my only thought was not waking him and having to face whatever the fuck that was.

I choose a pair of small heels and sit on the bed to strap them on. I had no idea what Alexander was planning but I already knew I wouldn't like it.

I meet him in the foyer, swallowing down the anxiety.

He looks casually my way, hands buried in his pockets. He nods to a guy behind me and takes my arm, guiding me out the front door. I suck in a breath of fresh air, turning my face to the slight breeze as it teases my curls. I'm ushered into the back of a black SUV, but it doesn't go unnoticed the number of guys that follow us out, piling into 4 more SUVs identical to this one. Alexander slides in next to me, looking down at his phone. The driver doesn't say a single thing to either of us, but he doesn't look like a normal chauffeur. Which probably means he's one of the copious employees Alexander has. He looks hard, unforgiving, and ruthless.

Perfect.

With a huff I slide down into my chair and stare out the window as we set off.

"Let's cover some rules for this evening, shall we?" Alexander drags my attention away from the moving scenery.

I roll my eyes which earns me a scolding look.

"Firstly, you try to run and I've given instruction to shoot first, ask questions later," he tells me seriously, "unless you want a bullet hole in that tight little body of yours, I suggest you don't leave my side. Secondly, you do everything I tell you to."

"You're a control freak, you know that?"

"Do you understand?"

"Yes sir," I grumble with another eye roll.

We're in the car for about twenty minutes but I recognize where we are the moment we pull up outside the club. His club. My door is opened and Gruff holds out a hand to help me out the vehicle.

"Well hi, Gruff," I give him my fakest smile, "such a gentleman."

"Gruff?" His brows draw down.

"Yeah, you know, because you're so grumbly and growly."

"What?"

"Never mind," I pat his cheek condescendingly which earns me a growl that makes me laugh, proving my point.

Alexander is shooting daggers at me, teeth clamped tight.

"Well come on then," I snap, "or are we here just to have a mothers meeting in the street?"

A couple of his men eye me, confusion pulling down their brows, "Such a smart mouth," Alexander tuts.

I'm guided into the club with Alexander on one side and Gruff on the other, Lex's hand is on the small of my back and I'm sure anyone looking in from the outside would see this as intimate. We don't enter through the main entrance though, instead through a side door that drops immediately to a set of stairs I almost tumble down. A hand wraps around my arm to stop the fall but not a word is spoken.

Twisted City   RIA WILDE

Gruff goes first, followed by me and then Alexander behind. I feel his presence like a shadow following me, the heat from his body consumes me, making it hard to breathe.

We enter through another door and what I'm seeing is nothing like upstairs. This is a completely different club, dirty, erotic, down right illegal. People snort white powder up their noses while others grope the women riding their laps, dressed in nothing but a pair of panties. Low music plays through unseen speakers and the scent of cigar smoke and whiskey permeates the air. There are security guards posted every few feet, watching the crowd. There are some very familiar faces here, the police chief, the port authority chief, even the fucking mayor.

Jesus Christ.

While their wives and children are at home these guys are playing with the underground criminals and it quickly dawns on me that Alexander doesn't just ooze power, he *is* the power. He runs this city not any of these guys. Not the mayor or the police, they answer to him, he's the one in control.

A girl dressed in a cute little baby-doll lingerie set sashays towards us though her eyes are for Alexander only. When she finally reaches us, her manicured nails tickle down the front of Alexander's shirt, fingers tucking into the holes between the buttons.

Jealousy stabs me hot and deadly, and I have to stifle the need to yank her hair. I'm not able to stop the growl though which has Alexander peering down at me with amusement.

"Lex," her voice is low and sultry while she eye fucks him

shamelessly. "Let me get you a drink."

Her brown eyes slip to me and one of her groomed brows quirks as she looks at me with disdain, her top lip curling.

My hands curl into fists, the nails biting into my skin.

"You can leave the newbie with Sasha, I'm sure she can train up the runt."

Alexander leans into her, and that jealousy explodes. Fuck. I feel unhinged. I avert my eyes, I can't watch this shit and can't show him it affects me. Even though I try, I can't help but bring my eyes back. His hand is on the back of her neck and she rolls her head back, desire, like a flickering flame burns in her dark eyes. I'm sure she'd mount him right here and right now.

Just when I don't think he can surprise me anymore, his hand squeezes the back of her neck and he jerks her roughly towards him. There's no lust in his gaze as he looks at her, hatred, no that's too strong, but it isn't friendly, "Watch your mouth." He warns.

"W-what?" She stammers.

"You are replaceable," he tells her, "No one will miss you, now, I think you owe Wren an apology."

Her eyes dart to me, "I didn't know she was with you." She pleads.

"Because you're not important enough to know anything." He releases her harshly and she stumbles in her heels.

"My apologies," she stutters before spinning and disappearing quickly, merging with the crowd to get away from Alexander.

Alexander drags me in close as we continue through the underground club until we hit an elevator. Inside it's just me, Gruff and him. The music from the club vibrates the steel walls but other than that and our breathing, the elevator is quiet. And tense. So very tense.

I practically sprint out when the doors open, putting distance between us. We are on a balcony, high above the dancers below. The music is loud, thumping through my body. I grip the handrail and peer down, if I could get down it would be so easy to slip into that crowd and disappear but I doubted Lex's threat to have me shot was empty.

I feel him step up behind me, caging me in with arms on either side of me, hands gripping the rail next to mine. His mouth comes down to my neck, where, so gently, almost as if he hadn't done it at all, he kisses the side of my neck.

My body stiffens with the heat that travels through my veins and I have to press my thighs together which earns me a deep vibrating chuckle. One hand releases the rail to hold my hip, fingers digging into my flesh, "You can fight it little bird, but eventually, you'll give in."

He's right. I've already proved, twice, that when it comes to him all my control slips right out the window. He does something to my body no man has ever been able to do.

He both terrifies me and intrigues me all at once. I should hate him, I should want to kill him, hurt him at least and yet I lean my back to his chest.

I know this man is a monster.

I know he's twisted. Cruel. Ruthless.

Everything about him should want me turning away from

him and running as fast I can and yet, his darkness entices me. It draws me in, speaks to parts of me I didn't realize I had.

I don't want to want him, I really don't but sometimes we don't get what we want.

I'll fight, because that's my nature but eventually we all know I'll break and he'll have me.

And just like the little bird he thinks I am I'll be stuck in his cage with no hope of ever escaping.

NINETEEN
Wren

I take it all back.

I want to kill him.

I stare at the glass in my hand and calculate the chances of being able to smash it and stab him with one of the shards.

"Come now, little bird, come sit your pretty little ass right over here," he taps his lap, daring me. I'm not sure if the challenge is to defy him or to do as he says.

"This chair is perfectly comfortable," I tell him, trying to sound sweet but missing the mark.

A couple of the guys around us grumble, unable to hide their amusement. Lex throws them a look that has them shutting up pretty quickly.

"It wasn't an option," he tells me, "do I need to come over there?"

My eyes dart around, so many people to be humiliated in

front of and he already has so much power, I don't want to give him more. I bare my teeth at him as I stand, stomping my way to him ungracefully. When I reach him, I throw myself onto his lap hard, making sure to land my ass right on his cock and my elbow on his sternum. He grunts and sucks in a breath all at the same time. Good. I hope that hurt.

"Oh I'm sorry," I purr, sliding a hand down his front, "was that a little rough?"

His men can't contain it now, they burst out laughing. Lex ignores them as his eyes burn into me, seething.

"You keep fucking pushing little bird and I'm going to snap."

I shrug nonchalantly and down the rest of my vodka cranberry. Another is put in my hand immediately.

His words and his body are at war with each other. Anger and frustration radiate off him but the thick, hard cock pressing into my ass tells me he likes this. He likes it when I fight him.

I squirm on his lap and his jaw clamps tight as his hand comes down on my exposed thigh, fingers digging into my flesh. "Easy."

"Scared I'll make you blow in your pretty suit pants?" I taunt.

Push. Pull. Push. Pull. That was our relationship.

"You think I won't fuck you right here, right now?" He rasps, "I'll let them all watch. I'll let them all know who you belong to."

The thought both shocks and arouses me.

I flush, from my cheeks, all the way to my chest and further than that. I feel myself grow wet between the legs as my libido takes the reins here.

His eyes flash like molten silver in the darkness, "That gets you off, huh? Knowing all these people here will see me fuck you so hard you'll forget your own name." His hand gently caresses my thigh, fingers teasing at the hem but not slipping beneath the dress. "Does that make you wet, little bird? Do you want my cock in you?"

I open my mouth to retort but my words are stolen when he slams his mouth onto mine in a kiss so possessing it consumes everything. My thoughts, my words, they disappear as his mouth devours mine, his tongue dueling, teeth clashing. There's nothing gentle here. No sweetness, just pure primal need.

His hand finally skims up my thigh, following the slit and then he stills, both his hand and his mouth.

"Where are your panties?" He rasps under his breath.

I grin against his mouth, "This dress doesn't allow for underwear."

The grip on me turns hard, punishing but not painful, a warning.

"You'll never do that again."

"You don't control me."

With a single finger he finds my slit, swiping the digit through my folds. The idea of this is wrong, so many people, so many eyes and yet the pleasure that makes my thighs tremble is a high I cannot resist. I feel my legs part to allow him in more and watch as his tongue traces his plump bottom lip.

His eyes narrow and he opens his mouth to speak but gets cut off.

"We have company," Gruff announces abruptly.

He snatches his hand away from my centre but continues to hold me, his eyes following the direction in which Gruff is looking, down towards the bar and dancefloor. Three men in suits stand menacingly but there's one who stands out. My father. Or who I thought was my father. Benjamin Lawson. He's staring right at me and there's nothing familial about it, he's furious, hatred pours off him as he stares at me. His eyes jump from me to Lex and back again.

"Who are they?" I hear Lex ask but I pay him no attention, my eyes stay trained on the man that raised me. Slowly, I see him reach into the inside pocket of his jacket.

"Lex!" I cry, grabbing him and pulling him to the ground just as a shot is fired. The glass panel of the balcony shatters into thousands of tiny pieces. Another shot has a man behind us hitting the deck hard. Our positions are suddenly reversed, with my body shielded by his.

Screams now overpower the music, the chaos and panic below palpable. Alexander's hands cup my head while his big body shields mine but he's shifting on top of me. We're out of sight of Benjamin but the shots keep coming.

A loud bang close to us makes my ears ring and then another, this one coming from directly above me. I twist my head, seeing Alexander holding out his gun.

The screaming continues but minutes pass and no more shots are fired.

"Get her out of here," Alexander growls as he climbs up off my body and then helps me to my feet. His eyes do a quick scan of my body, snagging on the cuts on my arms, hands and legs from the glass but I don't feel them. I don't feel anything other than sickness as I look down at the mass of panicked bodies, only seeing one.

Benjamin lays face down on the ground, a pool of blood blooming from his head. He's dead.

Grief robs my coherent thought. Despite it all, he was still the man that raised me, the man I called dad. We didn't have a great relationship, but we had something. And now he's dead. Killed by the man holding me as if I'm fragile.

"You killed him!" I scream.

"He tried to shoot you!"

Was he aiming for me? Why?

"Valentine wouldn't have sanctioned that," Gruff says, taking me when Lex hands me off. He tucks me into his side and I let him because if I don't, I'll end up a crumpled mess on the floor.

"No, that was rogue." Alexander looks back down, "Grab one of those guys he was with, we need answers. Now."

Gruff says something to someone and I'm handed off again. This one is unfamiliar and cold but he ushers me to the elevator as he is told to do and walks close to me as we make our way back through the underground area. It doesn't appear they heard the commotion upstairs, they all still sit and play and shove shit up their noses. We're paid no attention and then we're stepping outside. The cool air calms my heated skin. Screams and sirens echo through the streets of Brookeshill. I'm guided into a SUV and then we're peeling away from the sidewalk, leaving the chaos behind.

Silence settles like a hammer, deafening. The shots fired tonight continue to ring in my head and my stomach rolls.

I have no idea what to think. Why would the man that raised me try to kill me? Was it me or was it Lex he was aiming for? Maybe it was both. I don't know.

I don't know anything anymore.

Lex

This is a fucking mess.

I may have control over this city but shit like this looks bad. Cops have to get involved. Statements have to be made. It has to look like all the processes are being followed. The club is empty now, the lights on revealing the complete mess of the place. There're shards of glass scattered across the floor, blood on the chairs, the walls.

It wasn't only Benjamin that took a bullet tonight. A girl, no older than twenty-two is sat at the edge of the club, looking pale and sweaty as the paramedics stabilize her ready for transportation to the hospital. She took a bullet to the arm. Another is dead right along with Benjamin Lawson. Both bodies are covered but their blood still stains my floor. One innocent and one not so much.

He had aimed for Wren, while she was sat in my lap, he had aimed for her and if she had not done what she did it's likely her body would be beneath one of those sheets.

Ryker speaks to an officer downstairs, weaving some story while I try to figure this shit out.

I had confirmation that we caught one of the guys that bolted after the first shots were fired, he's currently unconscious in the back of a car being transported to the compound. They'll string him up out in the barn ready for when Ryker and I get back.

This wasn't what I had hoped tonight would come to.

I knew Valentine's men would show, I knew they would report back that Wren is looking awfully cozy with the enemy and maybe it would have ended up with said girl naked and willing under me. But that shits not going to happen now.

Benjamin Lawson is dead. We have one guy and the other guy is probably back in Valentine's ranks, reporting back.

But why shoot Wren? What was that angle?

Valentine wants his daughter back alive.

My mind whirls back to this so called Syndicate. I haven't managed to figure out anything about them but that'll change tonight. I had plans to interrogate one of Valentine's men and I have one ready and prime for the taking back at the compound.

As soon as this shit is sorted I'll be on my way. Appearances and all that shit require me to stay put for the time being but I'm itching to get back.

If only to make sure my little bird is okay.

TWENTY

Lex

"Get him conscious," I growl, wiping the blood from my hands on a rag I keep out here. Valentine's man sags in the chair, face a bloodied pulp but I'm far from done.

He's keeping his mouth closed for now but I can sense the crack coming, he'll break sooner rather than later.

"Where are you going?" Ryker asks, filling a bucket with cold water.

"To check on Wren."

Ryker laughs.

"What asshole?"

He shakes his head, "Nothing boss. You go check your girl."

I narrow my eyes but ultimately say nothing as I push out

the doors of the barn and head the short distance to the house. My eyes travel upwards finding the light in the attic bedroom is on but the curtains are drawn. She could very well be asleep but a half hour ago I saw her peering out the window, staring at the barn. My men were keeping her in the house to stop her from getting too close to what we were doing but she had to know what was going on.

Inside, I wash my hands and then head up the stairs. Her bedroom door is ajar, golden light spilling out into the darkened hallway and a soft whimpering fills my ears.

She's crying.

Pausing, I listen for a moment. Hearing the deep shaky breaths she inhales and then blows out. A sniffle. Clearing her throat. Eventually I push in, finding her sat on her bed, legs drawn up to her chest. She's still in the dress she wore to the club and dried blood clings to her skin. She hasn't even cleaned herself up. Shards of glass are still embedded into her skin, they glint in the light above.

"You haven't sorted yourself out," I growl.

"Go away."

She turns her face away from me, hiding her tears.

With a grumble I head back out and down to the medical cabinet, fishing out my first aid kit before going back to her room. I don't have time for this shit but clearly she isn't going to do it herself and like fuck will I let another person touch her.

"I said go away!" She yells when I re-enter.

"I heard you," I snap back, crossing the room.

I grab her ankle and force her leg flat so I can get a better look at her knees. The glass is just on the surface, a few shards here and there and other than a few grazes it's nothing to worry about. Fishing out the tweezers, I start plucking out the small fragments and put them into a cotton pad. I do her other knee and then her hands and arms until her skin is clean and the wounds have been flushed.

I meet her eyes, red rimmed and slightly swollen. The tip of her nose is pink and her cheeks are flushed and she looks…broken.

"You killed him," her voice shakes.

"I did what I had to do." I affirm, "you need to shower and sleep."

"You're a monster."

"I never claimed to be anything else, little bird."

She scoffs and turns her face away, "I hate you."

"I know."

I did what was right. Benjamin Lawson would have killed her had he had the chance. If I had left him alive, I had no doubt he would have attempted it again. I just needed to figure out why.

You don't live with and raise a child without growing an attachment regardless of whether they are biological or not. Wren was looked after, cared for, given everything she could ever need by the same man who pointed a gun at her tonight.

"You killed him," she repeats, sniffing.

I understood. I did. Regardless of the situation he was the only man she called father and I took that away, leaving her with nothing. The familial bond overshadows his betrayal. The fact that he failed means she's looking through rose-tinted glasses, unable to fully comprehend what he attempted tonight.

"He would have killed you."

"Then maybe you should have let him."

"I'm not going to let anything happen to you."

"It's funny," she snaps, "I was fine before *you* showed up. My life was normal. Now? Now it's a fucked up mess and I'm suddenly living in a nightmare where my own father wants me dead and the man I'm currently *fucking* wanted me dead only a few days ago."

She's too wired right now, too emotional and I currently don't have the patience to deal with it.

"Shower. Bed." I order.

"Asshole."

"Don't push me, Wren."

She climbs off the bed, wincing a little as the skin on her legs stretches and moves, disturbing the grazes. She comes to stand in front of me, tilting her chin so she's looking down her nose at me.

"I saved *your* life," she jabs her finger into the centre of my chest, "Even if he were aiming at me, that bullet would have hit you too or maybe he would have shot me and then shot you immediately after. I fucking saved you, but I should have let you die. It would have made sense."

"You're right," I grab her wrist, hauling her to me. She lands hard against my chest, "You should have let me get shot but you didn't, and I now owe *you* a debt."

"What?"

"You saved my life, I owe you."

"Then let me go."

"I'm sorry," that's genuine, "I can't do that, even if I wanted to this war is on your doorstep now."

"Because of you."

I nod, confirming.

She sighs heavily and starts to push against my chest, trying to remove herself from me. There's no fight in her, no push, no heat. She just looks defeated and that's on me.

Guilt sits heavy in the centre of my chest.

I've been a part of this life for thirty one years, most of those have been spent with blood on my hands, lives have been torn apart because of me, both directly and indirectly and I've never felt an ounce of guilt. I've never cared enough to.

And yet this woman, *this fucking woman* has crawled under my skin.

I fucking care. And I hate it.

"Shower," I order. "Bed."

She laughs without humor, "Sure thing, *boss*."

I watch her saunter out of the room and towards the

bathroom here on the top floor, hypnotized by the sway of her hips and then she slams the door. I wait until I hear the water turn on and then wait a little bit longer for the door to open and close and then I leave.

Back in the barn, Ryker has the guy awake. He's crying. Fucking pussy.

I grab a chair and slam it down in front of him, the sudden thud making the guy jump.

"What's your name?" I ask as I take a seat in front of him, placing my ankle on my knee and hooking my fingers behind my head casually.

This I can do. This I don't feel guilt for.

The man looks at me with glassy blood shot eyes, "Harry."

"Okay, Harry, we can get this over with really fucking quick, just tell me what you know."

"Fuck you Silver scum."

I laugh. "Wrong answer."

I hold my hand out to Ryker who places several paperclips in my palm. I begin to unbend them, straightening out the small rods of metal.

"What are you doing?" Harry stammers with wide eyes.

"Hand."

"No!" Harry panics as Ryker grabs his tied hands and drags them forward, forcing the fingers out flat on one hand. "No!"

"Are you going to talk?"

He doesn't answer.

I place one of the rods underneath the middle fingernail, pushing just a little, "Last chance."

"Fuck you!" Harry growls.

I jerk forward, embedding the paperclip so far down beneath the fingernail I'm sure it's touching his knuckle bone. Harry howls and I move to the next finger, doing the same thing on that one. Blood and tears mix together. I move to the next finger.

"Wait!" Harry cries, the third paperclip is already in position. I twist it a little, forcing it further down slowly, "wait!"

"Talk."

"You don't understand," he pleads, "They'll kill me."

"You're a dead man anyway, Harry, how you go, however, is entirely up to you."

He frowns.

I sigh, "You see, I'm just going to keep hurting you Harry, the longer your mouth stays silent the longer it will go on. I'll keep you alive but it's going to be painful. Want to know what I'm going to do next?"

His eyes are wide, begging for mercy. I have no mercy for him.

"Next, I'm going to use this little thing right here," I pick up the peeler from the floor. It's rusted and dirty but the blade on it is sharp, "And I'm going to peel off your skin, starting at your feet until I get to your face. If you talk, tell me what I need to know, I'll make it quick."

"I have a wife," he begs.

"And she's going to be a widow regardless. Your choice Harry."

"Okay," he sobs, "okay."

"There's a good chap." I nod, pulling out the paperclip still waiting to be embedded into his finger and throw it to the floor. "Now, why the fuck did Benjamin Lawson try to shoot Wren tonight?"

He swallows, "That bitch is a traitor."

My fist is quick to connect to his jaw, "Don't make me hurt you more, Harry."

He spits blood onto the floor and glares at me, "she's a Valentine and she's fraternizing with you. It makes her a traitor."

"How can the girl be a traitor when up until a few days ago she had no idea Marcus Valentine even existed."

"It doesn't matter. The moment she found out she should have put a bullet in your head."

"Well she didn't so I guess I win that one. Now answer the question, Benjamin Lawson raised that girl and now he wants her dead, why did Valentine order the hit?" I know he didn't but I have to ask anyway, cover all my ground.

"Valentine is a fucking useless piece of shit," Harry spits again, "ever since you took his girl he's been distracted. Edgy. Damn right nasty and is not meeting his end of the bargain."

"What bargain?"

Harry groans, "Valentine is working with another organization, one that has the power to take you out."

I laugh, "Sure they do, if they had the power why aren't they here themselves."

"How do you know they're not?"

"So this organization, what are the called?"

"The Syndicate."

"And so the Syndicate contacted Valentine and told him to start a war with a family that has more connections than he'll ever have. Why?"

"They promised him the city if he did it. But then you went and fucked it up!"

"By taking his daughter." I nod.

"Yes."

"Okay, so that doesn't explain the hit on Wren."

Harry winces as he fidgets in the chair but he doesn't actively speak. With the paperclips still in my hand, I grab one and jab it under his fingernail so hard and so fast it embeds all the way in, leaving just a glint of metal hanging out the top.

Harry screams.

"Talk!"

"Okay, okay!" Harry sobs, "We were tipped off that you had the girl at the club and the Syndicate contacted Lawson, told him if he got rid of the distraction he'd be rewarded. If he got you too, they would have killed

Marcus and put him in charge."

I sigh. Power like that will definitely turn a man like Lawson.

I glance at Ryker who's watching this whole thing with narrowed eyes and a locked jaw, "This Syndicate," I continue, "Why my city?"

Harry laughs then, manically, "Not just your city asshole. All of them. They're the biggest underground organization the world has ever seen and once they have you, because they will have you, they'll take down the rest."

I stand from the chair and pull out my gun, lining it up with Harry's head. I promised it would be quick and I'm a man of my word.

My finger squeezes the trigger without a second thought. The loud bang ricochets off the walls of the barn, the bullet slicing through muscle and bone.

But despite gleaming the information from him I don't feel any better.

In fact, I feel like shit has yet to really hit the fan but when it does, because it will, I will be ready.

I have to be.

TWENTY-ONE
Wren

The gun shot startles me where I lay in bed. My room is dark, my hair still wet from the shower and soaking the pillow beneath my head, but I didn't have the energy or motivation to dry it.

I knew they were doing something dodgy out in that barn and that shot just confirmed it. He just killed a man. Two in one night.

How many others have there been? How many lives has this one man destroyed. Tens? Hundreds? Thousands?

I swallow down the fresh wave of nausea and roll away from the window.

Silence settles around the house again, so quiet I could hear a pin drop until the door downstairs opens and closes and his footsteps echo through the halls. How fucked up does it make me to hope he comes to my room? How depraved?

Am I as bad as him?

Could I kill a man in cold blood?

The thoughts swirl in my head, I'm lost in them until the creak of my door opening has my eyes shutting tight. I know it's him. No one else would have the nerve to barge into my room, not because they're afraid of me but because they're afraid of *him*.

"I know you're awake little bird."

I sigh and turn my back to him, facing the window again. The door clicks shut and for a moment I think he's left but then the soft pat of his feet echo in the darkness and the other side of the bed dips down as he settles his weight there. I don't have to wonder for long what he's doing as he pulls back the sheets and settles his body behind mine.

"What are you doing?" I whisper.

"This is what you do when someone needs comfort, is it not?"

"You want to show me comfort?"

"Shh, little bird." His arms wrap around me, pulling me close and tight. His chin rests gently on the crown of my head while his body molds to the shape of mine.

This is weird.

This man is a monster.

And yet I am finding exactly what he said. Comfort.

Safety.

It makes no sense to feel safe with the devil but that's

exactly what settles over me and drags me into unconsciousness.

When I wake the following morning, my eyes feel like they're covered in sand and my head is clouded. His body is still a hard pillar behind me. We're in the same position as we fell asleep in and when I try to move out of his arms, they only band tighter around me.

"No, no," he grumbles sleepily, an air of boyish innocence lacing his tone, "just a while longer."

"We need to talk," I whisper.

"Jesus Christ woman," he growls, "it's not even seven."

"Would you prefer we spoke over morning coffee and breakfast in bed?" My voice drips with honey. Honey that's poisonous and will make your insides rot.

"Don't get fucking mouthy with me."

I swallow when I feel his thickness pressing against the base of my spine.

"I want to know what happened. All of it."

"I'm not at liberty of sharing those details with you."

"Then what are you are at liberty of sharing, hm? You killed a man last night. Actually two if you include Lawson."

Saying it out loud makes my throat feel scratchy.

"Yes."

"Who was the second?"

"His name was Harry."

"Do you feel guilty?"

Silence meets my question but then he sighs and answers, "No."

"You're evil."

"Evil has a lot of faces, little bird, what you and I classify as evil are very different."

"So what happens to him now?"

"He gets cleaned up."

"He disappears," I rectify.

"Yes."

"How long have you done this?"

"Always."

"And Lawson, it was me he wanted to hurt?"

"Yes."

"Are you sure?"

"If you need confirmation, Ryker was witness."

I scoff, "As if I'd believe he would tell me the truth."

"If I asked him to, he would."

"It's too early for this," I grumble.

"You wanted to talk," Alexander shifts behind me and then his body is gone. He sits at the edge, scrubbing his hands down his face.

"Well I apologize for wanting to understand how I fit into all of this."

"There's more going on than I realized but that's all you need to know." He stands and stretches, "You're safe here."

"With you." I deadpan.

His steel eyes trap me but he doesn't say anything, just stares, making me squirm in the bed. To break the stare, I climb out of bed and go to the bathroom, shutting and locking the door behind me. I lean against the wood, taking a deep breath.

When I come out twenty minutes later, my room is empty. The call for coffee is too strong to ignore and if this is how it's going to be I can't ignore it forever.

I dress in one of my favorite summer dresses seeing as the sun is blaring outside. I may not be allowed out the front door but I can sit in the window and pretend. Pulling my hair into a pony tail I rifle through the belongings he had delivered to the house, finding my pill packet.

I've missed so many, but I should be okay. I pop one out and swallow it down dry before stashing the packet inside my makeup bag and heading downstairs.

There's chatter in the kitchen, hushed voices and for a moment I think about hanging back and eavesdropping but the look I'm being thrown by one of Lex's guys has me reconsidering.

When I enter the large kitchen all talk stops. Three heads turn my way. Lex sits at the island, sipping at a coffee while Gruff AKA Ryker leans on the counter and the blonde who I now know is named Ainsley is perched on the counter, swinging her legs.

She cocks her head to the side, studying me before her eyes jump to Lex. His eyes peruse my body and one dark smudge of brow quirks in interest.

"Coffee," I grumble, stepping into the awkwardness. Ainsley moves out the way while I lean in to grab a cup and place it under the sprout on the coffee machine, but her eyes stay on me as if she can see right inside my head and pluck out all my thoughts.

"Ains," Lex's stern voice has her head snapping his way, "Can you do it or not?"

She scoffs, "Of course I can, I've already hacked his system once, getting back in will be piece of cake."

"Arrogance will get you killed," Gruff grumbles.

"Don't be a baby," she tuts, "I'm hardly facing down a firing squad behind a computer screen, plus I can hold my own." I feel her eyes back on me again. She's probably still pissed that I knocked her ass out that one time.

I'll do it again too.

When my coffee is done, I add a sugar and some milk and then saunter from the room again, leaving them to it. They won't discuss shit while I'm there that'll actually get me any valuable information, so what's the point in hanging around. I head towards a set of patio doors. There doesn't appear to be anyone around and I wonder how easy I could slip outside. Funnily enough my first thought isn't to run, I just want some air and some sun. I'm about to reach for the handle when the sound of gun being loaded has my head swiveling.

"Come away from the door, miss Wren," it's one of Lex's guys and the gun is pointed directly at me. He's not aiming for anything vital but it'll hurt nonetheless.

"I just want some air," I say to him.

"Orders are to not let you outside."

"Please" I beg, "I'll sit right there," I point to the set of chairs and table out on the patio, "You can even tie me down if you want. Just some air."

"I can't do that, Miss Wren."

"It's okay," Lex's voice startles us both, "Lower your gun."

"Sir?"

"Do it," Lex growls, "let her out."

The guy nods and holsters the weapon, frowning at me before slipping back into his position.

"Go ahead."

I pull the handle down and swallow, waiting for the shoe to drop.

"I can go?"

"On the patio, yes. But I think you know that if you run, I'll find you."

I knew it alright, and the thought exhilarated me. Maybe one day, I'll test the theory.

TWENTY-TWO
Lex

She curls up on the wicker chair, her summer dress falling lazily over her bent knees as she sips at the coffee in her hands. Her eyes are still slightly swollen though they look clearer than they did last night, not so clouded with emotion.

I couldn't expect her to understand, I couldn't expect her to be able to process what she saw like the rest of us would. She's been sheltered, kept in the dark and yet she's been a valuable player her whole life. It seems cruel to keep someone like her in the shadows.

If not me, it would have been someone else. Up until now no one paid much attention to Valentine, he was useless, not really a threat, more a nuisance until he decided to attack. Now I realize he's grown tired of being the little man in this world and is coming for the big guns. My city. Had he picked another city, another town, they would have picked apart his life too, found his weak spots and exploited them, who knows what could have happened to Wren then? There's so many ways girls like her could go missing and not every time means death.

This organization, the Syndicate, they are backing him and not knowing who they are or where they have come from puts me on edge. Being blind in a game like this has deadly consequences.

Leaving Wren on the balcony I head back through to the kitchen but bypass it instead and go to my study, pulling my phone from my pocket.

My father has been out of the game for months now, he left me fully in charge though I know he still has his fingers in the pot. There's no way in hell the old man would have just left. Even though his wife died and he was distraught, wrecked with grief, the city was his second love. Just like it was my grandfathers and his grandfathers. The Silver's own this city and have done for a long time, it's in our blood.

I dial my fathers number and settle down in the chair behind the desk, pulling up the camera feed, going to one in particular. It shows the back side of the house, positioned in a way that shows both the stretched lawn and the balcony where Wren sits. She's made me want *more*. An obsession I can't seem to shake, and I fear that if it is ever taken away, I'll never be the same.

She's as still as anything, the only giveaway that she's even real is the gentle way the wind teases her hair and her arms gently cradling the cup, bringing it to her lips every few minutes for a sip of her coffee.

The phone rings three times before he picks up.

"Son," he greets, his voice husky and rough from a lifetime of bad decisions.

"I need information."

"Well hello to you too."

"Hello," I grunt, "good enough?"

Me and my father didn't have a bad relationship, but it wasn't one filled with love and compassion either. No, I was raised on brutality and hostility. My mother was the one who showed me compassion. She was the one who nursed me and cradled me when I was a child, giving me at least some semblance of a normal childhood. I respect my father. I value him. But there was no compassion. The relationship between him and I seemed more like a business transaction, there was always an ulterior motive behind everything and even now, as I phone him and hear his voice on the other end of the line, I don't feel anything other than the need to find out more about this Syndicate. I didn't care to find out how he was doing, where he was or even if I'd ever see him again.

He chuckles, the laugh turning to a harsh cough, "What information?"

My eyes stay trained on the girl who's invaded my entire life. "The Syndicate. Who are they?"

"Where did you hear that name?"

"So you've heard of them?"

"Yes."

"What do you know?"

The line goes silent for a long time, long enough for me to pull the phone from my ear to check the call is still connected, "Not on the phone. I'm back in the city in soon.

We'll meet to discuss it then."

"When? I don't have time for this," I growl. "Where the fuck even are you?"

"That's none of your business." He huffs, "Soon, Lex. See you then."

He hangs up. He doesn't offer anything more or anything less. My hands curl around the phone as frustration and anger war with each other inside me. I was blind. I was fucking blind and I had no way of knowing shit. I had to hope Ainsley with her technical skills could get me something but I was losing patience.

There was no way in hell I was letting this shit go or stay in limbo for a damn week let alone an infinite amount of time. I needed to find who this fucking Syndicate was and end them. Now.

My eyes stray to Wren once again. One of my housekeepers has stepped out onto the balcony with her and is passing her a coffee. She smiles and takes it. As the house keeper turns back, her face lifts to the camera.

I don't recognize her, and I know all my staff.

Fuck.

I bolt from the chair and sprint through the house, drawing my gun from the holster at my back, clicking off the safety. I spot her walking casually towards me, when she notices me there, she halts mid-step, eyes growing wide.

"Down!" I bellow.

My voice startles Wren behind her, still cradling that cup of coffee. "Put it down, Wren." A sickness churns my gut, something akin to fear and panic.

She eyes me, the gun and then the coffee, her brows drawing together before she gingerly places the mug on the table and climbs from the chair.

"What's going on?" She asks.

"Down!" I yell again, directed to the intruder.

The commotion has drawn Ryker and Ainsley from the kitchen, the moment Ryker spots my weapon, he withdraws his own.

The woman before me lifts her hands slowly, bending her knees to lower herself to the floor.

"They made me," she cries.

I take a look at her, her skin is translucent, the bones on her face prominent as well as her collar bones and hands. She looks ill, malnourished. Her lips are cracked and her eyes are bloodshot.

"Face on the floor," I order, keeping my weapon trained on her with one hand, I beckon Wren to me with a curl of the finger on the other. The only reason I haven't shot her yet is because Wren is here. She's seen enough death in the last day, one more is not going to be added to the table.

Wren comes willingly though she is clearly confused. I tuck her into my side, turning my body to shield her.

"I didn't know she was your woman," the girl cries, "They didn't tell me that. They just said that she betrayed them, that she had to die and if I did it, they would let my sister go!"

"Do you know who I am!?" I growl.

She shakes her head.

I pass Wren off to Ryker who follows a similar move as me, tucking her to him and shielding her from whatever the fuck this is.

"What's in the coffee?"

"Cyanide."

Fuck.

They're not messing around. This Syndicate want Wren dead. A punishment to Valentine. I'd laugh if it wasn't so fucked up. Wasn't it me who had the same idea and now look at me, protecting the girl.

"Hands where I can see them," I tell her, "and then get up, slowly."

The girl raises her hands above her head and then slowly rises from the floor, keeping her arms above her head, "Ryker, take her to the barn."

"No!" Wren cries, "no don't do that."

"This isn't a time for mercy, little bird." I growl.

I hear the thud of someone's fist hitting flesh and I spin around, a blanket of fury making my blood boil so quick and fast I see red. Only what I expect to see and what I actually see are two very different things.

"She broke my fucking nose!" Ryker moans, cupping his face. Wren's eyes widen as she rushes towards me, but she isn't looking at me. By the time I realize what the fuck is going on, Wren has ripped the gun from my hand and has pulled the trigger. The loud bang in the small hallway makes my ears ring.

After the silence settles around us like a lead weight there are three thuds in executive order, one behind me and two in front.

TWENTY-THREE

Wren

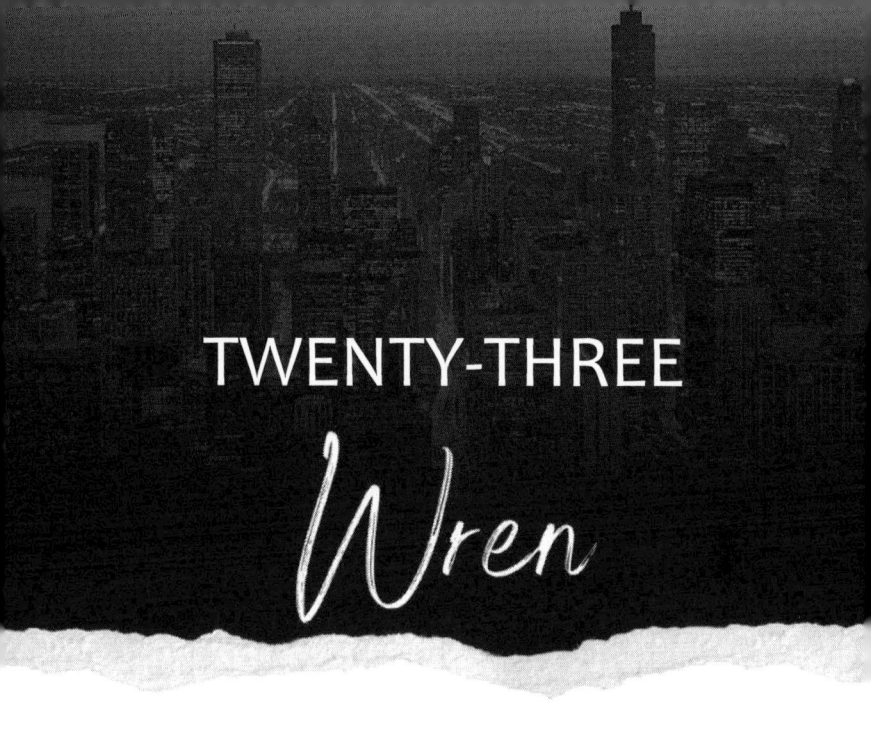

I spin around, my fist colliding with Gruff's nose. It's the only way to get him to release me and he's not expecting it which is why it connects with as much power as I can muster. I cringe at the sound of my fist connecting with his flesh, the cartilage breaking under the pressure and then the outburst of blood that streams from his nostrils. I ignore the pain in my knuckles as I rip myself away from his body.

I can't let them hurt her. She was only here because someone else put her up to it. That's not fair. They didn't give her a choice.

I can see clearly she's unwell, malnourished, in need of a good bath and some food, probably medicine too. I thought the same when she bought me my coffee – *my poisoned coffee* – and I thought it strange then. All the staff Alexander has employed here look healthy, happy even and it begs the question if they really know what happens within these walls. She didn't look like she fit but then what did I really know about any of this? So I didn't question it. Not until Lex stormed towards us like a demon sent straight from hell, his weapon drawn and directed at the girl.

I rush towards Lex, I'll beg and I'll plead until he gives her mercy.

But all that changes when I lock eyes with the girl over Lex's shoulder. She's suddenly pulled her own gun and has aimed it for the back of Lex's head. Her hand shakes, her eyes wide with both vengeance and fear and the next thing I know, I'm ripping the gun from Lex's hand and pulling the trigger.

She goes down hard. Quick too, the bullet hole in her chest blooming red immediately. Her hands hold it, the blood seeping through her fingers as if to contain a leak. When her body finally hits the floor she's staring wide eyed at the wall.

Oh God.

Oh god!

I killed someone. Shit. I killed her for him!

The gun slips from my hand and hits the floor. Lex stares at me, seemingly frozen as the gun rattles against the hardwood floor and then my knees give out. The pain, the guilt, the nausea of what I've just done crippling me. My knees crunch on the hard surface as a sob rips from my throat.

What have I done!?

"S-she," I stammer, shaking my head, trying to form

words while my tongue refuses to cooperate, "she was going to kill you."

All I can see is the young girl in front of me, she can't be much older than me, her hair is blonde, ashy but greasy and dirty. Her eyes are a deep blue color and while her skin is pale and sickly, she has an olive complexion, one that probably glows had she been healthy.

"Clean it up!" Lex growls but I can't see him. I can't see the others either, just the dead girl. The one I killed. For him. For Lex.

Why did I do that? That's twice. *Twice*! Why the hell would I save a man who wanted me dead only a few days ago, save a man who is keeping me here against my will. He's a monster and yet I don't want him to leave. I need him.

I've never needed anyone but for some sick and twisted reason *I need him*.

How do you need a man you've only known for a few weeks? How has he suddenly become so important to me that all his misdeeds don't even account for anything?

His body steps in front of mine, blocking off the image in front of me. With her out of sight the world comes back to me. I see Ryker step around me, Ainsley too but they keep a wide berth, making sure not to touch me. There's shuffling, the movement of something heavy being dragged across the floor but I can't see. Tears stream from my eyes, wetting my cheeks. I didn't think I had any left to give but I can't seem to stop them. I sob and I cry until Lex leans down and gently lifts me from the floor.

My legs feel like jelly, weak, like the bones have turned to mush but it's not painful. They just don't work. My stomach rolls.

When walking doesn't seem to work, Lex leans down and swoops my legs from underneath me, hoisting me into the cradle of his arms. My arms automatically loop around his neck.

"Don't look," he whispers, "Tuck your face to my chest. Don't look."

So much death. So much blood.

I cry into his chest, wetting his white shirt as he carries me through the house and towards his bedroom.

He gently places me on the bed where I immediately curl into a ball.

He must have gone into the bathroom at some point because now I hear running water but I didn't realize he had left until he's in front of me again.

"Come, little bird, sit up."

I do.

He slides my dress from my body, throwing it behind him and then removes my underwear. It doesn't feel sexual, but my body responds to his touch, nonetheless.

I'm sick.

Who gets aroused at a time like this? After they just killed someone.

I don't have time to think about that for long because the next minute he's lifting me from the bed and guiding me to the bathroom. The tub is almost full but the faucet is still running as he guides me towards it, coaxing me into the hot water. Steam rises from the surface and I sink down, letting the water run over my skin.

"Shh," Lex soothes, "It's okay."

"I hurt her," I whisper.

"It's okay."

I shake my head. How could it be okay?

"You're in shock. Wren, take a minute, breathe."

"Get in with me?" I ask, my voice quiet.

"You want me in there?"

I nod. "Please."

"Okay, give me a minute." He turns to leave but my arm dashes out, my wet fingers hooking against his shirt.

"No don't leave."

He puts his hand over mine and gently pries my fingers off. With his silver eyes holding mine he strips from his suit, revealing all his hard, lethal muscle and for a minute I forget. I revel in the brutal beauty of this man. I commit each scar to memory, each roll and flex of his muscles, the smattering of hair at his navel that travels all the way down to the pubic hair around his groin.

He moves with all the lethal grace of a lion stalking a gazelle. When he climbs into the tub and lowers himself behind me, the water level rises quick, spilling over the rim of the tub but he doesn't seem to care as his arms reach around and drag me to his chest, settling me into the cradle of his thighs as his arms gently stroke down my arms.

I never thought this man could do gentle.

"You make it look so easy," I say quietly. "how?"

"It wasn't always. But I turn it off, little bird, I don't feel."

"I killed someone."

"It's okay."

"It's not okay."

"Shh, little bird, relax."

Lex

This should never have happened. I'm distracted. That's twice now, in less than twenty four hours, that I have been distracted and people have gotten hurt.

I don't care much for the girl, despite her pleas, I wouldn't have shown mercy. There will be no mercy for anyone who comes for Wren.

Like this city, she belongs to me.

When Wren is finally asleep, her head in my lap while I gently stroke her hair, wild and unruly, I climb from the bed, turning out the light.

The shock will be with her for some time but she's strong and eventually she'll realize she did the girl a kindness. I wouldn't have made it that quick.

Twisted City

RIA WILDE

"How did she get in?" I ask when I hit the kitchen. Both Ainsley and Ryker are still here, Ryker now sporting a swollen nose with dark bruising starting to appear beneath his eyes.

"Here," Ainsley points to a camera feed from seven thirty this morning. Most of my house keepers stay on sight in the small annexes set down near the gates but some travel in. They are vetted and searched at the gates before being allowed entry.

I watch the feed and as the guard stops a vehicle I see her slip in while he's distracted. She darts left and tucks herself into a hedge line against the wall. It's another hour before she reappears again, further up the gardens, close to where Wren is on the balcony. I didn't notice her when I was watching the feed because she's not in direct line of the camera but is on the one looking from another direction. She seems to pause when she sees her on the balcony.

The girl was smart. She knew if she shot her there and then there was no way she would be getting off this land, so she slipped in through a back entrance. After that you can guess how she maneuvered through the house, posing as a housekeeper. No one would have questioned her, I have several members of staff here everyday, and she looks innocent and plain enough to fit right in. She probably avoided the kitchen Ryker and Ainsley were in, they would have noticed she didn't quite fit because they'd never seen her before, and they always know who I employ, so she would have gone to one of the other three kitchens in this place to concoct that little coffee she presented Wren with.

I'm too distracted. If it weren't for my current obsession with the girl sleeping in my bed upstairs none of this would be happening. I don't make mistakes, but I've made several now and each time they put her in danger.

I needed to end this.

Marcus Valentine needed to go followed by this Syndicate.

No one threatens what is mine.

No one makes an attempt on something that belongs to me.

I'm the motherfucking king and it's time I remind them of that fact.

TWENTY-FOUR
Lex

This was war. There's been more blood on these streets these past few days than there has been for years.

We Silver's had instilled enough fear into those who questioned us that there was no need for the violence. People fell in line wherever we went but now, now that was slipping.

Valentine's men line up in front of me, on their knees facing the water at the docks. In the distance a fog horn sounds, cutting through the mist that rolls across the dark waters. Around me containers are stacked high, cranes and forklifts abandoned.

I twist the silencer onto my Glock, my hands encased in leather gloves.

A whimper and a sniffle echo through the abandoned shipping yard.

Fucking weak.

Twisted City — RIA WILDE

And they think they can take over my city.

This shit is laughable.

"Eeny, meeny, miny, moe," Ryker taps the barrel of his gun to each of their heads as he sings the nursery rhyme, he repeats it a few times before stopping at the middle guy. There's five lined up in total. When the barrel rests on the base of his skull, the guy outright cries. His sobs ricochet around the yard, bouncing off the still waters of the docks. Ryker doesn't hesitate, he pulls the trigger, the bullet ripping through his skull like it's no more than butter. He hits the concrete hard, blood pooling from his face.

"So who's next, should we sing again?" Ryker taunts.

I've grown tired though. I pull the trigger four times, ending them. Five more deaths. Five more bodies. I'll take them all out one by one if I must.

"Dump them on the south side, make sure it's Valentine or his men that find them."

Ryker nods as I climb back into my SUV and head across the city, back towards the compound.

The radio is pulling the current news bulletin.

"Club Silver has reopened its doors after a gunman opened fire on the crowd. Two dead, one was student Robbie Hill and the other was the shooter himself. At this time, there is no known association to Club Silver or the owner Alexander Silver, but investigations are still ongoing."

I hit the button to silence it and instead listen to the tires of my car on the road. It's quiet, the streets empty bar a few other cars. It's too late for many people to be out but I could guarantee the city centre, namely the areas around my club would be packed. I avoid it on purpose, taking a few back roads to hit the highway that would lead me to the compound.

My bright white lights cut through the darkness until I eventually see the lights of the mansion like a beacon, drawing me in though I know it isn't the house making me put my foot down and speed up. It isn't my bed or the comfort of the four walls, it's her.

Wren fucking Valentine.

I'm well and truly fucked.

At the gates, I lean out and press my finger to the scanner, waiting for the green light and the beep to sound and then the gates begin to slide open. Since the incident with the house keeper there are constant guys patrolling the grounds. Call me paranoid but until this shit is over, I won't be making anymore mistakes or taking any chances.

I roll the car to a stop and throw the keys to one of my guys for him to put it in the garage and then take the steps two at a time, pushing the wide doors open. I scan all the rooms on the lower floor looking for her, but she isn't down here and as I climb the stairs the sound of soft cries and moans fill my ears.

I pick up the pace, heading up to the attic room where the sounds are coming from, throwing the door open.

Wren writhes in the bed, the sheets tangled around her limbs as she thrashes in her sleep. The cries are coming from her but she's alone in here. Alone with the demons plaguing her dreams.

She's been like this a few times since the house keeper and I don't know how else to help her. She hates me, or so she says but I know the truth.

It's me who brings her comfort, it's me who settles her dreams and allows her to sleep easy. She can scream and fight me for now, but the truth will eventually come out.

I cross the room and like every night, I scoop her up, pushing the covers from her body. She's damp from sweat, her skin sticky and like every night I take her down to my room, her grumbling and pouting like a child and shove her into the shower to wash away the dreams.

And like every night, she slips her head into one of my t-shirts that falls to mid-thigh on her tiny frame and climbs under the blankets, curling her body into mine.

Yeah, she hates me alright.

"You still fighting me baby?" I drawl into the darkness.

"I'll always fight you." She mumbles, pressing her mouth to my bare chest.

The touch of her lips to my skin sends a spike of pleasure down my spine.

"Careful little bird," I warn.

Her fingers curl into my stomach, her nails biting against my skin enough to make me hiss through my teeth as she pushes her hips forward, grinding herself against my leg.

I growl as I grip the hem of my t-shirt covering her body and rip it straight off, leaving her bare to me. With the curtains open I see her bathed in the silver glow of the moon, it caresses her pale skin, making her seem ethereal, like she has a halo of light around her. So fucking beautiful, all toned muscle and smooth curves.

She groans when I force her to her knees, bending her forward so her ass is in the air.

"You want this," I rasp.

Her answer is to back up, pressing her ass to my hard cock, straining to be free from my boxer shorts.

"My little bird," I coo.

"You're the devil," her voice comes out on a breath, barely audible above my own rough breathing.

My hand smooths down the curve of her spine, feeling each bump of her vertebrae until I find her waist, my hands cupping her sides. She's so tiny, so fragile. I could break her so very easily.

She moans as I press my erection against her centre, the warmth of her seeping through the thin material. Pulling back, I slide the boxers off and reposition behind her, pressing the crown of my cock to her entrance, warm and wet, ready for me.

"That's where you're wrong little bird," I tease her, pushing only an inch into her tight pussy, "the devil was once an angel and I've never been good. I'm the monster under your bed," another inch forward, "I'm the thing that goes bump in the night and stalks you in the shadows." Another inch and I begin to feel my restraint slipping as her warm core envelopes and tightens around my shaft. "I'm your motherfucking nightmare."

I slam forward, impaling her on my cock so hard she screams and her fists ball the sheets, nails scratching against the cotton.

I withdraw and slam forward again.

"Say it!" I demand on a growl.

"Fuck you." She cries.

Always pushing me. Always testing me.

"Say it!" I bellow, pounding into her hard. My fingers bruise her hips as my relentless thrusts jolt her body against the mattress, "Tell me little bird, tell me who you fucking belong to."

She moans loud, her cries of ecstasy causing my spine to stiffen, my balls to draw up tight, "Say it and I'll reward you baby."

She cries out when I withdraw, halting her impending orgasm. I tease forward, the walls of her pussy trying to clamp down and take purchase on my cock, "Say it."

I tease that sweet spot inside her with the crown of my cock, feeling her spasm, wanting – no – *needing* more.

"You!" She snaps, "I belong to you!"

"Good girl," I reach around and pinch her clit between my fingers while slamming into her hard enough to make her bones rattle. Her scream pierces the darkness of the bedroom.

Her orgasm is quick and violent, it clamps around my cock like a vice, holding me in place, drawing my own climax from my body with force.

I roar my release, my fingers biting into her flesh while she continues to spasm around me.

Spent and exhausted, I collapse down next to her, drawing her body into mine.

I liked having her this close, I liked her warmth on my skin, her breathing syncing with mine.

"I hate you," she whispers.

I smooth down her wild, still slightly damp hair, inhaling her sweet scent like it's a drug and I'm the addict.

She doesn't hate me. Not at all and the feeling is mutual.

The feeling is dangerous. It's what's likely to get me killed at the end of this but I've never been good with warnings.

I'm the king and this is my kingdom and all kingdoms need a queen.

TWENTY-FIVE
Wren

I hate you.

I hate you.

Those words leave my mouth far too often and yet every time I use them, I find I don't mean them quite as much as the last. No, hate isn't something I feel towards this man any more and that simply terrifies me.

He terrifies me.

He's a man that commands a room, commands respect, whether that be through fear or loyalty, he's lethal, brutal, vengeful and I'm drawn to that. His presence makes people cower, when he walks into a room he doesn't have to say a word for everyone to *know* the man is king.

His darkness calls to me. His violence and menace entices me.

Twisted City

RIA WILDE

I know how stories like ours end but I'm still the little idiot moth drawn to the flame, I find myself falling into him, waiting for the burn. There isn't much I can do to stop it, I'll just revel in the pain as the flames devour me.

His possessiveness, the way he handles me, both acting as if I'm fragile and the strongest woman he's ever known, I can't help but let my stupid heart fall for him. There's something so very satisfying about knowing he's a monster that is only soft with me.

His thick arms are banded around me, holding me to his chest, his heat enveloping my body like a caress. His breathing is soft and gentle, brushing the fine hairs at the nape of my neck as he breathes deeply in his sleep. It's still dark out, I can see the moon hanging fat and swollen in the night sky, silver light bathing the compound grounds.

I've seen more people this week than I ever have since being here, armed guards, men employed by Lex standing in the halls. They pay me no mind bar the odd hello but Gruff still isn't speaking to me after I broke his nose.

I apologized. He wasn't having it.

Gently, I roll onto my back and then turn again until I'm facing the man of my nightmares.

His beauty is cruel and unforgiving, merciless, all hard lines and sharp edges. My fingers tickle over the thick hair growing around his mouth and up his cheeks and then further up into his thick mane of hair, the strands soft between my fingers.

Slowly, I lean forward, allowing myself a kiss against his pillowy lips. When I pull away his eyes are open, staring at me, the silver irises so bright they rival the moon.

He reaches up and untangles my hand from his hair, pulling it down until my fingers hover in front of his mouth and gently, so very gently, his presses a kiss to every finger.

My heart stutters in my chest at the intimate way his lips press against my skin, the air from his breath caressing my skin almost as softly as his lips.

The room is silent other than the inhales and exhales of our breathing but in the quiet I swear a thousand words are said. Words neither of us would ever dare to vocalize. When he releases my hand, he brings his own to my face, feathering the tips down the side of my face, down the curve of my neck and over my shoulder. I'm still naked from our earlier adventures and I know he is. I press the palm of my hand against his sternum, feeling the muscles coil and jump under my touch. I love how he reacts to me, even from the first moment we met, there was no way he could hide his reaction to me, I felt it in the way the air around us charged with tension and electricity, in the way we both exploded like storms whenever we touched.

"Little bird," he mumbles, the first one to break this mutual silence.

"Twisted king," I reply.

His deep chuckle vibrates through me, "What am I going to do with you?"

I push his shoulders, forcing him onto his back and then straddle his narrow hips. My eyes devour his naked torso, his hard muscles, the definition around his pecs and the V that carves his hips. I feel him grow hard between my legs, his cock pressing into my sensitive flesh. His hands squeeze the tops of my thighs as his eyes narrow in on me.

Rolling my hips I rub against his shaft, pleasure shooting up my spine.

"I want you," I admit.

"I thought you hated me," he smirks, his fingers biting into the fleshy areas of my legs. When I grind my hips again his eyes roll back and his fingers tighten, his control becoming paper thin.

"Shut up," I growl.

That deep chuckle shoots straight to my clit and in one quick movement, he shifts my weight and pistons his hips, entering me in one swift move. I cry out into the darkness, feeling him stretching and filling me in the most painfully pleasurable way.

"Fucking ride me, baby," he growls, "let me watch you."

His filthy mouth fuels my need to own him, have him in everyway and with him buried so deep I begin to roll my hips, using his chest to help steady me. His breathing is heavy, and his moans fill the darkness. He takes his hand away from my thigh and runs it up the centre of my chest, through the valley of my breasts until his fingers curl around my throat. His hand tightens, fingers pressing in at the edges of my windpipe and he jerks me forward.

My mouth slams against his violently, his teeth pulling at my bottom lip, nipping hard enough to draw blood that dribbles onto my tongue.

"That's it," he rasps into my mouth, that hand still banded around my throat and now one in my hair, tugging my head back so my neck is stretched out and open for him. In this position I have no control, I have no way to move and he knows it. On my knees, straddled over his hips he pounds into me from below, holding my head back, the sting on my scalp and the pressure on my throat only adding to the pleasure wracking my system.

"You're such a good girl," he growls against my throat, "so good."

I can't talk, I can only scream for him, I can only let myself fall harder and harder with each deep thrust and whispered praise.

I wake to an empty bed and serious cramps. Guess I don't have to worry about the pill not working anymore. On a groan, I roll from the sheets and trudge across the quiet bedroom, slipping into the shower immediately. The hot water soothes the ache in my back but does nothing to stop the cramping in my stomach. I wash away the night, the scent of Lex on my skin and between my thighs before wrapping myself in a towel and heading up to the attic bedroom where I know I saw some of my toiletries in the bathroom.

I sort myself out and dress in baggy sweats and a sweater before tying my hair into a bun that sits atop my head messily. I need to go to the supermarket and pick up more things but I highly doubt Lex is going to let me go.

I no longer feel like a prisoner here, but I don't feel free either.

My feet shuffle back down the stairs and towards the kitchen where I hear the coffee maker whirring and spitting out coffee. It isn't Lex I find there though but Gruff.

"Gruff!" I beam at him.

He looks at me over his shoulder and heaves a sigh. The bruising on his face has gone down a lot since I hit him but he isn't over it clearly.

"Are we still sour about the whole nose thing?"

"You broke my nose," he grumbles.

I shrug, "I guess we're even."

"How are we even?" He exclaims.

"You kidnapped me."

He opens his mouth to say something but then promptly shuts it, his teeth rattling together.

"Where's Lex?" I ask, accepting the coffee from him.

"Busy, he left me watching you."

"I don't need a babysitter."

Gruff scoffs, "Trouble follows you Wren, of course you need a babysitter."

My brows pull low, I have no idea how all of this shit has been turned on me. I wouldn't even be a part of this mess if it wasn't for this asshole in front of me and the one currently off galivanting doing god knows what.

I try not to think about it too much.

This has all been a game for them, one that has gotten out

of hand. I wanted no part in it though we don't always get what we want.

My stomach cramps painfully. I'd always suffered with bad menstrual cramps for the first day or so of my cycle but it seems this one is really knocking me for six.

Gruff frowns, stepping towards me, "What's wrong?"

"Aw, look at the big scary man showing concern," I grit my teeth.

"Seriously, Wren, what is it?"

I wave a hand, "Don't worry. It's just mother nature taking her course."

Gruff visibly winces, taking a step back which earns a laugh from me. He has to be fucking with me. He's got to be.

"Can I, uh, can I do anything?"

I spin on the stool, facing away from him, my eyes suddenly colliding with the hall where I shot the intruder. Bile rises in my throat and I force myself back around.

I killed someone. My nightmares remind me of that fact every day, her face haunts my dreams, the sound of her body hitting the floor plays on repeat inside my ears.

"Wren?" Gruff presses.

"Yeah, actually, I need to go to the store."

"That'll be a no."

I narrow my eyes at him, forcing my mind away from the images trying to capture my attention, "What do you mean no?"

"You can't leave here."

My teeth grit so hard together the enamel feels like its chipping, "I need the store. I want to get some things. I can't stay inside this house forever, Gruff."

"Stop calling me Gruff," he huffs.

"Fine, *Ryker*, I need to go to the store. Take me."

He laughs, "No chance."

"Ryker!" I seethe. "Nothing will happen. Just take me to store, I'll even let you escort me round and you can bring me right back."

He's shaking his head before I've even finished my sentence, "So you can run?"

"I'm not going to run," it was the truth. Not because I wouldn't be able to, if we were out in public there would be undoubtedly every opportunity to make a break for it, but I find the need or want to run is gone. Again, terrifying, but I'm learning to take things as they come. These *feelings* for Lex stop those urges, they stop the need to get away and replace it with the desire to get closer, despite the blood staining his hands.

He scoffs again and the sound grates on my every nerve, "I swear to God." I don't finish the threat.

"What do you need? I'll go and leave one of the guys here to watch you."

I cock a brow, my lips curling with satisfaction. I've only ever seen men around here and while there are a few out there who would buy the shit I need, these guys aren't it.

Their fragile masculinity couldn't take the hit.

"Well, I need sanitary products Gruff, you know, tampons, towels. Maybe some heat pads and lots of icecream. Oh and chocolate. Maybe some popcorn?"

His face is a mask of horror, "On second thoughts, I'll send Ainsley."

He pulls out his phone and dials but after the fifth attempt, he huffs in annoyance, taps at his phone and puts it to his ear again but again, whoever he dials must not pick up because he throws the device down on to the counter and stares at me angrily like I'm the one dodging his calls.

"So are we going?"

"No, you'll have to wait."

I sigh dramatically and I really shouldn't, *really* I shouldn't but clearly I'm not above a little manipulation. "Well, fine, then, if you're happy for me to be in pain all day *and* bleed through then," I shrug, like it's not a big deal. I mean none of that shit will happen, I'm covered for at least today, "but I guess you'll have to explain that to Lex."

"Fuck." He growls. "Fuck."

"So, your choice, Gruff."

"Get your shit, you have ten minutes to get your shit and then we're out of there."

TWENTY-SIX
Wren

"I don't like this," Gruff says for the hundredth time since we pulled up outside the small supermarket and parked the giant SUV.

"I mean, we could have taken a less conspicuous car, you know?" I shrug like that's the problem.

Truth be told, I hadn't really thought this plan through, I just needed to get out the house and I did need the store. I didn't think about how nervous I'd be when I got there. After all, it's twice someone has tried to kill me, first my father, who's not actually my father and then a seemingly harmless housekeeper.

But realistically, how is anyone going to know I'm here?

Paranoia has no place inside my head so I tilt my chin up and pop the door. It's warm today making the sweats and sweater a bad move but I needed comfy rather than convenient.

"Hey, wait!" Gruff scrambles to get out the car and then he's right next to me, curling his hand around my arm, not hard or aggressively, more protective than anything else.

"It's okay," I tell him, patting the paw that circles my bicep, "let's just get what we need and go home."

He grunts and we make our way across the lot. I glance sideways at him, he looks out of place next to me, dressed in his pristine tailored suit, Italian loafers loud on the asphalt as his steps cover more ground than my little ones could ever hope to achieve. We look every bit the fucked up pair that we are. The air conditioning of the store hits me like a bucket of water, refreshing considering the heat outside and we move quickly to one of the aisles containing fresh produce.

"Doing some grocery shopping at the same time?" I ask.

Gruff drags me through the aisle, turning at the end until we find the one we are looking for. His nerves are rattling my own.

I realize there would be no real way of defending ourselves here, so open and public, it's not like Gruff could whip out his gun and shoot someone should he need to. No that shit is done behind closed doors with no witnesses.

They may run the city but there are still rules.

I stop at the section where the products are and pluck the bits and pieces that I need from the shelves, bundling them into Gruff's arms.

"This is a bad idea, Wren," Gruff tells me, I'm ready to

snap back with a retort but when I turn to Ryker I notice how very nervous he is. Shit, now my guilt is warring with the anxiety inside of me.

"It's fine, let's just get this and we can go."

"You don't need anything else?"

I grab some heat pads and a packet of painkillers and then shake my head, "This'll be fine, let's go."

He sighs with relief and we begin to make our way back down the aisle. A familiar face right at the end catches my attention.

"Shit," I hiss, grabbing Ryker and tugging him down another aisle, hiding.

"What!?" He hisses.

"I know him," I point to the familiar face at the end of the aisle. Griff, my personal trainer and self-defense teacher. Once upon a time I would have never questioned whether I trusted him but it's obvious that Valentine has had a lot of influence on my life if Lex is telling the truth. I still needed to learn it all but I knew enough.

Was it Lawson or Valentine forcing me into that training? Either way, neither of them could be trusted. Who was Griff really?

I used to trust this man without question but now as I look at him, I realize he's just like the rest. There's a darkness I hadn't recognized before, a way he holds himself, a controlled beast that when rattled will be unleashed.

"Who is it?" Ryker asks.

"His name is Griffin, I used to train with him."

"Okay, so what?"

"He was employed by my father."

"Which one?"

I roll my eyes, "Lawson."

"Who was likely instructed by Valentine."

I nod my agreement. I hated this. I hated that I didn't know what was real and what wasn't, who I could trust and who I couldn't.

He did this to me. Alexander Silver.

My life would have been fine had he never showed up.

But would I really want to go on without knowing him if I knew what I know now?

That was a question for another time.

Griff loiters at the end of the aisle, perusing the shelves and I spot a second man close by, a big guy and he's cornering a smaller man. Shit.

"We need to get out of here," Ryker says.

"No shit."

"Just dump the stuff," I say, "we'll come back later."

"No we take it," Ryker growls, "we ain't coming back out."

I'm sure if the moment required it, Gruff would use his weapons but I hoped it wouldn't come to that.

Gruff guides me the opposite way down the aisle, away

from Griffin, Ryker still clutching the haul of womanly products with bright pink and purple packaging in his arms. If nerves and adrenaline weren't causing chaos inside me I'd laugh at the situation.

We slip down an aisle a couple of rows down that would bring us out directly in front of the doors and make a beeline for it, that is until Griffin steps out in front of us.

His eyes are trained on me, hard and yet soft all the same.

"Wren," his eyes dart to the left just as Ryker shuffles the stuff in his hands to one side and reaches for his gun. I still his movements, hoping like hell it isn't a mistake.

"Griffin," I greet.

His eyes bounce between me and Ryker, calculating, trying to figure out what this is. I'm sure he's heard about Lex and me and everyone knows the man next to me is not Lex.

Griffin turns his attention back to me, scanning from the top of my head to the tips of my feet, "Are you okay?"

I frown but nod, "I am."

"They told me Silver took you, kidnapped and hurt you."

I knock my head side to side, "Some of that is true but I'm fine."

"What bits?" He growls.

I have no idea what the fuck is going on here, "It doesn't matter."

"You're not safe Wren," Griff says, looking to Ryker and then back at me.

"From whom?"

"Anyone."

Tears sting my eyes.

"You need to get out of here." Griffin steps closer, his brows drawn down low.

"Stop," Ryker growls, positioning himself in front of me.

"I won't hurt her."

"Like Lawson wouldn't?" Ryker snaps.

"I heard about that, I was told it wasn't true but it is? Lawson tried to kill you?"

"He did," I confirm.

Griff drops his head and takes a deep breath before seeming to come to a decision. He holds one hand out to Ryker and then gestures to his pocket, "I'm just getting a piece of paper and a pen."

Ryker grunts but nods and we both watch Griff reach into the inside of his jacket, to his pocket where he pulls out a small notebook and a silver pen. He rips out a piece of paper and then writes something on it.

Ryker shoves me harder behind his body when Griffin takes a step closer and hands us over the piece of paper. Ryker takes it but I see it quickly before he stuffs it into his pocket. A phone number.

"Remember what I taught you," Griffin says, "Use it and trust no one." His eyes bounce to Ryker again before landing on me. "Stay safe Wren, stay alive."

TWENTY-SEVEN

Lex

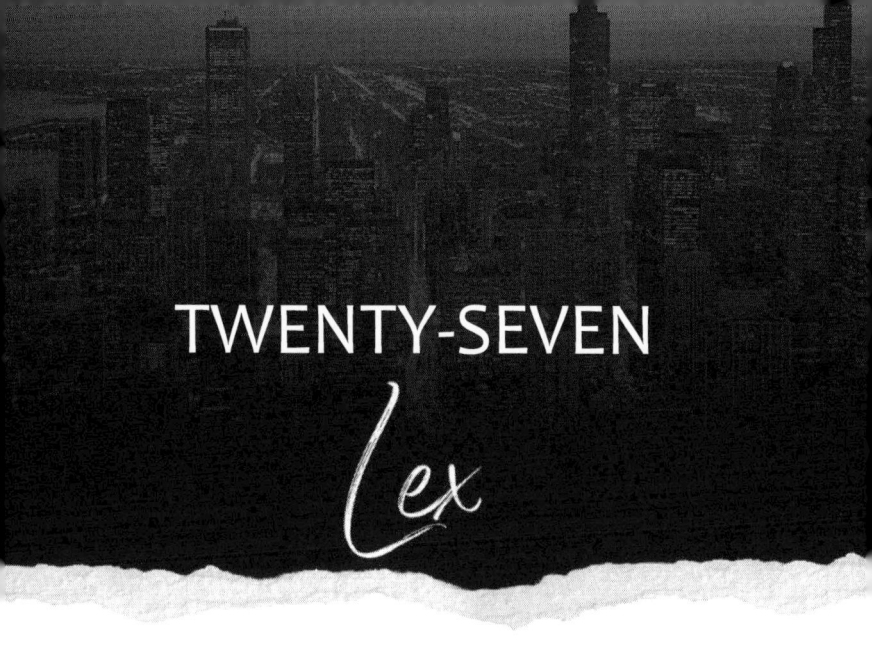

No matter which way I look, there's an enemy.

A fucker trying to take my kingdom, to take what belongs to me. I have them both for the time being, both Wren and the city but with all this new information I wonder if I can keep them both.

It's not gone unnoticed how distracted I've been. While my men don't outright say it – they would be stupid to – they look at me as if I'm walking a fine line of completely losing it.

Exhaustion tugs at me as I make the final few steps up to the mansion and when I touch the handle I can't help but feel some sort of sense of foreboding. I stare down at my white shirt that's not so white anymore, instead it's splattered with blood and dirt. I would have usually had Ryker with me today but truth was I couldn't trust anyone anymore.

I have a mole. In my fucking ranks, I have a fucking mole.

They've been feeding shit back to Valentine and the Syndicate the entire time. My plans, business dealings, fuck even how often I've been alone with Valentine's precious daughter.

He wants her back. Bad.

But something still doesn't sit right.

He abandoned her. Left her to be raised by someone else, that doesn't tell me he's a man who cares for her. He wants her for something else. I thought it was to take over the family business but I no longer believe that.

There's a lot I've learned about Valentine and everything tells me he wouldn't want a woman ruling his legacy. He's misogynistic, cruel with women and bigoted. He wants her for something else. Something big if he's ignoring the directions the Syndicate are giving him.

But what?

I open the door quietly, stepping into the foyer. Raised voices coming from the kitchen tell me that's where Wren and Ryker are.

"Just call it!" Wren yells, frustrated.

"We need to wait for Lex!" Ryker growls back with enough anger to make my blood boil. Friend or not, that's my woman. Mine. And no one speaks to her like that.

I shut the door quietly, despite wanting to barge in there and knock his teeth out for speaking to her that way.

"Why?" Wren sighs, "just call it! He didn't give it to you anyway!"

I step quietly through the hall, stopping at the threshold

but keeping myself concealed around the corner.

"Just wait, Wren."

"Wait for what?" My voice startles my little bird enough for her to jump in her seat. She spins around to face me, her wide green eyes first looking at my face and then the state of my clothes. Granted, this isn't the best way for her to see me, but it is who I am. She's a part of it now, whether she likes it or not.

"Lex," Ryker sighs heavily.

"What are we waiting for?"

"Ryker and I took a little trip today."

The news hits me like a truck to the body. He let her out the house! He knows how unsafe it is for her right now. My anger boils and my blood fizzes in my veins, furious and unrelenting.

"You took her out!?" I bellow. "Are you fucking stupid!?" I should get answers. I should find out why but all I see is red. He put her in danger. He took her out of this house. He could have got her killed or kidnapped. Fuck. I fly across the kitchen, my knuckles meeting his face like a rock to the skull. His head snaps to the side as blood sprays from his mouth.

"Lex!" Wren's voice is muffled to the rage booming inside my ears.

My fist connects with his cheekbone, and I raise my fist to hit him again but he manages to dodge this one, getting in his own hit. I spit blood onto the kitchen tiles, before taking another hit.

"Fuck you, Lex!" Ryker bellows.

"Enough!" Wren screams, scrambling her small body across the kitchen island before stumbling off of it to stand between us. If either of us want to go at each other again we'd have to go through her. She glares at me, squaring her shoulders in front of Ryker as if protecting him.

Jealously hits me hot and heavy, punching me straight in the gut.

"It's not his fault, I made him."

I scoff, "You're no taller than five three little bird and weigh what, a hundred and twenty pounds soaking wet, you're telling me you *made* him."

She rolls her eyes, "Don't be a sexist pig!" she snaps. There's so much fire in her eyes, so much heat warring with anger, "I will hit you."

"And I'll like it," I growl back.

"You two are fucked up," Ryker huffs, collapsing down into the chair, wiping his mouth on the sleeve of his jacket.

My hands shake with the unleashed anger but when Wren steps forward, no less angry and presses her palm to the centre of my chest, over the dried blood and against my rampaging heartbeat it sizzles. I stare down at her, nostrils flaring, trying to keep hold of those last remaining scraps of my anger. Anger is easy. You understand it.

This fucking feeling in my chest, this is not easy.

This is a complication. A mess. A distraction.

But I still raise my hand and place it over hers as I drag her closer with my other one. I press my lips to hers, a contrast to the war in my body and she kisses me back.

I'm in so much fucking trouble with this woman. So much so I'm not sure either of us are going to come out of this alive.

Wren

I feel his tension building in his muscles, the anger rolling off him in waves that send shivers down my spine. His knuckles are split, blood splattered across his skin. I guess that now matches the rest of him. His white shirt is speckled in rust coloured spots and I have no doubt his jacket and pants would be too, I just can't see it because they're black.

Why doesn't that repulse me?

I slip my fingers between two of his shirt buttons, feeling the searing heat of his skin against the pads of my fingers. His heartbeat is steady and strong, pulsing under my touch. He looks down at me, hoods of his eyes lowered, the silver of his eyes glowing.

Slowly, so very slowly, the corners of his mouth tip up in a resemblance of a smile. One brow cocks and he leans in, his breath whispering against my skin as his lips brush against the lobe of my ear.

"Did you miss me little bird?" He whispers so only I can hear.

Twisted City
RIA WILDE

Ryker is still grumbling behind me but in this moment we're alone, just him and me. Tingles run through my body chaotically, warming me, or perhaps they're warning me.

My nails bite into the firm skin on his chest and he retaliates by nipping my ear, scraping his teeth across the skin. Before I can lose myself in him, before I can forget everything I know is right, he pulls away and levels me with a look that tells me he is less than impressed.

"Where did you go today, little bird?"

"The store," I shrug pulling my hand back and curling my fingers into the palm of my hand.

"And what did you need at the store that someone else couldn't have gotten you? Do you understand how much danger you're currently in?"

He's speaking to me like I'm a child. And it annoys the shit out of me.

"Danger *you* put me in," I retort.

His eyes narrow, "Don't push me right now."

I scoff, "I had to go to the store seeing as I am female and females tend to have cycles. I required products to stop me bleeding all over your pretty furniture."

"That doesn't explain why someone else couldn't have gone."

I laugh out loud, the sound so violent in the quiet of the kitchen that I make myself jump, "Oh I'm sorry, your right hand over here can shoot people and torture them but he can't seem to go out and buy feminine products without turning green."

Lex's lips twitch as he fights his smile. He looks over my head to Ryker and I turn around, seeing him shrug. Pathetic.

"So what are you waiting for?" He presses.

I sigh. I wanted to phone Griffin the moment we got back to the house but Ryker wouldn't give me his phone or the number. Granted, I saw his reasoning but still, I was getting fed up being told what to do.

"I saw someone today, someone I used to be friends with. He told me to contact him if we wanted more information."

"It's a trap." Lex grunts.

"You're all very paranoid, you know that?" I cock a hand on my hip. "I trust Griffin." Kind of.

"Griffin?" Lex's eyes pin me in place.

Oh boy. Here we go.

TWENTY-EIGHT

Lex

Jealousy isn't something I've had a lot of experience with. There isn't much I don't have or don't get, I've never needed to be envious. I know what it looks like, I've seen it in action but this feeling in my body, it's wild and frantic. My heart beats hard, my scalp tingles and my stomach churns, all at the prospect of another man being in Wren's life.

One she so called *trusts*.

Trust is a fickle beast, once you give it someone they have the power over you. They can break you. Betray you. Kill you. And you're blind to it because of so called trust.

There's very few people I trust. I can count on one hand who they are and that's only because they have proven themselves.

Wren doesn't understand.

She trusts blindly. Freely. But she doesn't understand the

repercussions of misplaced trust, especially when involved in this life.

Griffin is from her old life, one connected to Valentine and if there is anything I have learned about that man and his men, all of them and I mean *all* of them are snakes.

I see the moment Wren decides to fight back. I've started to learn a lot about this woman, her tells, her triggers, and with her spine straightening and the rims of her nostrils flaring I know she's about to spit venom.

"Don't you dare," she seethes.

I smirk, the jealousy settling a little, "Don't what, little bird?"

"This," she waves her hand around, "This whole jealousy thing. You don't get to be jealous, asshole. I've known Griffin for years. *Years.* I trust him."

"Like you trusted Lawson?"

Her head snaps back and she strikes, her hand slapping across my face. The sting is sharp, tingles rushing over my cheek and jawline. Slowly I bring my head back, staring down at her. Ryker stands to intervene but I subtly shake my head as I step forward.

"Don't push me, Wren," I growl.

She does just that. She throws her entire body weight at me, trying to force me away but her slight frame is nothing on mine. I grab her, hauling her to my chest before I press her against the nearest counter, pinning her arms in place.

She thrashes around but ultimately, she can't escape me. She'll never be able to.

"You're a fucking asshole. I hate you!"

"Whether you like it or not," she struggles and I have to readjust to keep her in place, "you're a part of this now. You have to question everything and everyone. Lawson raised you, he fucking raised you and he tried to kill you!"

"It's your fault!"

It was. That was true.

But there was nothing to do about that now.

"Regardless, Wren, anyone and I mean *anyone* from your previous life, they don't exist anymore. All you have are enemies."

"And you? Are you my enemy?" She cries.

"No, little bird, I'm not your enemy."

"Then what?" She laughs manically, tears rolling down her face. I'm not entirely sure she even realizes she's crying but her lips wobble and her eyes glaze and something twists inside me. Like the blade of a knife being stabbed into my abdomen and then being twisted. "You're my knight in shining armour? You're here to save the day and we can live happily ever after!?"

Ryker quietly steps from the table, our earlier confrontation forgotten as he nurses his swollen lip and split brow. He looks at me with a mixture of shock and concern? He surely can't think this little thing could do me any damage. But then hell hath no fury than a woman scorned.

"I'm not that either," I say eventually now we are alone.

"Then what, Alexander Silver? What are you if not my

enemy?"

"Just yours."

Her eyes widen, the tears still spilling down her rosy cheeks.

"W-what?"

Slowly, I begin to loosen my grip on her, raising my hand as if I'm placating a terrified animal. I tip her chin back, forcing her to level her stare with mine.

"You belong to me Wren, you are *mine*. But where you are mine, I am yours. This is a two way street."

"You act as if people are things to possess."

"Are they not?"

She shakes her head.

I stroke my thumb across her plump bottom lip, grinning at the full body shiver it elicits, "Whether you like it or not, we are one. I'll never let you go. We rule together and those enemies, they are my enemies and we take them down. Together."

"This isn't war, Lex."

"Oh but that's where you are wrong little bird, there's always a war."

"But Griffin –"

"Is on your father's payroll," I interrupt, "and therefore cannot be trusted."

She shakes her head and huffs a breath, exasperated. "You

need to shower."

She isn't done with the argument, I know she isn't, she just doesn't have an answer right now.

"I do." I step away from her body, waiting and watching, expecting her to flee, when she doesn't, I tip my head, "join me."

She shakes her head.

"That wasn't a request, little bird."

Her eyes narrow and she purses her lips, "and you're going to need to learn to take *no* for an answer."

She spins away from me, slipping from the kitchen. I hear her take the stairs two at a time, bypassing my room to favor the attic bedroom. I'll remedy that later tonight but for now I let her go.

Before I head up to clean up, I go in search of Ryker, finding him hovering in the living room, nursing a scotch and an ice pack.

"I wouldn't have let anything happen to her," he tells me, spotting me in the threshold.

"This Griffin, what did you think?"

Ryker frowns, "I didn't get much of an impression, you want to contact him?"

I nod once, "contact him from a burner. Set it up. Somewhere public. I want him to come alone."

"The club?"

"Do it in a few days. There's a couple of leads I want to

follow before I contemplate using one of Valentine's men."

"He could have taken her out you know," Ryker tells me, "he wasn't alone, I spotted at least four others with him, he let her go."

"A false sense of security is what will get you killed, old friend."

He winces, "yes, boss."

I leave him with my instruction and head up, unbuttoning my shirt as I go. The blood on the shirt has seeped through, leaving faint red splotches on my skin.

Another dead end lead. Ainsley had given me names. Names of people supposedly linked to the Syndicate only they had fuck all for me, either that or they were more terrified of them than they were of me. And that was going to be a big problem.

I was still no closer to figuring out who they were and Valentine was only getting more persistent in his plots to get his daughter back.

Wren doesn't think this is a war, but this is going to be the bloodiest battle this city has ever seen.

And me, the twisted fuck that I am, was going to paint the streets red with their blood and stand atop the pile of bodies of those who dare question me.

The Syndicate may think they have me cornered, trapped with no way out and Valentine can believe all he likes that he has some hope of getting Wren back but if I am nothing else, I am resilient.

They can push and they can pull, but there was no way in this hell or the next I was giving up what belonged to me.

TWENTY-NINE

Lex

I head up to the attic bedroom after showering, finding Wren curled up in the centre of the bed. Her breathing is even and steady so I cross the room, looking down at her. She's curled on her side, hands beneath her face with her wild hair stretched across the pillow like flames.

I lean down and scoop my arms under her body. She groans but lets me lift her, cradling her to my chest as I leave the room and head back to the master bedroom.

"I can sleep alone," she mumbles sleepily, nuzzling her face into my chest.

"That's not how this works," I whisper back, kicking the door open and then placing her into the queen sized bed in my bedroom. She doesn't get up and leave, instead, she scoots herself into the middle and buries herself under the blankets, one eye watching me over the sheets.

I flick the switch and climb in beside her, pulling her closer, wrapping my arms around her. She sighs heavily and begins to circle her forefinger on my chest.

"You should not have left the compound," I say after a beat of silence.

"You can't keep me locked away forever."

"I can," I tell her, "do not forget who you are dealing with little bird."

"Like I could forget, Lex," she huffs, trying to pull away from me.

I don't let her go, not even an inch. "You belong to me and there are people out there who want to take you away."

"You make this hard," she answers. Life with me, it was never going to be easy for her. But she'd get used to it. And she'll learn her place.

We lay in silence until her breathing steadies back out and she relaxes against me, finally asleep again.

I don't sleep though. I lay there, staring up at the darkened ceiling with her in my arms.

Everything in me that feels for her seems too big, too strong, too fierce, forget just Valentine and the Syndicate, I'm sure I'd take the entire fucking world on if it meant her staying right where she is now.

It's become more than revenge. More than the city.

I'd never thought about taking a wife. Or I had, but in the sense of continuing my lineage but nothing more, with her though, I want it all. I want the marriage and the children with my surname and her fire. I wanted her to stand by my side with our enemies slain and the city at our feet.

On the bedside table my phone buzzes loudly against the top, the vibrations shaking the frame. I quickly reach out and snatch it off, glancing at the name lighting up the screen. My brows pull down. Ainsley didn't phone me. She phoned Ryker.

Gently, I pry Wren from my body and answer the phone, not saying a word until I'm out of the bedroom.

"Ainsley." I greet.

"I'm fucked."

The second floor of the house is dark but I know my men are around here somewhere. I don't go looking for them, instead I take the stairs and head to the office, settling in the chair behind the desk that's been in my family for generations.

"What's going on?" I ask.

"I did something, Lex," she breathes heavy down the line as if she's jogging. The sound of her feet setting a steady rhythm joins the sound of her ragged breath. "They're coming for me."

"Who?"

"The Syndicate."

My spine straightens as my hand curls into a fist atop the desk, "What did you do, Ains?"

"I need to get to you," Ainsley says to me, "But not now, they'll be expecting it. I have shit you can use, Lex. I have it all."

"Ainsley, how do you know they're coming?"

She laughs but it lacks humour, "I got the message loud and clear."

"Where are you going?" I slam a fist down, "We can protect you."

"No, you can't. Don't underestimate them, Lex, they are bigger than any of us could have expected. They have *everything*. Valentine is a pawn to them. Nothing more. They don't like getting their hands dirty but trust me, if they have to, they will."

"What did you get?"

"Everything Lex, all of it. I can't, not on the phone, when I can, I'll be back."

"And Ryker?"

"Tell him for me?"

"Do I look like your errand boy?"

She laughs, "You're an asshole. Please, tell him."

I sigh.

Ainsley wasn't supposed to be a part of this crew. She didn't fit. But I took her in anyway, thanks to whatever obsession Ryker has with her, and since then she's become as important as Ryker. A sister in arms.

"Sure. Stay safe, get me that information,"

"Yes, boss."

She hangs up. I try the line again a few minutes later and

all I get is a disconnection message. Good girl.

If she's right and the Syndicate are big enough to scare her off when she knows she has an army at her back, then clearly I am underestimating their power. I dial Ryker and relay her message before hanging up to Ryker cussing up a storm.

Ainsley is smart. She's a fighter. She can hold her own until I figure this shit out.

I'm still waiting on my father to give me what he knows but he's been ignoring my calls which tells me there's shit he's sitting on and keeping me in the dark.

And that pisses me off.

With no more to it, I head back up to Wren, finding her still in the same position I left her in. I have no hope of sleeping but I can hold her at least.

She's an antidote to calm the beast inside me. She pushes me, tests me, infuriates me but I always have a leash. One she has wrapped around her hand, holding me tight. With her, I don't worry about losing my shit, I don't worry about going too far. In a world where everyone bends to me it's nice to have someone to disobey me and test my boundaries.

With her warmth enveloping me like a blanket, I push further into the bed.

All this shit isn't going anywhere, it'll be here tomorrow so I take tonight. I take the peace and the warm body next to me, and I'll keep taking until it's ripped from bloody and broken body.

"You called him!?" Wren seethes.

Ryker sighs heavily.

It's been four days since Ainsley ran and Ryker contacted Griffin.

"Yes, Wren, I called him," Ryker confirms.

She purses her lips and glares at him, "Why didn't you let me do it? I doubt he was all that happy hearing from you."

"Because you're naïve!" Ryker snaps.

I shoot him a look to tell him to rein it in and while he doesn't like it, he nods subtly. "Look, Wren, we've been doing this a lot longer than you have, there are ways to deal with this shit."

Ryker turns back to me, sighing heavily, rubbing his temples. "Tonight. Eleven PM at the club."

"I'm coming!" Wren declares.

"No," both Ryker and I say at the same time.

"You can't keep me in the dark!" she snaps, "if you want me to be a part of this shit then I need to know. It would be good to understand what is coming after me. I'm a big girl, I can take care of myself and I need to be prepared."

I narrow my eyes, taking in the stubborn set of her jaw, the way she's begging with her eyes but her mouth stays flat and angry.

Fuck.

This fucking woman. She's going to be the death of me.

"Fine." I growl.

"What!?" Both Ryker and Wren say in unison.

"You can come but you do not leave my side, do you understand me?"

"Yes."

"Lex, you can't be serious, she's a liability."

"Watch your mouth."

"Boss, come on."

"Protect her at all costs. Get several men together, I want them all over the club, on the door, in the fucking bathrooms. I want every single person searched before they come in, no exceptions. Do it now. Get it sorted."

With a sigh, Ryker dips his chin and leaves Wren and me in the kitchen. She curls her hands around her mug and grins, satisfied with her win.

"Don't test me, Wren. I'm allowing this because you have history but if he so much as looks at you wrong, I will end him."

"Understood."

"Good girl."

She tries to hide the small smile my words elicit and the

blush that creeps up her cheeks makes my dick hard.

I've seen just how far that blush goes.

Cocking my head to the side, I watch her, the way she pulls her hair over one shoulder, her eyes looking at everything but me. Her teeth tug at her bottom lip.

"Little bird," I coo.

Her eyes rise to meet mine as I begin to unbutton my shirt.

"I'm going to shower. Join me."

I don't wait for an answer and my mouth tugs up when I hear her slip from her stool and follow after me.

She was mine. She knew it. I knew it.

I was never letting her go.

THIRTY
Wren

I watch his back as he climbs the stairs and then follow his body down the long hallway to the master bedroom where he proceeds to strip from his shirt.

I follow the lines of his well toned muscle, watching it flex and roll with all the lethal grace of a cat. The light catches the silver lines of scars that mark his skin but it adds to his brutal beauty. He doesn't once look back at me as he heads into the bathroom where he proceeds to turn the shower on.

I wait until I hear the door to the shower open and then I strip from my clothes and head through to the bathroom naked. He stands beneath the cascading spray with one arm outstretched, palm resting on the tiles and his head tilted down so the water hits the back of his neck.

I climb in behind him, running a hand up his spine, watching the muscles jump under my touch.

Twisted City

RIA WILDE

I had fallen in love with a monster.

A twisted king.

When you can't run from the monsters, you join them. You stand at their side and watch the world burn all around you.

My fingers trace the lines of his scars before whispering up to the bumps of his ribcage and following the curve until I can flatten my palm over his left pec, his heart beat a steady thump under my hand.

His body visibly shivers under my touch.

He's a glorious work of art, every single inch, all the way down to his blackened soul.

Leaning forward, I press my lips to his shoulder blade, the skin wet and slick under my mouth.

"Little bird," he rasps.

"Touch me," I beg.

Slowly he turns in the shower and grips my hips, eyes devouring every inch of my naked skin. His hands skirt up my belly, over my naval, following the curves of my body until he cups my breasts, fingers pinching my nipples, twisting them until it boarders the threshold between pleasure and pain.

When my mouth opens on a gasp he captures the sound with his lips, his tongue plunging in to duel with mine.

Desire shoots through me, the blood rushing to my core fast enough to make my thighs tingle and pussy clench.

My hair is slick and sticking to my back and my mouth is

swollen from his rough kisses when he drops to his knees, hooks one of my legs over his shoulder and presses his tongue to my clit, expertly flicking it with the tip in a way that makes my knees buckle. He alternates between teasing kisses and rough devouring, sucking the sensitive flesh into his mouth until I'm grinding against his face, begging for mercy. Begging for the release that keeps me constantly on the edge, teetering ever closer to the vertical drop that promises a world of pleasure and pain. When he inserts two fingers into me, I shatter. My cries echo off the walls, vibrating the glass panels that enclose us in the shower and when I don't think I can take anymore, he curls his fingers in my channel and draws another from my body, leaving me shaking uncontrollably. Slowly, pressing kisses up my stomach and breasts, he rises to his full height, pressing a teasing kiss to my lips before he roughly spins me and forces my hands out, pressing my palms to the tiles.

He kicks my legs out, separating them and lines his cock with my entrance.

"I dream of your pussy, little bird," he growls, the head of his dick nudging me open.

I groan at the filth leaving his mouth but the sound gets trapped in my throat as he pistons forward and spears me on his cock. He presses into my spine, forcing it to curve more so my ass juts out and with one hand holding me in position and the other gripping my hip hard enough to bruise he pulses his hips, pushing in deeper with each thrust.

He rolls his hips, slowing his movements, fingers kneading my flesh as he dips his knees and pushes in further, the head of his cock rubbing against the sweet spot inside me.

My eyes roll back in my head as he rides off the back of my previous orgasms, pulling my body tight, too tight, it'll snap.

"Yes, Lex," I moan, "Oh fuck."

"Tell me," he rasps.

"I'm yours," I need no prompting.

His hand slips up my spine as he fists my wet hair into his hand, curling the strands between his fingers near the root and tugging, pulling my head back so my throat curves. I boarder a very thin line, the biting sting of my hair being pulled only adding to the intensity building inside of me.

His fingers curl tighter, my scalp biting as his hips drive into me, over and over again, our wet skin slapping together obscenely loud.

"You're mine," he bellows, "only mine. *Always* mine."

"Yes!" my voice is strained as stars begin to explode behind my eyes.

"Come for me, little bird." He growls. "I want to feel you come all over my cock."

He pushes in so hard I feel my bones rattle and then I'm coming. No I'm flying. My whole body pulls tight and then… it releases.

My scream bounces back at me, my heart feels as if it's pounding straight through the wall of my chest, battering against my ribcage almost painfully but the climax continues to cause chaos through my body. My muscles spasm, my walls clench and my toes curls.

Lex grunts and roars behind me, his thrusts becoming

spontaneous but no less hard as he releases inside me. I feel him fill me up, my walls drawing every last drop from him.

His hand gently releases my hair and I drop my head forward, stretching out the taut muscles in the back of my neck. He's still holding my hips, his cock still buried deep inside me as he leans over me and presses the most tender of kisses to my spine, a complete contrast to the ruin he just caused.

Softly, he bands an arm around my waist and raises me to a standing position, his shaft slipping from my body as he presses my back to his chest. He reaches down and lifts a sponge and some soap, pouring the creamy liquid onto the surface and then sliding it over my pale skin. The soap is cold against my heated flesh but it feels so good. Goosebumps chase over my skin as he lathers it over my body, over the mounds of my breasts, across the tight line of my stomach. He moves my hair out of the way to get to my collar bones and throat, working the sponge over my sensitive flesh.

I don't stop him when he spins me and drops to a crouch, running the sponge over my thighs and then dips it between my legs. I jump when he presses the softness to my centre, washing away the evidence of him on my skin.

He tends to me like I'm the most precious thing in the world to him. Like I am a rare gem and should he take his eye off me for just a moment, I'll disappear.

The same hands that have killed, tortured, maimed are the ones working through my hair. He tips my head beneath the spray, wetting it further. He then squirts shampoo into the tresses.

"What are you doing?" I whisper.

"Loving you," he answers easily, his fingers working through the strands to bring it to a lather.

My eyes roll to the back of my head with each press of his fingers to my scalp.

I let him *love* me.

I let the nightmare that is Alexander Silver care for me.

THIRTY-ONE

Lex

Wren steps out of the attic bedroom, closing the door softly behind her.

"You look stunning," I tell her, eyes raking over the length of her. She's in a black silk dress with thin straps and a low neckline, the material teases her frame without being too tight and sits mid-thigh, giving me a good view of her creamy thighs. Her feet are strapped up in a pair of heels and she's pulled all her hair to sit across one shoulder, the tresses wild with curls that bounce on the mounds of her breasts.

Her eyes meet mine before dropping to my lips and then the rest of me.

We needed to make it look completely normal for our meeting with Griffin. If we turned up ready for war people would cotton on to the fact that we have an outsider in our midst, so I'm dressed in a charcoal grey tailored suit, the white shirt is unbuttoned at the top and I've buttoned the jacket. My hands are buried in my pockets but my hands twitch to touch her skin, to feel her softness beneath my fingers.

I take her arm when we reach the bottom of the stairs and head out into the unseasonably chilly night. Clouds cover the darkened sky, the moon suffocated beneath the thick blanket and a wind disturbs the oaks that line the property. Wren slides into the back of the SUV and I follow, pulling her back to me when she tries to sit on the other side.

She shakes her head but settles into my side anyway.

The gravel in the drive crunches beneath the tires as we begin to make our way down the long road.

My hand lazily draws circles on her bare shoulder, "I want you to be careful tonight." I tell her.

"I'll be fine," she sighs.

I can't help but feel like that's a lie. Not an intentional one but the sense of foreboding weighs on me heavily.

It's a set up.

An ambush.

Now that I have Wren, I couldn't bear to part with her. She was a drug and like all addicts I needed her more and more each day.

Was I selfish? Of course I was.

I knew keeping her with me was doing more harm than good, but the threat is there now, I can't simply hand her back. Marcus Valentine wants her for something, and I know it isn't to continue his fucked up legacy and the

Syndicate have now made attempts on her life twice. Both times being when she was with me.

I was losing control.

I couldn't let that happen.

Heading out tonight wasn't only for informative purposes, it proves to all the fuckers baring down on us that we are resilient. We won't be suppressed. We don't fear them.

This has been my city for a long time and the Silver's for longer than any of them have probably been alive. To get the key they'd have to pry it from my cold dead fingers.

"Little bird," I tip up her chin, "I know you will be, but I mean it, nonetheless, do not leave my side."

"As if you'd let me," she scoffs with a tease.

I push my thumb between her lips, suppressing a groan when she wraps her plump lips around the digit and sucks. "This mouth will get you into trouble." I warn.

She cocks a brow in challenge, "Will it get me into trouble, or you?"

I laugh, oh that mouth could get me into a lot of trouble. Her teeth graze over the skin on my finger before she releases it and leans forward to kiss my throat. When she pulls back her brows are drawn low, her eyes searching my face as if she's looking for answers to questions in her head.

"What is it?" I ask.

She shakes her head, glancing away, "nothing."

She's lying.

"Come, little bird," I pull her back, "what is going inside that head?"

"We're here," the driver interrupts, giving Wren the perfect opportunity to slip from my grasp and head out the door being held open for her on the other side of the car. My guy stands close, using his body to shield hers as ordered.

Did Valentine or even the Syndicate have this type of loyalty? To protect a woman even if that meant using your own body to shield her from any oncoming attacks? I doubted it.

He shows her to the door, me following close behind as we slip in. Ryker will already be here somewhere, and Griffin should be arriving in a little over an hour.

We head through the lower section of the club, weaving through the figureheads letting off steam where no watchful eyes can judge their actions.

"This city is truly corrupt," Wren comments when we step into the elevator that'll take us to the balcony. It's been repaired since the attack, the glass now reinforced incase that kind of incident were to happen again. It appeared the Syndicate didn't care whether or not this war was kept private, they are not directly linked and therefore cannot be accused. They sit in their comfy chairs in their offices, watching the mess they've created.

They believe themselves to be Gods.

We'll prove just how wrong they are.

"There's a little darkness in everyone," I say as the doors slide closed.

"Do you not feel guilty for this?" She asks with a frown.

"If it isn't us, then it'll be someone else," I tell her honestly, "we've controlled this city and the underground for hundreds of years, long before either of us were even born. The Silver's keep the streets clean."

She laughs without humor, "Hardly clean, Lex, you traffic drugs, guns, money."

"We do," I confirm, "but I personally don't do that, I just control those who do. If it weren't me then the drugs on our streets would be worse and dirty, the gun violence ten times worse than it already is. Gangs and pimps and dealers would rule here, we ensure that doesn't happen."

"You personally don't do that, but you'll kill someone."

"To those who deserve it, yes."

"And Valentine?"

"Valentine is a parasite, little bird, a small fish swimming with sharks. He believes he's capable of taking this city."

"So it's just a power trip?"

"No, he killed my mother. You were my vengeance until…"

"I became your pawn." She finishes.

"You're more than that now."

She sighs heavily, "You'll kill him?"

"Eventually but right now, I have bigger problems to deal with."

"Like?"

"The Syndicate."

She shakes her head, "It's all very political."

I laugh, "Yes."

"And what happens if I don't want any part of this?" She questions after a short silence, "will you let me go?"

"No," my answer is quick and snappy. "You're mine little bird, you'll realize that soon enough."

She doesn't say anymore on the matter as we step onto the balcony. Music thumps through the speakers and the dance floor is filled with bodies gyrating and pulsing to the music. The incident from a few weeks ago forgotten.

The stench of alcohol saturates the air around us but there's a tinge of something else in the air. Something metallic and stifling though I can't place it.

Ryker is lounging on the couch, a scotch in a small tumbler held between his fingers and resting on his knee. He's pinching the bridge of his nose, eyes squeezed shut.

We haven't heard a peep from Ainsley since she went into hiding. Ryker is frantic but it pushes this shit with the Syndicate. We need that information. She will be fine and will keep out of trouble until we can figure this shit out.

"Gruff," Wren plops herself next to my right hand and steals his whiskey, tipping it back before Ryker can stop her. "That's good shit."

"Yeah it is," Ryker growls, "And you just drank it."

I wave a finger to the server and gesture for drinks as I

settle into the couch opposite and beckon Wren to my side.

She stares at me, her face telling me all the things her mouth wants to. Basically, fuck you.

"Little bird," I drawl, "What did we talk about in the car?"

She growls but gets up, crossing the short space to throw herself down next to my side. I hook her around the waist and drag her close, holding her to my body.

"Any news?" I ask Ryker.

He shakes his head, "Griffin was spotted about twenty minutes away. They'll let him through the underground."

"Good."

Now we wait.

THIRTY-TWO

Wren

    Lex is tense besides me, he acts cool, collected but his body is coiled tight, like a snake ready to strike, his muscles hard, fingers squeezing the glass tumbler in his hand so hard I worry it may shatter.

He hates this.

The lack of control.

The threats.

This is a man who has had everything and never been questioned, now, it's different. The knots are unravelling and he's frantically trying to tighten them without understanding the whole picture.

I didn't understand any of it, how this world worked, how business is exchanged but I knew this wasn't how it was supposed to go. He was the self-proclaimed king and someone else was threatening to take his crown.

His fingers absentmindedly draw circles on my exposed thigh while he nurses his scotch.

"He's here," someone says besides us and both Ryker and Lex sit up straighter, eyes lasering in on the elevator doors.

Griffin.

When the metal doors slide open a few minutes later and I get a look at my old friend, I first feel relief and then that all goes out the window when I get a true glimpse at his face. He looks tired, ill, like he hasn't slept in weeks. His shoulders sag, his skin is pale and he doesn't look like the old friend I used to know.

There's an invisible weight on his shoulders.

"Search him." Lex orders.

Two men descend on Griff, forcing his arms wide and his legs apart as they pull and prod his body, searching for weapons. They withdraw a phone from his pocket and a notepad with a pen but that's all they find.

"You really think I'd bring weapons into the devils lair," Griff growls, "it may be stupid to be here, but I am not a fucking idiot."

"Sit." Lex demands, ignoring his statement.

I try to give him a reassuring smile, but he glances away quickly, unable to maintain eye contact. When he does sit, he finally looks at me and then at the hand still rested on my thigh, "You're with him, now?"

"Griff –"

"Don't speak to her," Lex hisses, "This is between you and me. Say what you have to say and then get the fuck out of my club."

"I'm here to help," Griff growls back.

Lex's muscles become increasingly tighter, like pressure under a lid, too much and he'll explode.

"Then help," Lex's fingers bite into my skin, "before I change my fucking mind."

"This is your fucking fault," Griffin roars, "if you hadn't fucking gone after Wren none of this would have happened. You pissed off the wrong man!"

Lex laughs though it's more manic than humored, "You think Valentine scares me?" He says in a voice so low I'm unsure if Griffin actually hears him, "Valentine is nothing. He has no power, no control. No loyalty," the last part of his sentence is spat.

"It isn't Valentine you should be worried about."

"The Syndicate, it's funny, everyone keeps mentioning this organization like they're the boogey man and yet they can't do the work themselves."

"Marcus got involved with the Syndicate a little over a year ago. They contacted him when he first took a shot at the city, telling him they could help. That they had the resources and the man power where he did not. He signed on the dotted line immediately. Wren here, was never supposed to be a part of this though. After a while, Marcus realized that the Syndicate would always be in control. They had him and his men. They were clever really."

"And so what? The Syndicate want the city?"

"Yes, they want you and your men under their thumb

whether they have to kill you or not. Marcus was their way in but that's no longer going to work for them."

"Valentine's an idiot."

"Don't underestimate him," Griff warns, "it's become more now. He is thirsty for power and he'll do just about anything to get it, including using his daughter as a bargaining chip. The Syndicate don't like the way he's running things, it brings too much attention but more than that, he's distracted, deviating from the plan and they are prepared to take out anything and everything that stands in their way. Including Wren. Without her, Marcus has no bargaining chip."

His eyes bounce to me and then back to Lex, swallowing visibly.

"What does he plan to use her for?" Lex asks.

Griff shrugs his shoulders, "Whatever it is, it's against the Syndicate and what they are working towards."

Lex

"Where do your loyalties lie, Griffin?" I settle back on the couch, holding onto the one thing grounding me right now.

I fucking knew there was something more to Valentine's need to get his daughter back.

He frowns when one of the girls working the club offers him a scotch, I nod when he looks to me for approval. Good.

He takes the drink and sips it, seeming to relax a little.

"I asked you a question," I press, "Where are your loyalties?"

With a swallow he looks to Wren and sighs as if he holds the world on his shoulders, "With Wren."

With Wren is with me.

"Why?" I ask.

He chews the side of his lip, his eyes touching every inch of her body and then settling on the hand I have on her thigh. The jealous beast inside me rears its ugly head. I know exactly why. It's obvious in the way he looks at her, with a softness only I'm allowed to look at her with.

She is mine.

"The reason why will get me killed."

"Son of a bitch," Ryker hisses.

"Look," Griffin raises his hands, "I'm not here to start anything, I'm here to keep her alive."

"Griffin," Wren has been quiet this entire time though she's been less than relaxed. She's nervous, fidgeting under my palm, "I don't want you to get hurt."

She cares for him deeply, hurting him will hurt her so I don't do that. I don't hurt him as much as I want to.

He shakes his head, "You need to fix this," he points at me, "you started this mess, you fix it."

Wren settles her hand on mine to stop me from beating the ever-loving shit out of him.

"I want you to get more information," I say through gritted teeth, "You pretend you're so far up Marcus' ass but you report to me now, do you understand?"

"Ha," Griffin scoffs, "I don't owe you shit."

"Then I have no use for you," I reach into the pocket, my fingers curling around the butt of the Glock I have stashed there. It has a silencer but too many eyes to really get away with it.

"Don't!" Wren grabs me, pleading, begging me.

Griffin isn't scared, he doesn't flinch under my venomous glare. "I will do it but not for you, remember that."

Silence falls between us, the music that thumps through the club pounding through my veins. Wren's hand squeezes mine atop her thigh.

"Please," she whispers in my ear, soft enough that only I hear.

Finally breaking away from the stare down with Griffin, I turn to her, taking in the wide eyes, glistening a little with unshed tears and the nervous way she gnaws on her bottom lip. With the hand not holding her leg, I reach up and gently pry her lip from between her teeth, smoothing my finger over the red, swollen skin to soothe the sting left behind.

"For you, little bird," I whisper against her mouth.

THIRTY-THREE

Lex

Griffin leaves, slipping back down the way he came. My mind goes over all the information he gave me, Marcus, the Syndicate. There's so many pieces of this puzzle and no image to follow.

"Can we dance?" Wren asks.

I look over to her, "You want to dance?"

She nods slowly and then shrugs, "I just want to relax a little."

I glance down at the dancefloor, at the mass of bodies, writhing and pulsing on the dancefloor. I spot my men, posed like security around the club and then glance at the door, at the three guys there searching bags and bodies before they can enter.

She's safe here.

I tip the remaining dregs of my scotch into my mouth and push up from the couch, taking her hand and gently tugging her up with me.

"You're dancing?" Ryker laughs.

"Shut the fuck up."

I jerk my head for two extra guys to follow us down. Ultimately, I could protect her better than any of these but knowing I have back up helps ease the sense of doom currently taking up residence in my stomach.

I don't scare easily. Fear isn't an emotion I'm used to, it was trained out of me at a young age. I don't get scared, people are scared of me. I was taught that the monster under the bed was myself and the only way to survive in a world like mine was to be the villain.

But Wren Valentine terrifies me.

She questions everything, she turns everything I've learned on its head and replaces it with shit I've never even dreamed about having.

She tells me I'm her nightmare but this little bird has it all wrong.

She's the nightmare.

Her hand is soft in mine, loose but there and I grip tighter as we descend the stairs and sink into the heaving crowd.

Finding a spot close to the back of the club, I pull her in close to my body, her breasts pushed against my chest as my hand slips around to hold her at the base of her spine. I feel the warmth of her skin soaking through the silk of her dress, her fragrance assaulting my senses.

I move against her, pressing further into her welcoming body. She's soft where I'm hard, warm where I'm cold. She's everything I can never be, making her the perfect fit by my side.

My lips tease across hers as we dance and her hands slide up my back, the muscles jumping, welcoming her touch.

With a sea of bodies and lights all around me, all I see is this woman. All I feel is her. She has come in and disrupted my controlled chaos, turning my life into a frenzied blur of images.

She has become my weakness and for that I am doomed.

There's absolute zero chance I'd let her go. I've tasted and I've teased, I've fucked and loved and cared for her and now she is mine.

Not Valentine's. Not Griffin's. Not even the fucking Syndicate's.

Mine.

My cock grows hard between our bodies, the shaft pressing heavily into the soft curve of her stomach. A stomach I'll have swollen and round as soon as possible.

She'll carry my child and she'll carry my name and she'll rule this city by my side.

She's the queen and all these fuckers can bow down to her.

"Lex," she whimpers against my mouth, the taste of cranberries lingering on her lips.

The air conditioning blows overhead, carrying a cool breeze onto our bodies. She captures my lip between her teeth, biting down hard enough to make it bleed and then she licks away the sting, sliding her hand between our bodies to grip my dick through the material of my pants.

I needed her.

I needed her here and now.

With a tug of her hand I lead her towards the offices behind the bar, only for personal use but I own the fucking club. The servers behind the bar pay us no mind as I throw the door open and lock it promptly behind us. The music continues to vibrate the walls, muffled and tinny now we are behind closed doors. The only window in the room rattles with the heavy bass that thumps wildly.

"Little bird, don't you know it's not nice to tease," my voice is a rasp, a husky baritone that forces a shiver from her body.

I revel in her reaction to me, the way her body wields to my touch, to my voice, to my every caress.

Wren steps forward and places a hand on my chest, pushing me back until I feel the chair behind my knees. I fall into it, slouching down until my knees are apart and my torso is curled. I rest my head against the backrest, watching my queen.

She takes a step back, the heel of her shoes clipping against the wood flooring.

"Tell me who *you* belong to," she purrs, lids hooded as she watches me slowly begin to unbutton my shirt.

My lips curl into a smirk, "Only you, little bird."

"Tell me what you want me to do." Her fingers play with the thin strap holding her dress up, pushing it down the curve of her shoulder and then back up while her other hand lifts the hem of her dress, bringing it up, up, until it shows the dips in her shapely hips and the thin lacy strap of her underwear.

She's so fucking sexy.

My erection pounds behind the zipper of my pants.

"You wanted to dance, little bird," I palm my cock, squeezing hard, "dance for me."

One side of her mouth tilts up and then she spins, showing me her back and the round curves of her ass. The dress clings to the curve, following the length of her spine and then the globes of her ass cheeks, making my mouth water.

She brings her arms up, lifting the mane of wild copper hair until it piles atop her head in a mass of chaotic curls. There's a sheen to her skin, a thin layer of perspiration that makes her skin glow in the lighting of the office, with only a lamp on in the corner emitting a dim orange light, her skin takes on a creamy, golden hue, dusted with fine, light freckles.

She weaves her body, matching the pace of the music, her hips swaying side to side, the dress creasing and bunching with her movements. Her calf muscles work as she bends her knees and lowers a little, dancing for me.

"Spin around," I rasp, biting the inside of my check to stop myself from taking her right now. "I want to see your face."

She does as she's told, slowly turning to face me.

There's a pink blush on her cheeks but it isn't from embarrassment, no, I see the darkness in her eyes, the way the pulse point in her neck batters wildly against her skin, like a butterfly trapped in a jar. If I were to slide my hand up her thigh and swipe my fingers through her folds I'm sure I'd find her wet, needy, ready.

She continues her dance, moving her body for me in a way that hypnotizes me. Her hands come up to the straps, dipping beneath the thin material to pull it away from her shoulders but then she drops them again, her hands following the mounds of her breasts to her ribs and her stomach.

A sudden popping sound echoes in the room, loud enough to drown out the music for a split second.

Wren stills in front of me, her eyes widening and instantly, I'm on alert.

My heart begins to pound in my chest as I scramble up from the chair, crossing the small distance between us and gripping the tops of her arms.

"Wren?" I question, "Wren, what is it!?"

Her eyes bounce between mine, her plump and swollen lips parted and then she tilts her chin, looking down between our bodies. I follow her gaze to where her hands are pressed to her stomach.

Red seeps through her fingers and when she pulls her hands away, I see her palms coated in blood.

No.

Oh fuck no.

With a small, frightful cry, her legs buckle beneath her.

I'm quick to catch her, stopping her delicate frame from

hitting the floor.

No, no, this can't happen.

I frantically search the room, spotting the perfect hole in the window where the bullet had come through before settling on a club uniform shirt folded on top of the desk. I grab it, pressing it to the wound pulsing blood in her abdomen.

She sucks in a couple of shaky breaths as I hold the fabric to her skin, trying to stem the bleeding.

"It hurts," her voice is steady, despite the shake in her breath and body, "Lex."

"I know, little bird," I can't think straight. I pat my pockets, looking for my phone.

She was safe. She was supposed to be safe.

I come up empty, my phone nowhere on my body but I need help. The music is too loud for anyone to hear me which means I need to get out of here.

Blood stains the crisp white shirt still half way unbuttoned, Wren's blood smearing across my skin.

This was no way the end for us. We had only just begun.

THIRTY-FOUR

Wren

The pain sears through my system as if it's lava rushing through my veins. My skin wet, sticky, the warm blood running off my skin. All I see is red.

Lex presses the balled up wad of fabric to my stomach, holding it over the hole that pulses blood but I can't focus on anything. The edges of my vision pulse with black and white spots, my head feels light, like I'm in the space before you fall asleep, where you're still conscious but barely.

I feel my body being lowered but that doesn't make sense, wasn't I already led down?

The hard floor presses into my back, putting pressure on the wound in my abdomen. The dizziness is chased away at the blinding pain and I'm not able to stop the scream that barrels from my throat.

Is this what death feels like?

Is this it now? I'll go out in a pool of blood with fire in my veins.

"It's okay, shh," Lex pants, "Just, breathe, okay?"

I've never seen him like this. This is a man who fears nothing and yet I swear that's complete terror in his eyes.

I don't like it. A sense of calm begins to wash through my system as I stare at his face. I suppose seeing his brutal beauty isn't such a bad way to go. With my fingers, I run my hand down the side of his face, frowning at the red streaks now marring his skin.

"You're bleeding," I croak.

He shakes his head and then stands, his feet pounding on the floor. I hear the rattle of the door and then the heavy music sweeps through the room like an angry wind but I don't mind the music.

I can sleep with noise, that doesn't bother me and even if it did, I'm so tired right now. So tired.

If I just close my eyes, I can sleep.

So that's what I do… I sleep.

THIRTY-FIVE

Lex

"No!" I scoop her up from the floor, wincing at how rough I'm handling her but I don't have time to be gentle. She needed a hospital. Now. "Don't you dare close your eyes little bird."

Anger pulses through me like a bull, red hot and furious. She doesn't get to leave me like this.

She doesn't get to fucking leave me.

"Wake up Wren," I shake her, feeling the warm droplets of blood running over my hands. How long has it been? Minutes? Fuck I don't now, it feels like hours.

The crowd in the club continues to pulse wildly to the music. No one turns our way, no one even bats an eye at the man holding a bleeding woman in his arms.

I turn to the door but the crowd is too thick to move through without either dropping Wren or hurting her further.

This is the Syndicate.

They got her.

I turn back and tilt my head to the balcony, seeing Ryker on the couch. He's still nursing a scotch, his head tipped back so he's facing the ceiling.

As if sensing my eyes, he slowly lifts his head and meets my stare through the glass.

It doesn't even take him a second.

He jumps up from the couch and begins to shout orders I can't hear over the music. It would be me doing this, but I can't seem to think, let alone talk.

I look down at Wren's sickly pale face, her eyes fluttering closed again.

"Wake up, baby," I shake her, "Wake up."

I needed to get moving.

I push around the edge of the crowd, forcing my way to the stairs and the only easy way out. Ryker is pounding towards me.

"What the fuck happened?" He goes to touch her and something in me snaps. I snatch her away, curling myself around her body as if to protect her though I know, deep down, it isn't Ryker she needs protection from.

It's me.

I caused this. She's bleeding out in my arms because of what *I* did.

That strange scent hits me half a second before an

almighty boom rattles the walls of the club.

Both Ryker and I, with Wren in my arms, are thrown off our feet with the blast, fire instantly erupting. Dazed, with my ears ringing I push onto my elbows, reaching for Wren.

She's face down on the ground, her wild cooper hair spilled around her like a fiery halo.

I feel the heat from the flames, can hear the screams and cries of the crowd and feel the stamp of feet vibrating the floor beneath me as they rush for the exit but my focus isn't on that, it isn't on how the fuck this has happened or who, it's only on her.

Pain pulses through my body at the same pace of my frantic heartbeat. I know I'm bleeding, badly but so is she. A red pool is blooming from beneath her body and red tendrils, like crimson snakes run ribbons over her pale skin, over her legs, arms and shoulders.

"Wren," my voice is raspy, "Wren."

With every single ounce of strength I have, I reach her, gently turning her body until she's laying on her back. Her chest rises and falls, and with ash clinging to her dark lashes, she blinks up at me.

She looks completely broken. Battered.

Bruises bloom across her pale skin, joining with the crimson that runs rivers over her body.

"You're okay baby."

"L-lex," she stutters, sucking in a wheezing breath.

No, no, "You don't get to leave, remember," I growl,

"You belong to me, little bird. I say when you are allowed to leave."

Her lips tip up into a small, pained smile, "I love you."

Those three words end me.

I don't deserve love, especially not from her.

I set out to kill her and I've just done that.

"No," I rise up onto my knees, my body screaming out at me, "No, don't sound like you're saying goodbye."

"It's okay."

"No!" I reach down, pushing her wild hair from her face, "you don't leave!" I grit out.

"Kiss me."

"Little bird," I beg.

I've never begged for a single thing in my life.

"Please."

With the world in chaos around me, I lean down and kiss her, tasting the metallic tinge of blood on my tongue.

When I pull away a sudden whack to my head has me falling away from Wren. My skull explodes with a pain so sharp my vision blackens.

Wren is flat on her back, staring at me as a single tear slips from the corner of her eye, running a clean path through the dust, dirt and blood that clings to her skin.

I try to get up but the fogginess in my head makes my

limbs too heavy, too weak to move.

Who the fuck hit me!?

Two legs step up beside Wren's body and through bleary eyes I follow them up to find Marcus Valentine standing over his daughter's body.

"Who the fuck did this!?" He bellows, "What good will she be if she's dead!?"

I hear people scurrying around, but I can't see past him and her, somewhere close by a fire crackles wildly, the heat of the flames making my skin too hot.

"Get the fuck away from her!" I growl, finally able to push up onto my elbows, though it's shaky and weak. When I'm there I roll, catching myself before I hit the ground.

A swift boot to the face has me crashing back down.

Get to Wren. I chant the words over and over as I try to push up again.

I keep my eyes on them, watching as I struggle as Valentine leans down and roughly pulls Wren from the rubble, throwing her around too hard. She ends up limp over his shoulder, blood dripping from her skin, mixing into the dirt that crunches under his feet.

"Burn it all to the ground," Valentine meets my eyes, "let them all burn."

His grin is nothing short of menacing.

There's nothing in his eyes, no soul, only darkness and death.

He's truly sold his soul to the devil.

"It's time my daughter and I become reacquainted."

And with those parting words he turns and leaves, taking Wren with him and I'm helpless to stop him.

PART TWO
TWISTED KING

THIRTY-SIX
Marcus Valentine

I stare down at the body, pale skin stained red with blood, blackened by dust and ash. The doctors rush around the bedside, inserting needles into her skin, pipes into the throat, bandages to stem the bleeding before they can get in to operate and fix this mess.

I feel no remorse as I stare at my daughters' lifeless body, at the translucent skin, slowly leaking life. I need her to survive, not because of the familial tie we share, I couldn't care for that, this *thing* is no daughter of mine. A traitor, a liar, a cheat. She may hold my name but that is all that links us.

But she has use yet.

My daughter, as vile as she is, is a beauty, nonetheless.

Her appearance has been whispered between the ranks of my men, and then further still, I've heard the tales of the

Valentine with copper hair and green eyes and I know how very valuable she is. What she can bring me.

Alexander Silver thought he would get to keep what rightfully belonged to me and here I am, proving him wrong.

He's likely ash and bones now, burned up and incinerated by the flames that I know are still devouring the building, the heat tearing through the club as easily as a knife slicing through butter. It's a shame he won't get to witness all the things I have planned for his precious little Wren.

It would have been satisfying to see the pain break the man when he watched me take his city *and* destroy his girlfriend right before she's shipped off to God knows where with God knows who.

I don't care what happens to her, but I hope she suffers.

All I care for is the resource she will bring.

I am not naïve enough to believe I can take this city alone.

Before, I chose the wrong person to help in my scheme to claim Brookeshill from the Silver's, now I've learned from my mistakes.

Any men left still loyal to Silver will perish, the rest can join my ranks and watch this city rise from the ashes under my rule.

The Syndicate will die.

The Silver name will die.

And once the blood on the streets has been cleansed, it will be my name they whisper, it'll be me they bow down to and my face that haunts their dreams.

So, while the doctors and the nurses battle to save the life that will help claim my rightful place, I turn from the room and pull out my cell, dialing the number only listed as Heart in my phone.

"Valentine," his English accent rasps through the earpiece.

"It's time."

THIRTY-SEVEN

Lex

My eyes sting with the smoke that swirls around my face, my lungs screaming for fresh air. Each breath burns as I inhale, my throat raw, a metallic coppery taste coating my tongue.

I can feel how weak I am, my limbs heavy with fatigue, body broken and bruised. Blood drips from my chin, my fingers, sliding over my ash covered skin like crimson snakes, mingling in with the dirt, rubble and dust beneath my palms. Fire crackles wildly to my left, the flames devouring everything they touch and it's only a matter of time until they reach me. I can feel the heat searing my flesh, making my blood boil and clothes cling to my skin, drenched in both my blood and sweat.

Bodies litter the ground, bloodied, burned, broken, eyes staring lifelessly at the ceiling where the disco lights continue to pulse green, red and blue across the club.

Twisted City — RIA WILDE

Somewhere close by sirens wail and horns blast, people talk and scream.

I push up though my legs are too weak to hold me, and I smash back down, grunting as the pain floods through my limbs, but I try again and again, one thought pushing me. One thought that erases all else.

Get to Wren.

Wren.

Wren.

"Over here!" I recognize the voice though it's muffled, like it's being spoken from behind a pillow. My vision blurs with my fight to get up, my head swimming but then hands grasp my arms and I'm hauled to my feet.

"Lex!" Ryker's voice shatters the fog inside my head, like the blast of a horn, it cuts through the mist until I can finally think clearly. His face swims before mine, forehead crinkled with a frown, a deep crease between his brows as he studies me, picking out every injury.

"Wren." Her name is a rasp from my throat, voice wrecked by the smoke and pain, a plea directed at no one and everyone all the same. My little bird. *My sweet little bird.*

"I know, boss," Ryker continues, dragging me towards the door. His feet kick at the bodies on the floor. People who were once dressed in their finest now lay bloodied and dead, some no longer whole and only vaguely resemble a human body, mangled and torn up, limbs missing, burns that have eaten away at their skin and muscle, exposing organs and bones beneath.

Death. So much death.

My chest constricts, my lungs squeezing and I hack, my body trying to rid itself of the toxins filling my lungs. I taste the coppery tang of blood on my tongue, mixed with smoke and ash. The stench of the dead and burning flesh assaults my nose but it isn't that that makes my stomach churn, it's the lingering scent of her on my skin, her blood now mixed with mine coating my hands. That's what makes my stomach roll. She's gone.

I will kill him for this.

I will Kill Marcus Valentine even if it's the last thing I do.

This is more than the city. This is more than my life. I will level this entire place to the ground.

They always talk about the monster who runs this city, they tell ghost stories to scare children into staying in their beds and stop teenagers from wandering the streets at night, and if it's the monster they want, then it's the monster they'll get.

I will tear them all limb from limb, I'll let their blood coat my skin, wearing it like a cloak and I won't stop until I have my little bird back in my arms.

When we finally make it through the exit I suck in my first breath of clean air, coughing onto the sidewalk with each inhale. The street is lit up and bathed in red and blue light, fire trucks and cop cars skewed in the road. Paramedics tend to those who were lucky enough to escape the carnage while firefighters tackle the raging inferno that has already burned through half of the building, and is now spreading to the buildings on either side. Even out here, I smell the potent stench of burning skin, and hair. My eyes sweep over the chaos, noting the panic, the fear that pales the emergency responders faces, the sheer terror in their eyes as they realize they can't save everyone and the people still trapped within those burning walls are going to be consumed by the raging flames.

It was carnage. Destruction.

A paramedic rushes to where we stand, takes one look at me with widening eyes, and grabs a hold of my arm as he steers me towards an ambulance waiting in the middle of the road as he shouts orders. "Get the fuck off me," I growl, voice raspy.

"You're bleeding a hell of a lot man," the guy says, "You need to be checked out."

"I'll give you two seconds," I warn, "Before I blow your fucking brains out."

I had no idea if I even still had a gun on me, the blast knocked the shit out of me but even if I didn't, I'd find one and I'd make good on my promise. The paramedic lets go of me quickly, too quickly and in the weakened state that I am, I stumble, almost losing my footing until I catch myself on the side of a cop car.

"You need to get checked out boss," Ryker comes up beside me, looking in a much better state than me. He's bloody and dirty, but he walks like he didn't just get blown the fuck up. Motherfucker is built like a steel giant.

"I need to get to Wren," I tell him, vision blurring as I limp at his side towards the underground garage where I know my guys parked the SUV.

Ryker doesn't argue, instead he helps me like the fucking broken boy I am and shoves me into the passenger seat when we finally get to the car.

I pull my cell from my pocket, "Fuck!" I growl, slamming a bloodied hand against the dashboard as the thing practically falls apart in my grip, the screen shattered, shards of glass falling away and landing in my lap.

There's no fucking time. Who the fuck knows where Marcus has taken Wren and if I don't get on it right the fuck now it could be weeks before he decides to resurface. I don't have weeks. Wren doesn't have weeks.

This ends now.

And if he so much as hurts a single hair on her head I'll be sure to make his death long and painful. They'll be no mercy, I will flay him alive and make him eat his own flesh.

My head pounds, a steady thump, thump, thump that mimics my own heart pumping in my chest. I should have been checked out, I'm no fucking use right now but Wren… She needs me. A King will always protect his

Queen, and I may have failed this time, but this motherfucking God is vengeful.

The drive back to the compound is rough, my consciousness slipping in and out the entire time and by the time we pull into the driveway, Ryker parking as close to the door as he can get, my lids are hooded and heavy and my body has all but given up. Numbness has started to creep in, through my fingers and my toes, blood dripping like a crimson river over my skin, staining the seat beneath me.

"Shit, Lex," Ryker hisses, pulling me from the passenger seat. I can't make anything out, the house ahead of me blurs in and out of focus, the gravel beneath my shoes crunches but it sounds as if I'm under water, drowning in the dark waters of the ports that surround this city, unable to break the surface. My legs barely carry me, limbs too heavy and sluggish. My feet scuff on the floor, tripping over the gravel as we slowly make it up the stairs and into the compound.

I can't die. Not yet.

Wren.

Get to fucking Wren.

Ryker drags me through the foyer, my blood dripping onto the floor, before he drops me unceremoniously onto the couch.

What the fuck happened!?

It was safe. *Safe.*

I flinch as the memory of Wren's shooting slams into my brain, the blood, so much blood, stemming from that hole in her abdomen, leaking out over her dress, seeping through her fingers. And then her crumbled and broken body, laying in the rubble of her own fathers making, staring at me, eyes wet with tears.

This shit, these fucking damn feelings are going to kill me quicker than the injuries currently sucking life from my body. Wren fucking Valentine was my undoing.

But she was also the damn thing that was going to get me off this fucking couch because she needs me.

I was *her* monster.

Her demon.

Her devil.

Regardless of whether I liked it or not, there was no way I'd be able to just let her go. No way I wouldn't tear this city apart just to find her.

Ryker begins to tug at my clothes, grabbing the lapels of my torn jacket to shuck it from my shoulders.

"Easy," I growl when his frantic movements jar the injuries littering my abdomen.

"Doc is coming," is all he replies, "I need to stop this bleeding, just until he gets here."

"I'm getting her back," I say to him once I'm stripped from the waist up, the air of the house cool against my skin. The blood seeping from my wounds chills as soon as the air hits it, droplets of crimson that feel like ice rolling over my skin. This wasn't only my blood though, this was her blood, on my hands, my face, my body. It was hers.

I've never cared much for human life, I've only experienced one death that gutted me and that was my mothers, but the idea of Wren never seeing the light of day again, never giving me shit or fighting me, it cripples me. It guts me from the inside out. The organ inside my chest no longer beats for me or this city, it beats for her. It thrums for her touch, her body and without it, the thing is useless.

She told me she loved me.

I didn't deserve that, not from her.

I didn't deserve that full stop.

Loving me would damn her to hell.

I would never let her go, she belonged to me, and now I know she has given me her heart, I'll do anything to get her back, damned or not.

This city has been my all forever, until she crashed into my life, kicking and screaming. This city was my only until she stole that away from me and replaced it with herself.

This was my own doing.

All the events that have led up to the now, that was my fault.

But even the Gods made mistakes. And that is what I am.

A fucking God.

I am king.

And it's time this king goes into fucking battle. It's time this king places his queen on the throne beside him.

I'm coming little bird and together we will bring our enemies to their knees.

THIRTY-EIGHT

Lex

"That fucking snake," I hiss.

"You called it," Ryker huffs, sucking on a cigarette. He's not a smoker but in the last few days he's had one hanging from his mouth near on every second.

Griffin was to blame for the detonation of the explosives.

That motherfucker was going to pay. I am not easily deceived but he had me. Did he ever truly care for Wren? I would have said so but watching him now, concealing himself in an alcove in the club, in a nice little safe spot as he pressed the button and caused the whole building to explode. The explosion happened in sections, first the door, making the exit impassable, then the bar, the patrons receiving drinks being blown to pieces in the process and then in the middle of the dancefloor. Fire erupted and chaos ensued as he slipped through the carnage, unscathed and escaped out a back exit while the rest of us burned.

This just proves how far I've fallen.

With the footage of the club, not publicly available to the authorities, I've picked out several faces employed by Valentine, though the shooting, I've realized, did not come from them. That was a whole different story and while his face is concealed beneath a hood and mask, I already know the man belonged to the Syndicate. A hired gun to do their dirty work.

"Find him," I slam the lid of the laptop down hard enough that I hear the screen crack, "I want him in that fucking barn by morning."

"Yes, boss."

Ryker gets to work, leaving me in the compound to stew on my decisions. There's zero chance of me being in the field for at least another couple of days, I know my limits and unfortunately, I am only mortal. Several deep lacerations, broken ribs, some minor internal bleeding, burns and a concussion later and I'm still standing.

The club is gone.

Burned to the ground, along with the hundred and fifty-seven bodies that succumbed in the attack. Only seven of my men died, the rest were innocents.

No one was truly innocent in this life, but they were innocent in this war.

I want Valentine to believe I perished along with them. A lot of the bodies in the club were so badly damaged, identities have yet to be announced, giving me the perfect opportunity to remain in the shadows for the time being. With me supposedly gone, there will be no need for Valentine to hide.

He's in hiding right now, but he'll come out soon if he thinks I'm dead, after all, if I'm not around, the city is open for him to claim. If I have to pretend to be dead for a few days then so be it, I'll wait, and I'll watch until he crawls out of whatever hole he is in. My men are on the streets, in every club, bar, building and shop, waiting for the moment he rears his ugly head.

There is a clock ticking above his head and there is only so much time left until it hits zero and when that happens, it'll be my face that sends him to Hell.

I pull the footage up on my phone, watching Valentine lift Wren from the rubble. She's so broken, my little bird, her wings crushed. She's lifeless over his shoulder, I can't even see a movement in her chest as Valentine carries her away, disappearing out the door before the emergency services show up.

I managed to track them to about three blocks away but after that, the trail went dark.

Not for long.

Valentine has underestimated me.

Severely.

"In the barn," Ryker drags me from my thoughts a few hours later. "We have Griffin."

That didn't take long.

I feel a cruel smile tug at my lips as I stand from the desk, ignoring the pain that shoots through my body with the movement. There is nothing inside of me but blinding rage, an anger so dangerous there won't be a single person left to utter the Valentine name.

"Grab the driver," I say to Ryker as I head out the room, towards the back door that'll lead me to the barn. Three men flank me while Ryker grabs the item I have asked for.

The night air is humid when I step out into it, the heat pressing down onto me, stifling, heavy. A sweat breaks out across the nape of my neck as I cross the lawn towards the barn. Impenetrable darkness surrounds us here, the only light this far from the house comes from the moon and the stars above.

I push the door open, the old wood creaking with the movement, hinges protesting. I'll have to sort that, I think casually as my feet scuff across the dusty floor, grit and dirt sending small clouds of dust to bloom in front of me.

Four men are strung up before me.

/ Twisted City   RIA WILDE

There's no kindness here, no chairs to be restrained to, instead they're tied up to the beams in the ceiling, arms together above their heads, tied at the wrists as they dangle there, only the tips of their toes brushing the ground beneath them.

Griffin is in the middle, his face a bloodied mess, swollen, blue with bruising and blood stains his clothes.

One eye meets mine, the other swollen shut and he curls his lip, baring his teeth to me. The other three hang there like the limp dicks they are.

With a blade in my hand, I press the tip of it into my forefinger, swirling the razor edge against the skin until a bead of blood wells to the surface and streaks down my finger. I ensure I hold my weight even though my muscles scream and protest, I don't show a weakness. Not in front of the enemy.

"I didn't think we would be seeing each other so soon, Griffin," I say calmly, sitting myself in the chair that's been placed directly in front of the bodies. I survey them. They look like animals, strung up for the slaughter, each one broken in some way.

"Fuck you, Silver."

I tut, sucking my tongue against my teeth, "You had even me fooled," I continue, "That's not an easy task so I will applaud you there."

"She wasn't supposed to be there," he hisses, "she was supposed to be on the balcony!"

I shake my head, "You Valentines' are always making mistakes."

"And what about you, huh, Silver? You're the reason Valentine has her!"

I stand abruptly, my fury boiling, "No, Griffin, you are. She was safe with me until you went and fucking blew up my club!"

"You really believe I would have left her with you?" Griffin sneers, "You're a fucking monster and she is innocent. She doesn't belong in this war."

"I really thought you'd be on her side, but you've been Valentine's little bitch this entire time."

"I have no loyalty to Valentine. I did what was necessary to get her away from you."

"And that didn't work out so well did it."

Griffin doesn't answer. I wonder how much he knows. Did he know the Syndicate had her shot only moments before he detonated those explosives? Does he know I held her bleeding body in my arms when he pressed the fucking button? Does he know where she is?

I retake my seat, kicking up my leg until my ankle rests on my knee, pushing down all those thoughts, calming the raging sea of emotions rising like a wave inside me. I pull at the cuffs of my white shirt, straightening the sleeves and then I twist the leather cuffs around my wrists, making sure the silver emblems are facing upwards. On one is a feather, a recent edition to honor my little bird, on the other, a wolf. Fierce. Loyal. Deadly and cunning. I hadn't worn them in a long time, an old Silver tradition I didn't see fit in the now however, I had recently changed my stance. We had never been defeated before and every Silver before me wore their cuffs like crowns. I would be no different.

Griffin watches me through his one good eye.

"Tell me Griffin," I drop my arms, linking my hands over my stomach as I lean back in the chair. I'm moving too much, disturbing my stitches, causing my joints to twitch and roll and jump, lighting fires under my skin as the pain bursts through my body. "Did you get a good look at what you had done? You claim to care for Wren and yet you blew up the building she was in."

"Fuck you, Silver, I care more for her than you ever will. You dragged her into this war, what happens to her now is entirely your fault."

"You're correct," I nod once, "I brought her into this, but I wasn't the one who handed her to her father. Valentine has plans for her, what are those?"

"You assume she is still alive."

Those words turn my blood to ice, it freezes inside my veins and causes my heart to slow down enough to make me truly believe I may pass out. She's not dead. She can't be. A roaring begins in my ears, so furious it drowns all else out as images of her body, pale, broken and dead flashes inside my head.

Not my little bird. Not my Wren.

I don't show any of that though. I don't show the emotion on my face or in my body as I lean forward, dropping my leg to the floor as I rest my elbows on my knees and rest my head in my hand, feigning boredom.

"Is she not alive, Griffin?"

The words are acid on my tongue, leaving a vile taste in my mouth. She wasn't dead. Valentine was using her for something, and he needed her alive. After everything that has been done to get her away from me and into his clutches, there is no way he's killed her. Unless she didn't survive the gunshot and the explosion. Panic claws its way into my chest. It is entirely possible that she did not survive.

His nostrils flare.

I grit my teeth as the next words spew from my mouth, "Tell me, come on, tell me how Valentine broke her so bad and dumped her body somewhere. Paint the picture for me. Tell me she is now just a corpse, rotting in a ditch somewhere."

He doesn't say a word.

He can't lie. Not about this and his silence is louder than any words he can speak. Wren isn't dead.

I truly believe he cares for Wren, in a twisted, fucked up

kind of way. He wanted to get her away from me, but he hadn't banked on the Syndicate getting their shot in first. He hadn't banked on her being so damaged afterwards she was easy picking for her father.

He wanted to destroy me, my men, so he could get to her himself, but shit doesn't always work out the way we plan.

"Your silence is awfully loud," I stand, "and now I need some information from you." I flick the tip of the knife towards him, using it to point, "we can make this easy, you just need to talk."

"She will hate you for this," he growls.

"She might, but ultimately, she'll forgive me. Do you want to know why, Griffin?"

He doesn't answer but his teeth grind together, his fingers twitching above his head.

"Because I have her heart, Griffin. She chooses me. *Me.*"

THIRTY-NINE

Lex

Ryker hands me the driver as I snatch up one of the timber screws from the stack to the left. Griffin watches, that one good eye narrowed in my direction. He tries to hide his fear but I smell it, I live on this shit. His fear is palpable, it coils in the air like a phantom snake, wrapping around us, making my heart thump with adrenaline, the blood course through my veins like a freight train.

The guy to his left is awake, he's as quiet as a mouse though, too afraid now he's in the vipers nest.

"So, Griffin, where is she?" I ask as Ryker casually lets the guy down, unhooking the ropes binding him to the ceiling so his body drops to the floor with a hard thud. Ryker's face is an impassive mask, mouth set in a straight, unemotional line but I see the darkness and vengeance in his eyes. He wants them to hurt, he wants to make them pay.

The guy groans, too fucked up to even fight or move on the dirty ground. The sound of a body being dragged across the floor fills my ears but I don't dare look. I keep my gaze trained on Griffin though he watches my man move the body to a steel table where he's then strapped down, his shoes and socks stripped from his feet.

"What are you doing?" Griffin asks, ignoring my question, eyes flicking from me to his guy.

"I think you're forgetting your place here," I back myself towards where his guy is prepped and ready for me. "Answer my question, *where is she?*"

"I'm not telling you shit, away from you is better than anything else."

"Even with Valentine?"

"He's the lesser evil."

"In this life, Griffin, choosing the lesser evil is not always the smart choice."

I line the timber screw up with the guys heel, pressing the tip hard enough into the skin that a bead of blood wells to the surface. "I'll give you one more chance," I say, "One more Griffin, I don't give many chances so think yourself lucky."

"Fuck you, Silver!"

But his eyes are wide with terror, his voice shaking with

the fear that rattles through his body like an earthquake. This is just the start of my revenge. Only the beginning of what I am going to do to those who have crossed me and Wren.

"I'll go through each of your men, Griffin, until I get to you, until I get the answers I want." I promise as I line the head of the driver to the screw and press down on the trigger. The sound is deafening to begin with but then the scream that erupts from the guy on the table overpowers that. His agony bounces off the walls, loud, painful, twisted. The screw slices through his skin, blood splattering as it spins through muscle and cartilage, vibrating against bone. The guy passes out long before I get it all the way in.

"You're fucking sick!" Griffin bellows, his fear a stench that stains the air. I breathe it in sharply.

The skin on my face is slick with blood, war paint that I smear over my face as I turn back to Griffin and a wicked smile pulls my mouth up. I no doubt look manic, a complete psychopath and if they didn't fear me before, they will now. "Tell me where she is Griffin."

"Fuck you!" He bellows.

I tut with a sigh and gesture for Ryker to wake the guy up. It takes a few minutes, but he eventually comes to, tears of pain rolling down his bruised face, leaving clean tracks on his otherwise dirty face.

"Griff, man," he begs, voice broken, "Tell him, please."

Twisted City   RIA WILDE

I line the second screw up, his limbs twitching, trying to escape but don't they know? There's no escape from me.

"Yeah Griff, tell me." I mock.

"I don't know!" he yells frantically.

I sigh, the driver dangling in my hand, "That's the wrong answer."

The screw goes in just as the first, bloody, loud, violent. My hands are coated in this guys blood, his cries of torture ringing in my ears like music.

I bounce from foot to foot, "Doesn't it make you feel alive, Griffin?" My laugh echoes through the barn, "doesn't it make you feel powerful? You hold all the keys here, Griffin, you can make this stop."

Griffin furiously lashes against his restraints, his body swinging. His hands have long gone purple from lack of blood flow, the wounds across his body clotted now and the blood dried to resemble the color of rust.

"You're a fucking psycho"

"You're probably right," I nod my head with a sigh, turning a little to watch Ryker unbind the guy from the table and drag his bleeding ass back to the ropes where he proceeds to hang him like a prime cut of meat. Blood drips down from the wounds in his feet, the skin blackened. I mean that shit's gotta hurt, right? "But I still don't hear you talking, so really, who is the bad guy here?"

"I don't know where she is, Silver!" He cries, "I don't know!"

"Why do I think you're lying, asshole?"

"I'm not!" He pleads, "He knew I found her and didn't tell him, the club was a test, okay!? To get back in his ranks. If I didn't, he would have killed me."

"You should have let him end you."

"I don't know where she is. He keeps moving, the last location I know about was in the city centre, an apartment block but underneath, it wasn't an apartment listed on any map."

"The address?"

He rattles off an address which Ryker writes down.

"That's good Griffin," I tell him.

"You're going to kill me, aren't you?"

"I am, Griffin."

He hangs his head, "You'll never find her, Valentine's smart."

"All you fuckers have underestimated me," I step up to him, pulling the knife from the holster attached to my belt, "Every single one of you. You've come into my city, started a war that you have no hope of winning and have expected me to what, give up? Let you all fuck me in the ass while you take my city and my girl?"

Twisted City

RIA WILDE

I nod to Ryker who makes quick work of finishing the other guys hanging from the ropes. They're no use to me, low in the pecking order, they'll have fuck all information I could actually use. Griffin's eyes widen as he watches each of them die, a single bullet to their foreheads, quick and easy. My face remains impassive. Taking life is as easy as the air I breathe.

We come into this life screaming, bloody, traumatic and it fits that we exit it the same way.

"You've called the monster now, Griffin, don't be surprised that he's answered."

I step up to him, tilting my head a little so I can look directly at his face. Fear swims in his eyes as I raise the blade and rest it against his neck. I don't waste a minute, there's no more words to say as my knife slices across his throat, cutting through skin, tissue and muscle, his windpipe opening up to me like a yawning jaw. Blood pours from the gash, sliding through the gaping wound and down his front, staining his white shirt red. His gurgles and muffled cries last only seconds as he bleeds to death, sucking in air that'll never reach his lungs and then his head droops and his body goes slack and the life finally drains from his body.

"Clean it up," I tell the men stationed sporadically around the barn, "make sure this one," I point to Griffin, "Ends up in public view. I want Valentine to see what he has done."

They get to work as I grab a cloth and wipe the blood from my fingers, the two bracelets around my wrists clipping together to make a tinkling noise that is almost melodic. Death permeates the air, the stench of blood and sweat heavy. Ryker joins my side as we exit the barn back towards the house.

"Ten minutes," I tell Ryker, "then we go to this address."

With the blood cleaned from my skin and the clothes on my back fresh, I step from the SUV, holding back the wince as my body cramps with pain. There's no time to recover, no time to sulk in the compound when my little bird is out there waiting for me.

The apartment building ahead of me looks like any other, a high rise but it's clean and tasteful, no wasters or low lives hanging outside. There is a security call button outside the large glass doors listing apartments from one to sixty-five but they are not what I am looking for. There's no button for an underground apartment but that's hardly surprising and from the research I've done, this building belongs to a real estate agency here in the city, one that isn't on my payroll.

I laugh to myself, cheeky fucker.

It's non-descript, to look at you'd never know there was a secret apartment below and so instead of going through the entrance, we round the building, my guys following and find the fire escape. It's locked but that shit is easy to get through and then we're in a stairwell. To the left is a set of stairs leading up to apartments above and to the right is a supply closet.

The building is silent all around us but the sounds of our boots on the hard floor echo up the stairwell. Ryker shoots the lock on the closet door and three guys slam through into the darkness.

"Clear!" One yells and we follow in, taking another set of stairs down to yet another door though this one is unlocked.

The apartment inside is huge, a ten-bedroom mansion fit onto one floor. Opulence and money drip from the walls, chandeliers made from crystal hang from the ceilings and art worth more than most cars people drive hang on the walls. I sweep through the place, finding it empty of any human presence but Valentine left a lot of shit behind.

He must have been tipped off that we had been given his location and ran. He gets it. I'll go to all and any lengths to get her back.

"Search it," I tell the guys, "I want everything empty. I want him found!"

They don't dawdle, splitting up to search the rooms while Ryker and I head through to the office room.

A huge oak desk sits against the back walls, and as it's underground, there are no windows so he's compensated by installing lights every few inches against the wall. A huge cabinet sits against one side, bottles of aged whiskeys and brandys sitting on the shelves. On the desk is a glass still half full with an amber liquid and there's a half smoked cigar in the ashtray though there's no laptop, no phone, only a note sat in the centre of the desk. I guess he knew I wasn't dead then.

> SILVER.
> GIVE UP. I HAVE WREN.
> GIVE ME THE CITY AND YOU CAN HAVE HER BACK.
> IF YOU DON'T, I CAN ASSURE YOU NOTHING PLEASANT WILL BE IN HER FUTURE.
> TODAY IS MONDAY, YOU HAVE UNTIL FRIDAY TO SURRENDER.
> CHOOSE WISELY.
> M VALENTINE.

FORTY

Wren

I've never felt pain like it.

My whole body is alight in agony, pure, unfiltered pain that runs through my bloodstream like wild fire ripping through a forest. My hands are restrained by leather binds at my sides, my ankles in much the same state at the bottom of the bed. To my left an IV drip is hooked into my arm and a machine beeps to match the pace of my frantic heartbeat. If I wasn't in this room, I might believe I was in the hospital, but hospitals don't look like this.

There are no satin curtains, or million dollar works of art hanging on the walls, there aren't crystal light fittings or fur rugs in a hospital. A window to my left shows a courtyard, I can see out onto a manicured lawn with a stone fountain spurting clear water into the air. The sky a perfect cloudless blue.

The door to the room bursts open and a woman, dressed in

blue hospital scrubs rushes to my side, silencing the machine still beeping wildly at my side. She checks the IV, picks up a clipboard attached to the end of the bed and then grabs some equipment from a box at the end on a counter.

"Where I am?" I rasp, my voice scratchy and hoarse from lack of use. Even talking hurts. Everything hurts.

Her eyes bounce to me, but she doesn't say anything as she positions the blood pressure sleeve around my arm and hooks something to my finger, pressing a button on a device she holds in her hand.

"I'm talking to you!" I growl, "Where I am!?"

"Please," She whispers, "I'm not supposed to talk to you."

"Who told you that?" I ask.

She shakes her head.

I don't remember much.

We were dancing, Lex and I, and then we took it to a more private area, the office.

I felt free, wanted, aroused and then, pain...

It tore through my abdomen, ripping through my gut and then blood. So much blood. I still remember the way the warm liquid seeped through my fingers, coiling around the digits and soaking through my clothes.

Lex was there. He was frantic.

The calm beast was finally rattled.

He looked... *terrified.*

I suck in a shocked gasp as I recall the way he looked at me, gone was the darkness in his eyes, the soulless stare and it was replaced with a fear so potent it took my breath away. He was scared for me.

After that I can't recall what happened. There was a loud bang, a boom really but what happened!?

"Where the fuck am I!? Where's Lex!?"

"Please," the nurse begs, eyes wide with fear.

"You can leave," a hoarse voice says from the doorway. My eyes snap to the newcomer.

"Who are you!?" I snap.

The guy steps into the room, dressed finely in an Armani suit, the color of midnight. His dark hair is streaked with silver but it's his face that gives away his age. Late fifties but looks much older with deep groves that wrinkle his skin. His eyes are the same color as mine, an emerald green flecked with gold and he's clean shaven.

I already know who he is, I see myself in that face, the eyes, the shape of his nose, but I want him to confirm it.

Lex is a monster. I've always known it, his darkness is something that swirls around him, it's his aura, his shadow. He's a terrifying creature but this man, it goes beyond that.

There is nothing there. No soul. No heart. No emotion. It's just a shell for a beast to inhabit but this beast cannot be tamed or reasoned with.

He looks at me like he would look at dirt beneath his Italian loafer, a speck, nothing, worthless.

You'd be stupid not to fear a man like Lex but not fearing a man like this would be lethal. Where Lex may hesitate, this one would not.

It's not because he looks particularly evil, it's all in the way his dead stare bores into you. It feels as if he's sucking out my soul, feeding off my life force.

"Oh, daughter," the sentiment is cold, it's not said with any fondness at all, "I've kept you away for too long."

My nostrils flare and I fight against the restraints holding me in place despite the pain wracking my body. The nurse flees the room, I can't even blame her. My fight or flight has kicked in and I've always been a fighter but right now I want to run, as far and as fast as I can away from this man.

My father.

Marcus Valentine.

He comes closer slowly, casually, with his hands buried into the pockets of his suit trousers, his watch glimmering in the light of the room. He stops at my bedside and picks up the chart, looking over it.

He whistles through his teeth, "It looks like you took quite the beating."

"He's going to kill you," I hiss through my teeth.

His low chuckle bounces off the walls.

"He has to find me first, but don't you worry, daughter," he reaches forward and even though I snatch my face away, his hand still touches my hair, pulling the strands away from my face and coiling them around his finger, the ringlets dull and limp. "I've made sure he understands what's at risk here."

"What did you do?"

"I've made him an offer he can't refuse, of course."

I meet his soulless eyes, trying to figure out what he means, what he's saying but there is nothing there. His face may as well be made of stone.

"What offer?" I breathe.

He tsks loudly, shaking his head, "Nothing to concern you, it doesn't even really matter now."

"Then why not tell me!?"

He cocks his head, his finger trailing down the side of my face that's sore and bruised, the skin of his finger snagging on the raised and dry skin on my cheek.

"You really are a beauty, Wren," he says absentmindedly before gripping my chin and forcing my head to the side, his fingers biting into my flesh hard enough that my cheeks cut against my teeth. The taste of blood coats my tongue. "You chose the wrong side, do you know that?"

"Any side is better than yours," I manage to grit out, despite the unrelenting grip on my face.

His fingers bite in harder and before I can even think, even react, he removes his hand and strikes it across my face, the pain flaring in my cheek bone.

Motherfucker.

"You're lucky," I bury it, the agony, the shock, I give him nothing even though the deep rotted fear shakes me to the core, holding my heart captive and the pain in my body makes me want to scream, "I'd kill you if I could."

He gets in my face, his nose pressing hard against mine, so close his face blurs and I can't make out a single feature. His breath reeks of whiskey and smoke, a stench so heady it makes me gag.

"You're all going to fall. You've made a mistake, daughter of mine and it's time you remember you're a fucking Valentine."

He snatches away from me, storming from the room.

"Get her ready," I hear him say.

"She's too weak," a feminine voice replies shakily, "She needs to recover."

"Do I look like I give a fuck!?" Marcus bellows, "*Get her*

ready."

It's minutes before someone reenters the room. Minutes of deafening silence and then the nurse from before scurries in, her head hanging low, a defeated sag to her shoulders.

She begins to unhook the machines, slowly, one by one before she heads round to the other side, placing latex gloves over her fingers.

"What's going on?" I ask her, hoping she'll answer me.

Her glazed eyes bounce to mine, shining with emotion, "I'm sorry."

"What is he going to do?"

"I don't know," she answers, "If you get the chance, you need to run, okay? Run, Wren, as fast as you can."

I'm not a runner. I don't hide from my demons or my enemies but the fear rolling from her makes me question everything I've ever known. I felt it when Marcus came into the room, the man wasn't just dangerous, he was beyond that. I didn't want to admit it but given the chance I'd likely run. I knew my boundaries and fighting off Marcus Valentine wasn't something I could do on my own.

There's a sting as the nurse pulls the IV from my arm before she presses a cotton pad to the small puncture hole, stopping any minor bleeding.

"Can you tell me what happened to me?"

"Concussion," she sighs, "a gunshot wound to the abdomen, we got the bullet out and it managed to miss your organs, so that's good, you lost a lot of blood though. There's a fracture in your wrist, several lacerations, bruising, swelling."

Shit.

I felt weak. I felt hurt. But those injuries weren't something I could simply get up and walk away from. I was in no state to fight. No state to argue.

And I knew, I *knew* Valentine had much worse planned for me.

There was the promise of violence hanging in the air and that was all for me.

FORTY-ONE
Wren

Valentine's man drags me from the room, still dressed in a hospital gown and I can feel my limbs protest with the movements. My abdomen twinges and pulls, the stitches moving too much, I can feel the wound beginning to reopen, the warmth of my blood seeping through the front of the gown.

"Stop," I beg, but he doesn't, if anything, the grip on my arm only increases, his pace becoming faster to the point my feet drag more than step across the carpet. It burns my bare feet and the pain pulsing through my body makes the edges of my vision turn black, a thick fog pushing in at the sides.

We walk for what feels like forever, down endless corridors and past opulent rooms, until we hit a door and I'm forced down a steep flight of concrete stairs. The steps are freezing beneath the soles of my feet, grit and sharp gravel biting into my skin. When we make it to the bottom, the hallway before me is barely big enough to fit two people side by side, the light dim and almost murky. We only stop when he roughly twists me and shoves me into a small room.

The door slams behind me, the noise ricocheting off the walls. A single, metal framed cot sits in the centre of the small cube of a room, an old dirty mattress on top with a single, thin sheet folded at the bottom. No pillows.

The light buzzes overhead, dangling there from a wire that has seen better days. There's condensation on the walls, tiny beads of water that cling to the concrete walls and it smells of mold and rot, the stench of death permanently etched into the walls. There are dark patches staining the floor and the color gives away to what it was that was spilled.

Blood.

A lot of blood. Through the door I hear feminine whimpers, cries for help, screams and sobs. There are more women down here, I didn't get a good look when he dragged me down here, too focused on trying not to pass out from the pain but now I'm alone I hear them. I hear all of them.

What the fuck is this place? I swallow down the panic and fear rising like bile in my throat and scan the room once more.

Apart from that rotten bed, there isn't much else in here.

There's a sink that used to be white but is now stained brown and yellow, the tap constantly dripping water. There are no windows in here but I'd already figured that. We were underground, way underground with no way out apart from that one door we came through.

I press my hand to my abdomen, looking down at the red splotches. With the door closed, I pull up the gown to check it out. There's a thick padded plaster over the stitches, but the blood has seeped through that and onto the gown. I carefully peel away the edges, hissing as the adhesive tugs at the bruised skin around the edges. The wound is clean but it's bleeding, not terribly but I can see the stitches have pulled away. The area around where the bullet tore through me is purple, black, yellow, matching the rest of my body. Bruises and scratches cover a lot of the parts of my body that I can see but I didn't doubt the parts I couldn't see looked in much the same state if how sore I was, was anything to go by.

Pressing the gauze back down gently, I trudge to the bed, gritting my teeth as I lower myself onto the cot, too weak to care about the state of the furniture. I suck in a breath, holding it as plumes of dust puff out from the mattress, stinking of rot and decay and only when it settles do I let out the breath.

"Please," I hear a voice just outside the door, "Please no!" The voice appears young, far too innocent to be in a place like this. Loud bangs and further cries echo down the halls, growing quieter as whoever it is, is dragged further away.

My stomach rolls at the hideous ideas forming in my head,

prostitution rings, human trafficking being the main ones. Girls went missing all the time, never to be found again and it's things like that, the insidious darkness that prays on young girls and women that usually get them. Most get falsely declared dead, no evidence to ever suggest such a thing happened and once they're declared dead, they're forgotten, leaving them to this evil.

This world is a cruel, harsh place, the people in it even more so. There are monsters everywhere, there's no escaping them and sometimes you have to join them in order to survive.

I've chosen my monster.

And it isn't Valentine.

He may be my blood but he is not my family.

Given the chance I will pull the trigger myself.

Exhaustion tugs at my consciousness and I can feel my body sagging, bowing over to the side as I try and fail to fight the grips of sleep. The sheets smell of damp, a musky sent that makes it hard to breathe easily but it doesn't stop my eyes from falling closed.

Just five minutes. I can take five minutes to rest.

I bolt up in the bed to the sound of a scream so gutting it tears through me. Goose bumps rise on my arms and my stomach churns with the noise. Very male grunts and groans fill in the gaps between the cries and I have no doubt in my mind exactly what is going on here.

Twisted City

Valentine truly was evil, dabbling into this sort of thing is a sure way to have your soul ripped from your body.

Bile rises in my throat, burning my tongue but I don't vomit, there's nothing in me to even bring up, so I sit there and I listen, unable to help the poor girl down the hall.

Eventually her cries die down, becoming gurgled and muffled but the man in her room continues, his booms of pleasure turning my blood to fire. I want to kill him. The burning rage blinds me, makes me into something I've never been and I welcome it.

I welcome that darkness, the claws of it seeping into my mind as I imagine ripping the mans' throat out with my bare hands, watching him bleed on the floor. Reveling in the warm, crimson liquid coating my skin, relishing how quickly the light drains from his eyes.

What would Lex do? Tear out his organs while he made him watch? Cut off his cock and feed it to him?

Lex was a lot of things, but I knew he wouldn't do this. The man may be evil, but this level of evil is saved for the likes of Valentine. The ones so deprived and soulless not even hell would want them.

A door slams and before, I couldn't figure out where the sounds were coming from, but the slam is right next to me, the room over. It'll be why her cries were so loud and his grunts so nauseating. His feet pound heavily on the concrete floor and my heart leaps up into my throat when they stop right outside my door.

I swear I hear his heavy breaths through the door. My fear is thick but there is no damn well way I'll let him touch me.

I brace, fully prepared to use any means necessary to protect myself and hold my breath, waiting. After a few *long* seconds, their footsteps retreat and they head up the steps, the door slamming as they close it behind themselves.

I climb from the cot, my legs weak, barely able to sustain my weight as I creep towards the door, pressing an ear to it. The handle doesn't move as I press it down, but I already knew that, I wasn't stupid enough to believe they'd leave it unlocked.

"Hello?" My voice is quiet, too quiet so I speak a little louder. "Hello?"

A cry answers me.

I wait for a guard or something to bang on the door, demanding silence but when that doesn't come I speak again, "What's your name?"

Her sobs break me, it's filled with an anguish that goes soul deep, fills your body with so much sorrow you could weep for years.

"Tessa," she replies.

"How long have you been here, Tessa?"

I was going to get this girl out, all of these girls out, even if it was the last thing I did.

"I don't know," she sniffles, "A long time."

"Can you remember the day you were taken?"

Three breaths of silence and then, "December eighteenth. My twenty second birthday."

Six months. She's been here *six months*.

"Okay, Tessa," I say, trying to put as much comfort into my tone as possible, "We're going to get out of here, okay? Do you hear me?"

"We're not," she replies.

"We are."

"No, we're not. We're all going to die down here."

Not a fucking chance.

I had no idea if Lex was coming and it didn't even really matter if he was, I was no damsel, I didn't need rescuing, I mean a little help would be nice, but I was getting out of here with or without him. There was no way I was dying like this, like a rat in a sewer. And none of these women deserved this fate. I was getting us all the fuck out of here.

"Hey!" A boom of a voice shatters the delicate silence between us, "Quiet down!"

Tessa whimpers. These walls are paper thin, the doors even more so. You can hear everything, the footsteps, doors creaking, floorboards groaning above. It's why I notice the second set of boots hitting the steps. Slow, calculated, casual and then his voice penetrates the wall and my blood runs cold.

Father is back for another visit.

"Is my lovely daughter causing problems already," he tuts as if I'm a petulant child, "well, I suppose it's time to teach the girl some manners."

The words are so carefree, so casual and nonchalant you'd simply think it was a father scolding a six year old and not a twenty three year old.

The last visit wasn't pleasant.

This visit is going to make that one look like a walk in the park.

FORTY-TWO

Lex

A twisted grin tugs at my mouth as I rise from my crouching position, cocking my head as I stare down at Jameson, or what used to be Jameson. You could hardly recognize the man now.

I flick my eyes to Ryker who stares down at the man impassively, like this is an everyday occurrence to him. But I guess it is, in this life, shit like this happens all the time.

Okay, maybe not, but we're not shy to the scent of death.

Jameson has been crucified to the wall inside Valentine's old apartment. A big old *fuck you* to Valentine.

Ha.

He thinks he can threaten me.

No.

Did I believe he'd do something to Wren, damn right I did but I also wasn't stupid enough to believe he'd simply hand her back either.

That little note was a bluff.

He wants my city, but I know he won't give Wren back.

Would I give it up for the woman?

Probably.

And that shit terrifies me.

Jameson's white shirt is no longer white but stained scarlet red, the buttons undone to reveal a large 'S' that's been carved into his chest, the wound so deep you can see the layers of fat that cover the muscle underneath. I'd like to tell you he was long dead when I graffitied his skin, but he wasn't. His screams of pain still ring inside my head, his pleas for mercy left unanswered as the tip of my blade sliced through his skin. He should have known there would be no mercy in this.

We did at least, manage to get some information from him before he croaked it.

An English organization, no names but there were plenty of English that could be the culprit. It would take some time to figure out who it was that was working with the vermin, but off the top of my head I couldn't think of one that would sink so low or be so stupid. They were all big. The English and the American's had very little do with each other.

There was no need.

He wouldn't give up the location of Valentine, not for love nor money and I had to hand it to him, that was loyalty. He still had to die.

Blood runs down the walls and I dip my finger into it like it's paint, smearing the thick substance over the note Valentine so lovingly left for me.

I have left one in return

RUN

That's it.

Because if he didn't run, if he didn't heed my warning, there would be only pain in his future. I wasn't going to let him live, even if he did run and I would chase. I'd make a game of his demise, a sport for my entertainment and fuck, would that be entertaining.

My little bird was missing from my side, from my bed, her attitude and her soft body was absent, and I was slowly going crazy without her.

I don't know how it happened, or when, but she was under

my skin, in my black soul, a light cutting through the shadows that is my life.

I *needed* her and I've never needed anyone.

This shit sends men like me batshit, like an addict gone too long without a fix.

I didn't know where she was. I knew she was alive and that at least settled some part of me but how bad was she injured? What was Valentine doing to her?

It was these questions, the ones that haunted me when I tried to sleep, when life became quiet, the silence too loud, while I was waiting and watching for the next lead, the next word, the next anything where I pictured her. And I saw what he was doing. I saw her bleeding, bruised, broken. I saw her spirit and her fight leave her wild eyes and it pumped me full of rage.

It was blinding.

I allow my mind to wander back to catching Jameson, I revel in his screams, how we dragged him from his comfy bed in the south side of the city, how he kicked and he screamed while tied up in the trunk of the car. He threatened us to start with but those threats soon turned to pleas. I replay how Ryker held him down as I slammed paperclips under his fingernails, remembering the feel of his blood on my skin. But it was only when the tip of that knife sliced through his flesh, permanently marking him with the S that he started to talk but it still wasn't good enough.

He eventually died, sooner than I had wanted but a fitting end for him at least.

This apartment has been turned upside down twice, the remnants of the last time still strewn across the floor, glass smashed, holes in the walls, papers crumbled and littered over the varnished hardwood.

Jameson was useless.

They're all fucking useless. A sudden burst of fury has my fist slamming into the wall next to where Valentine's second hangs. He's long dead, gone cold and blue and yet I wish I could see a flinch. I need the fear. The fucking terror. It drove me. I wanted suffering and pain. *I wanted them all to fucking pay.*

My men back from the room as my anger bursts from my body, what wasn't destroyed before now is, the desk, the furniture, even the hundred year old bottles of whiskey on the shelves. All but Jameson and the note except now it's embedded into his sternum, held there by my switch blade.

Blood coats my hand like a second skin, warm, slick, crimson. I feel it on my face, my throat.

I've never lost a single thing in my entire life, but I was losing everything now. Every-fucking-thing.

I can feel emotion clawing at my windpipe, my tongue, drying it until it sticks to the roof of my mouth, my heart pounding inside my chest to the beat of a frantic drum.

Wren. Wren. Wren.

That's what my heart shouted.

I never thought something would become more important than my city. Than my family name but he has. She *is*.

"Lex," Ryker steps into the room, the only one brave enough to face me down in this current state. I pick up a bottle and launch it across the room, a scream erupting from my throat, the bellow ricocheting off the walls to fill the space with an echo of my anguish. My rage. My pain.

He's just another body, not necessarily in the way but a body there anyway. So easy to destroy. A life that can be snuffed out beneath my thumb with just a simple flick of my wrist.

I'm this fucking close.

I imagine what it'll be like when I finally have Valentine in front of me. What it will feel like to inflict wound after wound onto him.

He's smart to hide.

I wish he wasn't, but I had to hand it to him as much as I didn't want to.

There wouldn't be anything to stop me if I saw him. I wouldn't care if we were in public, fuck they can broadcast it for the nation, I'll kill him still. I'll make the whole fucking city, the whole country watch as I enacted my vengeance.

A calmness settles over me as I tilt my head side to side,

working out knots that have formed in the muscles. Rolling my shoulders, I loosen the muscles in my back and flick a glance back at my work.

I give it an hour after we leave before this little scene is put before him.

I'd love to stick around and see just who it will be to deliver my message but I have no time.

For every day my little bird is missing from my side, I'll triple, *quadruple* the amount of damage I do to his men.

Going for his right hand now was a little hasty, I should have waited but my control, it was slipping. And he can only be to blame.

Taking a deep breath through my nose, I close my eyes, inhaling the stench of death that tinges the air with a metallic tang, it was the smell of a man losing himself to his own demons.

And this time, there was no pushing them down. No restraining them. No concealing them from the people of this city.

They wanted the monster.

I'd give it to them and make them wish they never even stepped foot in this city.

This was war.

And it was a war I wasn't going to lose.

FORTY-THREE
Wren

"Ten years," that's the greeting I get from my father as he steps foot into my little cube of a bedroom, "Ten years I've known that man. Do you understand how hard it is in this way of life to have someone like him stay loyal to you for so long?"

After he came to my room earlier, throwing around his air of menace, he didn't act on it. He promised to show me some manners and never delivered.

I stand from the cot, holding in the wince that wants to give me away as my body twinges in pain. I was weak, that much was obvious, we both knew it but showing that weakness, that vulnerability was another thing.

I had no idea what he was talking about and wasn't going to ask.

Twisted City

RIA WILDE

He stands in the doorway, a menacing shape blocking my escape but I can see into the hall beyond him.

What I failed to notice before was the door opposite my room, no doubt the same door that's repeated all the way down this hall. They look to be originally painted green but with age, they have deteriorated and now rust spots and peeling paint make up their exterior, an ugly shell to hide an even uglier interior.

My father, Marcus Valentine was a trafficker. Amongst other things.

I wonder idly, as we stand face to face, the air between us sizzling with suppressed rage and fury whether we could have ever had a connection.

I mean, at the end of the day, this man is a part of me. His darkness is in me one way or another, but I don't look at him like I want him as a dad.

Benjamin Lawson was my father. He raised me. Granted, he wasn't much of a father either and tried to kill me, but he was still more of a father than this man would ever be.

Did I regret it?

Not even a little.

I wanted nothing to do with this man.

This monster.

"Restrain her," Marcus says, jerking his chin towards me.

Twisted City

RIA WILDE

Two men enter the room, holding heavy set chains as they advance towards me.

"What?" I say, "Afraid I might hurt you?" My voice rings with all the confidence I don't have, but my body gives me away as I start to back up, the edge of the cot hitting the backs of my knees.

He laughs, "Oh daughter of mine, you don't scare me. This is so you don't move too much. That'll take away from the fun."

My nostrils flare as a healthy dose of fear injects itself into my bloodstream. I can't show him that weakness, I can't show him how much he terrifies me.

There's no hope of fighting them off, no hope of winning any battle with them as they wrap those chains around my wrists tightly, the metal cutting into the skin and drag me towards the wall next to the bed. They link the chains to the steel hoops I failed to notice in the walls, pulling them tight so my arms are stretched out at my sides and on my knees, my face pressed to the damp wall.

I'm not able to control my breathing, I can't stop the frantic way my heart pummels inside my chest, beating against the walls of my ribcage, so hard I wonder if it's possible for it break through the bone.

I pull at the restraints, hearing the metal clang loudly, the sound mingling with the footsteps drawing closer. Measured. Leisurely.

"Ten," Marcus muses.

I finally give, "What are you talking about?"

"Alexander Silver wants you back," he answers.

Lex. *My monster.*

I say nothing as I laugh though nothing is funny.

"If Lex wants me back, *Valentine*," I spit the name as if it doesn't belong to me too, "You best give me to him."

"He's not in control anymore."

Or so he thought.

Lex was smart, too smart, calculating, categorically evil, and Marcus was underestimating him badly.

Lex would be on a war path.

To get to me.

He'd made it clear I belonged to him, I was his, no matter the cost and he may not have said the words, but I knew what I was to him.

I shouldn't want the man who kidnapped me in the first place, my heart should not beat for the man who set off a chain of events that would ultimately lead me to this very moment but clearly my heart wasn't very smart.

Not that I could blame it.

I had fallen in love with the darkness.

I wasn't going to fight it. Not anymore.

He could have me.

All of me.

Possess and claim and keep.

I was Alexander's.

"Ten," Marcus repeats.

I hear rustling behind me, but the restraints restrict my movements, I can't look back to see exactly what is happening.

I don't say a word.

"Ten," the number is repeated and then hands grab at the back of my gown, ripping it away from my body until it falls away, revealing my bare back.

The first lash of the whip is a shock and I'm not able to hold in the scream that unleashes from my throat.

The second is just as much of a shock and the third. I hear them counting.

A lash for every year.

The thin strip of leather whips against my skin, ripping it open. I feel blood and sweat rolling over the surface as the wounds open with each new laceration.

At four, the pain becomes unbearable, my consciousness begins to slip, I clutch at it but it's loose and slimy, never quite staying in my grip.

My head sags forward on the fifth and while I still feel the whip hitting my skin it's almost warming, like it's gone from pain to something else entirely. I know it's there but it's happening to someone else. I see it. I hear it.

Six.

I'm sure I'm going to die.

Seven.

I see Lex's face, his fathomless, silver eyes, his amused smirk, the wicked gleam.

Eight.

I feel his hands on my body, soothing the cuts, kissing away the pain. His teeth nip at my flesh before his lips kiss away the sting.

Nine.

Fight little bird, his words penetrate through the fog inside my mind. *Come home to me little bird. Stand by my side. Be my queen.*

Ten.

You are mine.

You belong to me. Only me.

Twisted City

RIA WILDE

I wake stuck to the sheets, the wounds on my back clotted and scabbed over, fused to the dirty fabric under my back.

Sweat makes my hair cling to my forehead and my skin is on fire but that's nothing compared to the pain in my back, it makes the gunshot wound still healing in my abdomen a walk in the park.

I'm starving. Dehydrated.

At this point, I'm not entirely sure Marcus wanted to keep me alive.

Perhaps he just wanted me to suffer for as long as possible.

At this rate it would be forever before he put me out of my misery.

I pull myself from the sheets, squeezing my eyes closed as the sheets snag at my skin, reopening the healing wounds on my back.

I feel a trickle of blood run down my spine as I head towards the sink in the corner of the room on unsteady legs.

Turning the faucet, a spurt of dirty colored water bursts from the pipes, filling the stained basin with brown colored liquid before it finally clears.

I wasn't about to drink it, not yet at least but it would be good enough to get some of the dirt off my face and aid in cleaning the dried blood on my spine that was making my skin too tight and causing it to pinch.

As I wipe the blood from my skin, I notice how eerily quiet it is, so silent you'd hear a pin drop outside the door. The light is on in the room and there doesn't appear to be a switch to turn it off. The electricity buzzes through the wires, the bulb flickering every now and then. There was no peace in this place.

No retreat.

I knew I wasn't going to die down here, that was too easy. But there are some things that are worse than death and that was the path Marcus was leading me down.

FORTY-FOUR
Wren

For every one thing Lex did to retaliate against my father, Marcus gave it back to me ten fold. Lashes to the back, beatings, starvation and dehydration. All I was told was that Lex was destroying it all. Valentine had lost nearly half his men in recent weeks at the hands of Lex and his men, buildings and warehouses destroyed, burned to the ground, men gutted, murdered and mutilated beyond recognition. They don't hide the information from me, it's spoken aloud outside my room, them discussing how crazy Lex has gone. He's killing everything in his path.

Before I would have been disgusted, shocked and scared, but all I feel now is an adoration for the crazy bastard. He was bringing death to Valentine's doorstep and I knew he wasn't going to stop. I didn't know if he would ever find me or get me back, part of me is sure this is where my life ends but there's a glimmer of hope, a small beacon shining in the shadows surrounding me that it's only a matter of time before I'm back with Lex.

I've lost count of how long I've been here, days, weeks, months? I had no idea. The slipping in and out of consciousness doesn't help, every time I don't know how long I'm out for and there's only so much the human body can take before it starts to shut down. Not just in body but in mind too.

Give up, the small voice inside my head urges, pleads for it if only to stop the suffering. If you shut down, shut it all off then the pain inflicted won't touch you. It won't matter because you won't care. And if you don't care, death isn't so scary. If you just let the pain take you, if you just let yourself slip into that darkness, you won't ever have to emerge again. There will be no more pain, no more suffering, just a peaceful darkness where nothing can hurt you.

The threats. The graphic images, the screams and the cries, they won't matter because you don't feel anymore. You don't care.

I know if that happens everything I was before, everything I had, including my feelings for Lex will just vanish. That's if I didn't die first.

Not because they didn't matter anymore but because I wouldn't have the capacity to deal with them.

The mind is fragile.

It always has been, us humans like to think of ourselves as these super beings, strong, powerful, smart, but we have so many weaknesses. Emotion being one of them, it's what controls most of us, even those who claim not to have it are controlled by it in some way. Greed. Courage. Fear. All emotion.

Lex tried to claim he was emotionless, he acted as if nothing mattered but everything did. His city. His control. His power. It sent him over the edge and if that isn't emotion then perhaps, I've been wrong this entire time. With everything I have learned in my twenty-three years, it's that humans react on pure basic instinct. Survive. Fight. Live. By any means necessary.

It's amazing what we are capable of when given the circumstances. How many stories have you read about women murdering their attackers? Children no older than ten or eleven killing their parents just to survive.

We want to live. To Survive. We think we could never do such a thing but the balance between good and evil has always been a precarious thing. A slight nudge to the other side will tip the scales and once you're over that edge, there's no turning back. You're in a free fall, that abyss, that darkness ready and waiting to swallow you whole.

The wound in my abdomen doesn't feel as painful today, it's not as tender, doesn't seem as if I'll rip my body open if I move too much or too quickly which is a good sign. My bones aren't fairing the same fate. I ache. All of me, from the top of my skull to the tips of my toes. Muscles scream in agony from all the positions I've been contorted into, from all the flinching and tensing that's inevitable when you know pain is coming.

Twisted City

RIA WILDE

No amount of preparation would get me ready for what Marcus had planned for me.

It's like he took pain and notched it up a level, figuring out new ways to torture without causing too much damage. It was punishment to Lex but to me too.

Despite being raised as a Lawson and not a Valentine, I must be punished for turning on the family name. It made zero logical sense but, in this world, what was logical and rational didn't always mean what was right for them.

You're a Valentine. He'd chant through his beatings, *Wren fucking Valentine. Act like it.*

But I'd never be a Valentine. I'd rather be nothing at all.

The screams of the girls surrounding me only settles that further into my brain.

I'll let him break me and beat me and make me empty before I ever submitted to him.

It doesn't feel like much time has passed when I'm visited again. I'm still healing and sore from the last visit, the blood barely dry on my skin but the gleam in Marcus' eye this time is like none other. It's wicked and evil, devious, like the devil has entered his body and is about to inflict damage.

I brace, standing on my bare feet. The grit on the floor bites into the skin on my feet and my muscles twinge wanting rest but there is no rest here. There will be no reprieve for me.

"Your man never learns, Wren. You must not be too important to him if he keeps doing what he is doing knowing each time he does it, I punish you."

I scoff, "You don't know Lex at all."

"He's weak. Useless and unfit to run this city anymore if a bit of cunt is what has finally tipped him over the edge."

I square my shoulders, tipping up my chin.

I belonged to Alexander Silver, he doesn't share, he doesn't give up what is his. This city, it's his, and me, I belonged to him too.

It was obvious.

He wasn't a man that thought rationally, he knew what Valentine was doing and he was lashing out, unable to stop himself. If you cage a wild animal you expect to get bitten and Lex was no different. There was nothing grounding him without me by his side.

He would get to me. Eventually.

I just hoped I wasn't too far gone when he finally found me.

Lex

Blood.

So much blood.

It covered her pale skin, turning the creamy color crimson, streaking paths over her curves like snakes. She looked too pale, too thin. Her face was away from the camera so I couldn't see her face but even her hair looked limp and lifeless.

He was killing her slowly. Her heart would always beat but my little bird was being ripped away, piece by piece, shard by shard. Feather by feather.

She's strong.

A fighter.

A queen.

But there was only so much she could take.

This seemed like it may be the final straw.

The V carved into her thigh is raw and gaping, the edges of the wound bruised and swollen. He'd cut into her with a blunt knife, the edges of the wound are too rough and jagged for it to be a clean cut. There are bruises littering her skin. Purple and black showing the newer ones and yellowed and green ones showing the old. He's beating her.

Hurting her.

The need to maim has never been stronger but it's a cold kind of fury that settles over me in this second.

I'm past being angry. I'm past being uncontrollable.

It just simply *was*.

The updates on Wren have been hammering in a nail for weeks. The frustration of not knowing where she is only adding to the pressure. Eventually I was going to boil over to the point of no return.

My little bird has been crushed. Her wings were breaking.

And I couldn't find her. *I couldn't find her.*

I don't think in this moment, I just unleash my rage onto the man in front of me. My fists pound into his flesh, his bones and skin breaking with each slam of my fist. I feel my own skin break from the hits, but I don't feel the pain, just the warm blood of his and mine mingling together as I kill him with my fists.

When his body sags unconsciously I still don't stop. Not until his chest stops moving and my skin is slick with his life essence.

I was close.

I knew I was.

I was coming little bird. I was.

She just needed to hold out a little longer. Stay strong a few more days.

Twisted City — RIA WILDE

My fist slams into the man's face beneath me, my knuckles raw and bloody but it's nothing compared to the mess in front of me. The images tear through my mind and a scream unleashes from my throat as I slam my fist down again, what was left of him breaking under my rage.

Ryker drags me away from the body when his face no longer resembles a face, just bloodied pulp and I breathe heavy, clenching and unclenching my fists. I don't feel better.

He's permanently marked *my* woman with his initials. The large V on her thigh will never go away, a constant reminder of how I fucked up.

The streets of the city were turning to chaos. To ruin.

This war was getting bigger and bigger each day, so much blood has been spilled in the last few weeks than it has in years.

Not even the rain can wash away the damage.

The Syndicate have been quiet since the attack on Wren at the club. Why would they need to get involved, after all, their two problems were ripping at each other's throats. They're probably waiting to see who wins this and then will aim for the victor.

It was clear Valentine was a loose canon.

Ainsley has disappeared. There's no way to find her, track her or contact her and I need that information she has. I won't be able to use it right now but when Valentine is dead and the war has been won, the city won't settle into peace.

Enemies don't just disappear.

They just sit and wait for the right opportunity, the right time to strike but I'd be sure to be ready for them.

And I'll have Wren by my side.

My queen.

My little bird.

"Clean it up." I order the men lingering at the edges, faces unable to hide their fear, it shines in their eyes every time they look at me, their minds wondering when I'll finally snap at one of them.

They are smart to be cautious with me.

I haven't heard from my father despite his promise to give me what he knows about the Syndicate. His phone has been disengaged but I know he's still alive. He may be out of the city and away from the carnage, but my men talk. He still has ties in this city and he's pulling the strings. Making my messes go away, watching, observing.

It's why I haven't lost my shit with him yet, because despite his sealed lips, he's still helping in all the ways he can.

I can feel the tension leave the room with me, the heaviness easing as I step into the cool air of dawn. Sirens wail in the distance and dogs bark from the houses a few streets down. It's early morning, the city still sleeps, oblivious to the battle raging all around them.

One way or another, this was ending now.

The only way I wasn't getting to Wren was if I were dead.

FORTY-FIVE
Wren

Hands scrub at my skin, not in anyway gentle or soft, the bruises and cuts ache and sting with each pass of the sponge but I've become numb now. I don't feel the burning sensation of my skin ripping or the tenderness across the bruises.

My mind is gloriously blank.

The screams of the girls all around me does nothing to me anymore. Valentine's threats roll off my skin like water lapping at the shore.

His words don't bite, his threats don't elicit fear.

I'm simply nothing.

Dead but still breathing.

The same hands washing me grab at the dirty gown covering my too thin frame and rip it off, leaving me naked on the bed. I should be worried these men will do something to me, harm me in the same way, abuse the situation but they don't, instead they continue to wash my skin, removing the dried blood and dirt caked on me like paint. My eyes drop to the large V carved into my thigh.

This way you'll never forget who owns you. Not Alexander Silver. Not his men. Me.

He branded me.

Permanently marking me with his initial. My initial.

But it wasn't the brutality of the act that finally broke my mind.

No, I kicked and I screamed and I slashed at him while he sliced the blunt edge of the knife through my skin. I even managed to get myself some slight satisfaction as my nails left angry welts in the top of his hand.

What finally broke me was what happened after.

The memories, the only memory that occupies my mind now, begins to play. Like a fucked up film playing on repeat, the stop button broken and the movie on a loop.

I felt the blood rolling down my thigh, dripping onto the floor beneath where I was restrained to a chair. I thought it funny how every interaction with the man I was always restrained. He worried what I might do.

Smart man, I had pictured a thousand ways to kill him with my bare hands. I've imagined ripping his eyes out with my fingers and strangling him with my hands, I've pictured how his eyes would beg for mercy and how he would fight but ultimately lose.

All the lessons I was forced into had taught me several

ways to kill a man with only my hands. I could even make it look like an accident if I wanted.

The pain of the knife in my flesh was like nothing I'd ever felt. The bullet in my abdomen was nothing compared to the prolonged torture of a blunt edge ripping through your skin, but I kept the pain out of my voice as I told him all the ways I wanted to hurt him.

When he was done and I was marked with the V, he looked at me like I was merely a possession, a pretty little doll on his shelf, not like I was his daughter, his flesh and blood.

"All the girls are branded," he explained, "but only my daughter gets a special kind of mark."

"Fuck you." I spat.

"So disobedient," he tutted, "So mouthy. Don't you know women are to be seen and not heard? It is the only thing you're good for."

"You're disgusting. I can't wait to watch you bleed."

He just grinned maliciously as he jerked his fingers over his shoulders, notifying the man standing behind him to do whatever it is he asked for earlier.

"Perhaps a little motivation, hm?" He cooed, "a little persuasion. My plans are far too precious to be ruined by a bitch of a woman who can't learn to keep her trap shut so maybe this will help you learn your place."

I swallowed, knowing I wasn't going to like what I saw.

Even preparing myself for it wouldn't have ever set me up

for what happened next.

The man behind him disappeared for a few minutes, but when he returned, he wasn't alone. He dragged a small woman in with him, dressed in a blue summer dress, she sagged in his grip, her straight blonde hair hanging around her face like a limp curtain, areas matted and bloody. Bruises mark her skin, cuts and grazes down her arms, her legs. Her feet are cut up, nails on her hands torn and bleeding. Marcus continued to grin as he took measured steps back.

"I believe you two have met," he told me, reaching beneath the mane of disheveled tresses to grip the girls chin. My heart pounded inside my chest and dread settled deep into my stomach as he jerked her face up for me to see.

Rory.

My best friend.

Her face had been beaten black and blue, one eye swollen, a gash across her right cheekbone, and her bottom lip split and fat. Her one good eye widened when she saw me, and a sob of pure and utter agony escaped her throat. I'd never forget that sound.

"I believe you've been listening, these walls are rather thin after all." Marcus cocked his head to the side, "my men seem to enjoy this one along with the pretty little thing next door."

The scream that echoed through the room after that could only be described as inhuman, I wailed, the pain blooming so fast and furiously it exploded out of me.

Twisted City

RIA WILDE

It was just me before. I didn't know these women, as much as it made me sick, I could disassociate myself from it but not Rory. Not *my* Rory. My innocent best friend who had managed to escape a life of hardships to come out on top. Not my friend who loved life, loved to laugh, loved to explore. She was as innocent as a child. And he had her.

He had ruined her.

All the screaming, the memories of the cries and pleas beat like a drum inside my head. I had listened to the demise of my best friend and I had done nothing.

"Wren," she sobbed, bloody spittle drooling from her swollen bottom lip.

Marcus reached down and gripped the hem of her dress, dragging it up almost to her underwear, and there, on her right thigh was a brand. Not cut in like mine but burned, scorched into her skin like they do to cattle.

The burn is weeks old, healed over but still raised and angry, the skin around it blackened.

"Let her go!" I screamed.

His fingers continued up, tracing the edge of her underwear, "Perhaps I should give it a go."

"Get your hands off her!"

Aurora just stood there, she didn't fight, didn't scream or cry. Her eyes are glazed over, dead, soulless. They did this to her.

"You want it to stop?" Marcus continued, pulling at the strap so it comes away from her hipbone.

I knew what he wanted.

My submission. My willingness to do what he asked.

No questions. No fighting.

I could feel the numbness seep in at the edges to begin with. There was no way I wasn't going to do what he asked. There was no question as to whether this was right. I'd save her.

"Yes."

His hand came away, "then you be a good little girl."

"She stays in here with me," I told him.

He laughs, "you are in no position to negotiate, daughter."

"Then I'll scream and I'll scream. Kill us both. Do it, you coward."

His nostrils flared.

"I'll fight. I'll make sure I do everything I can to stop whatever it is you have planned. I don't believe you won't harm her the moment my door is closed, the only way I will behave is if she stays in here with me."

Marcus growled, grabbed Rory and launched her across the room, causing her body to slam into the wall with a hard thud. With a whimper she sunk down to the floor.

There were no more words. No more threats. They untied me and pushed me back towards the bed before leaving and bolting the door behind them.

I didn't waste a second. I moved to where Rory lay crumbled on the floor and gathered her into my arms.

The only way I could save her was by sacrificing myself and the only way I'd ever be able to comply with my fathers wishes was to become a shell. To become nothing.

"I'm so sorry Wren," Aurora sobbed, "I'm so sorry."

But she had nothing to be sorry for, this was my fault.

I smoothed my hand down her dried and dirty hair, trying to soothe her and when she stopped crying, I guided her to the bed, gently nudging her into it.

"Sleep," I told her, "You're safe here."

She may have been safe with me but what will happen when I eventually leave? Marcus wasn't planning on keeping me here, I knew that much at least, when I was gone who would look after her?

If I didn't do something she'd die down here.

I come back to the present, eyes flicking to the top of the bed where she sits with her legs pulled up to her chest, still in that blue dress. Her eyes are wide, full of fear as she watches Valentine's men manhandle me. They tug a white dress over my head, forcing my arms into it roughly and pulling it down to cover my body though my wounds are hardly concealed.

When one of them wraps their beefy hand around my arm and yanks me to my feet, I let him, the pain in my body only reminding me I'm alive and nothing more. I'm not scared. I don't fear what is going to happen next.

I don't allow thoughts of Lex.

I only think about the girl behind me and how doing this stops her pain.

I follow, like the little willing captive up the stairs to the warmth of the house and further through to a den like room where I'm positioned in the corner of an office.

And that's where I wait to learn what's to happen to me next.

FORTY-SIX
Wren

I'm standing for what feels like hours, my legs ache from the prolonged position and I'm growing tired. The room is too warm, and the scent of cigar smoke and whiskey tinges the air. Marcus sits behind a giant desk, clearly trying to compensate for *something* with his fingernail tapping incessantly on the hardwood. Two guards stand at the doorway, staring straight ahead at the wall behind Marcus' head like the good little dogs they are.

A radio crackles and then a raspy voice sounds through the speaker.

"He's here, over."

Marcus stands abruptly and smooths his hands down the lapels of his dark suit jacket, tugging at the collar to straighten it out. He fidgets with the cufflinks and then pats at the weapon he has tucked into a holster at his back. He's nervous which means whoever is about to enter is clearly more dangerous than this man.

That should scare me. It doesn't.

His eyes dart to me and he curls his lip as if what I have to offer is less than favorable.

Whatever.

He did this to me.

"Stand up straight," he barks.

With a roll of my eyes, I do as he asks and link my fingers together in front of me, hiding the twitch.

The door to the den opens and a flurry of activity happens, men dressed nothing like the ones in this house file into the room. These guys look casual in dark jeans, dark tees and leather jackets or hoodies. They're tattooed, rough around the edges but the air around them crackles with power. They're not people to be messed with. It's completely silent until the final man steps into the room and finally, *finally,* my body reacts. Fear makes my heart pound harder, makes my palms sweat and causes my throat to become dry. It's hard to swallow, a lump the size of a golf ball now sitting there. I peel my tongue from the roof of my mouth, my blood roaring in my ears as my heart thumps wildly.

He's dressed like the rest, in a pair of dark jeans but he wears a white tee and no jacket. Dark tattoos cover both arms, from his fingers all the way up until they disappear under the cuffs of his t-shirt. They snake up his neck, there's even a small one on the side of his head, barely visible with the short dark hair growing over it.

His eyes are the lightest shade of blue I've ever seen, like the Caribbean sea with the sun bouncing off the calm waters. His sharp, stubbled jaw is clamped tight, the muscles in his cheeks jumping with each grind of his teeth. A straight nose with a piercing in one nostril and lips, full and far too soft looking for a man like him are pressed into a flat line. To look at directly, you wouldn't say he was a huge man, not when compared to the beefcakes Marcus employs or even against Lex and Ryker but he was athletically built, toned and lithe. His clothes fit him perfectly, outlining the hard lines of his abdomen. He surveys the room, first looking at Valentine's men, and then at Valentine. A quick appraisal later and those eyes made of ice land on me. He surveys me from the top of my head to the tips of my toes. He narrows his eyes each time he comes across a bruise or cut, and I can't help but squirm under that penetrating gaze.

I don't feel like I'm in danger when he looks at me. No hostility, no imminent threat which probably means I really am fucked, well and truly.

"Mr Heart," Marcus steps forward, towards the man he's just referred to as Mr Heart and his gaze snaps away from me back to my father.

"Don't," Heart growls, his English accent strong, sophisticated, curling his lip and stopping Marcus in his tracks, his arm still outstretched ready to shake his hand.

"Kingston," a melodic feminine voice scolds softly and I look behind him to see a woman stepping in behind him.

Kingston's nostrils flare and his hands ball into fists at his sides. He doesn't seem pissed that she's just interrupted him, if anything his whole demeanor has just switched from killer to protector. The woman comes up next to him, close but not so close it says intimacy and I study the newcomer.

She's gorgeous. Long, black hair falls around her face like silk, the lights in the room bouncing off the tresses and her skin is flawless but incredibly pale. Her eyes are the same color as Kingston's, a blue so icy they freeze everything they touch and her pouty, full lips are painted blood red. She has a snow white vibe about her if snow white had all the lethal grace of a lioness.

She's lithe like the man beside her, tall with a slender yet toned frame, dressed in skin tight black jeans and a white blouse that flows over her torso and a pair of black boots with heels that if I wore I'd likely break an ankle.

She doesn't survey the room like Kingston did, instead her eyes home in on me instantly and soften. Surely that can't be right. Why would they be softening?

"Marcus," Kingston grumbles reluctantly, "This is my sister, Isobel."

Marcus appears to like Isobel very much if the way he's devouring her with his eyes is anything to go by. His tongue may as well be hanging out of his face.

A few of Kingston's men step closer to the lone female in their group, shoulders squaring, a warning to Valentine to back the fuck up.

I'd laugh if I could.

"You did not mention you'd be bringing a female," Marcus drags his gaze away from the woman and lands back on Kingston.

I can't gage him. Is he friend of foe?

I scoff internally. Of course he's foe. Look at him.

There may as well be a neon light flashing above his head that reads DANGER in big bright letters.

"Is that a problem?" Kingston's mouth tips up at the edge, a smirk knowing Marcus will never admit that he doesn't think women belong on the same level as men.

"Not at all."

I can't stifle the laugh.

The slap across the face is quick and painful. I didn't even see him cross the room until his hand was striking me. The pain burns in my cheekbone and unable to control my basic instincts, I lash out, though I don't get far. Not even a finger to his skin as he steps back to a safe distance and one of his men restrains me.

Marcus glares at me, promising me punishment for that later.

Fuck.

When I look back to the Heart siblings all I see is amusement. Isobel watches me with so much glee you'd think she was a kid on Christmas and Kingston peruses me with an air of respect.

"You're Alexander Silver's woman, are you not?" He asks me directly.

"She's nothing." Marcus snaps.

"Was I speaking with you?" Kingston doesn't even turn to look at Valentine, keeping his icy gaze on me, urging me to talk.

Swallowing, I nod, "I was."

"Was?"

"I hardly think I belong to him now."

Kingston laughs, "Oh you belong to him alright. It's nice to finally meet the woman who brought the king to his knees."

I don't sense malice in his words, and it just confuses me more. Kingston Heart was an enigma.

He turns back to Valentine, "Brave of you to mess with a Silver, Valentine, what makes you believe I'd also want to fuck with that family? You do know who they are, yes?"

"We had a deal," Marcus sputters.

"Now, now, Valentine," Kingston chuckles, "don't get ahead of yourself. I never said anything about backing out of the deal. I just want to make sure you understand what you have gotten yourself into."

"I am aware," Marcus growls, "Now, do you want her or not? If not, I have a list of buyers more than willing to take her in exchange for resource."

"Ah," Kingston holds up a finger, "but none with resources like mine, right?"

Marcus glowers, "no."

While the men are talking Isobel has edged closer, so close in fact she's standing directly in front of me.

Marcus has taken notice, "Is she for you or your sister?" The slimy smile that drags up his mouth is nauseating.

Isobel sneers in his direction but keeps her eyes trained on me, cautiously lifting her hand to whisper her fingers over the blooming bruise on my cheek. Her face is soft, almost kind as her eyes drop down my body. "What did he do to you?" She whispers.

I swallow and frown. What the fuck is going on here?

"I'll take her and I'll give you want you want," Kingston confirms, forcing me to look away from his sister to the man himself. I was being sold. Like fucking livestock.

"I'll make your life hell," I warn him.

Kingston smirks, "I hope you do."

Isobel gently grips my arm and begins to drag me towards her brother.

She's suddenly stopped by one of Valentine's men who snatches her arm, pulling her roughly towards him.

The sounds of guns being withdrawn and safety catches being switched off has my spine straightening.

Kingston has a gun directly aimed at Marcus while Marcus has one pointed at Isobel and me.

Well fuck.

"You don't take the woman until I have what I want."

Marcus barks.

"I think you're severely outnumbered here, Valentine. I'll kill you and your men in three seconds flat. You think we're the only ones on this property right now?"

Marcus' eyes widen a fraction but he stifles it down quickly, "And I'll kill your precious little Isobel."

Kingston's nostrils flare as he cocks his head, "Belle, let go of the girl. We'll be back for her."

"But –" Isobel starts.

"Now, Isobel."

She lets go gently and sighs heavily before joining her brother, the gun following her the entire time.

"I'll have what you need brought to you by tomorrow night. I don't want a hand on her."

Marcus cocks a brow, "She still belongs to me until you deliver, Kingston, I'll do as I please until then, if you don't want her touched you best make the delivery quick."

Big words for a man who trembles in this guys presence. But it's all about looks and they can be awfully deceiving.

Kingston's smile is cruel, "Let's go," he orders his guys before his eyes bounce to mine, "We'll be seeing each other again real soon."

FORTY-SEVEN

Lex

"Where?" My hand slams down on the table.

I had enemies coming out my fucking ears, everywhere I turned there was someone, another fucker trying to take over my kingdom. Take what belonged to me. Kingston fucking Heart was in my city.

I'd never met the bloke but I've heard enough and I needed him gone before he could cause too much fucking stink in these streets.

Why was he even here? What the fuck could Brookeshill have that he wants.

I wasn't scared of the guy but I wasn't stupid either. The biggest underground organization in Europe with ties *everywhere.* Kingston Heart and his sister were nightmares whispered on the wind and it didn't matter which side of the line you were on, if you got in their way you'd be crushed before you could even blink. They made a lasting impression wherever they stepped. There was a reason I didn't associate with the likes of them, I may be strong, and I may have this fucking city, everyone in it and my resources and contacts may be vast, but they were a whole other level.

And they were in my fucking city.

"Spotted down on the northside docks," Ryker grunts, swiping through the image surveillance we had managed to get, "they weren't doing shit though. Just standing there."

I look down at the images. There are fucking hundreds of them here. To look at, Kingston didn't appear to be much, a little menacing but that was it, but I knew better than to believe he was harmless. Oh no, that man made even the devil shake.

It was possible that him and I could have gotten along at some point, but not now. Not now that he has stormed my city uninvited.

"Does anyone know where they were before that?" I ask, swiping through more images. Kingston lazes against the barrier, drawing in from a cigarette while his sister talks on the phone. Even though I've never met them in person, I know damn well out of the two of them, Isobel is the most unhinged. Fucking batshit actually. The stories, Jesus Christ, the fucking stories of the men she's strung up using nothing but their fucking balls and the tales of their DIY castrations.

Most of their life is private, where and how they were raised, their parents, all of it. One minute they weren't there and the next they were fucking everywhere, taking over Europe like a plague.

Twisted City

RIA WILDE

I had to respect them at least.

Ryker shakes his head, tapping the images with the tip of his finger, "Before this they hadn't been seen. Do you not think that strange?"

It wasn't merely a coincidence that they were here. With Valentine and the Syndicate breathing poison into my city, there was no way they were simply here for a vacation. They had a part in this but where, I didn't know. Could they have been the English Jameson mentioned before he died?

I flick to another image and stop dead. Kingston is staring directly at the camera, one brow cocked and a smirk on his face. In the next picture he's holding up nine fingers.

What the fuck.

What the hell does the number nine have to do with this.

After that image it's just a picture of him checking his watch and then rounding up his guys, heading towards a convoy of dark SUVs. They headed out the city and haven't returned since. That was early this morning and it's now eight the same evening.

I press my fingers to the bridge of my nose.

Valentine hasn't sent any more images of Wren. I've had nothing since the last one and his men have disappeared off the streets. All the hideouts we've found them at previously are empty. Everyone has just fucking vanished.

I'd take that as a good sign usually but not this time round, not when my little bird is still missing and Valentine is still trying to take the city.

Twisted City

RIA WILDE

Now with the Heart's here, I know it's all connected.

But how?

Fuck I hated not being in control.

It made me crazy.

She made me crazy.

I had her at my side and it turned my whole world upside down and now she's not there, everything I've ever known doesn't make any sense. The only thing that matters now is getting her back. I'll pile the bodies and I'll stain the streets until she's here. Where she belongs.

My phone buzzes in my pocket and I pull it out to see an unknown number calling.

"Silver," I answer.

"Son," my fathers voice crackles through the speaker.

My anger spikes, "How nice of you to finally reach out," I growl.

"Go to the study," he orders, ignoring my tone.

I comply as much as I don't want to, walking away from Ryker who still studies the images in front of him, trying to piece together Heart's movements.

"You're making an awful lot of noise," my father tells me after I've locked the door and taken a seat at the desk, pouring two fingers of scotch into my glass.

"Yes well, people are fucking with things that do not

belong to them."

"We're not talking about the city," it isn't a question, a statement which I do not deny. "All of this for a woman."

Again, I say nothing because there is nothing to say.

"She better be fucking worth it, Alexander. I didn't raise a bitch."

"Ha," I laugh without humor, "Not that I need to justify my actions old man, this is my Kingdom now, but she is worth it."

"Good. Then you need to know that the Syndicate are in your ranks."

I had my suspicions. I didn't know who or how but they were here.

"I know."

"I can't say much, Alexander, I'm being monitored to see how much I know but they are deeming this old man useless now I'm not in the city."

"Who are they exactly?"

"The Syndicate have been around longer than even the Silvers, a small organization initially but they amassed a following. They're a parasite, coming in and killing off the hosts before taking over the body. They want the world. They do it silently but I've been watching them for some time."

"And you didn't think to warn me of this?"

"I didn't think they'd come for Brookeshill so soon."

"Wonderful."

"Like all things Lex, they have a weakness. They live for their anonymity, they're businessmen, by day they're like any other fucker on the street, they have wives and children, day jobs but by night they're killers and thieves and scum. They want power and money and they'll go to any lengths to get it. Drugs. Humans, you name it, they'll do it."

"Fuck."

"They don't live by the same rules as we do, son. Nothing is off limits. There are no laws, no moral code, they take and take and they'll use any means to get it. Stand in their way or cause a problem for them they'll take out the issue. Like your little girlfriend."

"Why get Valentine to do their dirty work?"

"Valentine was an easy pawn to them, he was hungry for your throne and while they'll do anything to take what they want they don't like getting their hands dirty. They know they can't simply take you out without losing the city and the loyalty, if Valentine does it for them and claims the city, your men will either die with you or swear new loyalty to him if they want to keep the money rolling. It's war, Lex."

"You should have warned me," I growl.

"I'm warning you now." He says, "take them out. All of them."

"I'm fucking trying!"

"Five five five, south street, it's a safe house only I know about. When –" *not if,* "you get your woman back, put her there until this is over. She's your weakness Lex, and they'll use it. Hide her."

Silence settles between us.

"I understand."

There is no goodbye as he hangs up and for a moment I sit in the quiet, sipping my whiskey.

But I should have known the quiet wouldn't last. It never fucking does.

The alarm sounds on my phone just as Ryker bursts through the door, "We've got company."

FORTY-EIGHT
Wren

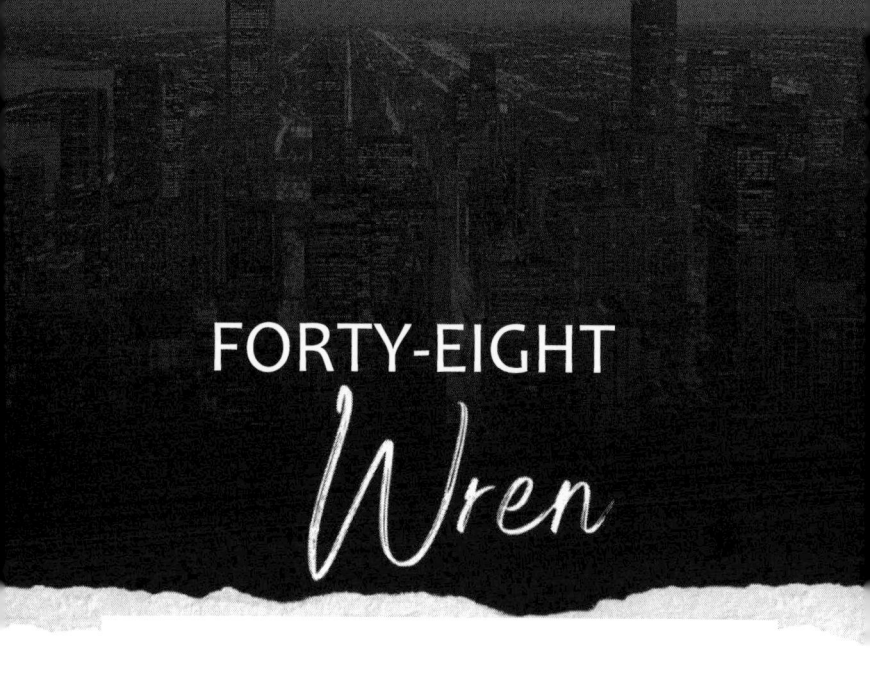

Two hours earlier.

Despite his threat, Valentine didn't lay a finger on me. I was shoved back into the room minutes after Kingston and his men left and I've been here ever since. Rory is doing better, her wounds now healing but her mind still needs to be fixed. It's too often I find her staring at the wall, her eyes filled with horror as she remembers all that she's endured since she's been here.

She wakes often, screaming and lashing out and those nightmares trickle into her waking hours. I don't know if she'll ever be the same again.

"What did he do?" She asked an hour after I was put back.

I shake my head, not wanting to tell her I'll be leaving. I didn't want to think about what they would do with her when I was gone, and I was trying to think of ways of either negotiating her release or convincing Kingston to take her with us. It was obvious he wouldn't allow it, this wasn't a package deal, whatever he was trading with my father made him as bad as everyone else. He came here because he wanted me. No-one could be trusted.

The door opens a crack and two sealed bottles of water are rolled in before the door slams shut once more. I grab them and throw one over to my best friend, breaking the seal on mine and taking a sip.

"How did you end up here?" I ask instead.

She looks down at her hands, "I don't really know. It was a few weeks ago I guess, I'm not actually sure how long it's been but I was coming out of school, it was quite late because I was grading, when someone hit me. When I woke up, I was in that room down the hall."

She sniffles.

"Don't tell me the rest, Rory, I don't need to know that."

"They hurt me," she whispers. "Real bad."

"I know," I cross the room to sit next to her, "I'm going to get us out of here."

It's amusing comparing this experience to the one with Lex, I'm determined to get out of here, but where was that determination when I was strapped to Lex's bed.

I lift my water bottle to my lips, but a sudden boom causes me to flinch, making me drop the open bottle onto the floor. The walls shake and the ceiling above me vibrates, dislodging dust and dirt that rains down onto us. Another boom has all the lights going out and with the fact that we're underground and there's no windows the room plunges into a darkness so deep I can't see my hand in front of my face.

Rory screams next to me, snatching out to wrap her dainty fingers around my arm painfully, her nails digging into my skin.

There are a few beats of silence before the sound of gunfire comes. The loud pops make my ears ring and the shouts and hollers coming from above leaves my brain scrambling to keep up. Feet pound against the floorboards above us, frantic, panicked and the gun fire continues.

I pry Rory's fingers from my arm as I climb from the bed, my bare feet scuffing across the floor. A door slams close by and then footsteps are drawing closer quickly. Before I can react the door to the room swings open, letting in a tiny amount of light from the emergency lighting I hadn't realized had been installed into the ceilings of this underground prison. Marcus's face is shrouded in menacing shadows and the gleam of a knife catches in the dim light. He lunges forward, slicing the knife into my flesh. I manage to dodge but it still cuts through my skin, just below my ribs, deep enough for a well of blood to pour down my side and hip, staining the white dress crimson. I cry out as he grabs my throat having dropped the knife in our scuffle.

"No one gets you!" He growls. "No one fucking gets you!"

I try to frantically suck in air as his palms crush my windpipe, all the while Rory screams, her fists slamming into Marcus's back but it's useless. She's too weak to fight him off and me, I'm losing too much blood too quickly.

Fuck.

"Get off!" Rory cries. "Get off!"

A door slamming has Valentine's hands loosening and then they come away entirely as he spins and runs.

Runs.

The fucking coward.

I collapse onto my knees, sucking in breaths as my blurring vision follows his dark shape out the door. I blink once, twice, staring at my freedom. The door is open. We can get out.

I clutch Rory's hand, pushing onto shaky legs as I clutch my side, trying to stem the bleeding.

I should be dead. I will be if I can't stop myself from bleeding out.

If I die though, I will be out of this house. Even if that death happens on the front porch, I'll be free and so will Rory.

I make a step towards the door and that sense of freedom dies as a body fills the doorframe.

"Hello, Wren," Kingston's smooth English accent sends a warning shiver down my spine.

Will someone give me a fucking break!?

Men run behind him, opening doors, the metal clanging of

keys loud as it echoes through the halls. There's still the odd pop of gun fire up above but it's obvious Kingston is the winner here.

"You're hurt," he comments, with a cock of his head as his eyes drop to the blood seeping through my fingers, "I don't think Silver will be best pleased with me bringing you back broken."

Confusion has my head snapping back, "W-what did you say?"

"Let's go, Wren," he curls his fingers, beckoning me forward.

It may be fucking stupid, real dumb but I go, grabbing Rory as my weak legs carry me towards the man that I have no doubt has been the star of many a nightmare.

When I get to him, my legs give out but he doesn't let me hit the floor, no, his arms snatch out, grabbing me before I can break my nose on the concrete.

"Not pleased at all," he tuts, mostly to himself as I'm dragged back into a standing position and hoisted up. Fog clouds my mind, coming in heavy at the edges but I can tell I'm moving, or maybe I'm floating.

"Don't you die on me, love," Kingston says, "I need you alive and kicking."

"You're going to use me too," my voice is weak, small.

"It's more of a peace offering," he tells me.

"W-why?"

"Your man has a lot of power, I'll be stupid to get on the wrong side of him but I need his help."

"You're taking me to Lex?"

"I am, love, now stay alive," he orders, "I hate it when people die on me, especially since I've gone to all this trouble."

"Rory..." my voice trails off.

"All the girls here will be taken care of," Kingston says.

I know the moment we step outside.

Cool air washes over my feverish skin and even in my current state it lights something inside of me. My lungs expand as I suck in the fresh air, feeling the wind on my face, teasing through my limp and unwashed hair. Freedom.

I'm free.

A numbness begins to spread through my body as Kingston continues to carry me away from the house but I don't fight it. I'm not going to die inside that house, inside that prison. I'm not going to be left to rot in a ditch. I'm free. I feel myself being lowered, the pain in my side a dull throb compared to the fog inside my head.

"There goes the car seats," a feminine voice chimes from somewhere in front of me.

"Shut it, Belle," Kingston orders, climbing into the back with me, "drive. Now."

The movement of the car has my stomach rolling and I gag

though nothing comes up and then my eyes roll back, my consciousness slipping.

"Oh no you don't," Kingston shakes me roughly as he presses something into my side, "What did I say, love? Stay alive."

But that shit was easier said than done when all I wanted to do was sleep.

FORTY-NINE

Lex

Present

I grab my gun from the holster at my back and then snatch the other from where I've attached it under the desk, my legs pounding against the floor as I dart out of the office, towards the front of the house.

Oh, we had company alright.

There was a small fucking army in the compound grounds. The gates at the front of the house didn't fucking stand a chance against the convoy of SUVs barrelling down my driveway.

Fuck.

Heart was here and he was making his presence known.

"Hold your fire!" Someone booms from outside, a body stepping from the closest vehicle with their hands raised.

Twisted City

RIA WILDE

"It's a trap," Ryker hisses.

"Hold your fire," I growl out the order.

"Where is Silver!?" The English accent has my eyes narrowing though it isn't Heart shouting towards us but one of his men.

One of my guys raises his pistol, "Hold it for fucks sake," I hiss, unfolding my body until I'm standing. Ryker rises with me, I can see it in his face that he thinks this is a bad idea and I don't know why, call it intuition, but something is pulling me towards the door.

I open it, my gun still in hand and raised, ready to fire but I don't pull the trigger.

When the guy spots me he lowers his weapon and steps to the side, nodding his head once.

Heart steps from the vehicle but it isn't him I'm interested in.

Oh no.

It's the broken body he has cradled in his arms that has me moving.

My little bird.

The threat, the dangerous, very real possibility of having a bullet between the eyes in the next three seconds is lost on me as I cross the space, the gravel crunching under my feet until I'm directly in front of Kingston Heart. Blood coats his hands, his forearms, the front of his t-shirt but he doesn't matter as he simply hands the girl to me. Her body is too cold, too thin, too *still*. There's too much blood. Too many cuts and bruises. Her chest barely moves with the shallow breaths that she inhales through slightly parted pale lips. Dying. She was dying.

"A doctor!" I boom, "Now!" Crippling fear takes a vice like grip around my heart.

There's a flurry of movement behind me.

"If a doctor isn't here in ten minutes, I'll kill you all," I stare at every face I can see, the promise of my words penetrating deep inside their brains. I would do it. For her, I'd kill them all.

To my surprise, Heart lets me leave but he, his sister and a few of his men follow. I wasn't going to stop him.

I owed him.

He did this for a something in return, there's no way a man like him, so much like myself did this out of the kindness of his heart.

There is no compassion in his soul. Strategy. Ruthlessness. Intelligence. All of them but never compassion.

He's king where he comes from like I'm king here.

Having Wren back in my arms feels like I've come home. It's a sense that burrows deep into my soul, swelling my chest until I feel as if my lungs and heart will burst right out. It's not a feeling I'm used to.

It fucking terrifies me.

Upstairs, in the master bedroom, I gently lay her onto the bed, placing her head on the pillow so her hair fans out around her head like a halo of fire. It's not glossy or wild like it usually is, just limp, weak.

Her pouty mouth is pressed into a thin line and her skin is almost translucent beneath the lights in the bedroom. The prominent bones of her collar and ribs protrude from her skin like sharp edges.

"Get out!" I bark at the men that followed me in and all but Ryker leave, clicking the door closed.

"Kingston Heart is downstairs, Lex," he warns.

"Do I look like I give a shit?"

"Lex," Ryker starts.

"Get the fuck out!"

Ryker stops in his tracks as he makes his way towards me and Wren. Panic has started to crawl through my body, it makes my scalp tingle, my palms sweat.

This much emotion I can't control. "GET OUT!"

"Lex," Ryker tries again, fucking pushing, always fucking pushing.

A loud crash echoes through the house which distracts us for a moment, "I'll deal with it."

My nostrils flare, "you do that."

When I'm finally alone, when silence settles like a heavy weight around me, I sit on the bed, pulling my broken bird into me, resting her head in my lap, smoothing back the hair from her face.

Twisted City   RIA WILDE

"You left me little bird," I whisper, "you fucking left me."

Her lips part and her lashes flutter but she doesn't open her eyes.

"I'm going to make him pay for this, mark my words little bird, you'll be standing at my side while we watch his heart beat in my fist. I'll make it rain, little bird. For you. Always for you."

"Lex," her voice is as soft as a summer breeze, "Alexander."

"I'm here."

A small whimper escapes her lips as her body shivers against me and a single tear slips out the corner of her eye, rolling down the side of her face to disappear into her copper hairline. Her breathing is still too shallow, her breaths slow.

I hate seeing her like this. No fight. No strength. As much as I fucking loathed her attitude and her push, I wished for it now. I needed her venom if only to teach her a lesson, I needed her fight and her strength if only to prove I'd always own her, always have her.

I wanted to both devour and soothe her broken frame, to love her and worship her while I claimed her. Made her mine.

I'd ensure the whole fucking world knew she belonged to a Silver and fucking with her was fucking with an army bigger, better and stronger than any of our enemies.

I'd make her a Silver, have her at my side, a crown atop her head and make them all bow down. They'll bend the knee and kiss her feet like she fucking deserved.

The doctor arrives seven minutes after the threat, sweating, his eyes wide with fear, his equipment tugged in behind him by the nurses he's no doubt managed to blackmail onto his payroll.

Doctor Gerald Whitmore was a seedy old man but a good doctor, he's patched me up many a time and I had no doubt Wren was in capable hands.

"Mr Silver," he greets, swallowing nervously.

"Fix it."

"You know that is not how this works, Mr Silver," he steps towards us and instinctively, I bend, covering my woman, baring my teeth like a fucking animal.

"You'll need to let him at her," a strong English accent says from the door.

"Heart," I growl.

"In the flesh," his arms stretch out at his sides, palms facing towards the ceiling, "She took a beating Silver, you want her to live, the good doctor is gonna need to see her."

He's right. I fucking hate it.

Reluctantly, I uncurl myself from her and retract enough to let Whitmore in. He tugs at her clothes, pulling the fabric away from her skin and the urge to protect makes not ripping his throat out almost impossible.

"Look at me, Silver," Heart drawls, "stop picturing all the ways you could disembowel the doctor."

Whitmore audibly swallows.

"What the fuck do you want?"

I allow the distraction, trying to ignore the doctors hands on Wren's body. She needs this. She needs to live. To breathe. To survive and the only way that is happening is with him.

"To talk, Silver."

"You've come all the way from London to talk?" I scoff.

"Amongst other things," Kingston nods, "now isn't a good time but I'm not going anywhere."

"And what's stopping me putting a knife through your throat?"

Kingston smirks, eyes bouncing to my woman, now half naked and bleeding across my sheets. A growl leaves my throat. The only warning I'll give.

"You're a man of code, Silver. I gave you something and you don't like debt."

"And I don't like fuckers walking in on my turf, regardless of whether you've done something for me."

Kingston nods slowly, "I get that but unfortunately for you, I don't give a shit. We need to talk, don't make this harder than it has to be."

I have too much going on to pick a fight with a man who owns half of Europe and despite the fact that he's busted in on my fucking turf, I did owe him for bringing me Wren.

"Fine, now leave. We'll talk when I'm ready."

I don't wait to see if he accepts that, just turn back to my girl. My eyes fall to the healing wound in the centre of her abdomen, the healing scar where the bullet ripped through her skin. There are old and new cuts all over her, dark and fading bruises and the wrapped thigh with blood spots staining the white makes my blood fucking boil.

"I'll be here a while," the doc says.

And so I wait. I settle into the chair across from the bed and wait while the doc fixes up my woman, unable to focus on anything other than her. All the problems, they'll still be here tomorrow but there's not a guarantee she will be.

Wren

I hear his voice. A deep soothing baritone that both scares and excites me. It's the type of noise that brings a surge of memories to the surface, his hands on my body, his tongue on my skin, teeth grazing, nails biting. It isn't real. It can't be.

I'm in hell.

But the memories, they keep torturing me as his breath brushes my ear, the smell of whiskey on the air. His possessive growl, his ruthlessness, his violence, his demons. They caress my body like hands, making me *feel*.

Twisted City — RIA WILDE

I don't want to feel. I can't. Not in this life.

If I feel, I'll die and Rory won't ever be free.

"I've been looking for you, little bird," his growl is barely audible, a whisper in the darkness, taunting me, "You left me, but I came looking. I'll always come looking."

The absolute sorrow that overtakes me in this moment is crippling. Why am I being tortured with thoughts of Lex? Why is it him haunting me?

The sob echoes in the darkness and for the first time, everything hurts. My head, my body, my heart. All of me is on fire as agony rips through me.

And as if to haunt me more, as if I haven't suffered enough strong arms band around me, gently, barely even touching my skin but there nonetheless and a mouth is pressed to my hair.

"Shh, I've got you, little bird," are his whispered words. "Shh now, that's it. Good girl."

But while I quiet, the pain continues, eating away at my soul. I'm left to the demons and the nightmares while I hallucinate Alexander by my side.

FIFTY
Wren

    Something isn't right. It isn't the smell of coffee or the voices in the room with me, it isn't the familiar scent of Lex's aftershave or the soft sheets beneath my body, it's the steady presence at my back. The soft hand on my body, the feel of another person breathing behind me, the steady rise and fall of their chest pressing into my spine.

No.

This isn't right. My eyelids feel heavy as I try to open them, the burning light coming in through a window right in front of me scolding my retinas. What the fuck? There's a window? Daylight and trees and grass.

I curl my fingers, feeling the soft cotton yield under my grip and squint, trying to get a look of the room without notifying anyone around me that I'm awake. My skin feels too tight for my bones and my throat is dry, but I don't dare move or make a sound. The walls are white with a pair of navy curtains hanging at the window, the bedside table is one I recognize, dark colored with a lamp on the top and drawers. Everything is so similar. Is this just another way for Valentine to torture me? Give me what I want only to burn it to the ground later.

Footsteps sound, heading away from me and then a door is closed, the soft click making me jump where I lay, still with that body pressed behind me.

A few beats of silence where the only sound in the room is my frantic breathing but then that rough voice is whispering against my ear, the hint of mint brushing against my nose.

"I know you're awake, little bird."

My heart stops beating, the breath ceasing to continue as I push away from where I'm led on my side to position myself onto my back, it hurts and my skin pulls and twinges with the movement but nothing right now is going to stop me from seeing the face behind me.

I swallow as I start at his clothed legs, dressed in a pair of black suit trousers, his ankles crossed and then work my way up to where his black shirt is tucked into the pants, a black belt with a silver buckle holding it together. I follow the line of the buttons before they stop, creating a V to reveal the hard expanse of his chest, prominently lined muscles and bronzed skin, and then further up his throat, noticing the way his Adam's apple bobs as he swallows. The hard line of his jaw twitches as he grits his teeth and then I see his mouth.

His beautiful, dangerous mouth, set in a straight line.

When I meet his eyes the whole world stops. Silver orbs

bore down into me, filled with so much emotion it gives me whiplash. I've never seen him reveal so much in his face, but it's there, as if it's typed into his skin with ink. Pain. Regret. Fear.

His eyes bounce between mine, but this can't be real, can it?

His dark hair is slicked back away from his face, but one tendril falls across his forehead which creases with a frown as he looks at me.

Is this a dream? Am I dreaming?

His finger comes up to caress the side of my face, the very tip, following the line of my cheek, across my jaw until it brushes over my bottom lip.

"Lex?"

One side of his mouth tips up, "Hello, Little Bird."

Fuck the pain. Fuck the obvious injuries, I scramble, trying to get to my knees but his firm hand holds me down, pinning me in place.

"Let me up!"

This earns me a grin as he flips himself, getting to his knees, the mattress dipping beneath his weight. He cages me between his arms, face hovering above mine.

"I've missed you little bird and I've never missed anything in my entire life."

"Kiss me damn it!"

His eyes bounce between mine but whatever he was looking for he must find because his mouth crashes down on mine possessively. His hands may be gentle, he may be holding himself away from my body but his mouth is not in any way soft as his tongue pushes in through my lips. Fuck he tastes good.

It's been too long.

I never thought I'd miss the man, I didn't even think I'd ever need a man, but I needed him. I needed him as much as I needed air to fill my lungs. We're inexplicably linked, his demons and his darkness caressed my soul.

He rips himself away, practically throwing himself off the bed to get away from me, but I just lay there. Part of me believes this is still a dream, still a nightmare but my swollen lips, the wetness there transferring to my fingertips as I brush my fingers across my mouth seem all too real.

I find him breathing heavy at the edge of the bed, "Don't do that again."

"What?"

"You're injured, Wren, this," he points between us, "This ain't happening."

"Are you fucking kidding me?"

His eyes narrow, "Just because you're incapacitated right now doesn't mean I won't put you over my knee the moment you're less *fragile*."

"Don't make promises you can't keep."

He grins, his white teeth almost gleaming when compared to the bronze tone of his skin. Goddamn he's so fucking beautiful.

I try to push up onto my elbows but the pain in my side cripples me. I cry out, squeezing my eyes shut as my blood roars. Fuck, that hurts.

How the fuck did I even get here? I remember the loud bang, Valentine attacking me and then Kingston. After that, I don't remember a single thing.

Oh God. Rory!

Ignoring the pain, the agony that wants to pull me under, I get up onto shaky legs, pushing away the blankets. There's no time to think about the fact that I'm dressed in a pair of leggings and a t-shirt that's three times too big for me. Where is Rory?

"Stop!" Lex booms.

Had he been talking? I'm halfway to the door but I stop, my knees shaking, threatening to buckle under me.

"Where the fuck do you think you're going?"

Lex appears in front of me, his nostrils flaring, anger palpable.

"I just got you back little bird and you're trying to run away already?"

"No," I swallow, "no, you don't understand."

He steps up and curls a finger beneath my chin, "Tell me." My eyes meet his, swarming with emotion, with something far too deep for my mind to comprehend.

"My friend, Valentine, he had her and…"

"Shh," He brings me to his chest, "She's safe. All the girls are."

"Where?"

"Not now, Wren, you need to rest."

"Alexander," I grit out.

"Fight me, Wren, I dare you."

I didn't have the energy to fight him. Not even with words, as much as I wanted to lash out, to demand to know where she was I couldn't. I was so tired. In so much pain.

"What happened?"

He guides me back to the bed just as Ryker comes into the room with a bowl of soup and a couple of bottles of water.

"Good to see you awake," he comments, a gentle smile curling his lips.

"Hi Gruff." His eye roll makes me smile a little but it's the scent of the soup that really gets me going. My stomach gurgles loudly, cramping painfully, reminding me how little I've eaten in recent weeks.

He leaves the soup on the side, hands me a bottle of water and then exits while Lex settles into the bed next to me.

"So?"

I drink half the bottle of water while he just watches, head cocked to the side.

"Eat."

"Just tell me."

"Eat."

"You're so fucking bossy."

But I let him help me into a sitting position, trying to hide the wincing while he does, and then the tray is placed on my lap. He lowers the spoon, filling it with the red creamy liquid before lifting it and bringing it to my mouth. I open for him, letting him pour it into my mouth and onto my tongue. A groan sounds in the room. Lex smiles, his pupils dilating as he watches me eat, watching my mouth, my lips as they wrap around the spoon. I'm so taken by him and the food that I've eaten half the bowl before I realize it and come to my senses.

"Tell me, Lex."

With a sigh and the loud clang of the spoon hitting the side of the bowl, he explains the whole thing reluctantly. Kingston and his sister, Isobel, belong to a huge organization based in Europe and while Lex doesn't know why he wants his help, the reason I'm here is because of him.

Kingston wants Lex so he used me to get to him.

I should feel angry that I'm simply a pawn, yet again, in a war that is not my own, but I just feel grateful towards the man.

Kingston helped bring me back.

I owed him.

But I also knew that debt wouldn't land on me, that's not how this world works. The debt is on Lex, it will always be on Lex until he pays it back. But I had no idea if whatever price Kingston was asking was going to be too high, even for the Twisted king of this city.

FIFTY-ONE
Lex

I watch Wren as she sleeps, still too fragile and pale for my liking. Cleaned and clothed now, she doesn't resemble the girl I lost in the club. There is something different about her. The trauma of what happened doesn't appear to have hit her yet but you don't go through what she did and come out of it with your mind in one piece. I am waiting for the time it hits.

I know it will. With an absolute certainty. She is not built for this, not yet anyway, she may be with time, but right now, she is still the same girl I took from her apartment all those weeks ago.

There are purple and blue bruises mottling her skin, too many cuts and grazes to count, swollen limbs and stitches with white bandages covering the wounds. She is lucky to be alive.

After eating plenty she fell into a quick sleep, exhausted but it was good to see a little fight in her.

Twisted City

RIA WILDE

I take the syringe of antibiotics and insert it into the canular the doctor inserted into the top of her hand, administrating the medicine followed by a dose of painkillers that should keep her asleep for a little while. She'll hate me for it but I'll take it if it makes her better and keeps her safe.

Reluctantly, I slip from the room and close the door behind me, motioning for two of my guys to station themselves outside the door. I wasn't taking any chances. Keeping them here wasn't to keep her in the room, more to keep anyone who wasn't me *out*.

I take the stairs down quickly and find Ryker in the kitchen, his hands cradling a tumbler of whiskey while he hangs his head as if exhausted.

"What the fuck is wrong with you!?"

"That chick is batshit," he huffs, throwing back his drink.

He was referring to the blonde Kingston so lovingly deposited on my doorstep a few hours after bringing Wren to me.

Aurora Barrett.

If Kingston is to be believed, she went through some shit back at Valentine's compound, and the only reason she is alive is because of my little bird. Something I'll be having words with her for when she is well enough to hear them.

I knew the girl was important to Wren, you don't sacrifice yourself for someone you don't know but then this is Wren, so fuck knows what she would do.

"Can't handle a little blonde?" I taunt, grabbing the bottle and pouring myself a drink before handing it back.

"She needs help." He says seriously.

"I don't have time for this shit," I growl at him, "I want Valentine's head."

"How is she?"

"Alive."

"Have you set up your meeting with Heart?"

"He's headed back to London for now but he'll be back next week," I sigh.

Whatever he wanted he was keeping it locked up tight. Kingston Heart, in his own right was a man not to be fucked with, he didn't scare me, not even a little but he had power. I recognized it, like for like, after all, recognize one and other.

It wasn't important right now. *She* was.

I've had men out, searching, tearing this city apart looking for Valentine or his men but it's like the man has disappeared yet again. The Syndicate are radio silent but this war is far from over.

While Valentine licks his wounds the Syndicate are looking for another way to destroy my city.

No leads, no answers, no anything.

Everything was out of my control.

And I hated it.

I wanted blood.

I wanted pain.

I wanted vengeance.

A loud bang vibrates the ceiling above my head followed by loud yelling and grunts. Wren's friend was awake.

"Fuck," Ryker hisses, "how is she awake!? The doc gave her enough sedative to knock out a horse."

I didn't have the patience to deal with Aurora. I gave that shit to Ryker, if it were anyone else, I wouldn't give a fuck about her safety or health, I would have shoved her into the nearest hospital – *maybe* – and left it at that.

But I'd already determined that Wren was my weakness and I needed something to help bring Wren back when her mind can't handle the demons anymore.

I knew she was mine, she had admitted it but there is only so much I would be able to do. I may be a monster, evil, but my little bird was my tether and I would do anything for her.

Let it be said, even the devil can be tamed.

Ryker doesn't bother with a glass, he simply lifts the bottle from the table and swigs directly from it before shoving back from his chair and stomping from the room.

The call from my father rings in my head.

Five, five, five, south street.

A safe house.

Twisted City

RIA WILDE

Taking Wren there would be the safer option, but I wouldn't be able to stay. Not when the battle continues to rage on the streets. I wasn't sure if I'd be able to part with her now that I had her back. I throw the rest of my whiskey back and head back to the room. My men part to let me inside.

The room is shrouded in darkness, a small amount of silver light drifting in through the crack in the curtain but I see her shape writhing on the bed. Silently screaming as her dreams torture her in her sleep. So very broken.

Closing my eyes I try to settle the boiling rage before I cross the room and tug her into my lap, cradling her and restraining her to my chest to stop the thrashing. I can see speckles of blood seeping through the white bandages on her abdomen and her hair is slick with sweat but for whatever reason, be it pure insanity or not, she settles against me, the nightmares chased away by my presence.

Perhaps she was more broken than I thought.

Wren still sleeps when light streams in through the window the following morning. I worry about leaving her. I stare down at her face, tracing the lines of her nose, her cheeks, her perfectly shaped mouth with my eyes, unable to get enough.

Every emotion inside me feels too big, too important and I've no idea how to deal with or control them. I had always been taught that these feelings would be my destruction and now, as I stare at her, as everything inside me knots up so tightly I worry it'll snap, I understand why. This was nothing but obsession. I am *obsessed* with her. What the fuck do I do with that?

Gently, I pry her arm from my body and slip to the edge of the bed, running a hand down my face. Wren whimpers behind me but ultimately stays asleep as I drag my ass to the bathroom for a shower.

I have to harness this. Use it to my advantage. With how strongly I feel for my little bird it could bring some serious consequences, like seeing Valentine crucified on the tallest building of this city. He cannot hide for long, rats like him never go far and all I need to do is wait patiently for him to resurface.

I can do that.

I can wait.

Afterall, the sweetest meal comes to those who wait.

FIFTY-TWO
Wren

I wake in a bath of golden sunlight, it streams in through the window, the curtains pulled back and a window open to let in a gentle breeze that caresses my overheated skin. My body hurts, bruises, and cuts and old wounds, pulsing with new and old pain that I fear will never go away.

A glance at the clock tells me it's a little past one in the afternoon but I have no idea what day it is. I don't know how long Marcus kept me locked in those cells beneath the house, how many days, weeks or even months passed before I was finally freed.

It's tough to remember everything, it's like since I've been back with Lex my mind has shut down on itself, as if, now it knows I am away from the imminent threat it can take a seat and turn off, no longer having to think too much in order to survive. I didn't blame it, part of me wanted to curl right back under this blanket and shut off.

Twisted City   RIA WILDE

Sitting up in bed, I stare around the room, the room I've shared with Lex on so many occasions but cannot remember the last before the blast. So much has happened, so much still happening and I can't work out my left from my right.

I run a hand down my face, frowning at the needle sticking out the back of my hand, strapped down with white medical tape.

My eyes narrow, I don't think so.

Ripping the tape off, I gently slide the needle out of my skin, watching as blood wells from the new hole in my hand. I press a hand to it to stop it from dripping everywhere and climb from the bed, heading across the room to the bathroom. Scents of Lex fill my nose, spicy and intoxicating, a familiar aroma that helps memories of his hands on my body fill the blank spaces inside my head.

There was one emotion pumping through my system, one feeling that kept my heart a steady thump inside my chest and that was having my revenge.

Lex might think he'll get to strike the final blow, but Marcus – *my father* – will die by my hand. He doesn't get to do this to me, *I will kill him.*

He has severely underestimated his own daughter and instead awoken something inside of me I feel has always been a part of my soul. A darkness that matches Alexander's. I always wondered why I felt attached to him somehow, always worried about why his breed of brutality spoke to me in ways I was never able to understand but now I know. And it's because I was born to be like him. To stand at his side. To rule and reign.

Twisted City

RIA WILDE

I stand before the mirror, in nothing but a tank top and a pair of white panties, all my wounds on show to me. The bruising on my throat, the shadows cast across my face from the number of hits and beatings I took at the hands of both Marcus and his men. At the gauze covering the slice in my side and another covering my thigh.

I stare at that one.

I can see dots of blood seeping through, staining the snow white bandage red but I can't remember what's under there. My head cocks to the side as I try to piece together the events that left me with this particular wound. What happened here?

I should probably leave it, but I have to shower anyway – *I really need to shower* – so unwrapping these bandages is a must.

I peel the tank top from my torso and do the one on my side first, keeping my eyes trained on the task rather than the scar that mars my abdomen from where I was shot. The wound in my side is still too raw to be left open but I can get away with it for an hour or so. I move to my thigh next, grabbing one end of the gauze, I start to unwrap it, taking each inch as slowly as possibly. My heart starts to pound furiously inside my chest, a sweat breaking out on my brow and between my breasts.

I know this is going to be bad. I already feel it, a sense of dread settling into the pit of my stomach as I continue to unroll the white material. Around and around it goes, only a few layers left before I can see what damage is lying underneath.

Finally, it falls away from my skin and drops to the floor, a puddle of white material mottled with red splotches.

Twisted City

RIA WILDE

Tears prick my eyes as I get a look at what that bastard did to me.

My own father.

I stare for the longest time, the tears welling in my eyes never spilling over, tracing the deep cut in my thigh, shaped in a V. He fucking branded me. Like livestock. Like cattle.

I am forever marked down as a Valentine. But I am not a Valentine.

I am a Silver.

Bile rises in my throat, a burn as my stomach churns, threatening to heave up anything that's in there though I doubt there will be much.

This can't stay. This needs to go.

Taking a deep breath, I meet my eyes in the mirror and realize what I must do.

Steeling myself, I nod and turn the shower on, letting the water heat to a near point of scolding before I step beneath the spray. It feels good, the water cascading over my overly sensitive skin, my muscles beginning to relax as the water soothes away the tension.

Other than the sound of the water, the bathroom is silent and even beyond that, I can't hear anything. It's in this moment the sounds of screams haunt my waking hours, shrieks of pure terror, of pain and suffering, it's the sounds of male grunts accompanied by the cries of the women they're torturing and the noise of blades and gunshots that fill the silence.

Twisted City   RIA WILDE

My knees are weak, too weak to keep me upright beneath the spray as these memories, memories that bounce around inside my head, one moment they are there, a pure vivid video replaying itself, the next they're gone, replaced by something else. Faces. Voices. Smells.

Rory.

Oh god. Rory.

Did she get out? Did I save her? Why can't I remember anything?

My sob is silent as I drop to my knees under the spray of the shower, the water hitting my spine, plastering my hair to my face. All my cuts stretch and pull as I move to sit under the spray, making me wince. Taking a deep breath, I try to calm my mind, try to push back the images to let in some light. Rory was safe. She got out.

Valentine did this.

He fucking did this.

I wanted to hold his heart in my hand. To watch the life drain from him and I wanted to laugh and revel in it.

Everything up until this point has been a chain of events caused by him.

I wanted him to suffer.

The first thing I needed to do was get rid of this brand. It probably gives him joy to know that even if he doesn't have me, he still owns me in this way. His claws are in my skin and the only way to remove him is to remove this.

Twisted City — RIA WILDE

Sucking in a deep breath, I swipe at my face, closing my eyes to calm myself once more before I wash away the memories and turn off the shower.

Wrapping myself in a towel, I pick up the bloodied gauzes I left on the floor and shove them in the trash can just outside the bathroom door before I shut it and lock it behind myself. The mirror is steamed up, my reflection a blur of color in front of me but I don't need to see myself to do this.

I dry myself and stand there, on the cold tile floor in nothing, staring at the V carved right there into my thigh. It's still raw, not even knitted together properly yet, barely a scab. I close my eyes, the memory of how he did it slowly coming back to me, how he restrained me to a chair and carved into me with a knife. I remember his face, the twisted smile on his face, the look of pure joy in his eyes as that knife cut into my skin. He reveled in my pain just like I was going to revel in his.

I run my fingers over the wound, the flesh soft and easily split as my nails scratch and disturb the dermis trying to grow over the top. I won't let it scar this way. I'd rather have a huge messy scar than the V carved into my thigh.

Lifting Lex's razor from the holder by the sink, I begin to pry the parts apart. First the handle, and then the casing that holds the blade in place. My fingers bleed from where the edge of the razor slices against my skin but I don't stop until the small little blade sits in my hand.

I stare at it for a while, this gleaming silver blade in the palm of my hand, used for nothing else but to shave the hair on Lex's face. But it's sharp and it'll do the job I need it to do.

Twisted City

RIA WILDE

In the time it has taken to dismantle the blade the mirror has cleared and I can see myself. I don't recognize the person that stares back at me. My red hair is slicked back from my face, dripping wet from the shower and leaving pools of water on the tiles beneath my feet, there are dark shadows under my eyes, even my freckles are dull and faded as if them too have simply given up. I'm too skinny, the bones of my collar and ribs protruding too far out of my skin, and my hip bones are sharp.

I lift my foot and rest the heel against the marble counter, remembering how I sat on that very counter, with Lex standing between my legs while I tended to *his* wounds. Swallowing, I line the blade against my thigh, but I don't intend to slice. Slicing won't get rid of the brand, I have to peel back this entire area to get rid of it. It'll leave me with one hell of a scar but rather that than this.

I grit my teeth and push, feeling my skin, still too sensitive, the nerves alive and exposed, peel away. I push, tears pricking my eyes with the pain as I push from the top of the V all the way down to the bottom, leaving a line of exposed flesh, bleeding and raw about ten centimeters long. Blood trickles from the new wound but I don't stop, I move to the next section, imbed the blade and push.

My teeth grit together, grinding inside my mouth loud enough to be heard.

Vaguely I am aware of a voice sounding through the door, a deep baritone that calls to me but I can't stop now. If I stop, I wont restart.

"Wren!"

I continue still.

"Wren!" this time my name is accompanied by a loud thud, the door to the bathroom rattling as something heavy is rammed into it.

I continue.

"Wren, I swear to fucking god! Open this fucking door!"

I don't.

I finish this line and move onto the next just as the door to the bathroom slams open, the wood finally succumbing to the wrath of Alexander Silver.

He stands in the threshold, sweaty, out of breath and fucking angry.

And I make that push with the blade, slicing through my flesh to rid myself of the brand.

FIFTY-THREE

Lex

I head into the bedroom, feeling exhausted after the lack of sleep the night before. I expect to find Wren in the bed, still sleeping. Doc had said she would sleep a lot, to recover from all the shit she went through with Valentine but when I enter, I don't find her in the bed.

The sheets are rumbled, a breeze blowing in through the open window, the curtains swishing as it does. There are small splotches of blood on the white cotton and my eyes frantically search the room for her until they land on the dustbin outside the bathroom, filled with the used bandages from her wounds and the bathroom door closed.

I cross the room and press on the handle, finding it locked.

Her breathing is heavy from the other side, so loud I can hear every intake and exhale of breath. Can hear how it's filled with pain, a rattle of air that pushes forcefully from her lips.

"Wren!"

She doesn't respond.

"WREN!"

My shoulder slams into the door.

She doesn't respond to either my voice or my need to get in.

"Wren, I swear to fucking God. Open this fucking door!"

I get no response and I flip, a rage with no off button. I slam my shoulder into the door, once, twice, three times before the wood splinters and the lock comes away. The door slams into the wall on the other side, cracked down the middle and dangling from its hinges.

"What the fuck are you doing!?" I boom, unable to completely understand the picture before me.

Wren, naked, wet, bleeding, the blade from my razor grasped between her fingers as she runs the long edge down her thigh, peeling the skin away over the top of that fucking brand Valentine gave her. Her fingers ribboned with blood, sweat on her brow, dripping down her spine.

She meets my eyes, but I don't see anything there, just a soulless, dead and broken stare. Her eyes are bloodshot and her face twists with pain as she continues to mutilate herself.

Fuck.

"STOP!" I boom.

It's as if she cannot hear me.

I have no choice, I cross the space between us and rip the blade from her hand, feeling her blood mingle with mine as the same blade cuts into the palm of my hand.

"Get off me!" She screams, her fists pounding into my shoulders.

"What the fuck do you think you're doing!?"

"I'll fucking kill him!"

She thrashes and convulses as I grab her, hauling her over my shoulder as I take her back into the room, throwing her naked onto the bed. Her eyes are wild, my little bird isn't there at the moment, instead, she's being drowned by whatever this is.

She tries to get up, but I force her back down and as I hold her there, I reach across and open the top drawer of the cabinet by the bed. Her blood stains the sheets, runs over my skin and seeps through my clothes. Her eyes are wide, face twisted in anger, in pain and in sorrow. Tears leak from her eyes, sliding over her temples and into her hairline.

The nightmares might manifest themselves, the doc said, *it's unusual but not unseen in cases like this. If she doesn't calm, sedate her, it'll be like a reset for her mind.*

I've done a lot of bad shit in my time, but this feels wrong. While I may not understand all this shit going on inside of my body, I know don't want to do this to her though I see no other way.

Again, she tries to get up, but I stop her, throwing her back down on the bed and using my weight to keep her there.

"I want to kill him!" She sobs, "But I need this gone, Lex, please. Take this brand off me!"

Her cries twist like a knife to the stomach.

"Please!"

"I'm sorry, baby. Forgive me."

I plunge the needle into her arm, compressing the plunger so all the medicine is deposited into her bloodstream. Her eyes widen, a look of shock and betrayal crossing her features before the sedative quickly takes hold and her arms drop, thudding against the mattress.

I see more tears pool in the corners of her eyes as she realizes what I have just done and then her lids shutter closed, and her body goes slack. Those tears continue to slip from her eyes, haunting me.

"FUCK!" I roar, climbing away from her and launching the needle across the room. "FUCK!"

There's a sudden whirl of activity as Ryker and several men storm into the room and I snap. A different type of fury fills me, this is primal, this is an explosion of protective rage that does not discriminate. Everything and everyone is a target.

"Get the fuck out!" I withdraw the gun from my side and level it at the nearest guy, I don't know his name, I don't care as I pull the trigger and shoot him. I move to the next guy but a quick hand lowering my arm abruptly stops me from shooting him too. The other men leave quickly, dragging the injured guy from the room as they depart, fleeing, until its only me, Ryker and Wren left here. I didn't kill him at least, a flesh wound at most.

My chest heaves with each inhale of breath, my eyes wide and teeth bared.

He doesn't once turn to look at her. He keeps his eyes solely trained on me. "Fix your woman, Lex."

My nostrils flare as anger and confusion and pure blinding rage run through my system like a rampaging bull. I watch him leave, his shoulders tense, spine ramrod straight and the click of the door closing is as loud as the gun I just fired.

Ryker's comment wasn't one to shame Wren, it was one of understanding. He knows what's happening to her and to me, something that would never happen to me. I have a weakness, one I've had for months now and I also know he'll be there to protect her with his life as much as I will be.

She lays sprawled on the bed, medicated and asleep, naked body with all the cuts, the bruises and scars Valentine subjected her to on show to me.

I see the canular discarded on the floor where she ripped it from her hand and also the new wound on her thigh where she tried to rid herself of the brand and realize this is way beyond my capabilities. Sighing, I pull my phone from my pocket and text Ryker, instructing him to get the doc here as soon as possible and in the meantime, I dress her, careful to avoid the wounds on her body.

A short time later, Wren now covered in a pair of my boxer shorts and a large undershirt, the doc arrives. He surveys her where she lays in the bed, the wound badly dressed by my hand but at least I've stemmed the bleeding.

"What happened?" The doc asks.

"Fix it."

He sighs and gets to work, first on the leg she mutilated. He unwraps the gauze I put on to stem the bleeding and sucks in a breath. "What happened?"

I shake my head, refusing to bring the images back to my head, "She tried to rid herself of the brand."

"This poor girl."

My brows pull down as the doc brings all the supplies he needs from the case. "She didn't deserve this."

He starts to clean it up, putting antiseptic fluid and other ointments onto the wound, wiping gently over the top and around the edges, "She could need a skin graft here." He says.

"Do what you must."

The doc sighs, "Do you think maybe she would be better off without you?"

This is the type of comment that would usually switch me in a matter of seconds but his words hit some deep rooted part of me that knows he is right. This, *this whole entire thing,* is my fault.

"Yeah, doc, I know."

He gets to work, and I leave him to it, positioning myself

in the chair across from the bed, not interrupting him as he fixes up my little bird. When she's wrapped and medicated, he nods his head once and exits, leaving me with my sleeping woman.

There's a pile of medication on the cabinet next to me that I know I'll have to force her to take but right now I can watch her as she sleeps, as medically induced as it is.

At least like this she slightly resembles the woman I lost in the club all those weeks ago.

Her hair, now dry and wild like I remembered fans around her head like a fiery halo, her dark lashes resting on top of her cheeks as she dreams, hopefully something more pleasant than whatever is plaguing her every other time. The sedation will wear off soon but I can appreciate this time now.

She'll hate me when she wakes.

I knew whatever animosity she felt towards me was long gone, I knew I had her but how much damage is this going to do to the already precarious balance we had. Regardless of whether she wanted nothing to do with me, regardless of if she kicked and screamed and fought me, she was mine. I had her. I was never letting her go. I would not lose her again.

At my side is where she belonged. At my side is where she will stay.

FIFTY-FOUR

Lex

I wake to a grumble, a distressed sound, a mixture between sorrow and pain and when I open my eyes the room is in absolute darkness.

"Wren?" I ask.

"Stay the fuck away from me." Her voice is weak and yet her words hold a punch so hard I feel it in my gut. When had I become so weak that a woman could do this to me? I didn't hate it. Not when it was her.

She loved me, I knew she did and despite my belief that I was incapable of feeling the same, I loved her too.

She was mine. Irrevocably mine. There was no escape, no mercy, there was no way I was ever going to let my little bird go.

"That isn't how this works, little bird." I stand from my chair, stretching out the muscles that have been sat in the same position for too long.

"You drugged me!" I hear her climb from the bed, feel the anger radiating from her in waves that meet my own. Rage because she hurt herself. Rage because Valentine hurt her. Rage because this was a war I was losing.

"I did what I had to."

"You have no right!" She screams. I see her silhouette standing at the side of the bed, bathed in the moonlight streaming in through the window and I stand to match her stance.

"I have every right little bird or have you forgotten you belong to me now."

"I belong to no one."

"Do not test me now, little bird."

"Or what, Lex? You'll drug me again!?"

I storm her, finding her body in the darkness as if it is a beacon for my eyes and body. Her sharp intake of breath makes my heart rate spike and so quickly, in a way I know will not do her harm I have her pinned to the wall, her face cupped in my hand. My fingers sink into her flesh, holding her still, tilting her face towards mine as I press my nose against hers with my teeth bared.

"You think you can hurt yourself and get away with it?" I growl, "You think I'm going to sit here and watch you mutilate this body, this body that is *mine!*" My anger courses through me and I slam my free hand against the wall, the thump loud to my ears, "What you do with it is on my authority, how it is treated, worshipped, loved and pleasured is my responsibility."

"Fuck you!"

"You want me to fuck you, little bird, help you remember how it feels to be owned?" My cock twitches and I grind my hips forward, pressing into that sweet, sweet place between her legs. I hold her tightly, no space between us as I push her harder against the wall.

Her breathing becomes erratic, her heartrate pumping so wildly I feel it against my own chest.

"You want that? Did you miss me?" My lips brush across hers, barely a taste and yet fire erupts deep within my soul, "Have you missed my cock, baby? Let me help you remember how it feels for my dick to slide so deep into your fucking pussy that you forget your own name and the only thing you remember is me, the only name you scream, will be mine."

"Lex," her voice is a broken whisper, a mix between a cry and a moan.

"Let me help you forget," my tongue runs down the side of her face, the taste of her salty tears coating my tongue, "let me help you forget, *everything*."

"Yes."

I need no more convincing. I need her as badly as she needs me. I rip her from her clothes, shedding the material until I feel her body under my hands, the soft skin, the dips and curves. I have to be careful not to hurt her, but I can't stop myself. I unfasten my pants, grabbing my cock when it is free to pump my hand up the shaft, rubbing the bead of precum over the crown before smearing it across her lower abdomen. Fuck, I need her heat. I want her pussy convulsing on my dick. I want her to forget it all, Valentine, the club, the pain and torture, I want the only thing she remembers is me, my name, my body, my cock. I grab her, pushing her up the wall until her legs wrap around my hips and her arms loop around my neck. My mouth sucks at her breasts, the wild beat of her heart pulsing against my tongue and I line up to her entrance, sliding in home and finding it wet, welcoming and ready for me.

"I see you did miss me, little bird," I rasp against her throat, pulsing my hips, "I missed you too. I've been crazy without you."

"Lex," she cries, rolling her hips so her clit rubs against me, smearing her arousal over my skin the same way I did hers. My fingers knead her ass, the flesh pliant beneath my grip as I pound into her, her walls clamping and convulsing on my cock.

"Tell me little bird or have you forgotten."

When she doesn't answer I pull us both away from the wall, spinning and dropping us both to the bed, settling myself in the cradle of her thighs, knees to the edge of the mattress.

"Say it!" I growl.

I let one leg – the inured one – drop to the mattress and then force the other up further, holding it at the back of the thigh, opening her up further for me to slam my hips forward. Our hips clash as I penetrate deep.

Wren screams, her back arching from the bed.

Twisted City

RIA WILDE

"Little bird," I coo, "Tell me."

"You," she cries, "I'm yours!"

"Good girl," I drop down to my elbows, nuzzling my nose into her hair as I roll my hips slowly but no less deep, "Such a good girl."

Her nails score my back, drawing blood as I lose myself in her. I'd been without her for too long and I vow, here and now, as my balls tighten and her walls clamp down around me, her orgasm drawing my own from my body, that she'll never leave my side again. I empty myself in her, my teeth biting her flesh, her scream echoing from the walls and then we lay there, in the darkness, in silence.

"I need it gone," she whispers, "This doesn't change anything, Alexander, I want this mark off me, and if you do not help me, I'll do it myself."

My hand strokes up the centre of her chest, through the valley of her breast until my hand caresses her delicate throat, "Do not make threats, little bird, I will help you, but you must first heal."

She swallows against my palm, "I'll kill him." She declares.

"I hope you do little bird, I want to see you bathed in his blood."

She curls into me, wincing a little in pain so I get up and move to the cabinet, grabbing the painkillers and antibiotics the doc left. Surprisingly she takes them with ease and curls up at my side, resting her head on the soft spot between my neck and shoulder. Her breath fans across my chest, her hair draped over my arm while her finger lazily draws circles on my stomach. She sleeps and for the first time in weeks, I do too.

I would complain that the morning is here too quickly however I find no such thing when I wake to Wren kissing her way down my stomach, over the ridges of my abdominal muscles, all the way down until her mouth hovers over my cock.

A grin curves up my lips as her eyes flick to me, a life there I didn't see in her before. Here she looks wild, free, a little mischievous as her tongue slips from between her lips and she licks me from the base all the way to the tip.

When she wraps her mouth around my dick, my hips surge from the bed, seeking the heat of her tongue as she sucks, swallowing me down until I hit the back of her throat. I wondered how long I'd get to keep this version of Wren before the nightmares begin again, how long her mind will remain here rather than in the past, remembering all the things Valentine did to her. I don't think she'll truly be free of her horrors until we see Valentine dead and it's something I'll give her. My gift to the queen of the city. Slowly she draws away from me, dropping to her knees at the edge of the bed and I stand, staring down at her as her small palm wraps around my cock and she retakes me into her mouth.

"That's it, little bird," I praise, slowly pumping my hips to match her pace, tangling my hand into her hair and wrapping the copper strands around my fingers, "such a good girl, on your knees for me."

She hums on my cock, forcing herself down further, enough to make her gag reflex kick in but I don't give her a reprieve, I fist the hair the back of her head tightly, forcing her back down, reveling in the feel of her on my cock. I'll have her every way. Her nails dig into my thighs as I begin to fuck her mouth, her eyes watering, tongue lapping and licking.

"You're going to fucking swallow it," I tell her, teeth gritted and voice nothing more than a primal growl, my orgasm impending and she gives the barest of nods. My grunt, a moan of pleasure as her other hand slides up the inside of my thigh to cup my balls echoes through the room, her hand squeezing almost to the point of pain, and I can't control it. My orgasm whips through me and I spill into her mouth with a roar, coating her tongue, her throat as my cock pulses wildly, my balls emptying themselves into her willing mouth. I withdraw myself and she smirks up at me, one brow raised as she gently wipes her lips with the tips of her fingers.

"On your fucking back," I order.

Never taking her eyes from mine, she lowers herself gently until she's laid completely bare on the carpet.

"Touch yourself."

Her hand slips down her stomach, fingers falling between her thighs as she spreads her pussy and gently caresses her clit, swollen and ready. Her arousal glistens, coating her fingers as she plays.

"Keep your eyes on me," I tell her when her lids threaten to close under the pleasure of what she is doing to herself.

She slips a finger inside, using the heel of her hand to apply friction at the same time, and rolls her hips, the sweet sound of her arousal loud in the otherwise quiet bedroom.

I'm already growing hard again watching her and so I wrap a hand around my cock, pumping it to the same speed she fucks herself with her finger.

"On your fucking knees!" I order, "Now!"

Slowly, she rolls before raising on her knees, spine arched so she's still able to toy with herself and leaving my cock, I drop behind her, pushing her hand away in favor of my tongue. She pushes her ass back, wanting more of my mouth on her pussy so I spread her and punch my tongue into her entrance before licking and sucking at her flesh.

Before she can climax, I pull away, rising up onto my knees and reveling in the view before me, even bruised and a little broken, she's a fucking angel for the devil to feast his eyes upon. Her ass, on show for my eyes, spine curved, body heaving with each labored breath. I run a finger down her ass, through her cheeks, finding her virgin flesh, teasing with the tip of my finger.

She sucks in a breath as I tease it forward, finding resistance. "Lex," she moans.

"It's coming."

I smear some of her arousal up through her cheeks and then line myself up with her entrance, slamming forward as my finger teases and slips in, making her spine arch further, her ass pushing back.

"Yes!" She screams.

I fuck her like this, her body meeting mine thrust for thrust, slamming, and biting and screaming, her cries of ecstasy bouncing off the walls and meeting me, spurring me on to go harder, faster. Skin slaps together, bodies grinding, finding a high I'll never be able to find unless I'm buried inside of her body, hearing her moans, tasting her pleasure.

I hold her hip with my spare hand, my other still at her ass, fucking her virgin flesh with my finger while my cock pounds into her body relentlessly. The carpet burns against my knees, my fingers tightening as she draws out the pleasure.

"Oh, God," she cries, "fuck."

"Not God, little bird," I pull from her ass and lean forward, licking my way up her spine, tasting the salt on her skin, as I continue to roll my hips, pushing into her hard but slow, "But your very own fucking devil."

"Lex," She cries, "Please!"

"For you, little bird, anything," I straighten, tuck one hand around her hips to pinch her clit roughly between my fingers and then fuck her hard and fast, slamming into her again and again. She screams my name over and over as we both tumble over that edge, disappearing into the abyss of our own making.

FIFTY-FIVE
Wren

I feel a wetness slipping down my thigh, a warm, thick liquid that tickles as it rolls over my skin.

"You're bleeding," Lex grumbles, pulling out abruptly. I wince at the loss of him, dropping down onto the carpet, the pain a sudden onset that grips me and has my body alighting in raging flames. It was too much too soon, but even so, even with my nerves lit up like a live wire, I can't find it in me to regret it. Not when Lex consumed me so thoroughly, not when the feel of him pressed against my body, buried so deep inside chased away the darkness and shadows that continued to plague me. When Lex comes back into the room he's dressed in sweats, bare chested, and surprise, he doesn't look happy.

His eyes narrow in on the blood streaming down my thigh but if he thinks I'm going to apologize for what I did, he can forget it. They're all thinking I'm weak, broken, unable to understand what I'm doing but I haven't seen anything as clear as I do now.

Alexander Silver was both my monster and my savior, but he wasn't the villain in my story. Not yet at least, the villain, the evil, the darkness in my story was my own father. I knew this. Did I go about it the right way? No, but I don't regret it. He doesn't get to win. He doesn't get to *own* me in this way. I don't belong to him. *I belong to me.* Lex likes to believe I belong to him and while he has my heart and my body, I am still me.

I will always be me.

Without saying a word, Lex kneels on the floor next to me, unwrapping the bandage from my leg, slowly, as if afraid of what he is going to see on the other side. I wasn't afraid. It was a start of getting my revenge.

He did this to me, but it won't break me.

But I *will* break him.

He's underestimated me.

And that was his second mistake. The first being crossing Alexander in the first place.

My thigh is a mess. The skin raw, open and weeping clear liquid along with the blood, oozing from my flesh like a leaky tap.

"You ever do something like this again," Lex growls, his teeth grinding, the threat left hanging in the air between us.

I roll my eyes, gritting my teeth as he starts to clean up the wound with alcohol. The breath hisses through my teeth as he swipes across the open wound, cleaning away the blood.

"I'm serious Wren," He pins me with a look so icy, my heart stutters.

"I understand."

His eyes narrow but ultimately, he says nothing and continues to clean me up before wrapping the wound in a new gauze and shoving painkillers and antibiotics into my hand.

"Come downstairs," he orders, "Eat with me."

I nod and watch him leave, dragging my naked ass from the floor in search of clothes and brushing my teeth. When I'm dressed in loose fitting pants and a sweater, my hair tied in a knot atop my head, I take the stairs and step into the hall, greeted by a mass of huge bodies, guns strapped to their hips, poised, ready, lethal. They each nod their head at me as I pass them, watching in a way that feels protective, like they're ready to leap in front of a bullet for me. It freaks me the fuck out.

When I turn into the kitchen, I don't find Lex, but I do find Ryker.

"Gruff!"

His eyes widen before settling back down, a small tilt of his lips giving away his pleasure at seeing me. I knew he liked me. The burly fucker.

"Wren," he nods.

"Oh, don't be so serious, Gruff, we're alive."

"Barely," he grumbles.

"Oh, shh," I pout, heading for the coffee machine, "Where's Lex?"

"Dealing with shit."

I cock a brow, "Care to elaborate?"

"Not particularly."

I make my coffee and sit opposite him, cocking my head as I take in the tiredness in his face, the dark shadows beneath his eyes and the downward turn of his mouth. I mean the guy had a face of stone, but this was more.

"What's going on with you?"

"Has your friend always been this difficult?" He blurts.

"My friend?"

"Aurora."

The blood drains from my face, my heart rate plummeting and I have to grip the table to stop myself from falling from the chair.

"Where is she?"

"I'll take this," Lex's deep baritone fills the room like a blast from a speaker.

Gruff's eyes dart from me to Lex before he nods once, plucks his coffee from the table and exits.

"Where is she, Alexander?"

I stand, still using the table for support.

My best friend was here, under the same roof.

"Safe."

"*Where!?*"

"Come, little bird," he beckons me with a curl of his finger, and blindly I follow, crossing the space and watching his body before me, slowly take the stairs and turn at the end of the hall. I forgot how damn big this place was and it feels like several minutes pass before we stop at a door.

"Is she in there?"

"Yes."

"Let me in."

"Wren, she isn't the same girl you remember."

"Alexander. Let me in."

He closes his eyes and unlocks the door, pushing it open and stands back, allowing me room to enter.

The room is darkened by the curtains drawn though not so dark I can't see inside. A bed, some drawers and a couple of doors leading to an en suite and walk in wardrobe. There's a shape on the bed, a curved womanly shape that lifts the white sheets from the mattress, moving steadily with a person breathing deeply.

"Rory?"

The person on the bed goes completely still, any and all movement ceases to the point I worry they have stopped breathing but then a voice cracks the silence, so small, fragile, cracked and hoarse, "Wren?"

"Yeah, Rory, it's me."

"Where have you been?"

I stop at the end of the bed, feeling Alexander's presence behind me but not too close, allowing me some space to speak with my friend.

"I've been sick." I wouldn't tell her exactly, but I'm sure she knew it wasn't an illness.

"Me too," she sighs heavily.

"Are you okay?"

A long silence draws between us, and what I thought would be a happy reunion between two best friends is turning worse with every second that passes between us.

"I don't know." She answers.

"Can I help?"

"I think you put me in this mess, Wren, I was doing okay, ya know?"

The words shatter my heart, "I'm sorry, Rory, I didn't mean for this to happen."

"But it happened, and that's, I'll survive."

"Rory…"

"They raped me, Wren. *Raped* me. Countless times. Over and over. I was choked. Beaten. They chained me up and spread me open so one, two, three men could come in and do whatever the fuck they wanted and then I find out that the man who had me kidnapped in the first place is *your father*. He watched. He watched it happen. And every time he watched he spoke about how this was going to happen to you. How all of this was going to happen to you, and I couldn't bear it Wren. I didn't want this to happen to you, so I tried to tell them we didn't know each other. That we weren't that close but then you went and did that stupid fucking thing and gave yourself up. To what? Protect me? Why!?"

"I'll always protect you, Rory."

"What did they do to you?"

I suck in a ragged breath, "Enough."

"Wren, I'm sorry. If it wasn't for me, maybe you wouldn't be here either."

"Don't!" I growl. "Don't you fucking dare!" My voice goes up a pitch as emotion clings to my every being, threatening to overtake me but I will not allow Marcus Valentine to have any more of me, even if he is not here to see it. "None of this is on you. I will protect you no matter the cost, there is nothing you can do about it."

Lex's hand wraps around my shoulder, a calming presence to settle the rising storm within me. It works, I fear it'll always work. I scoff inwardly, how things have changed. I met a monster only a few weeks ago and yet it is the same monster that settles the demons brewing inside of me.

His breath strokes my neck, warm and scented with smoke and whiskey but not unpleasant, "Easy now, little bird."

"Is this him?" Rory asks.

"Yes."

"This is your fault," she hisses.

Lex stiffens behind me but stays quiet. I know it's for me, but I can't help but feel defensive over him. He is my demon. My devil. His sins are my own. When I whisper to the darkness, it's his voice that answers.

"Rory, there is a lot you do not understand."

"Please leave." She suddenly requests, "I don't want to talk anymore."

"Rory..."

"Please," her voice cracks, "now I know you're alive and

okay, I can sleep."

"Okay," my own emotion clogs my throat, making it rough and raspy, "you sleep, Rory. We'll talk tomorrow."

She doesn't answer me so Lex steers me from the room, guiding me out the door and then closes it softly behind him before locking it.

"You're keeping her prisoner?" I hiss under my breath.

"No little bird, she is a danger to everyone and herself, she needs to be kept here until we can be sure she is safe."

"Why?"

"Because she means something to you, Wren, and what you care for will always be important."

I fall into his chest, trying to stop the tears from falling but failing. I don't want to cry. I don't want to feel anything but this much emotion is too much to stifle. Marcus Valentine doesn't deserve this and yet I do it anyway, crying into Lex's chest like he's my lifeline, the only thing keeping me afloat in turbulent waters.

His hand smooths down my hair, his other arm holding me as close to his body as physically possible.

"Shh now, little bird, you will have your vengeance."

I picture it, I taste it on my tongue. Valentine, *my father,* bleeding out before me, not from a gunshot or an easy wound but a wound that would cause a slow, painful death, I taste the copper tang of blood on my tongue and feel it running over my skin. It's the only thing that stops the tears. Knowing that his days are numbered, and it is only a matter of time before I have him before me.

"Promise me." I say suddenly.

"What little bird?"

"That when the time comes, I get to kill him."

"Wren…"

"Lex, I need to do it. For me. For you. For your mother." I stare up into his silver eyes, seeing the confliction there, the need to protect, "he took so much from me, so much from you and I want to do it for you and *me*."

"We will see."

I don't push him, as much as I want to, this is something that will need to be discussed. I laugh at myself, had I thought this would become of my life only a mere few weeks ago? Planning a murder? Planning vengeance for both me and a man I deemed a devil but became so much more than that between then and now?

He presses the most tender of kisses to my forehead and then steers me towards the stairs, "Let's eat."

I agree and follow him down the stairs, watching all his glory move and ripple, the muscle and the sinew, an unleashed fury buried not so far from the surface.

And he was mine.

FIFTY-SIX

Lex

I watch her from across the table, those dainty hands, her small and yet undefeatable body, the way her eyes have seemed take on a steel coating as if the world could come at her but she would stand atop it all and break everyone who dare try to defeat her.

It's a far cry from the girl Kingston delivered to my arms. A far cry from the girl I thought I would never get back.

All it does is make me harder than a fucking rock inside my pants.

My little bird is not so little anymore. She's a fucking phoenix, rising from the ashes to destroy our enemies. She's a goddess, a formidable presence that when crossed will simply explode to protect what she loves the most.

She wraps her perfect lips around the fork to slide the piece of meat from the tongs into her mouth and flicks her eyes to me, quirking one brow as if to ask me what is going on inside my head.

We needed to discuss things. Things separate to the shit burning our kingdom to the ground around us. Things that simply cannot be ignored.

Did I deserve her dying words?

Of course not.

Was I going to ignore them? That's a big fucking no.

"Little bird," I coo, finishing my dinner and placing my cutlery on the plate before me.

"Twisted king," she smirks.

I laugh, leaning back in my chair as I watch her across the table.

She finishes her plate and then leans back in her chair, cocking her eyebrow, "Something the matter?"

"We need to discuss things."

"What is there to talk about?"

"Back at the club," flashbacks of the fire raging around us, the blood spilling from her body, staining the ground beneath where she lay freezes my tongue. My eyes squeeze shut. Her, right there, a wound that should have been fatal spurting blood from her abdomen, rivers of crimson running over her pale skin, her breath slow and shallow. Her dying and me not being able to save her. Her being ripped from me.

A body before me brings me back to the now and when I open my eyes I see her there, fiery hair, emerald green eyes, holding a fire that only belonged in hell within them but dulled, soft, warm as she stares up at me. "Tell me."

"You said you loved me. Was that true?"

I couldn't help but feel like a little boy at this point. But I had to ask. I needed to know.

She sits back onto her heels and cocks her head, a small, devious smile curving her lips, "Why, Lex, are we feeling a little insecure?"

"Little bird, do not push me."

Her smile only curves higher on her mouth but she does not toy, she leans forward, pressing her delectable mouth to mine, "Yes it was true."

"You love me?"

She sits back but far from relaxed. "Yes. Lex, I love you, though I'm sure it'll leave me as damned as you are."

A grin carves my lips.

"Don't be so smug."

"How can I not?"

"Because I doubt this is a victory."

"It is a victory, my little bird," I drag her to my lap,

positioning her in a way that means she has to straddle my lap and feel how much her words affect me, "for I have won the most prized possession of all."

"What's that?" she breathes, mouth hovering above mine.

"You."

I waste no more seconds, I slam my mouth onto hers, pushing my tongue between her lips, tasting her, claiming her once more. She was mine as much as I was hers.

"I am in love with you too," I admit, "I never thought it possible, but I love you, little bird. All and every part of you."

"Alexander," she breaths, rolling her hips.

My cock grows ever harder.

Shit. The things she does to me should be forbidden.

"And so the monster can love, after all," she presses her mouth to mine, tentative, soft and unsure.

"Who thought it possible," I chuckle, letting my hands roam down her curves to cup her waist. When my hand brushes her wound, she winces, body tensing on mine.

"Are you finished?" I ask.

She nods so I guide her from my lap and towards the stairs, up to the master bedroom and then the bathroom where I begin to draw a bath. I pop a couple of pills from the packet the doc left including the antibiotics and cross to where Wren sits on the bed. She takes them without argument, following them down with some water before I guide her to the bath, helping her strip from her clothes.

The marks on her body cause my heart to speed, a rage so hot and blinding rushing my system. I don't know if I'll be able to give her what she wishes for with Valentine. I have no idea if I'll be able to stop myself when the time comes.

She climbs into the steaming water, eyes squeezed closed as the water washes over the wounds on her body but once the sting settles she relaxes, leaning back and submerging herself more. I sit on the edge of the bath, just watching her, witnessing the stress lines on her face ease, her brow relaxing and her mouth flattening as she fully settles. Her copper hair floats on the surface of the water, and the steady rhythm of her breathing gently ripples the water.

Unable to stop myself, I lean forward, following the curve of her jaw with the tip of my finger. She leans into the touch, lashes fluttering as I move down her throat to her collar bones, her smooth skin so warm beneath the pad of my finger.

"Come in here with me," she whispers.

She keeps her eyes closed as I strip from my clothes and only when I'm ready, she sits up so I can slide in behind her. She leans back against my chest, rolling her head to the side to look up at me.

"Have you heard from Kingston?" she asks.

My nostrils flare, "While we are naked together, little bird, please refrain from muttering another man's name."

She smirks, "That's not the answer I was looking for."

"I see you still cannot hold your tongue." I kiss her forehead, "he'll be arriving in the next few days."

"Do you know what he wants?"

"No, but let's not think about that right now," I push her wild hair away from her face, "let me love you, little bird."

Her eyes go soft as I lean down to kiss her perfectly delectable mouth. I was never going to get enough of this woman.

FIFTY-SEVEN
Wren

I lay in the dark, staring up at the ceiling. A gentle breeze teases the curtains at the window and Lex's soft breathing is a comfort at my side and yet I cannot sleep. Every time I close my eyes I see him, the deranged look in his eyes, the malice and evil rooted so deep the only way to cure it is to put him down.

No one knows where he is. His men have scattered, his usual hide outs left deserted like no one was ever there. How does a man disappear like that?

Part of me wonders if he's already been taken out and while that should bring me a little comfort, it just twists my gut. I still hear the screams of the girls he had down in that prison, the cries and whimpers, the grunts and groans, I fear they'll haunt me forever. I know the girls are now safe but forever changed.

My mind wanders back to Rory, locked away in a room in

this very house.

She may be free of Valentine and the sick fucks he has employed but she's not the same girl.

But then neither was I.

Slowly, I push back the covers and slip soundlessly from the bed, careful not to disturb Alexander. He stirs momentarily and I hold my breath, waiting to see if he'll wake but when he doesn't, I grab one of his shirts and slip it on before creeping to the door and opening it, wincing when it creaks in the otherwise silent house. Looking over my shoulder, Lex still hasn't woken so I slip into the darkened hallway and wait.

I'm not stupid enough to believe we were alone in this house but there was no one immediately in the area so I continue until I'm outside of Rory's bedroom.

The lock on the door is open which causes me to pause, but instead of questioning it, I push on the handle and go inside.

There's a light on, its dim ambience casting a dull orange glow throughout the room. The large bed is centered on the far wall, close to a window and when I look over, it isn't just one shape I see in the bed, but two.

Rory's pale blonde air is fanned out on the pillow behind her, and she is curled on her side, pressing into a much larger body which holds her protectively. I recognize Gruff immediately, his shaggy hair a mess on his head, his thick arms banded around her, so big they make her look more pixie like than anything else and they look…*peaceful.*

What the actual fuck?

"Sneaking away in the middle of the night," Alexander whispers behind me, making me jump. One hand comes down onto my arm to steady me while the other covers my mouth to stop the scream as he gently coaxes me back out the door. "Anyone might think you want to run away from me still, little bird."

He takes his hand away, "No, I just," I frown, looking back at the door which Lex is pulling closed, "What the hell is that?"

Lex pinches the bridge of his nose, "Ryker is helping her."

"By fucking her!?" I hiss under my breath, "fuck, Lex, do you know what she went through!?"

Anger courses through my veins, I wanted to go back in there and rip Gruff out of that bed if only to protect my best friend.

"They're not fucking," Lex growls, "Now, back to bed."

I huff but let him push me back towards the bedroom, confused as all hell. "I don't understand."

"Nightmares."

"Huh?"

"She's suffering with night terrors, Ryker appears to keep

them away."

I puff my cheeks, filling them with air and then blow it out harshly, still not grasping this whole thing. Ryker. Lex's second hand, a man almost as ruthless as Lex, giving comfort to a broken girl…

"Don't think too much about it."

Lex shuts the door and pushes me towards the bed, "Why aren't you sleeping?" he asks.

"I couldn't"

The back of my knees hit the bed and I sit, staring up at him as he advances, body shrouded in shadow and only a slight glow lighting up the harsh edges of his face. He looks both terrifying and delicious all the same.

"Have I ever told you how much I like you in my shirts?" He muses, leaning forward to pluck the top button open, "but not as much as I like it off."

I don't stop him as he flicks all the buttons on the shirt open and I still don't as he pushes the material to the side and gently pushes me back so I'm led flat on the bed with my legs dangling over the sides.

I don't see his eyes taking in every inch of me, but I feel them as they caress me, as thorough as his hands, looking at all of me like I'm a piece of art hanging on a wall. I may have felt that way before but I'm scarred now, wounds and bruises littering my skin.

As if sensing where my thoughts have just gone to, Lex snaps, "Don't you fucking dare."

I swallow.

He drops to his knees so suddenly I don't have time to keep up with his movements and then his mouth is on my stomach, pressing kisses over the almost healed wound in my stomach, right on top of the raised and angry pink skin. He moves over my stomach and chest, kissing each bruise and cut before he moves to my neck, my shoulders, arms and then he's at my legs, pressing butterfly kisses to the inside of the thigh where Valentine branded me.

Arousal heats the space between my legs and my stomach knots, pushing those thoughts from my mind as his mouth drags across my thigh, kissing all the areas where I'm now marked. He doesn't give a fuck.

When his mouth lands on my pussy I gasp, the sound loud in the quiet room. His tongue swipes from bottom to top, the flat edge of his tongue dragging through my folds before stopping at my clit and sucking it into his mouth, the sound obscene and dirty and yet oh so right.

My hands fly to his head, fingers gripping his hair to hold him in place as he flicks his tongue, sending me higher and higher.

The king is on his knees for me.

"Shit," I hiss.

His fingers suddenly thrust inside of me, curling and

already finding that one sweet spot inside me, rubbing it expertly until my thighs are shaking and I'm gasping for air, begging for both mercy and more.

I'm right there when he suddenly pulls away.

"Do you want more?" He asks.

"Yes," I beg, "Please."

"Who do you belong to, little bird?"

"You. Always you. Only you."

"You're such a good girl."

He slides his boxers from his hips and down his legs before dropping down once more to kiss me between the legs and then he's lining himself up to my pussy, sinking in torturously slow.

My eyes roll back in my head as he fills me and continues to do so at a pace that will kill me if he doesn't do something.

When he's fully sheathed, he drops down to his elbows, holding himself there as he rests his forehead against my own. He begins to pump his hips, sliding out before slamming back in still too slow for my liking.

"Fuck me," I growl, "I want you to *fuck me*."

His mouth slams down onto mine, his tongue forcing entry as he continues that slow, torturous pace.

When he pulls away, a wicked grin tugs at his mouth, "say please."

"*Please.*"

"Anything for you," he chuckles darkly.

Pushing up, he stands at the edge of the bed, dragging me further down the bed and forcing my ass up before he slams into me so hard my bones rattle.

"Like this, baby?"

"Yes!"

He slams his hips into me, our skin slapping together, the sound echoing in this quiet space. Perspiration wets my skin and my whole body coils tight, ready to snap at any moment.

"I want it," Lex growls, "I want to feel you come on my cock, now, little bird."

"Lex," I rasp.

He fucks me like I'm his lifeline, like I'm the air that fills his lungs and the blood that pumps through his veins and he continues until he's drawing out a climax so shattering I'll never be put together again. Stars burst behind my eyes and all my muscles cramp and then release, my pussy contracting wildly, ripping a scream from my throat so loud I'm sure the whole house hears it.

"Fuck!" He roars, fucking me harder, more relentlessly before he slams home once more, and then stills, his climax filling me, his cock jerking with his release.

For a few minutes we lay there in the dark, bodies stuck together, breathing hard and fast.

Lex fills the silence, "Don't you ever think you are anything but perfection."

I don't have a chance to respond when he pulls away from me and crosses the room, slamming the bathroom door which has been replaced since he rammed his way through it only a few days ago. I lay there in the dark, feeling him leak onto my thighs and wait for him to return.

FIFTY-EIGHT

Lex

This much rage has no output, no way to be released. There's only one thing I know that will remedy it and he is still yet to be found.

My hands grip the marble counter, my chest heaving with each breath I take, trying to steady the fury I feel sliding through my veins. I can still smell her on my skin, my cock is still wet with her arousal, the sweat beading on my skin and yet fucking her has not released a single ounce of this tension.

And I know why.

It's no longer a game to keep the city, no longer revenge for the murder of my mother but it's something else entirely. It is justice for my woman, it is ensuring she never has to see his face unless it's ripped away from his shoulders.

I splash cold water on my face once I've calmed a little more and then climb into the shower, allowing the heat to release some of the tension coiling my muscles. I hear the door open and Wren enter but I don't turn to her as she climbs into the shower behind me, wrapping her arms around my waist and leaning her cheek to my spine. Her breathing is a balm on my soul, her presence a beacon cutting a path through the darkness.

One hand is flat against my abdominal muscles, the other resting over my left pec, my heartbeat beneath her palm.

I take in a deep breath, dropping my head so the water hits me in the back of the skull.

We stay like that, her curled and plastered to my back while I calm, fingers gently whispering against my skin.

Wren eats her breakfast quietly, seemingly lost in her head as she takes small bites of the toast on the plate in front of her and gently sips her coffee. Dark shadows line her eyes from lack of sleep but overall, she appears to be getting healthier once more, the weight she lost in the time she was with Valentine slowly filling her back out and the glow under her skin becoming more vibrant every day. I'm sifting through emails when Ryker stumbles into the kitchen, still sleep mused and in the same clothes he wore yesterday.

Wren instantly shoots to her feet, crossing the space between them before she's jabbing her finger in his face, "I swear to god, if you touch a single finger on her body, Ryker, I will kill you."

"Excuse me?" Ryker squares his shoulders, on high alert. He won't touch Wren but it raises my hackles nonetheless.

"Rory."

Ryker's head snaps back, offended, "What the fuck is your problem!?" He growls.

"Watch it." I snap.

"No," Ryker hisses, "why the fuck would you even fucking say shit like that? I'm not your fucking father, Wren."

I stand from the table abruptly, stepping up to Wren as she takes a step back, her hands clenching at her sides, "Enough!"

"Then why the fuck are you sleeping with her?" Wren growls.

"Because she's fucking scarred," Ryker furiously taps at his temple, "She's broken. Won't sleep. Won't eat, won't even fucking shower and for whatever *fucked* up reason, the only way I can get her to calm is if I fucking hold her!"

I had told Wren this though I couldn't blame her for not believing me, but she didn't know Ryker like I did. There were lines we wouldn't cross, even for us, the Silver family have never used or extorted women, let alone human beings for profit, it wasn't something that interested us. The skin trade was a seedy, dirty place to be and there were better ways to make money.

Valentine however wasn't just trading, he was *in* it. Allowing his men in on the business, letting those girls be beaten, tortured and raped before he sold them off like livestock, something that would have happened to Wren had Kingston not been the one to 'buy' her in return for protection.

The reminder turns the breakfast I ate sour. I fucking owed him.

I hated debt.

Fucking hated it.

It was worth Wren's life and I'll pay, even if I loathed the idea.

"I need to see her, maybe I'll be able to get through to her," Wren murmurs, leaning back on me further, Ryker's words sinking under her skin.

"I'm not sure that's a good idea, Wren," Ryker softens, reaching out to touch Wren's arm.

She stiffens but doesn't pull away and he drops his arm, flicking his eyes to me.

When was it that women became more important than anything else in this business?

Twisted City

RIA WILDE

Before, I would have done everything to see this city thrive, burn everything to the ground to ensure the Silver name stayed on top but now, I'd level the entire thing to the ground if it meant keeping my little bird safe.

Fuck.

"I've known her since we were teenagers, we've been through some shit, I can help."

With a sigh, Ryker shrugs and looks to me for approval. With a nod, I let Wren go, watching her as she quickly marches from the room and around the corner.

"Aurora isn't the same person."

"I know but Wren needs to understand that herself."

"There's nothing in the room she can hurt her with," Ryker huffs, dropping into the seat Wren vacated, "I've had word that Kingston has landed."

I pinch the bridge of my nose, "We need this shit sorted, the sooner the better. I have rats to kill."

"You not think it odd that Valentine is untraceable? Even when he was hiding, there was still a trace, now there is nothing. Not even his men have been spotted, it's like they never existed."

"The fucker is a coward, gone completely underground since he pissed off both us and the Hearts. If he knows what's good for him, he'll turn his gun on himself."

Ryker scoffs, "that won't happen."

"No," I sigh, "this city is going to shit."

"We'll get it back," Ryker taps his knuckles on the table, "best go make arrangements for the King of England."

My laughter is a quick huff of breath through my nostrils and a shake of my head.

I watch him leave and then I'm left with my thoughts, my mind whirling back to the safe house.

It would be wise to ship both Wren and Rory over there, give them twenty-four seven protection, security, weapons, and everything they could ever need to ride out this storm. I'd lose my fucking mind if something were to happen to Wren again and with Valentine still at large and the Syndicate breathing down my neck, I can't help but feel like it's inevitably going to happen, only this time round would she survive?

Beyond this shit, I have plans.

Plans for her and me, plans that involve continuing this line of Silver's, plans to have her with my ring on her finger, my surname gracing her name, and her swollen and pregnant with my child.

I want it all.

And for the first time I don't think I'm going to get it.

FIFTY-NINE
Wren

    I don't knock as I turn the key and open the door. Darkness greets me on the other side and a noise akin to a child weeping, not a tantrum or a wail, but a soft, sorrow filled cry, one that seeps into your skin and buries itself into your soul. It's a cry of pain, pure, unadulterated pain and with each sob and intake of breath I feel that pain burrowing its way into my marrow.

"Aurora?" I whisper to the darkness.

With the curtains drawn all the way and all the lights off I can barely see into the room, but I can just about make out the outline of her body beneath the blankets on the bed.

The sobs stop when she hears my voice and she rolls onto her back, inhaling sharply.

"Why are you here?"

"I want to help, Rory, please let me help."

"There's nothing you can do, Wren."

"They hurt me too," I say to her, "and I would do it again, take it all again if it meant protecting you."

"But it didn't protect me, did it?" She snaps, sitting up abruptly, "Because before I even knew you were there, they had already done everything you'd never even dream of happening to you. They'd already taken *everything*. They ripped me apart."

"I'm sorry."

"Why?" She asks.

"Why am I sorry?"

"Yes, why are you sorry, Wren?"

"Because this never should have happened."

"Did you do it?" She asks. "Did you strap me down and hurt me Wren? Did you tell them to take me? Did you tell them to take turns?"

"No, Rory."

"Then why are you sorry, everyone keeps saying they're sorry. Sorry it happened. Sorry no one came sooner, but ultimately, what does an apology fix?"

I stay silent as she sits there in the middle of the bed, her body barely visible in the shadows of the bedroom but her breathing is heavy and filled with so much grief.

Ryker was right. She was broken and I didn't know how to help. I wanted to help. I wanted to fix it.

I would never be able to take it away but I wanted to get revenge, I wanted to get her through this.

"I came from nothing," she continues, "I had nothing, but I was starting to get something. I moved away from the only place I knew as home, to get away from the trouble I knew would follow me if I didn't. I was going to be a teacher, Wren. A teacher but how can I ever do any of that now?"

"You still can, Rory, this does not define you." I cross the room and pause before her, "can I sit?"

She sighs, "Sure."

"Ryker," I say, "He's helping you?"

She shrugs, "Some."

"What else can we do? Whatever it is, I'll do it, Rory."

She needed a therapist, a doctor, she needed help and I couldn't give her everything, but I would do as much as I possibly could.

She deserved the life she was fighting so damn hard for, she deserved everything she had worked to get and this, I needed to believe this was only going to be a set back, a huge one, one that will stay with her forever, but I knew she could be what she wanted to be.

I knew it. She just needed to believe it. It wasn't that easy, I knew that, I was suffering with my own troubles that would no doubt stay with me forever, like this will her, but there has to be a way I can help her.

I climb onto the bed, shimmying my way towards her before I pull her into a huge hug, so fierce I hope she feels it right down to her soul.

"It's going to take time," I tell her, not letting go, "It'll take time, but I know, *I fucking know* you. I know you can do this. I know you hate me right now. I know this is my fault, I know I dragged you into this but I'm going to be here, I am going to help you and give you everything you need. Whatever it is you want, you need, you ask for, I'm going to give it to you."

"Wren," she cries, turning her face into my shoulder.

"I know, Rory. There's so much darkness in this world, but you already knew that, look where you came from and look at what you have achieved."

"I hate this feeling."

"What feeling?"

"It isn't even about what happened," Rory says, "I can deal with that. I can move on from that, over time, you know?" She pauses, "It's the idea, the fear, that it'll happen again."

"It won't happen again," I growl fiercely.

"You can't know that, and I'd rather be dead than do it again."

My heart stutters in my chest, an overwhelming panic settling into my skin, "Don't say that."

"I mean it."

Rory finally falls asleep, her head resting on my stomach as I smoothed her hair, and gently I move her from my body, positioning her head on the pillows before I climb off, leaving her curled on the bed. She appears to be sleeping soundly but I'll be back in the next thirty minutes to check on her again.

I will stay by her side every minute of every day if that's what it takes. My father will not take anything else from me.

I gently close the door but don't feel the need to lock it. She shouldn't be locked away, she needs freedom, normality, there is no need to take her from one cage and place her in another, no matter how gilded it is.

I take the stairs slowly, pressing my fingers into the centre of my forehead, trying to ease the tension I feel building there.

I'm not paying any attention when I hit the ground floor and head to the kitchen which is why the voice that greets me catches me off guard.

So off guard I'm sure my heart stops beating inside my chest.

"Hello Wren."

The English accent has goose bumps crawling over my skin, the very same voice that spoke to me as I bled out in his arms. The very one that I was sure was going to be the continuation of my suffering and yet turned out to be the very opposite.

My eyes clash with Kingston's, the icy blue a cold that appears too warm, a contrast and contradiction given the circumstances.

"You."

I knew he was coming. I knew he would be back and yet seeing him here, in the flesh is something else entirely.

My memory serves me well in remembering him, even with all the shit that has fallen between us, the tattoos, the casual and yet dangerous demeanor he wears around him as if it were a cloak.

His fingers turn a crystal tumbler of amber liquid on the table, and he leans casually back in the chair, spreading his knees as he looks at me with a smirk.

"I expected a better reception for the man who saved you."

Lex growls beside him, slamming his glass down so hard on the table the crystal cracks, allowing a steady flow of golden liquid to seep from the splices.

"Now, now, Silver," Kingston chuckles, "your woman does not interest me."

"Well, you did try to fucking buy her."

"Have we not gone over this?" Kingston sighs, "It was for you, I needed an in and she was it. Valentine is just a fucking idiot. Who sells their own fucking daughter?"

A pair of heels clicking on hardwood draws my attention from the man sat at the table. Isobel saunters in, holding a flute of champagne, her jet black hair dead straight and hanging around her face. Pale skin and blood red lips are the first things I notice and then it's the blue of her eyes, so similar to Kingston's.

"Oh!" She beams at me, "look at you!"

She heads right for me and before she can even reach me there is a flurry of activity, bodies jumping up, intercepting hers from mine and then there's Lex, forcing himself in front of me, holding me to his back with one arm while his other pulls at the Glock he has concealed.

Kingston, all the while just leans back in his chair and tucks his hands behind his head, grinning. As if this is the funniest thing to happen to him in a while.

"Well," he comments, "A little touchy aren't we, my sister here is just very fond of Wren."

"Your sister needs to back the fuck up!" Ryker threatens, I

hadn't noticed him come up on my other side, teeth bared.

"It's okay," I say, "I trust her."

And it was true.

I didn't believe she would hurt me, there was something about her, something seriously unhinged, something *dark* but I truly believed that darkness stemmed to something else entirely.

Lex looks to me, I see the confliction, but I also know he wants to give me my own say, my own rule and when I plead him with my eyes, beg him in a way that will only ever be between the two of us he sighs heavily and stands taller, straightening himself and forcing himself to relax a little though he doesn't put the gun away.

"At ease," he orders.

The men around me straighten, tucking their weapons away, all but Ryker and Lex. They sit, though they keep their weapons in view at all times. Isobel cocks a brow, looking at each and every one individually before she huffs and shrugs her shoulder, continuing towards me. Her hands cup my face the moment she is within touching distance, and she stares at me intently, eyes bouncing between mine, "So much fire."

"Hello."

She grins, her teeth a stark contrast to the red staining her lip.

"I am so happy to see you well, Wren."

My brows draw down, there was something about this woman, something that didn't scream *off,* but unusual. It didn't feel unsafe, but I was also starting to understand that people in this life, they wear many faces.

"Heart," Lex barks, "tell me why you are here."

I cock my head, it appears I arrived right at the nick of time. I wanted to know exactly what it was that Kingston desired.

SIXTY

Lex

I didn't fucking like this at all.

Heart grins, eyes on his sister and Wren but then slowly moving them to me. "The Syndicate."

My teeth clamp tightly together, the muscle in my jaw aching, "What about them?"

"Well, it appears you have some information on them, I want it."

I scoff, "I have fuck all."

"That's not true, now is it?" Heart licks his teeth, his glass of whiskey dangling between his fingers before he throws the liquid down his throat and pulls out a cigarette, placing it between his lips where it just dangles there.

My mind whirls back to Ainsley. I have no fucking idea if she is even still alive, I haven't heard from her in weeks.

She has or at least *had* the information but where it is, I had no fucking idea.

"You're referring to Ainsley," I lean back in my chair.

"I am," he confirms, "she got into the Syndicates servers just before we managed to breach it, downloaded everything. The breach alerted them, and they locked it down before we could get anything, but I know your girl got that info. I want it."

"Why?"

"Let's just say the Syndicate have a lot to pay for," he growls, eyes flicking to his sister who still appears to be infatuated with Wren, cooing and touching her hair. Wren looks at ease with the attention if not a little confused, but Isobel wasn't a threat to her, probably to me and the other men in this room but not Wren.

It wasn't a secret her distaste for men in general though no one knew why exactly.

"Well, Ainsley is not around at the moment," I tell Heart, "Though, should she come through with the information, I'll have a copy sent to you."

"That's not really going to work for me, Alexander," Heart says, lighting the cigarette between his lips.

My eyes narrow, "And what'll happen if I can't provide it?"

His eyes flick to Wren and before anyone can even move

or even so much as blink, I have my gun at his temple with the safety off. "I wouldn't even let the thought cross your mind, Heart."

"A deal is a deal, Lex," he turns, not an ounce of fear in his eyes as he stares at me, "I did you a favor, you owe me, if you cannot pay up, do you not think it fair I take back what I gave you?"

I hear his men levelling their guns at me, at Ryker but not at Wren, my own men preparing for a fight that cannot happen.

"You shoot me, Lex, I get her anyway, my men will snatch her right from your grasp and ship her off to somewhere you'll *never* find, even if I'm dead."

"I thought you weren't interested."

"Can we all stop talking like I'm not in the room!?" Wren snaps, stepping away from Isobel to come closer to me.

"Stay where you are!" I order.

"Fuck you, Lex, Kingston, you're asking for something we don't have."

"Then get it," he snaps, "I don't care how you fucking do it, I want that information!"

Isobel sighs heavily and dramatically, throwing herself into a vacant chair at the table. She snatches the bottle of whiskey from the table and unscrews the cap, sipping directly from the bottle.

"You boys want to get your dicks out?" She smiles manically, licking the whiskey from her lips, "Someone grab me a ruler, we can settle this."

Wren pinches the bridge of her nose before she curls her delicate hand around my forearm and begins to push down, trying to get me to stand down.

"This won't do anything but start a war, Lex," she whispers.

She was right. Reluctantly, I drop my weapon and haul her to me, tucking her against my chest.

"Bloody hell," Isobel huffs, "Do you wanna piss on her too? Make sure everyone knows that she is yours? Kingston, stop being a fucking arse, we didn't come here to fight."

King grunts and waves a hand, his guys following his silent order to stand down.

"Look mate, we're not going to take your girl, regardless, the skin trade is not something I'm interested in. I need the information on the Syndicate, Ainsley has it."

"When she turns back up, I can give it to you."

"Ainsley will come through," Ryker pipes up.

"She fucking better," Heart growls, "until she does I think I might stick around a while. Brookeshill is quite delightful." His words are dripping in sarcasm, tongue laced in venom. He was a fucking piece of work.

"Little bird," I lean down and whisper to Wren, "Go upstairs, wait for me there."

Her head snaps back. "I don't think so."

Isobel laughs.

"Don't push me, Wren, please, I'll be happier if you were away from this fucking mess."

She wants to fight me, I know she does but ultimately she backs down even if she is far from happy about it.

"Why don't you show me around?" Isobel suggests, standing from the table.

"Leave the bottle," Kingston demands.

Isobel flips him off as she saunters from the room, holding the bottle with Wren trudging behind her, grumbling under her breath.

When the girls are gone, I sit across the table from Kingston, "I haven't heard from Ainsley in weeks."

"She's alive." Is all King says.

"And you know this how?" I ask.

"Your girl is good," he says, "but not that good, we tracked her down in Chicago a few days ago, I have men watching her."

"So why not get the information yourself?" I snap. It was a bluff, I needed that information as much as he did.

"You think she'll just hand it over?"

That was true.

"I mean I can force it if you wish but I don't make it a habit to hurt women."

"Don't you fucking touch her!" Ryker roars.

I slap my hand on his chest, a warning to shut the fuck up. Kingston smirks.

"I've got no problem with you Silver, in fact," Heart leans forward, placing his elbows on the table, "I respect the fuck out of you and your family. It's not often one family can keep reign over a city for the amount of time you have but unfortunately, our two families have now become linked, you have what I need so I gave you what you wanted."

"Wren."

"Women, ay?" He laughs, "weak spots."

I scoff my laughter.

"I'll give you what you need, Heart but I can't do so until Ainsley pulls through."

"I won't be going anywhere." Heart pulls his phone from his pocket, "I'll get someone to pass a message to your girl, anything you want me to say?"

That damn smirk on his face was fucking infuriating, second to the fact that he had connections I didn't know about and means to do it in my fucking city.

"Yeah," I stand, "tell her to get the fuck home, she's needed."

A sudden scream follows my sentence, "Get the fuck down!" Is all I hear before a loud boom shakes the house.

SIXTY-ONE
Wren

"This place is gaudy," Isobel comments, swiping a single red fingernail over the frame of a painting hanging on the wall before her eyes drop to the fur rug lining the corridor.

She wasn't necessarily wrong. I don't answer her and have no intentions of showing her around either, I feel like the only reason she offered was to get away from the tension and testosterone saturating the air in the kitchen. I couldn't blame her but I was fucking pissed at Lex.

He forced me into this life, into his world of bloodshed, violence and danger and yet the first sign of trouble he's ushering me out of the room like I'm a precious doll.

I'm not precious and I'm not a doll. I may have been innocent before but that girl no longer exists. If he wanted me at his side then he had to have me there a hundred percent.

Twisted City

RIA WILDE

I wouldn't be a delicate woman on his arm or a piece of ass people can look at, I'll be just as fierce as he, maybe not as ruthless but I'd have people whispering my name and turning to watch me like he has.

"Hey, what's that?" Isobel draws me from my musings, and I turn to look at where she's peering out the window, looking down the long drive to where the gates are.

I thought it pretty self-explanatory, I mean they're only gates so I cross the hall and look out the window, "That's just –" oh fuck.

A car is barreling down the drive, the gravel kicking up behind the tires. They weren't slowing down and instead of following the drive around they continue over the lawn, cutting huge trenches into the garden, heading right for the kitchen.

Shit.

I grab Isobel's arm and push her towards one of the back rooms before I sprint back towards the kitchen, not caring where she lands or if I hurt her.

"Get the fuck down!" I scream just as the car smashes through a wall in the house.

I dive to the left, my body smashing against the table, my head colliding with the wall as I slump to the floor. The impact isn't too far from me, and I can see the headlights of the car, lights shining through the dust raining all around me.

Twisted City — RIA WILDE

My ears ringing, I vaguely hear doors slamming and then feet on the ground but it isn't that, that pulls me from the fog in my head trying to drag me down, it's the sound of a scream so filled with terror is turns my blood cold.

Rory.

I had no idea what the fuck was going on, but I could guess who had orchestrated this and there was no fucking way I was going back to my father.

I shakily climb to my feet, covering my nose and mouth in the crook of my elbow and duck around the corner, watching two guys step through the rubble, weapons drawn. They don't even try to come this way, instead head right for the kitchen where Lex and the rest of the guys are.

Idiots.

Rory continues to scream but I know I can't go to her yet, instead I follow behind the two attackers, quietly approaching and staying out of sight as they prepare to enter the kitchen.

Gun shots start ringing, loud bangs that make my head pulse and ears ring even more and a flurry of movement keeps me pinned to the wall, trying to be as silent and still as possible for fear of a gun being turned on me. I've been shot once, it wasn't fun.

One guy goes down while the other continues to shoot wildly into the room, shots being fired back but the only thought flowing through my head was that this guy couldn't die.

He was employed by Valentine.

And I need Valentine.

With the loud pops of the gunfire I'm able to creep up on the guy undetected, lifting a large China vase from the ground I raise it above my head as high as I can and smash it down with all the force my body can muster, slamming it around the back of his head hard enough for the vase to shatter into a million pieces, scattering amongst the rubble and stone littering the floor from the destroyed wall.

The guy hits the deck hard and then the gun fire ceases and all eyes turn to me.

Kingston is the first to snap out of it, storming to where the guy lays in the dust, a steady stream of blood seeping from the gash in the back of his head. He's still breathing at least.

Kingston has every intention of shooting the guy and making that breathing stop.

"No!" I scream, jumping forward, "You can't fucking kill him!"

"Why the fuck not!" Kingston bellows.

"Because we need him to find Valentine!"

"Get him in the fucking barn!" Lex orders, rushing towards me to check me over. A few scrapes and bruises but I'll live. Isobel limps towards us, not because she's injured but because she appears to be missing a shoe but other than that she doesn't have a single hair out of place.

What the actual fuck!?

With all the chaos now over, the screaming from upstairs travels through the halls, reminding me that I needed to get to Rory.

I rush to the stairs but two arms band around my waist, hauling me back. Lex's breathing is heavy and hard in my ear, fanning my hair until it tickles against my skin and then Ryker pushes past, taking the stairs two at a time.

"Let him deal with this!" Lex growls.

"Get the fuck off me Lex." I snap. "Stop fucking telling me what to do!"

His hand comes around my throat, holding me further back on him, his fingers squeezing my windpipe, "Little bird," he rasps, "Let's not play fucking games."

"I'm not fucking playing," its hard to speak with his hand on my throat and even despite the current situation, being in this position with him, his dominance and need to control leaves a heat in its wake, one that reminds me every fucking day how fucked I am for this man.

But Rory needs me, and I can revisit this shit later.

I slam an elbow back into his stomach, shocking him enough for him to let me go and before he can grab me again, I dart to the stairs, too quick for him to catch me. I climb the stairs to his curses, joined by a chorus of laughter from Kingston and his sister.

"Shit, Silver, you got yourself a wild one," Kingston's voice becomes distant the higher in the house I get.

"No! I can't go back!" I hear as I round the corner on the hall, my feet slipping on the hardwood. "I can't go back."

"Put the gun down, Rory, you're not going back."

My heart sinks.

On shaky legs I make it to the door and tug at the handle, pulling and pulling but the thing doesn't fucking open.

"Open the door!" I scream.

Lex is at the end of the hall, storming towards me, his face a mask of pure rage but I don't give a fuck about that, he can be angry later.

"I can't," she sobs. "I can't go back, you don't understand."

"Will you shoot me?" Ryker asks.

My heart sinks further.

"Put the gun down."

"You're going to send me back."

"Rory!" Ryker shouts.

"I'm not going back!"

"No!" Ryker booms.

Rory's scream is followed by a gun shot.

Both Lex and I freeze, the air being sucked from my lungs.

The thud of a body hitting the floor makes me jump.

She shot him.

She shot Ryker.

SIXTY-TWO
Lex

Wren begins to pound on the door, throwing her whole body weight against the wood but the thing doesn't budge.

"Rory!" she screams, "open the fucking door."

Shock and anger course through my system, "Move." I order.

She does as she is told, moving to the left as I position myself in front of the door and kick it, once, twice, hearing the wood crack and splinter under the force, on the third kick the thing swings open. I don't enter straight away, I push Wren behind my body and withdraw my gun, entering with it leveled ahead of me and ready to be used.

She fucking shot Ryker.

The smell of blood, metallic and coppery permeates the air

of the room and I find Ryker on his knees, leaning forward with blood pooling in front of him.

Only when I step further in, it isn't his blood staining the carpet, but Aurora's.

She lays in the middle of the floor, a hole in her temple where she turned the gun on herself.

"I couldn't stop her."

A scream lashes through the room, as sharp as a whip, "no, no, no," Wren sobs, dropping down beside her friend, knees hitting the puddle of crimson seeping out the side of Aurora's head, "Call an ambulance!"

"Little bird," I try. There was no coming back from this.

"Call a fucking ambulance!"

"She's dead, Wren." Ryker says.

"No!" Wren manically shakes her head, pressing her hands to the wound as if that'll somehow bring her back. "She's not, she can't be."

Sobs make her voice quake and she sucks in air, trying to fill her lungs as grief robs her of oxygen. Her face is crumpled, eyes wide and pleading, tears streaking down her cheeks.

Closing my eyes, I sigh.

"Little bird," I soothe, stepping behind her to rest my hand on her shoulder, smoothing her sweat dampened hair away from her forehead.

She collapses back against my legs, blood coating her hands and arms and legs and she screams. Her cry hits me straight to the soul, earth shattering and grief stricken in a way I have never and will never want to experience.

Her pure, unfiltered emotion feels as if it'll shatter windows, her cries no doubt heard throughout the house. No one comes though, not Kingston, not Isobel, knowing when to interfere and when not to.

Carefully, I drag Wren from the floor, holding her to me as she buries her face into my chest and continues to cry. Bloody handprints stain my shirt, dirt and ash mixing with the crimson. She lets me guide her from the room and I signal for Ryker to get some men in here to clean this up before I shut us away in our bedroom.

She doesn't make it to the bed, instead choosing to sit in the middle of the carpet, bringing her knees to her chest as if to contain everything inside of her. She wraps her arms around her legs, holding on tight as she rocks, staring vacantly at a spot on the wall.

"Let's get this blood off you," I say to her, "Okay?"

She nods once, mute and follows me to the bathroom, stripping from her blood drenched clothes which land with a wet slap onto the tiles and then she steps into shower before the water has even warmed. The water sliding from her skin is tinged red, circling at her feet before it drains down the plug, but she continues to stare at the wall, arms limp at her sides, letting the water hit her.

I don't undress as I climb in with her, turning the temperature up a bit further to try and rid her of the goose bumps that have taken purchase on her skin. I help wash the blood from her skin, my clothes sticking to my body but she doesn't appear to be here, stuck inside her head.

When she's cleaned, I guide her out, wrap her in a towel and sit her on the bed. I'll do everything if I need to.

"He did this." She says as I come back from the wardrobe with a fresh pair of leggings and one of my shirts.

"Valentine," she affirms, eyes finally meeting mine. "This is his fault."

I nod.

"Where is the guy?" She asks. "The one from earlier."

"In the barn."

I wait for the wince, the grimace, but it never comes.

"I want to come."

"Wren–"

"No!" She snaps, cutting me off. "I let you push me out that room earlier. I let you do that but you want me here, you have to let me in. I'm not going to fucking sit in this little cage you've built for me, I'm in or I am not."

"It's not that simple." I growl.

"Then make it that simple!"

She sighs, stepping up to me, her eyes clouded and misty, tears still making her eyes watery, "I fell in love with you. You. Despite the shit you do and the blood on your hands. You fucking kidnapped me and yet I still fucking love you. How fucked up is that!" she laughs, "You're a twisted, ruthless motherfucker, Alexander and I'm still fucking here."

I swallow.

"Let me fucking in. Teach me."

This was a bad fucking idea.

"Wren," I try once more.

"Alexander."

She wasn't budging. There was no movement, no negotiation. Anyone else, there wouldn't even be the time of day, her, I'll give her everything. What was it Kingston said? Weak spots. Like showing a predator your jugular.

There was no doubt she was that one spot that'll kill me before anything else and everyone knows it.

How can I protect her if she's there with me? My enemies would use her to hurt me, would take her and ruin her and break her just to get to me.

"I can't be a pawn anymore," she says so quietly, "I can't do nothing anymore."

I drop my head, "Fine."

There's no celebration, no eager thanks because she may as well have signed our death certificates.

"After tonight, we're moving," I tell her, handing her the clothes.

She puts them on.

"Where?"

"I take it you're opposed to moving to a safe house?" I try.

She glares at me.

"The penthouse in the city."

"Okay."

When she is dressed, she pulls her wet hair into a ponytail, her hands shaking but she's pushed all that grief behind a mask of determination. She wants Valentine's destruction and she'll do anything to get it.

"You don't have to do this," I tell her, sliding my hand into hers.

"Yes, I do."

She doesn't look at me, but her hand holds mine in a tight grip, palm sweaty and a tremble in her fingers. She's afraid.

I squeeze her hand and force us to stop in the hall, pinning her suddenly to a wall. Caged between my arms, she stares up at me, my sweet little bird with glassy green eyes and a somber look on her face.

I feather my fingers down her face, unable to get enough of her. Her eyes flutter closed beneath the touch, lashes flickering against the apples of her cheeks and she leans in to my hand.

"I will always protect you," I tell her, "You will always be first."

"Your city comes first," she breathes, pressing a kiss to my palm.

"Not anymore, little bird."

Her eyes open and she stares up at my face, checking for deceit in my words but she'll find none. I never thought it possible. Weakened by a woman, brought to my knees by a single female who started out as a means to an end but became my queen instead.

"I love you," I whisper against her mouth.

She melts into me, fusing her lips to mine.

When the kiss turns heated and my cock grows hard, pushing against her lower belly I pull away. There could be no distractions with what is to come tonight. I needed to have my head in the game, I needed to protect Wren and get what we both needed to end this once and for all.

Her teeth drag against my lower lip, and she spears me with a glare, "let's go."

"After you, little bird."

SIXTY-THREE
Wren

The first thing that hits me is the smell.

Blood, sweat and piss all mingle together to create a stench so heady it makes me gag. I wretch, my stomach cramping and my throat constricting.

"You don't have to do this," Lex calmly states again, placing his hand on my spine to soothe me.

But I did have to do this, for if I am to stand by his side I need to be just as formidable and ruthless, someone not to be fucked with no matter how delicate I may look.

I inhale through my mouth rather than my nose, pushing down the need to vomit and straighten. My chin tilts up and I steel my spine.

This is for Rory. For me. For Lex's mother. For all the

women Valentine has hurt and tortured.

I drag my eyes across the dusty floor of the barn, noticing the dark spots that are forever stained into the ground. Blood. This is what this city lives on, thrives on it. Blood and pain and corruption.

And I am now sitting beside the king of chaos himself.

The man I had hit over the head earlier dangles from a hook suspended from a beam in the ceiling of the barn, arms chained with steel above his head. He's been stripped to his boxers and blood covers every available inch of his body, there's barely any skin showing through the crimson paint covering him. His head hangs, chin to chest and his eyes are closed though his chest moves with each labored breath that wheezes through his lungs.

Ryker stands to the side, a hammer of some sort dangling from his hand and blood splatters over his face and arms, staining his white shirt. His eyes are dead. Void of any emotion and it's the first time I realize he's just as formidable as the man next to me.

He doesn't seem as ruthless but with the almost satisfied and content look he holds on his face, he appears to be enjoying the torture.

His eyes meet mine and he nods his head.

"Well, well, well," Lex steps away from me, "What do we have here?" The voice, the demeanor, it's like nothing I have ever experienced with him. He holds himself differently, his voice not even slightly resembling the one I heard back in the hall as he declared his love for me. "A Valentine rat."

The guy in chains startles, the steel links clanging together loudly, echoing through the barn and spooking a couple of rats that had been hiding behind some cabinets on the back wall. They scurry out, darting from their safe shadows for safer spots outside.

I had always wondered what this barn looked like. Worn and depleted from the outside and that was exactly how it was on the inside. Bare walls, dirty floor and a few rusty and old tables scattered around the space, holding a variety of weapons, from daggers to hacksaws. There's a couple of chairs laying about but not enough to hold a party.

"Kill me and get it over with." The guys spits.

"Oh no," Lex wags his finger, "When is it ever that easy?"

The guy curls his lip, eyes bouncing between him and Ryker before his evil gaze lands on me.

His bloodshot eyes do a once over on my body and then another only slower, following each line and curve of my body until he reaches my face and curls back his lip, "such a shame Valentine wouldn't let us have a taste of your pretty little cunt."

I stifle the need to recoil. I am not afraid of him.

His head snaps back so suddenly and so hard I'm amazed his neck doesn't break but he drapes forward, blood dribbling from his mouth as he laughs, "May as well let her go now, Silver, she won't be yours forever."

Another hit.

The guy laughs.

"I imagined what it would be like," he heaves, "to taste that pretty little pussy."

He was taunting Lex, forcing his hand, making him lose his cool enough for him to snap and kill the guy. It was what he wanted, and he was getting exactly that. With each word uttered against me, Lex's patience and anger was waning thin.

"I wanted to know if she would scream or lay there silently, accepting her fate. Tell me, Silver, is her pussy tight like I imagined? Does it feel like heaven when you sink into her body? Does she scream?"

Lex tenses beside me but I quickly grasp his arm before he strikes.

"I watched her, bloody and broken and beaten," the guy taunts, "I imagined what it would be like to sink inside that sweet body as I pressed on her windpipe. I could picture the way her eyes bulged and she fought me as I choked her to death and fucked her like the simple little fucking woman she is."

Lex's muscles are so rigid and coiled, it's only a matter of time before he snaps again.

I pretend to be horrified at the words and while they *are*

repulsive, I find them not nearly as terrifying as they should be. He didn't do it because he is simply a dog. Following orders. Always following orders. He wants Lex to kill him, so he doesn't talk and using me is the quickest way to get there.

Feigning terror, I bury myself into Lex's neck which instinctively has his arm coming around me in a protective embrace, trying to shield me from the darkness.

Doesn't he know he introduced me to it. He whispered in my ear and called me forth. And I answered. I was always going to answer.

"He is baiting you," I whisper so faintly I worry he may not hear.

When his fingers dig into my flesh, I know he heard my message.

The guy continues anyway and risking a glance over my shoulder I see his eyes perusing my body like I'm a prime cut of meat waiting to be eaten.

"Fuck," he smirks, "let me have a taste before I die," he says, "Just show me that cunt, dripping. Make it wet for me, let me imagine what she might taste like."

"You want to see her wet?" Lex asks, finally understanding. A calm wave washes over his face, relaxing his features and schooling his expression. Gone is the rage, the fire burning in his eyes, replaced by blissful indifference.

My eyes squeeze shut. I hated this. It made me sick, but I knew it had to be done.

"Yes."

Lex feathers his fingers down my side before releasing me, ushering me back as he advances on the guy hanging from the ceiling.

"That, unfortunately, is not on the table," Lex says, "You been in this game long?"

"A while."

"Then you should know that *my wife* is a no go for scum like you."

"Your wife?" the guy scoffs. "You married the tramp?"

"Mm-hmm," Lex nods, lying but I would be a fool if I didn't like being called his wife. "So, let's strike a deal, shall we? You tell me what I want to know and I'll make it quick."

"Fuck you."

"Where is Valentine!?"

"Torture me all you want, I'll never talk."

Lex holds out his hand and someone places a thin steel blade in his palm. The handle is leather bound, black with a single strip of white material that wraps around the hilt and has a dangling silver emblem hanging from the knot. I can't make out what it is from here but whatever it is, Lex thumbs it lovingly and I can only assume it holds value.

Alexander suddenly plunges forward, burying the thin blade into the abdomen of the prisoner and he wails, blood pouring from the wound and covering Lex's hand.

"Where. Is. Valentine."

When the guy quiets he snatches the blade from his stomach, wiping it on the dark material of his pants.

"Fuck you, Silver."

"I'm in!" A sudden yell from a guy I hadn't even realized was in the same room as us, fills the space and Lex's grin is telling. It's menacing and corrupt and bloodthirsty.

Ryker steps up next to me, a huge presence but I don't feel unsafe around him as he presses his hand to my shoulder and squeezes, his silent condolences for Rory. But it was more than that too, it was his way of showing me he was here. He had my back. I had his protection.

I am glad he didn't die.

I am glad she didn't shoot him, but I would have preferred neither of them being hurt.

Her death makes my gut churn, the sadness, the sorrow makes everything inside me hurt. I should have saved her. I should have done more but she died anyway. Permanently erased from the world and with her death, I lost a little bit of light.

A cell phone is pressed into Lex's palm by a guy I've

never seen before and then he scurries from the room.

"Do you know what I have here?" Lex asks.

I'm impressed. Despite his injuries, the blood seeping from various wounds, the bruises blooming on his skin, the guy stands tall, head held high and he shows no fear.

Lex holds up the cell phone, "Last message. Received at seven twenty three today," He mocks a cough to clear his throat, 'let me know when it is done. Wire transfer ready.' By someone named V. That doesn't happen to be Valentine, now does it?"

The guy stays quiet.

"It's okay," Lex shrugs, "I don't need you anymore."

I don't have time to grasp the meaning of his words before he pulls out his gun and shoots the guy in the chest.

The guys eyes bug out of his head and his head angles down to look at the wound in his chest. Blood spurts and dribbles from the wound, streaming over his skin like a leak in a tap.

And then he is dead. Gone.

Like he never existed at all.

Lex turns to me, the gun still dangling from his fingertips, "We have him little bird." Fingers trail down the side of my face, "It's time you have your vengeance."

SIXTY-FOUR
Lex

Wren's face remains impassive, no emotion showing there but her eyes give her away. Shock. A little fear but she inhales a deep breath, closes her eyes and when she reopens them, she looks at the dead man like he is nothing but a doll.

Good girl.

She leans into my hand as I put the gun away and then I'm hauling her to me, slamming my mouth onto hers. She kisses me back, hard, rough, teeth scraping and biting. The copper tang of blood hits my tongue from where she split my lip with her bite and then she licks it clean, soothing the sting.

Holy fucking shit.

"Let's go," I tell her, needing her away from this place and alone with me.

I leave the guys to clean up and walk back to the destroyed house, a draft blowing in through the smashed wall. King is still in the kitchen, his legs up on the table as he takes a puff of his cigarette, a bottle of whiskey dangling from the fingers of his other hand, "Shame about the wall." He comments. I narrow my eyes on him, noting the thin trickle of blood now dried on the side of his brow.

He's going to drive me insane before I've got the information from Ainsley. I pack a small suitcase for Wren and me while she sits on the bed, watching me move through the room, collecting things. I don't take much, just the essentials for the time being, anything else can be purchased. With a bag and my little bird, I head to the garage, guiding Wren to the passenger side of the Maserati.

She runs a finger down the side and smirks at me, "nice ride."

I grin and open the door, watching her climb in, green eyes stalking me.

Justice is so close I can taste it on my tongue. Ryker will give the cell to one of our tech guys who'll trace Valentine and then once I have his location, we'll strike.

There's no games this time, as soon as I have him in my sights, he's dead.

Twisted City

RIA WILDE

It feels like years since I've been at the penthouse though everything is exactly how I left it. Plush grey carpets, white walls save for the left side of the apartment which is just glass looking down onto the city below. We are far enough up that we don't get the noise of the streets below, no traffic or loud sirens, just a gentle whistle of the wind as it blows passed the glass. I place the bags in the corridor and hit the house service button, they'll prepare the bedroom and put away our belongings before disappearing again. Everyone in this building is here because I deemed it so, the staff, the residents.

Wren is looking at everything and nothing at all, eyes sweeping over the plush interior, the couches and bars. It's modern and sleek, lavish with the marble units and large leather sectional positioned in front of an open fire.

I head to the bar and pull out a bottle of whiskey and two tumblers, running them beneath some water to rid them of any dust before I throw in some ice and pour the amber liquid over the top, the frozen cubes cracking as the fluid hits them.

Wren stops at the windows, leaning over to press a button that allows the panes to slide open to a balcony. She steps out onto the slate tiles and places her hands on the rails, peering down at my kingdom. *Our* kingdom.

"The city seems so different up here," she murmurs, voice almost swallowed by the wind, but I hear her.

I place the drinks on the table to the right and step up behind her, pressing her into the rails.

"Different how?"

"Like it isn't full of men with too much power and not riddled with corruption."

I grin against her neck, stifling the need to sink my teeth into her throat as she angles her head to the side to allow me better access.

My cock presses into her ass and my hands grip the railing beside hers. "Do you like it?" I ask.

"Mm," she breathes, pressing back harder.

Shit.

I spin her so she's facing me, wild hair being teased by the wind and make quick work at ridding her of her clothes. Goosebumps chase across her skin, nipples puckering in the cold.

"You look so beautiful with the kingdom at your feet," I rasp, sliding a finger over the mound of her breast. If the cold bothers her she doesn't show it, instead she arches her spine, pushing her chest out for my palm to squeeze. "So fucking beautiful."

I continue my way down her body, slipping between her legs to rub the pad of my finger over her clit, finding her wet and ready for me. Always so ready for me.

"All for me," I muse.

"Lex," she moans.

I step forward and lift her, backing up until her ass is on the railing and the thirty floor drop right at her back.

Her eyes bug out of her head and her nails bite into my shoulders, gripping tightly as the fear of falling makes all her muscles tense up.

"Lex!" She screams.

"Yes baby?"

"I'll fall!"

"You think I'd let you fall, little bird?" I step between her legs, holding her tightly as I kiss up her throat.

She whimpers, a mixture of fear and arousal. Her pulse jumps wildly under my lips and her thighs shake but I feel her wetness seeping through the thin material of my shirt.

"Does it scare you to know that it could end at any moment?" I murmur, "That this could be it?"

Her nails bite even harder into my skin but she rolls her hips, rubbing her pussy against me, searching for more.

"Hold on," I tell her with a grin.

I let go and her legs wrap around me, along with her arms, holding on as if I'd ever let her go. If she falls, I'll be going with her.

Using one hand I unbuckle my belt and unbutton my pants, tugging them down until my cock is free. I guide it to the entrance, feeling her warmth envelope me, sheathing my dick as I slide in slowly.

"Does it turn you on to know that death is just one slip away and yet you know it'll never come because I'd never let you fall."

"Alexander," she moans.

"That's it, baby," I pull out and then slide back in, a sweat breaking out across my skin as I pull at my own restraints. "How does it feel to be fucked in front of our entire kingdom?"

Nails biting into my flesh I slam into her, holding her as her body slips further back on the railing. It's dangerous and sexy as fuck, reckless in the most delicious way.

I fuck her with the city at her feet, her body precariously close to the edge and slipping back with each deep thrust. The sound of our skin slapping together is drowned out by the wind but her moans of pleasure echo deep inside my bones.

"Fuck, yes," she cries, "Lex!"

"You like it, little bird?"

"Yes, Lex! Yes!"

My hands bruise her hips as I hold her there, thrusting my hips, fucking her and watching her, eyes closed, mouth parted as she loses herself to the sensations. I watch her breasts move with each thrust and can't help myself as I lean forward and capture one between my teeth.

She cries out, her climax slamming into her full force. Her thighs tighten around me, limiting my movements as she holds me flush to her body, cock buried to the hilt inside as her walls clamp and spasm around me, but I'm not done yet. I need more. When she calms, I help her from the railing and spin her, bending her so her face is over the railing and she's staring down at the street below. One hand on the back of her neck, holding her there, the other squeezes her ass as I slip back inside.

She moans as I bury myself to the hilt and then pull out, slamming forward again, keeping that hand pressed to the back of her neck. I fuck her hard and fast, relentlessly and brutally, slamming into her hard enough that she jerks forward with each thrust but she pushes back all the same, her cries getting louder as she climbs to her next orgasm.

"Come for me, little bird," I tell her, "I want another."

"Yes," she cries as I let go of her hip and reach around, teasing her clit with my fingers.

"There's my little bird," I whisper against her spine, the hand not holding her neck dancing over her body, memorizing each curve and dip and edge, "There's my good girl." I whisper my praise against her flesh, "Are you my good girl, little bird?"

Not waiting for an answer, I straighten, keeping my hand on her neck, slowly withdrawing from her only to slam back home once more, "Look at our city, my love, look at our city while I worship its queen."

Her legs wobble as she climaxes once more, drawing my own from me. Her scream is swallowed by the wind and my roar is hollered at the sky. My muscles bunch and tense as I spill into her, her pussy walls squeezing me for every last drop.

We stand there, breathing heavy, bodies sweaty continuing to stare down at our city.

I press a kiss to her spine, "Forever may we rule."

SIXTY-FIVE

Lex

I step from the bathroom, my towel wrapped around my hips to find Wren curled up in the middle of our bed. Her hair is damp from her own shower and one of my shirts covers her slim body. She stares towards the wall of windows, looking out at the skyline.

Lights blink on the horizon and right in the distance you can see a cargo ship coming into port.

"What are you thinking?" I ask, dropping the towel to put on a pair of gym shorts before I join her on the bed.

"Rory," she sniffs.

I sigh and run a hand down her spine, "I am sorry about your friend."

"She has a sister," she says, "I guess she'll never know what happened."

"Ryker will take care of it."

"How?"

"He'll think of something."

"She'll just be forgotten, buried like everyone else in this life. It'll be a wound left open, no closure."

"No Little bird, she won't, I'll make sure of it. She will get the burial she deserves."

She inhales deeply and turns to face me, her eyes red rimmed from her recent tears. I wish I could take it away.

I reach forward but my phone ringing loudly from the dresser halts my hand. "Go on." Wren says with a gentle tilt of her lips, staying exactly where she is, so I do, climbing from the bed to pick up the call, keeping my eyes on her.

"Lex." I answer.

"We have him," Ryker says on the other end, his voice rushed and breathless, "pinging you the address now."

My phone buzzes against the side of my head and I pull it away, reading the address, "next city over." I comment.

"When do you want to hit?"

"Tonight, I'm not giving him a chance to move. Get some men, meet at the penthouse in an hour."

I hang up.

Wren is climbing from the bed, throwing the shirt from her

body as she searches for different clothing.

"You're not coming," I growl.

"Like fuck I'm not."

"Yeah, what's going to happen if Valentine gets you again, hm? You think he's just going to kidnap you? He'll kill you, Wren."

"Probably the same thing that'll happen to you, Lex," she hollers back.

"Don't fucking push me, this is final. You. Are. Not. Coming."

"Fuck you, Alexander. You leave without me, and I'll find my own way there."

"Wren," I try, lowering my tone, "I can't have you with me."

"You're not taking this from me," she pulls on a pair of leggings and a sweater, "I'm coming."

"And what if something happens to you?"

I hated this. I fucking hated it.

"Give me a gun and a knife. I'll be fine."

I lick my teeth, narrowing my eyes, "Tell me little bird, are you prepared to shoot a man?"

"I shot you," she fires back.

"But not to kill," I retaliate, "You shot me yes, but you couldn't kill me. You couldn't kill the man that kidnapped you. Hurt you. Kept you in his house. You couldn't end the one life that would have stopped this whole thing."

"That's different."

"Valentine is your father."

"No, he is not." She snaps as she tilts her chin up, staring at me, "I am *not* a Valentine."

"A Lawson?" I say.

"No."

"Then what?"

She stomps her way towards me, my very own little ball of fury, she stabs her finger into my chest, "I am a fucking Silver."

Hearing her say it makes my cock jerk in my pants. Holy fucking shit.

I push away the burning desire to seal that fate and say, "How can you be sure you'll put a bullet in his head if the time called for it?"

"I want to see his heart, Lex. That man deserves to die. I want to do it."

I curl a finger beneath her chin, pressing a kiss to her lips, "I don't want you there, baby."

"You don't have a choice."

"There's always a choice."

"Not this time."

I sigh and cross the room, pulling out a box from beneath the bed. Inside is a handgun, small and light and I hand it to her, along with a box of ammo. "This was my mothers. Her preferred weapon of choice."

Wren weighs it in her hand and then tucks it into the back of her leggings.

I pull out a knife next, a dagger of sorts with a leather hilt and a sharp as fuck blade that glints in the low lighting of the room and hand it to her.

"Don't cut yourself," I grin.

She presses the tip of it against the side of my throat, the point nicking my skin enough for blood to well quickly and roll down the side of my neck.

"This'll do." She smirks.

I wipe the blood with my palm and cock a brow as she leans forward and licks it from my fingers, "Let's go."

Fucking damn siren.

Ryker climbs from the front seat and hops in the back as I

climb behind the wheel and Wren slides into the front.

"Thirty minutes east," Ryker says from behind, "guys are en route."

"We kill him," I tell him, "No hesitation."

"Yes boss."

"Hi Gruff," Wren looks back at him, peering between the two seats. In the mirror I see him raise a brow and shake his head. "How's the nose?"

"Healed but sore."

She laughs turning back around and settling against the chair before turning her face to the window to watch the city roll by.

I reach across and squeeze her thigh, the shape of her legs clearly visible with the tight fitting pants, "Are you sure you're ready for this?"

"Never been more ready."

About ten minutes from our destination, Ryker passes something to Wren between the seats and with a frown she takes it, staring down at the piece of paper between her fingers.

I risk a glance over to find a picture of Wren and Rory, dressed in bikinis in front of a swimming pool. It appears to be somewhere abroad though I can't tell where exactly, but they look…happy.

Wren's fingers flex on the image, "Where did you get this?"

"I guess when Valentine took Rory, she had a handbag or something, one of Heart's men retrieved this from a bunch of other personal belongings they found in the house."

"We were in Egypt," she says, "a year ago now."

"I'm sorry, Wren. I tried," Ryker says.

"I know," she answers. "it's not your fault."

Wren stares down at the image for a little bit longer before she tucks it into the glove compartment and steels herself, lifting her chin and pushing back the emotion that I can see trying to force its way out.

That's my girl.

Was I worried? Of course I fucking was, but I had to give this to her.

I squeeze her thigh once more before returning both hands to the steering wheel and stopping a few streets down from our destination.

There's a number of dark SUVs lining the street, my men. When I climb out, they all do too and to my surprise, Kingston and a few of his men join us.

"Heart," I greet.

"You didn't think I'd miss out on all the fun, did you?" He grins.

"No Isobel?" Wren asks.

"She's a little busy," he says, eyeing her. "I'm sorry about your friend." He says to her gently, showing a side to him I didn't think existed.

She nods and swallows, curling her fingers into the palms of her hand. With a final look at her he turns to me, nodding once.

"Kill everyone," I tell them, "no prisoners. No survivors."

That's the only plan. I don't care how it is done, but they're all meeting the reaper tonight.

SIXTY-SIX
Wren

The building anxiety within my body makes my hands shake, I'd like to say I am not afraid of Valentine, but I'd also be lying. Of course, the man scares me, the things he did, the things I heard, there's no going back from that.

We walk silently towards the destination, a row of guys in front and a number behind and Lex never lets go of my hand. The building comes into view, an abandoned motel by the looks of it, deserted and run down with the old sign hanging from a pole.

Litter and debris is scattered across the parking lot, being disturbed by the gentle breeze but other than that, it is quiet. No lights shine from within the depleted building, no sign of life and for a minute I doubt the intel Lex has received.

Was Valentine even here?

Was it a trap?

Lex silently orders his men to scatter with a flick of his finger and then it's just me, Lex, Ryker and Kingston. I look around, searching for the others but they are out of sight, having merged with the shadows, disappearing. Lex steers me towards what would have been the front entrance of the building.

The front doors are off their hinges, dangling from the frame and Ryker moves one aside so we can enter. Inside smells like rotting wood and dust, a stifling smell that makes my throat close up and eyes water.

"Wren," Lex hisses, "behind me, Ryker and King take that hall."

I don't say a single word as they follow his orders, vanishing down a long, dingy hallway that cuts sharply right and I drop in behind Lex, following blindly down a corridor that's darker than the pits of hell.

It's silent between us other than the steady rate of our breathing but a slight creak in a door frame to the left has my feet pausing on the threadbare carpet. Lex doesn't hear it but I do.

I pause, turning my head towards the sound, my brows pulling low.

I can hear Lex walking further and further away from me but I'm so focused on this sound that I can't help myself, like sleeping beauty drawn to the spindle, I turn and make my way towards the source of the noise.

A barely there glow from beneath a door has my hackles

rising.

I know, I *know*, Valentine is there.

I press my hand to the handle, prepared to push down but a sudden body behind mine stops me.

"Hello, daughter," Valentine's rancid breath huffs passed my nose as his hand comes around my throat, pressing the edge of a blade to my windpipe.

I expected to be paralyzed with fear, with dread, with a doom so stifling it would stop my heart, but I just feel *pissed* off.

My nostrils flare and my teeth grit as he steers me away from the door, back towards the corridor where Lex continues to search, the razor edge biting into my skin. He isn't alone either, there's two guys with him, silent with guns drawn, going ahead before the two of us do. Searching for Lex. I swallow, the movement of my throat making the edge of the blade cut into my skin.

The two guys suddenly raise their guns, aiming ahead of them as Lex's footsteps draw closer.

"No!" I scream, knowing they'll shoot first. Lex's steps stop and silence settles around us.

"You stupid bitch," Valentine bellows, pressing the edge in hard enough to cut into my skin. I feel blood rolling down my throat, seeping into the collar of my sweater. "Go," he orders his men, "I want him alive."

They silently obey his order, their steps careful as they advance down the corridor, avoiding the glass and debris scattered across the floor.

Valentine keeps the blade on my throat but moves the other to the back of my head, roughly grabbing a fist full of hair and yanking my head back hard enough I feel my neck crack.

"Move," He hisses, shoving me forward, towards a closed door. "Open it."

I do, nostrils flaring as I try to figure out a way to get the fuck out of his hold without him slicing me open.

Once inside the room he just pushes the door to, leaving it slightly ajar and positions us in the centre, holding me tightly against him, my back to his front. His breathing is heavy and uneven, his heartbeat erratic, giving away his fear. I feel myself smile, just a small tilt of my lips knowing in these last moments he would know nothing but fear.

The silence around us is abruptly shattered with several loud gunshots. The shots echo through the depleted building, bouncing off the crumbling walls and ricocheting inside my head. My heart pounds harder, my fear for Lex making my eyes sting with emotion.

Valentine's hold tightens on me as footsteps begin to approach, a slow and even pace, casual and yet with each thud of their foot, the tension around us seems to get tighter, like a rope is being pulled and any minute it'll snap. Thump. Thump. Thump.

Twisted City

RIA WILDE

The steps stop outside the door and it feels like minutes pass before anything happens. Valentine's breath puffs chaotically at my ear and even my own increases, wondering what the fuck is about to happen.

The door is pushed, and it opens slowly, so slowly, the hinges creaking and then there he is.

Lex stands in the threshold, eyes wide but not in fear but with a crazed sort of rage that makes everything simmer rather than boil. There are blood spots on his face, on his shirt and his gun dangles loosely in his grip.

His head cocks to the side as he takes us both in, eyes scanning me from my feet, all the way up my body, checking for injury. His eyes snag on the blood on my throat and when he finally meets my eyes, the man I know is no longer there.

No, the man staring back at me is the very one that is whispered on the wind. The devil in this concrete jungle. His eyes slide from me to Valentine slowly, casually.

"Here's what's going to happen," Valentine says, his voice shaking with the fear I can feel pounding against my spine. "You're going to leave. Both here *and* the city, once I know you're gone, I'll send Wren back."

"You believe me stupid, Valentine?" Lex cocks his head again in that way of his that makes him look like a predator sizing up his prey. There is no hate or anger masking is tone, everything about him is just so measured. Easy. Like I don't have a knife held to my throat and he didn't just kill two men.

"You have no choice." Valentine presses the blade harder into my neck and I wince, squeezing my eyes closed.

"Let her go and I might consider not killing you." Lex says, and my eyes home in on him, pupils blown so wide his eyes appear black.

I hope he's fucking bluffing.

Even so, there was no way I was letting my father leave here alive.

Keeping that blade to my throat, Valentine pulls a gun, aiming it at Lex, "Or *I'll* just kill you both."

Lex is quick to level his own gun, eyes pinging to me where I stay trapped against Valentine, a silent message. *Stay very, very still.*

We stand there for minutes, no one talking, no one moving, "Let her go." Lex growls.

Pain explodes in my right ear, travelling through my skull as a gun is fired right next to my face. It's so sudden, so abrupt Lex just stands there, his brows pulling low while blood blooms like a growing rose on the front of his shirt, and then he stumbles, legs barely able to hold him up as he droops and drops to the floor.

He shot him.

"NO!" I scream.

A rage I've never felt before fills my body, turning the blood in my veins to lava as I see red. All my training, every ounce of it comes back to me in a flash and I use it, managing to get Valentine's blade away from my throat. Legs and fists fly as he tries to take back his advantage, all the while, Lex lays there on the ground, moving, trying to get up, his blood dripping onto the carpet.

I kick the gun out of Valentine's hand and he lunges for me, slicing the blade towards me. I dodge the knife, managing to avoid it penetrating but the edge slices across my arm, cutting through the fabric of my sweater and then across my flesh.

The pain barely registers as I rip my own knife out, holding it out in front of me as he circles. My fingers flex on the hilt, I am so ready for this. *I am so ready.*

He lunges forward but I dodge again, managing to come up the side of him and I don't think, only act as I plunge the knife into the side of his throat, straight through the artery and then the windpipe.

My father stills. Blood coats my hand, my arms and the front of my clothing as Valentine drops the blade he was holding to favor holding his throat.

I pull the blade out, watching the blood spurt from the wound, coating me even further.

I thought killing someone like this would do more. I thought I'd feel quilt, sorrow, grief, but all I feel is fucking powerful. I took him. I killed him.

I got my revenge, for me, for Rory and for Lex.

I watch him sink to his knees, his blood spewing down his front and onto the floor. His eyes meet mine, so similar to my own and he reaches forward, fingers curling into the front of my sweater while his other hand still holds his throat. He's so weak the tug barely even moves me. I lift my chin, my breaths coming heavy as I look down my nose at where he is dying on his knees in front of me.

I reach down and take his hand, pulling it away from me and stare at him. His mouth forms the word please and I smile, "Goodbye Valentine."

Lifting my leg, I press the sole of my shoe against his chest and kick. He tumbles back, landing with a loud thud into the dirt. I watch the remaining bits of life drain from him, pooling in puddles around his throat.

Dead. Finally fucking dead.

"Little bird," Lex rasps.

My head snaps around and I rush towards him, dropping down to the side and looking for the damage. A bullet hole, straight through the upper section of his shoulder, a through and through. It hasn't hit anything major but there is a lot of fucking blood, but I had to wonder, how much of it actually belonged to him.

"Kiss me." He growls.

I press my hand to the wound and stifle his hiss of breath with my mouth. Both of us covered in blood, Valentine's blood pooling in the dust and the dirt beneath our knees, I kiss him and I don't stop.

His one good arm comes around me, pulling me to his body and I straddle his lap, kissing him harder, deeper, a fiery need taking possession of my body. Adrenaline and lust warms me through and I roll my hips against Lex's growing erection. His blood seeps through my fingers, warm and wet but I still don't stop.

"You did it," Lex breathes against my lips.

"Lex," I moan.

We're both covered in blood, injured, tired and yet I *can't* fucking stop. I need him. I need him now.

"Fuck me," I whisper.

The vibration of his growl travels to the back of my throat and then he's lifting me from his lap to unbutton his pants and pulls them down while I do the same with my leggings before I sink onto his rigid length, burying it until I feel him pressing so deep inside me I see stars. Our skin, wet and crimson slides together and I ride him, hard and quick, the need to release stronger than anything I've ever felt.

"You look so fucking beautiful," he growls, eyes a little manic, taking in my blood stained face.

I gyrate my hips, lifting from him only to slam back down again, crying out as my body begins to build for a release.

"Shit," I cry.

"That's it," Lex growls.

My orgasm hits me like a truck, shaking my bones and muscles and forcing me to still on top of him, my head dropping and burying into the crook of his neck, twitching as it rockets through me. Lex doesn't stop though, he lifts me slightly so he can piston his hips under me, chasing his own release and when he comes with a roar, we both collapse onto the ground, breathing heavy.

After a few minutes, I slide off him, dragging my leggings back onto my legs and wincing as I feel him seep from my body. My eyes land on Valentines' dead body, still and lifeless, his eyes staring straight ahead, the blooming puddle of blood growing bigger with every second while he just turns grey.

Lex grunts as he gets to his feet, leaning heavily to the left and pressing his hand to his shoulder. He'll live but I'm sure it hurts like fuck.

I prop myself beneath his arm to steady his walking and then head towards the door.

It bursts open before I can reach it and I find Ryker and King barging into the room, breathing fast and heavy.

"Where the fuck were you!?" Lex growls.

"On the other fucking side," Heart snaps back. "This building is practically a fucking maze!"

Ryker stares down at the dead enemy and instantly sags in relief. He's dead.

He's finally fucking dead.

"Leave him for the rats." Lex orders.

I didn't see any better way than that. He didn't deserve a 'clean up' or even an unmarked six foot hole. He was vermin food, nothing more and nothing less.

It was over with him.

We had won.

SIXTY-SEVEN
Lex

After the doc finishes cleaning me up, I lay back onto the pillows, turning to face Wren who is curled on her side, freshly showered.

"Are you okay?" I ask.

She nods her head, "It feels surreal to be over."

I sigh. It wasn't over. Not yet. The Syndicate are still at large, invisible and yet pressing in none the less. Heart is staying in one of the hotels in the city, waiting for me to come through with his payment and while he had told me he didn't want a war, I suspected his patience would only go so far.

"Rory was buried today," I tell her, cupping her face in my hand.

I would destroy the world for this woman, including my

city, I'd level it all to have her right where she is now.

"Where?"

"In the Silver crypt," My finger strokes across her bottom lip.

"Thank you."

I nod. "I'll take you one day."

Images of the battle back at the hotel flash through my mind, Valentine with the blade against her neck, the manic and violent light shining in his eyes. Wren slicing through his throat like an avenging angel, watching as his blood coated her skin and never once grimacing or flinching. And then her riding me, urgent and chaotic. Her need filling me, pulling me up and the taste of her sweetness on my lips.

"Marry me." I say.

Her eyes widen, "Excuse me?"

"Don't pretend you didn't enjoy being called my wife, little bird," I grin, sliding my thumb between her lips, "be my wife. Be a fucking Silver officially."

She sucks at the pad of my thumb, tongue rolling around the tip and then she pulls away, "you want to marry me?"

"Yes, Wren."

She grins, "Shouldn't there be some grand gesture, you on your knees, a ring?"

"You want me on my knees for you, little bird?"

She cocks a brow playfully.

With a grin to match hers, I slide from the bed, dropping to my knees, "I'm already there, baby," I admit. "I'll always be on my knees for you. I'd burn it all for you."

"I don't want you to burn it all," she breathes, leaning towards me.

"But I would."

"Yes," she whispers, "Yes, Lex, I'll marry you."

The light of morning has started to bleed onto the horizon, turning the black sky grey and while a new day may be beginning there's too much shit hiding in the shadows.

I will be marrying this woman but only when this city is back under control. Only when I know she can rule at my side with no threats. I kiss her with the sun rising over our kingdom, and I vow to keep her as far from this as possible.

"Come now, Little bird," I coax, "stop asking so many questions."

She glares at me, lips pursed as I gesture for the door of the elevators. My eyes peruse her body, the smooth skin of her legs, the hem of her dress sitting just above the knee, long enough to cover the mark on her thigh, the skirt flared before becoming tighter on the torso, neckline high but not high enough to cover the sharp lines of her clavicles. Her mass of wild copper hair is pulled across one shoulder, untamable but it's her face that catches me off guard.

I expected some guilt over what she did last night, disgust or horror at herself for killing a man but her green eyes are clearer than they have ever been. She squares her shoulders and straightens her spine, tipping her chin to the ceiling, showing off that slice on her throat like it's a victory badge and not a wound that could have killed her.

She was going to be formidable.

"I don't like surprises," she grumbles reluctantly taking my outstretched hand. Her flat sandals hit the marble floor of the foyer and I press the call button for the elevator. I keep her hand in mine as we step inside and it takes her all the way down to the lobby.

"Where is everyone?" She asks as we walk across the spacious area, all windows looking out onto the bustling streets of Brookeshill.

"Who?"

"Well Ryker for one? Or any of your other men?"

"Why would they be here?" I smirk, turning just before the entrance doors and heading to a set of stairs that will take us to the underground parking lot.

"Well don't they come everywhere with you? Like

bodyguards?"

I laugh at that, unable to stop myself I halt us on the stairs, grasping her and pinning her to the wall, ignoring the twinge of pain in my shoulder, "Do you think I need a bodyguard little bird? Who do I need protection from?"

Her cheeks flush and her lips part, a reaction to my proximity, "I just thought…"

"What kind of leader would I be if I couldn't take care of myself or my woman?"

"I don't need protection," she frowns.

"You are correct, but I'm going to give it to you anyway."

She kisses me gently and then pushes me off her body, tilting her head and raising her brows, "Where are we going?"

"You'll see."

I take her down to the Maserati, opening her door for her to step in, "Where were these manners when we met?"

I pinch my tongue between my teeth, "I'm not sure but I quite enjoyed having you restrained. Maybe we'll revisit that later, play a little."

Her eyes widen and then she shakes her head, averting her eyes.

I chuckle and close the door before rounding the hood and climbing into the front. The drive across the city is quiet,

Wren watches the city roll by through the window until I'm pulling into a spot outside a huge building in downtown. She frowns but says nothing when I open her door and hold out a hand to help her from the car.

The building ahead of us is lavish and modern, and the door is opened for us, a man dressed in a pristine black suit waiting patiently for Wren to go ahead.

"Mr Silver," he greets me, "It is wonderful to see you again."

"It is not me you need to impress Mr Livingstone." I quirk a brow at the guy, noticing the light sheen of sweat dotting his forehead, the slight tremble in his hand as he reaches out to greet Wren.

"Miss Wren," he bows his head.

She takes his hand, "What's going on?"

Mr Livingstone frantically looks to me, eyes wide.

"Have you forgotten already Little bird?" I tilt her chin up, stepping between her and the old man, "We were engaged just last night."

"So?"

"So, an engagement usually comes with a ring."

"Oh," her plump mouth forms a little 'O' as she realizes what we are doing here.

"Pick anything," I tell her, "Or all of them, I don't mind."

She huffs out a laugh and shakes her head.

"This way, miss Wren," Mr Livingstone directs, "I think I have the perfect ring for you."

She frowns but follows after him as I watch on. They stop at a glass counter and he reaches underneath, unlocking the back to pull out a piece of jewelry I can't really see from this distance. Her fingers dart to her mouth to contain a gasp as her other hand whispers over the ring.

I gently step up behind her, looking over her shoulder.

The ring is beautiful, an oval cut ruby surrounded by glittering diamonds and a platinum band, the stones large but the ruby is truly a masterpiece. The deep red color reminding me of her wild hair.

"We'll take this one," I tell him.

"What?" Wren gasps.

"Of course sir," Mr Livingstone says quickly, "Is there anything else?"

I laugh, "Is there a set to go with this?"

"Yes sir, a necklace, earrings and bracelet."

"I'll take them all, also did you get that piece I asked you for?"

"Yes sir."

"Lex, you can't just buy that! Did you see the price tag!?"

"Do you like it, little bird?"

"Yes, of course, it's stunning but–"

"Then it is yours."

"But Lex," she starts but I cut her off with a kiss, "I'll buy you the whole damn store little bird if that is what you wish for."

"Lex," she breathes into my mouth.

"Sir?" I look over to the old man who holds out a set of jewelry on the counter, the ring holding centre place.

I pick it up, "We can resize if required," he tells me.

"Your hand, Wren."

She holds it out for me, and I slip the ring on to her finger, the band a perfect size for her dainty little fingers.

She stares at it, her hand resting in mine, the ring positioned and then looks to me, eyes glistening, "Don't go crying on me, little bird."

SIXTY-EIGHT
Wren

I stare at the ring on my finger, unable to withhold the emotion. How did this happen? How the fuck did we get here?

"Don't go crying on me, little bird," I look at Lex's face and I cry anyway. Lex swipes the drop from my cheek and places his thumb between his lips, tasting it. There is no regret there this time.

"Now you're always mine," he whispers and then turns me back to the set on the counter, the diamonds and rubies glittering where they sit in their velvet boxes. "Bag this up," Lex orders Mr Livingstone, "and bring me the last piece."

"What did you get?" I ask.

"You'll see," he grins.

When Mr Livingstone comes back out he places a rectangular box on the counter, opening it up to reveal a thin leather strap that has a wolf emblem and next to it, a feather.

He pulls the sleeve of his shirt up, showing his own cuffs with the same emblems.

"The wolf has always been a signet for the Silver family," he explains.

He lifts it from the box and positions it around my wrist, tying the leather strap. "All the Silver's wear them."

While Lex pays for the jewelry I wait at the door, watching the city, still shocked at how we became this.

His captive turned fiancé. I was well and truly in love with the devil, the monster that haunts this city, and I was falling into his darkness. I thought I'd lose myself to it, to his abyss but I'm finding myself there instead. There are parts of me I didn't know existed, parts of me he has coaxed from the deepest parts of my soul. A protectiveness, a ruthless edge that appears whenever he is near. Not against him, but for him.

I thought murdering Valentine would haunt me. That my dreams would be bloody and violent but there's a sense of calm that has washed over me ever since I plunged that knife into his throat. A wash of serenity.

He's gone but I know Lex's battle is far from over.

I'll be standing at his side the entire time.

I'm here now, he wants me with him, on top, then I'll be right at the head of the war, standing next to the king.

My fingers play with the emblems on my new bracelet, pushing them both up and down the leather strap, "It suits you," Lex says, turning down the street towards the penthouse. His phone buzzes in the centre console but he ignores it, instead leaning over and grasping my hand, thumb stroking the newly placed ring on my finger.

After parking, we head up, a relaxed silence between us but I can almost feel the hum of anticipation vibrating between us. He's restrained but he twitches, fingers tapping against my skin.

I smile, knowing what's to come.

As soon as the door closes, I'm pinned to the wall, his mouth fused to mine.

"I'm trying to be better," he rasps, "but the moment that ring slid onto your finger I wanted you bent over and open for me right there on that counter."

"Don't be better," I urge, "never be better."

I feel him grin as his teeth nip at my skin, his phone buzzing again. Once again, he ignores it. He pushes up the hem of my skirt, hands skimming the intimate curve of my hip as his fingers squeeze my flesh. Heat floods me, warming my centre as he follows the line of my thong before slipping in the side and swiping against my clit.

"I love how wet you get for me, little bird, even when you didn't want to, you were so responsive for me."

I grind against his hand.

"Bend over," he rips himself away from me, "I want your ass in the air, little bird, let me see you."

"Where?"

"The couch," he jerks his head to the living area, "face the windows." I do as he orders, leaning over the back of the couch, placing my palms flat on the other side of the back rest. When he steps up behind me, he flips the skirt up and tugs my panties down my legs.

"You look so fucking sexy like this," he growls, tracing my spine with his finger, down to my ass and then through the cheeks before he slides that finger inside.

His phone buzzes again.

He drops to his knees suddenly and then buries his face between my thighs, tongue swiping at my clit with the full width of his tongue.

My legs threaten to give out at the sensation rocketing through me.

His phone starts ringing.

"Lex," I moan, trying to get him up.

"Shh," he whispers against my pussy.

He pushes one leg further out, sliding his hand down so it's cupping the back of my knee and then forces it up, opening me up further for him. "Don't move," he orders, taking that hand away and bringing it up, sliding two fingers inside me before putting his mouth to me again.

He sucks and he licks, pumping his fingers in and out of me curling them to tease at the sweet spot inside.

"Holy shit," I whimper, legs shaking, "Lex, I'm going to come."

This time when his phone rings I barely hear it over the roar of my blood in my ears but it's still there, that damn ringing phone.

"You taste so sweet, little bird," he rasps.

With the vibration of his deep baritone washing over me, mixed with the incessant flicking of his tongue, I come apart at the seams, shattering instantly. I cry out for him, but he doesn't stop until he's drawn every last second of my orgasm from my body.

Gently, he slides my dress back over my ass and helps me stand, my arousal still coating his mouth.

"That was just the start, baby," he grins wickedly.

His phone rings.

He rips the thing from his pocket, glaring at it, "What!?" he barks into it.

His jaw tightens with everything spoken down the line to

him, his eyes pinning me where I'm barely held together, leaning against the couch.

"Fuck," he growls, "I'll be there in ten."

He hangs up and steps towards me, crouching in front of me, "Unfortunately little bird, we are going to have to wait," he taps my ankle, sliding my foot into my underwear and helping them up my thighs. When he gets to my pussy he presses a gentle kiss there and then pulls the thong all the way up.

"What's going on?"

"It appears we have a package."

We walk down to the car while Lex explains the situation with the Syndicate, from start to finish, "is Ainsley there?"

He shakes his head.

"Where is she?"

He shakes his head, "I don't know."

I have more questions than answers but don't voice them as we make our way to the compound, my mind whirling over all the information I've just been given. Lex's hands are tight on the steering wheel, his brows set low in a frown.

Is this what life is going to look like for us?

A constant battle.

Enemies around every corner.

My finger plays with the engagement ring on my finger, pushing it side to side.

The compound comes into view, the side of the house completely destroyed though it appears Lex has already had workers start on the rebuild.

There are several cars in the driveway, large black SUVs and a number of Lex's men hovering at the door waiting for orders.

The tension is wound tight but Lex even more so. The car crunches over the gravel and then he stops. Before he can climb out, I grab his hand.

His head whips around to me, a frown pulling down his brows. I lift his palm and press a kiss to his hand, "We'll destroy them all."

SIXTY-NINE
Lex

Ryker sits in the kitchen, nursing a scotch. He's staring down at a brown envelope in the middle of the table, sealed shut with no address on the front.

"When did it arrive?" I ask.

"This afternoon, a worker flagged me down when I came to check on the work."

"Hand delivered?"

"Mm," Ryker grunts, "We missed her."

I pick up the envelope and open it, sliding out a pile of photos.

Wren steps forward, looking over my shoulder as I begin to sift through them, my smile hardly contained at what I'm seeing.

People. *Important* people, all of them in precarious situations, I stop on one, the mayor of London, head buried between the thighs of a blonde haired woman when he has a wife and two children, a few politicians and high ranking CEO's. These people are from all over the world, huge cities, countries, there's even a fucking priest. I stop on one image, a guy in a suit, holding a gun to a woman, her son dead next to her.

"I thought they didn't get their hands dirty," I comment.

"I guess they will if they need to."

"Who is this?" I ask, tapping the photo.

Ryker looks over, "I believe that's Graham Edmonds, Edmonds Enterprises."

"Interesting," his reach is far, owning several well established and successful businesses across the world, a range of hotels and restaurants and is in real estate. I lift the envelope and tip it upside down, a flash drive thudding against the top of the table.

Without a word, I spin in the kitchen and head down to the office, hearing Ryker and Wren trailing behind. At the computer I load it up and slot the drive into the port, waiting for the contents to download. Wren stands at the other side of the office, looking around, taking in the paintings on the wall and the hundred-year-old whiskeys lining the shelves. She looks out of place and small, but I know this is exactly where she belongs.

Thousands of files drop, one by one, a list of sins to be

used, extorted and bargained with. "She fucking got it all didn't she," Ryker comments, amusement lining his tone.

"She did." I agree and I knew exactly how to use it. Going through each file, I pull up tax evasion, drug and money trafficking, skin trade, everything and it's all tied to names. Names of the very people running cities, offices, senators, politicians. They're all corrupt. They're all dirty.

They were clever really, from the dates on these files, this has been going on for years and they've never been caught. There's never been an arrest. Most of their crimes are done using various different groups, some gangs, but I can see how they are taking over cities. Taking down the ruling bodies and inserting themselves in their place, taking over the drug routes, the money and gambling and inserting their own dirt, their own schemes.

Skin trade and trafficking is something us Silver's have never been interested in but the Syndicate, they were all for it. It was their main source of income and no doubt where Valentine got his inspiration.

A number of sex houses dotted around the world, girls used in various ways, images of them drugged, some dead, others frothing at the mouth all the while these guys in suits watch on with smirks on their faces.

I make a copy of all the information, saving it to a second flash drive and remove the drive.

This would take some time and I needed the Syndicate to come to me, I wasn't going to go looking for them. With Valentine gone, they were probably making a new plan but this time, I'd be ready for them.

I store the flash drives in the safe in the penthouse and then go in search of Wren, finding her in the bathroom, drawing a bath. Her hand swirls through the water, mixing in bubbles, the stones in her ring glinting in the bright over head lights.

I press a button to dim them and then strip from the shirt I have on, wincing with the movements in my shoulder.

"All that shit I saw today," she comments as I brush her hair away from her face, "You're going to make them pay, aren't you? The trafficking, it's disgusting."

"It is, I agree, but organizations like the Syndicate are like a hydra, you cut off one head, three more rise to take its place. I plan on keeping them away from this city but I can't do much more than that."

"So it continues?" She grits her teeth.

"There's going to be plenty of shit in this life that you're going to see and not agree with, if you weren't here, it would still be happening, you would just be blind to it."

"I wonder if that would be better," she murmurs, switching

the water off. When she turns to me her hands go to the large white bandage covering the bullet hole in my shoulder.

She peels it away from my skin and finds a new one to replace it with, being careful not to disturb the stitches. When that is complete, she slips from her clothes, stepping over the rim of the tub to submerge herself into the water. A long exhale escapes her lips as she slips all the way down until the bubbles touch her chin and her lashes flutter against the apples of her cheeks.

I perch on the edge of the bath, watching her, patches of pinkened skin peeking through where the bubbles separate on the surface of the water. Perspiration dots across her forehead and a thin tendril of hair sticks to her clammy skin.

Reaching forward, I slide it off her face, watching as the water takes it.

"What's the plan?" She asks after a few minutes of silence.

"The plan?"

"For the Syndicate? How do you exactly plan to keep them away from the city?"

"Don't worry about that, little bird," I say to her, standing from the tub and heading for the door.

"Is this how it will always be?"

I stop in the threshold, looking over my shoulder, seeing her leaning out the bath, hands curled over the rim, watching me with narrowed eyes.

"What do you mean?"

"Keeping me at arms lengths? Married to you but not involved in your life? Do you expect a dutiful little wife?"

My lips kick up into a smile, "You are a lot of things, little bird, but a dutiful little wife is not going to be one of them."

She stands from the water, steam rising from her body and bubbles clinging to her skin, sliding over the smooth surface. Her eyes are narrowed on me.

"Then what will I be? If I am kept in the dark, what good am I to you?"

"You are not a pawn anymore."

"No, I want to be a player. I want to know what your plan is. I want to help."

"And I'd rather keep you here where I know you'll be safe."

"And what about you? You think I'm going to be happy day in day out, knowing something could happen to you?"

My chest twinges, I do understand but memories of her missing, away from me, the images and videos of her, beaten and tortured. It's the very reason I'd rather her stay away from this. While the Syndicate wanted her dead because of Valentine, I cannot be sure they would not continue to make attempts now that he is gone.

I'm not suggesting her stay away forever, I knew a life like that would never satisfy a woman like Wren, but for now, I wanted her to be safe.

"I've lost you once," I sigh, "I cannot lose you again."

Her eyes soften as she climbs from the bath, wrapping her beautiful body in a white towel. She walks towards me, dripping water onto the floor before her arms wrap around my neck and she presses her lips to the centre of my throat, forcing my chin up.

"They would have to rip me from you," she whispers. "And I'd rather die than be away from you for even a moment."

SEVENTY
Wren

I may not like what I am seeing, it may make my gut churn and my heart squeeze painfully inside my chest, reminding me constantly of my time spent with Valentine, but I can't stand back and watch it all from a sideline.

I need to be involved. I need to know I am doing something. Lex is right, I would be blind to it if it weren't for him and if what he says is true and that information is to be believed, the Syndicate is bigger than even Lex can take on. The idea that they would continue to get away with exploiting girls the way they were didn't sit easy but maybe, just maybe, this could be the start of their downfall.

They've been unchallenged for so long that us, the Silver's pushing them back may make others realize that they aren't so powerful after all.

I needed to be there, standing at his side, not for me, and

not for Lex either, but for Rory and for all those girls down there in Valentine's keep.

I wanted to see them suffer for their hand in it.

Lex wasn't going to make it easy though and that pissed me off.

Have I not proven myself? Have I not shown what I am capable of?

I am not a weak little girl. I don't shy away from the blood or the violence, even when it makes my skin crawl, I watched a life be taken, I've taken a life. I can do this.

I *want* to do this.

I step from him, looking up into those pensive grey eyes, unable to read exactly what it is he is thinking.

When I think he may say something he simply steps from me and heads for the bed, unbuttoning his pants as he goes. I sigh, drying myself off and then dropping the towel in the hamper by the door, following him into the bedroom.

He lays beneath the comforter, hands behind his head, watching me, but I am watching the city. Even at this hour it is still alive, the streets below thumping with activity, cars and revelers and while the noise is muffled this high in the clouds I can feel that energy.

This is what it is to stand on top of a kingdom. To have the ground at your feet and the people before you bowing down to your every whim. Most of the citizens of this city don't even know that it is Lex that rules them, but should they step out of line, they will surely know who their king is.

I always knew there was darkness. Shadows. Demons.

I hadn't expected the level of corruption I'd witnessed but I am hardly surprised.

I step out onto the balcony, a smaller, separate version to the one in the living room, the cool wash of the night breeze cooling my heated skin. My hands wrap around the railings and I watch it all. I feel the burn of Lex's stare at my back but he makes no move to bring me back inside.

I stand for a little while longer, watching the world roll on by, realizing I'll never be the same again. I'll never have that innocence of believing the world was all sunshine and rainbows. I'll never be able to walk these streets without wondering about what kind of monster lurked in the shadows, beneath the ground and in all the dark corners.

I am forever changed and for it, I will be stronger.

I'll never be weak again.

I turn back to Lex, lounging on the bed, the muscles of his arms tense in the position he's in, veins snaking around his forearms and further up. Bronzed skin, glowing in the low lighting of the room and in even more stark contrast compared to the pristine white bedding beneath him.

I narrow my eyes.

I head towards the drawers on the other side of the room, reaching in to withdraw a dagger I'd found in here previously. Surely, he couldn't think I'd go long without exploring. The steel glints in the lighting, the sharp edge cutting into my skin as I run the pad of my finger across it.

"Wren," Lex growls.

I watch the blood bead and roll down the length of my finger before I cross the room and put a knee on the bed.

"You think I cannot handle what this life will bring," I say in a low voice, crawling up the bed, between his parted thighs where I then sit back on my heels, the blade held in front of me.

His eyes bounce from me to the knife, his brow cocking.

"And what do you think you're doing right now, little bird?"

I cock my head, my lips tilting up into a smile, "Reminding you of the woman you took all those weeks ago."

He smirks.

I crawl over him, straddling his thighs and then his hips, feeling the hard length of him through the sheets beneath my core.

"It really should disturb me that a woman holding a blade turns you on."

His hands come up to cup my sides before he suddenly

yanks me forward, "What will you do?"

With my mouth whispering over his, I bring the blade up his body, purposely positioning the tip to face downward so it grazes over his bare abdomen as it goes. He hisses in a breath as the tip slices through his skin, and dropping my gaze down, I see a thin line of blood beading where I've cut into him. Barely anything, a scratch that'll close and heal in no time.

I stop and rest the tip of the blade against his throat, "I am stronger than I have ever been," I tell him, watching his pupils dilate, becoming so dark it almost drowns out the light, "More powerful."

"You are," his Adams apple bobs as he speaks, scratching the blade across his skin.

"And yet you wish to keep me in a cage?" I whisper, "Am I still your prisoner, Alexander?"

One side of his mouth tips up, "No."

"Then put me next to you," I demand, "Show them just how strong we are together."

I am no threat to him, the blade I hold to his throat is merely a prop, nothing but a thing that'll never be used against him. I mean I don't mind seeing him bleed a little.

"Formidable," he whispers before he strikes.

I am flipped, the knife knocked from my hand and positioned in his and then pressed to my throat, "Well doesn't this bring back memories, little bird."

Instantly, warmth pools between my thighs. Don't ask me why but being dominated and subdued by him makes my stomach knot and my pussy clench like no other.

He grinds the length of him against me, the blade pressing just a little harder against my windpipe, "And what now, Wren? Are you still strong?"

"No," I breathe.

"No?"

When I shake my head the edge of the blade slices into my skin and I feel it come apart, blood welling and rolling over the surface, pooling in the little dip between my clavicles. Alexander snatches the blade away, "What the fuck!?" He growls.

"I am not strong here, Lex," I admit, "But neither are you."

His eyes snap from the blood on my throat to my eyes, widening, sensing the truth.

He had always been weak for me and would always be weak for me, but it would also be his strength and him, mine.

He had to understand how good we could be together if he truly let me stand at his side.

A duo to take down an army if only to protect our other halves.

His mouth slams down on mine violently teeth nipping at my lips, tongues dueling.

"Okay," he rasps, "okay!"

His hips grind against me eliciting a low, guttural moan to rip from my throat.

"I love how responsive you are to me," he whispers against the shell of my ear before dipping his head to lick up the trail of blood on my throat. It stains his lips as he brings his head back to watch me through hooded eyes. "Always so ready, so wet."

I roll my hips, sliding over his length.

My eyes roll back as I go, the pleasure making my insides clench.

There's a clang of metal before his hands are dropping, tugging his boxers down his thighs.

"There'll never be enough time in this life to enjoy this," he growls before slamming forward, sliding inside me so deep I feel him in my stomach.

I cry out, my legs lifting and widening to allow him more access. He pulls out slowly, pressing his forehead against mine and thrusting his hips. One arm wraps behind my thigh, holding me in position and then he truly fucks me. Slamming in again and again, so hard my bones rattle and his mouth leaves hungry kisses against my throat, sucking and biting.

"Lex," I moan, lifting my hips a little to allow it in just that little bit further.

"Fuck," he rasps, "So good. So fucking good."

He fucks me hard, relentlessly, drawing an orgasm from my body so intense I'm sure I'll never recover and I know now, I know that he will accept this.

Despite whatever danger he believes I'll be in, he knows he cannot keep behind a shield.

Where he goes, I will always follow.

SEVENTY-ONE
Lex

Wren stiffens next to me as we sit on the opposite side of the table, the restaurant around us busy, the talk loud and boisterous but the table we join is the complete opposite.

Kingston nurses a glass of wine as his eyes watch us take our seats before him. Isobel grins at Wren like a child might on Christmas morning and suddenly leans across the table, snatching Wren's left hand.

"Nice rock!" She beams, fingering the stones on her finger, eyes wide, "so pretty."

Wren carefully tugs back her hand, "thank you."

"You'll make a fierce queen," Isobel comments.

"It's taken you far too long to come to me with this

information," Kingston muses, rubbing his bottom lip with his middle finger, the rings there catching in the light, "seeing as you've had it some time now."

"A few days," I agree, ignoring the fact that he already knew I had it.

"And why is it only now I am seeing it?" He asks, flicking his eyes to Wren, "was my trade not valuable enough?"

My nostrils flare, "Don't push it, Heart, I don't care who you are, you're on my territory."

His laughter is light.

"Don't mind my brother," Isobel tuts, "he enjoys an argument far too much and does it often."

"It just seems that your brother is an asshole." Wren comments, her fingers curling into a fist atop the table as she glares at King.

"I am so very pleased I turned up when I did," King suddenly says, "A fire like yours should not be snuffed out quite as soon as Valentine had intended."

"Enough," I snap, "I have your information."

"I know you do," he leans back, waving over a waiter, "But let's eat first, I'm fucking starving."

I didn't have time for this shit.

I wasn't particularly fond of the Heart's. Kingston was infuriating but powerful, a ruler with an iron fist. With no information on the man, it made him unpredictable. He overthrew a notorious ruler for the throne, opened new trades and businesses in Europe and has never been challenged. Most don't like him, but they leave him be mainly because he'd flatten an army in a second and never blink an eye.

Isobel was chaotic. A charming and kind exterior that hides something a lot more insidious underneath. There's a darkness in her eyes that screams violence but again, like Kingston, no one knows much about her.

Even if I didn't like them, they were fearsome and respectable, and I had to accept that this trade was worth it. He could have used Wren as a bargaining chip, blackmailed me into handing over the information, instead he did something not many men would have done in this line of work.

After ordering food, King forces the conversation onto lighter topics, steering away from anything Syndicate related. Wren has relaxed a little next to me, talking to Isobel about the tattoos that adorn her skin.

It's only after we have eaten and the restaurant has emptied a little more that he holds out his hand.

I pull the flash drive from my pocket and hover it above his open palm.

"What plans do you have with the information?" I ask.

"It does not concern you," King replies, "But I will not use it until your business with the organization is done."

"You're going back to the UK?"

"Tonight," King confirms, "There are matters to be addressed and I've been gone too long."

I drop the flash drive into his hand, "That has everything Ainsley uncovered, including scanned electronic copies of the images she got."

"Thank you," King dips his chin in a nod and stands, Isobel following. He steps away but stops at my shoulder, his hand suddenly falling there, "For the record, I meant what I said, I respect you and your family however," he pauses, bending, "I respect your woman a hell of a lot more for what she has endured. Take care of her."

And then they're gone.

"They freak me out," Wren comments, picking up her wine glass to take the last sip of red liquid in the bottom. Ryker drops himself into the vacant seats opposite us.

"I've ordered men to follow them to the airport, make sure they actually leave."

I nod my agreement, "Good, I want them gone before whatever shit goes down with the Syndicate."

"Do you trust them?" Wren suddenly asks.

"The Heart's?"

"Mm," she nods.

"Isobel is a bit of funny one," Ryker comments.

"They've kept their word," I say, "There's no reason for them to stay. I trust they'll leave, whether they come back…that's a different matter."

It's late, Wren and the city sleep but energy flows through my system making it impossible for me to rest. Too many variables and not enough intel keeps me on edge. With no idea where the Syndicate are or how many players they have keeps me awake. I trust my plan will be enough, an organization like that, with as many people as they have won't take a threat like this lightly.

The only problem, I didn't know how to find them and the waiting game was killing me. They would come, of course they would but *when?*

My fist flies into the leather bag, forcing it to swing violently against the impact and then I hit it again, trying to burn some of the excess energy.

"Lex," Wren's voice forces me to pause.

I grip the bag, stopping its swing and look at her from over my shoulder. My eyebrows rise at her attire, a pair of tight black leggings and a sports bra, her copper hair pulled into a ponytail that swings like a pendulum as she walks towards me.

"Trouble sleeping?"

"Something like that," I comment, eyes roaming down her frame, taking in the curves and mischievous grin pulling at her mouth. She is so much healthier now, her weight back to normal, the injuries healed or almost there.

"Spar with me," she says, taking a position on the mat, "burn some of that energy."

"I don't want to hurt you, little bird."

She laughs, "you won't hurt me."

She drops into a fighting position and raises a brow in challenge, "are you scared?"

"Oh, little bird," I laugh, joining her on the mat, "do you like a challenge?"

"Always," she grins and lunges for me, jumping so her legs wrap around my waist and then she throws herself back, bringing me with her. I suddenly fall forward with the momentum, hitting the mat on my knees but her body doesn't join me. She somehow manages to remove herself, leaping away and landing in a crouch in front of me, a smirk on her mouth.

I get back to my feet and crack my neck before I charge her, grabbing her around the waist to slam her down onto the mat, my hand cradling the back of her head to save it from the thump.

She doesn't lay there and take it, thrusting her hips up hard enough to wind me and then she flips me, straddling my hips with her hands around my throat.

"Too soft," she mocks on a whisper, "I'll win every time."

"Little bird," I rasp, my throat working under her palms.

"Yes, *my* twisted king?" She licks my bottom lip, "I'll accept a surrender if that is what you wish."

"Never," I growl, my fingers wrapping around her wrists.

And so we spar. We spar until we're too tired to go anymore, too exhausted to think of anything more than just sleep.

And I forget everything until the morning sun wakes me and the trouble truly begins.

SEVENTY-TWO

Lex

"They left," Ryker confirms standing on my left.

I nod, not saying a thing as I watch the man in the suit approach, followed by another who is far more threatening than the suit who stops a mere few feet in front of me. It isn't a coincidence that they sent word the moment Heart and his entourage were airborne.

Wren holds herself by my side, chin tilted defiantly.

"Wren Valentine," the man greets, looking her up and down, starting from her feet, all the way to the top of her head, "A surprise to see you so well."

My anger begins to simmer, just beneath the surface, not an explosion but I doubt it'll take long.

"You'd be surprised at what I am capable of," she snaps back, "Do not believe me weak just because I am a woman."

He licks his teeth, dismissing her before his eyes land on me, "You are proving quite the complication, Silver."

"Isn't that a shame," I lie.

He cocks a brow and grins, "I am here to talk of surrender, no more bloodshed."

Ryker bursts out laughing besides me and then sobers, "Oh, you're serious," he looks to me, "He's serious."

"You have the advantage of knowing my name," I say, "what is yours?"

"Eric Ward," he replies.

"Eric," I repeat, "What's your business?"

"A truce," he grins, "If you will."

My eyes flick to his man behind him, a mercenary, hired blade to make sure things here don't go sour. I didn't believe he was the only one available to him, I had no doubt there would be many, including a few snipers but as long as my plan worked, they'd all be leaving with no blood spilled tonight.

The compound is drafty, a late summer breeze drifting in through the gaping hole in the structure. "Valentine's body has been recovered," Eric tells me, spinning on his heel to start inspecting the space, running his finger over a shelf as if to inspect it for dust, "Quite the violent death."

Twisted City

"He deserved it." Wren says, her voice even and steady.

"Maybe so." Eric agrees.

"Speak your terms," I order.

"Surrender and no one else has to be harmed," he turns to me, "We can work out a deal where you continue to sit on a throne but ultimately, this city belongs to us."

"So, you can traffic more girls?" Wren steps forward, seething, "You are disgusting."

"You'll learn," Eric hisses, "You don't belong in these ranks, woman, you are nothing more than a wet cunt and easy lay."

"Enough!" I roar, "And if I do not accept?"

"Then you, your bitch and everyone involved will be seen to an early grave."

The way he says it, so calmly, as if a destruction of an empire is merely an everyday occurrence.

I was starting to understand though. They knew Ainsley had the information, but they had no clue that she had managed to deliver it to me already.

I had the advantage.

"Compelling words," I mock, "But I do not accept."

"Then you are a fool," Eric spits.

"Am I?" I ask.

Eric narrows his eyes, cocking his head.

"You see, I think I have something worth more than this city is to you."

Eric pales, "Is that so, Mr Silver?"

I hold a hand out and a simple brown envelope is placed there. Before I can even bring it to me a gun is drawn and aimed at my head.

"I wouldn't do that," I warn.

As if my words are a signal, the gun is aimed at Wren. She doesn't even flinch, if anything she stands taller and puffs out her chest, a cruel smile curling her lips.

It's the completely wrong time to get turned on but my dick twinges anyway.

Fuck, she's feisty.

"That'll end in much the same way." I tell him. "Should we see what we have here?"

The gun is not withdrawn but no shots are fired so I proceed. My heart pounds inside my chest. I don't care for my safety but Wren's. The barrel pointed at her makes me sweat though I keep it collected, cooling my expression as if the threat on her life is nothing more than an inconvenience.

I turn and head to the nearest surface, opening the envelope and spilling the contents onto the side, revealing a number of compromising images.

"This is you, is it not?" I ask, fanning the photographs so each one can be seen.

Eric looks down at them, "This is nothing." He snaps.

I laugh, "No, but this," I pull my flash drive from my pocket, "this is enough."

"And what?" Eric laughs, "You'll go to the police?"

With everything backed up to my server I place the drive on the counter next to the images, keeping my hand over it, "No, but I will release it. I won't have to go to the police, I won't have to do anything at all. You've pissed off a lot of people over the years, before the police can even get to you or any of your associates you'll be ripped apart by the people and the families you've destroyed. They don't know who you are, they've never been able to figure it out, but this information will give them everything they could ever need."

With my hand still covering the drive I feel the cold metal of the gun press into my temple, "There is nothing stopping me." Eric warns.

I can't see Wren but I can feel her panic. I sense it down to my bones, feel her presence drawing closer.

"Do it. See what happens when I die." I laugh, "You're done, Eric. This city is gone."

"I don't think so. Shoot him!"

"No!" Wren screams.

"I die, it's released anyway." I rush.

I hear the safety catch, the movement of his clothes as he prepares to fire. The seconds that stretch between feel like hours but then Eric yells, "Wait!"

A long minute of silence stretches between us.

"What do you mean?"

"I mean," I turn into the gun, staring at Eric, "you shoot me, you shoot Wren, you hurt any one of us, then the world sees this. I have a clause in place, you see. I die, you do too."

"You're bluffing."

I wasn't, "Try me."

"So that's it?" Eric asks.

"You leave, I keep it safe, you stay away from *my* city, your information and your identities remain hidden from the public."

"How can you be trusted?"

"I can't," I admit, "But are you willing to take the risk?"

"How many people have it?" He asks.

"Enough."

"They wont like this."

"That's a shame," I say.

Eric waves a hand, disarming his guy but I don't relax, not yet.

"Ainsley," I continue, "She comes home."

"I can't do that," he says, "she's far too valuable."

"Then we don't have a deal."

"I can't promise you a single thing, Silver but I know your *Ainsley* is an asset."

"Then what can you promise."

"Your city." He growls, "We leave, in return you keep the information you have concealed."

"And Ainsley?"

"She belongs to the Syndicate now."

"No!" Ryker growls.

I had to think bigger than this. Ainsley was smart. Lethal. She could handle this.

"Fine."

"Fine!?" Ryker hisses.

I ignore him though I know he'll be pissed but this is what needed to be done to take the enemy off our turf. I'll figure out another way to get Ainsley out of this mess.

"Do we have ourselves a deal?" I ask.

Eric pauses but then huffs, "Yes."

I don't dare relax, not until I watch the man exit my grounds and then have men follow him until he passes the city limits. I don't relax until I know he's far away from Wren and far away from me.

This city remains in the Silver hands and I'll be dead long before I see it anywhere else.

SEVENTY-THREE
Wren

It doesn't feel like a win, it simply feels like we're pushing the inevitable.

My guilt weighs heavily on my shoulders, guilt for Ainsley having to stay on the run and guilt for all those girls trapped inside the Syndicate.

The city may be safe for now, but I'll continue to push on Lex to do more.

Ryker sits on the couch, elbows on his knees staring out the windows while a scotch dangles between his fingers and Lex stands in the kitchen, pensive, brooding, thinking about everything that happened back at the compound.

I pass Gruff, touching his shoulder. He offers me a small smile but continues to stare out the window, no doubt thinking about Ainsley. I had to wonder what was going on there. Was it something more than just loyalty? When I reach Lex, I smooth a hand down his spine, feeling his muscles relax as my touch soothes him.

"Little bird," he whispers, dragging me forward until I'm in front of him and caged in his arms, his mouth resting in my hair.

"I think we should reach out to Kingston," I say after a few minutes of silence, "offer our help in taking them down."

"We aren't vigilantes," Lex mumbles.

"No, but I'm not comfortable leaving it as it is knowing what I know."

When Lex says nothing, I push from his chest and stare up into those steel eyes of his, "I'll do it myself. I don't need your approval."

His mouth tips up, "no, you don't."

"Okay, good." I nod once, "Then you won't mind that I've already contacted Isobel."

His chuckle rumbles through my chest, the vibration of it sending a swarm of butterflies to flutter in my stomach, "Why am I not surprised?"

I wasn't bluffing. I reached out to Isobel a few hours ago. After Eric left, taking his hired gun with him, I found their number and called her. She wouldn't go into details, she wouldn't tell me exactly what it is they were planning but she accepted my offer of aid should she ever need it.

Kingston still terrified me but I trusted he would do what was right in this situation.

Lex's hands skim down my sides as he leans down and kisses me gently, "Go on to bed," he tells me, "I'll be through in a moment."

I look to Ryker and then nod, leaving them to it as I head through to the bedroom and strip.

Rory would have wanted me to try everything I could to stop this organization. I didn't believe taking them down would put a complete stop to the exploitation of these women but I knew they were a big player and it would help.

Sliding under the sheets I turn to stare out at the twinkling lights of the city, the docks further beyond and let myself breathe for a minute.

How everything has changed.

How my life is a far cry from what it was only months ago.

I know I've made the right decision.

SEVENTY-FOUR

Lex

"You threw her to the wolves," Ryker accuses, throwing back his scotch.

"Ainsley will be fine," I tell him, "But I have not thrown her to the wolves."

"What do you call it?" He snaps.

"What would you have me do?" I growl.

He sighs and places his face in his hands, shaking his head, and then he abruptly gets up, heading for the door without a word. It'll take him a few days but he'll understand I did what was necessary for this city.

When he's gone and the silence settles around me I finally stand and head for the bedroom, finding Wren tucked under the sheets in our bed.

Her wild hair spreads across the pillow, the color a stark

contrast against the white of the pillow.

It was over for now.

Valentine was gone, Wren was safe and the Syndicate have backed off.

I wasn't stupid enough to believe it was done, that they wouldn't try again but for now, I could actually sit back a little.

Stripping, I climb in behind Wren, pulling her closer to me. Her naked skin brushes against mine, warm and welcoming and when my hand runs down the length of her, she shivers under my touch, turning to face me.

I capture her mouth, kissing her roughly and pressing her back into the mattress, touching and tasting her skin.

Her fingernails scrape down my back, biting into my skin and I growl into her mouth, my need for her burning with each second that passes. I settle between her thighs, my cock pressing into her warm and sensitive flesh. Her back bows off the bed, her breasts pushed out and I capture a nipple between my teeth, nibbling at it as my other hand slides down her stomach before sliding through her folds and finding her clit. Her arousal smears across my fingers, making it oh so easy to tease her and have her panting under my weight. I slide a finger inside, capturing the gasp that leaves her lips with my own and unable to wait any longer, I position my cock at her entrance and slam forward, burying myself all the way to the hilt.

Her cries echo through the darkened bedroom, mixed with

the quickening tempo of skin hitting skin as I fuck her.

She was mine. She would always be fucking mine.

A queen.

The light in the darkness of my life.

"Lex!" She screams, widening her thighs but I grab one leg and force it back, lifting it so her ankle rests on my shoulder.

"Who do you belong to?" I grin against her mouth.

She laughs but it cuts off as I shift my hips, pushing in at a slightly different angle, rubbing up against that sweet spot inside her.

"Who?" I press.

"You!" She breathes.

"Do you want to come?"

"Yes!" Her nails claw at my skin, "Yes, *please.*"

I suddenly pull out of her body but before she can protest, I grip her hips and spin her, tugging her up so she's on her knees. My hand resting on the base of her spine, I reenter, the feel of her warm pussy enveloping me making my balls draw up and pleasure to shoot down my spine.

"Fuck," I rasp, sliding in deep and reaching around to pinch her clit between my fingers. She bucks back, crying out but then begins to move herself, sliding herself up and down my shaft searching for that high.

I watch, my fingers working over her flesh as she becomes tighter and tighter until she finally snaps. Her cry of ecstasy echoes through the penthouse and when she finally calms, her body drops but I don't stop. I fuck her hard, pushing her body into the mattress with each deep thrust until my release stills my hips and I spill inside her.

With her head turned, she looks at me over her shoulder, breathing hard.

Slowly, I brush a piece of hair from her face, letting my fingers linger on her cheek before I lean in and kiss it, whispering into her ear, "Are you ready to rule, little bird?"

"With you," she sucks my finger into her mouth, "always."

EPILOGUE
Wren

6 months later.

The clip of my heels on the marble floor sets a steady beat as I descend the stairs and head towards the ballroom. A band has been set up in the corner, playing upbeat music but no one dances. Waiters buzz between bodies, offering glasses of champagne and tumblers of whiskey to the guests.

I spot Lex standing close to the bar speaking with the chief of police while Ryker leans against the wooden bar.

I start heading for him, the sight of him in his tux doing all sorts of weird things to my body. My dress, silver in color and tight at the top flows into a flattering A-line skirt that reaches my knees and my hair has been coiled away from my face, hanging down my back.

Twisted City

RIA WILDE

"Mrs Silver," A man stops my advance on Lex and I turn, narrowing my eyes at the gentleman.

"Yes?" I didn't recognize him but there were many faces I didn't recognize here tonight.

His eyes do a scan of my body, lingering a little on my stomach before he meets my face again, "I wanted to reach out," he says "I'm Detective Scott."

I cock a brow, "Okay?"

"I've been working on the missing girl case," he continues, "I understand you've had a lot of involvement."

I see Lex over his shoulder, eyes narrowed on the detective's back and it doesn't take him a minute to put his drink down and close down whatever conversation he's having with the chief to start making his way over.

"I haven't been all that involved," I say to the detective, "Merely provided some finance to help with the case."

"It has helped," he nods, "but I do not understand."

"What is it you're not understanding?"

"The men," he rubs his mouth, "we had leads and well now, they appear to be missing."

"Oh, that's a shame, what do you think happened?"

I knew exactly what had happened. It wasn't enough to simply have these *men* caught, they'll do time, not enough time and then walk away. That wasn't how I wanted this to work and Lex agreed. The police being involved was a complicated matter but a necessary one.

"I think you know," He grumbles, "your husband is not a good man is he, Mrs Silver? But you, you *were* good."

"I think you may be mistaken detective."

"Detective," Lex's hands comes down hard on his shoulder, fingers curling, "It's a little late to try and scare her off me, we're already married."

"Good evening, Mr Silver," the Detective snatches away from him, "I wasn't scaring her, just curious."

"Have you not got a case to crack?" Lex mocks, "now if you excuse us, my wife needs a drink."

Alexander takes my hand, tugging me gently away from the detective and towards the bar where Ryker waits. I do a quick scan of Lex's body, spotting the splattering of blood just beneath the lapel of his jacket. I huff, stop him and readjust the material, covering the evidence of his activities before the event started a few hours ago.

"You couldn't find a minute to change," I scold, pulling and smoothing the material down as I shake my head.

"I was late," he shrugs, "and we all know how my wife hates waiting."

"Why were you late?"

"There were complications," he simply says, "it got messy."

"I can see that."

"It is dealt with now," he tells me, "what did the detective want?"

I grin, "Nothing at all really, inquiring about the missing leads."

After we tipped the police off to the missing girls and exposed an entire underground ring of skin trafficking in the deepest, darkest parts of the city we've been following and funding the investigation. The Syndicate had their hands in it but are still not directly linked but the biggest blow came when Lex discovered one of his most trusted men having his hands in the scheme. He knew he had a mole but he hadn't expected this one. Dawson and his family had been here for as long as Lex and his family had but Dawson wanted more.

"Trying to warn me that the man I am married to is not a good man."

"He is not," Lex agrees, leaning down to kiss me tenderly, "But he is utterly devoted."

When he pulls away, he does a scan of my body, hands coming forward to rest on the growing bump on my abdomen. He smooths and tightens the material of my dress, revealing the swollen area before he rests his hand over my naval, rubbing his thumb in circles.

"Have I ever told you how beautiful you are pregnant?"

"Only a few hundred," I laugh, leaning into his hand.

Twisted City — RIA WILDE

"I'll be sure to keep you this way for a few years."

A laugh bursts from me, "I think not, this one is enough."

"Oh no, little bird," he teases, "I'm thinking at least three."

I shake my head, his hand gently caressing my bump before he guides me and sits me in a stool at the bar.

"You realize there is an audience," I breathe as his mouth descends onto mine, his tongue slipping between my lips.

"Let them watch," he rasps, "It can't help just reminding them all that you belong to me."

"Like they could forget."

"So much sass, Mrs Silver," he tuts, "do you enjoy spoiling all my fun?"

I push him away though his hand still lingers on my stomach. It's been like that since he found out I was pregnant the day after our wedding.

He promised me I'd always be his first. His only. His queen and he's kept his promise. Just like I promised to always fight him but love him later, to be his light even on the darkest of nights.

But there was one thing I was certain of. No matter how hard or dark our life got, I'd always stand by his side.

EXTENDED EPILOGUE
Wren

(The events in this extended epilogue happen 3 months after the ending of Savage Heart)

The club opened up before me, the paint fresh on the walls, the floor a gleaming black marble. One wall was completely taken up by the bar, the back of which was a mirror that stretched down the entirety of it. Behind it, the staff, dressed in fine black uniforms served the waiting customers efficiently, preparing cocktails and spirits in crystal glasses. Everything was black, silver and red, from the booths that were deeply set into the walls, the benches made of a soft red velvet, the table before them black with silver edgings and candles that flickered from within silver holdings.

Club Silver had risen, quite literally from the ashes, the scars and scorching from the bombing long gone, replaced by ornate and intricate fittings. No detail had been missed.

Twisted City
RIA WILDE

On the front of the bar, carved from something that looked like shiny black stone was a wolfs head, the detail and mastering of the piece making it appear realistic, as if a wolf was truly staring back at me.

Lex places his hand at the base of my spine.

"Welcome to our new club, little bird," he says, dipping down to whisper the words into my ear.

"It's beautiful," I breathe, fingers brushing over the sheer red curtains that hang around the booths set into the wall. I look up, trying find the balcony Lex favored when he was here, but there was no balcony, no plush sofas where girls served drinks and men did business, instead the walls stretched up and up, all black until it was just the high ceiling.

"No balcony?"

"No," he smiles down at me, "I thought of something better."

I cock a brow and match his grin, my stomach knotting at the sight of the desire that swims in his grey eyes. His brow kicks up and he reaches for my mouth, pressing his thumb into my bottom lip, "When you look at me like that, my love, it makes me regret ever letting you leave our bed."

"We had to for your grand opening," I swallow, pressing my thighs together as if to stop the ache brought on from the memories of only a few hours ago, when my husband worshiped my body like I wasn't just his queen but a goddess, licking and kissing every inch of my skin, caressing all of my scars, bringing me to the peak time and time again and continuing to do so as if he simply couldn't get enough of me.

Our daughter Aurora was with Ryker back at the compound. Even a year later it was still such an odd sight seeing the big, growly gruff turn into a teddy bear around my daughter. It was like he was a different man, not one who reveled in the torture of those who threaten us but a simple man enjoying time with his closest friend's child.

"It will go on with or without me," his lips move against the shell of my ear, and he pulls me closer, pressing me into his body hard enough that I feel exactly what he wants to do to me.

"You can behave for a few hours, Lex," I chide, not meaning a single word of it.

"Let's get you a drink," he breaks away and straightens his jacket, keeping his body angled in a way that hides his hard cock against me.

We don't have to wait, the crowd parts to let us through, the security Lex had employed for us and the club keeping close. Lex wouldn't take any chances.

Not again.

I catch my reflection in the mirrors behind the bar, seeing the light bounce of the glossy, copper tresses that surround my face. I'd done my makeup in a dramatic smoky look with a deep red lipstick to match, and my dress is a dark emerald green made from satin, short on the hem but with a halter style neckline. It hugs all the right places, cinching at the waist and following the curves of my hips until it cuts off, showing off the new tattoo that I got to cover the scars left by Marcus on my thighs. The fresh black ink, an intricately designed wolf symbol, is a stark contrast to my pale skin.

Lex orders us both a drink while I survey the room, at the press gathered close to the entrance to get pictures of the VIP guests invited to Club Silver's grand reopening, at the various groups of people carefully selected. All the women are dressed pristinely in expensive designer cocktail dresses, the men in labelled suits with shoes that shine in the dim lighting of the club.

I recognize several of Lex's men, my men now too, stationed throughout the large space, their weapons concealed but there were many on each of them. While the Syndicate was mostly gone there were still a few left remaining, gone into hiding since Hunter and Isobel sacrificed themselves to blow the building up with them all still inside. There may not be a leader anymore but plenty still wanted revenge against the people who caused the dangerous organization to crumble. Namely Tobias' son, Garrett, who was still unencountered for. The rings they had dotted around the globe were being raided, girls as young as fifteen being freed and given back to families who have been searching for them for years.

They were no more but the smoke would take a while to clear. We were all aware of that.

We had stayed in contact with Kingston this last year, but it had been silent on that front for about three months now, though we knew he was still thriving with his wife, Eleanor, running London.

It was an unexpected collaboration, the Silver's and the Heart's, but the two families, us and them, we were unstoppable, powerful. Everyone knew it.

I take my drink from Lex, sipping on the fruity cocktail

while he guides me through the crowd towards a pane of opaque black glass.

"What are—"

"This is the something better," Lex cuts me off, pressing a switch on the wall. Suddenly the glass clears to reveal a whole other room, or rather booth, I suppose, but one much larger than the others in the club. There were three tables with high walls between them to separate them off, the couches red velvet like the others but larger and donned with cushions. The tables were long and glistening in the low hanging silver chandeliers that dangle in each section.

"How did you do that?" I ask, watching him press on a section of the glass that then opens up like a door. He ushers me through. Instantly the noise of the club is dimmed, muffled by the glass that stretches from floor to ceiling.

"It's switchable glass," he explains, guiding me towards the luxurious booth, "When charged with electricity, it becomes opaque, no one can see in or out, but when it's off, it's as if you're looking through a normal window."

I take a seat in the booth, nursing my drink and watching the crowd through the glass. I feel Lex's eyes on me from across the booth and I slide mine to his, seeing how hooded they've become. He slouches back, half his body hidden beneath the table, and he lifts his hand to run his thumb across his bottom lip.

"I believe there was a rule, little bird," he rasps, dipping his eyes to my chest and back up, "In this club, you already have an assigned seat."

I smirk, "Everyone already knows I belong to you."

"No harm in making sure," he cocks a brow in challenge and taps his thigh, "Come now, little bird, come sit your pretty little ass over here."

I grin, unable to hide it as I remember how he said those words to me before, when we were on much less hospitable circumstances.

I stand and shuffle around but obviously, I'm not about to give the man exactly what he wants. I throw myself onto him, landing in his lap hard. He lets out a grunt and rush of air, hands coming to my waist.

His fingers dig into the flesh as he yanks me back, right onto the hard length of his cock pushing up through his trousers into my ass. "My vicious little bird," he growls, "That wasn't very nice."

I wiggle on him, teasing his erection and he groans, the sound sending a jolt of heat right between my thighs. I was always ready for this man, my king.

"You want me to fuck you right here?" He whispers against the shell of my ear, "Where everyone can see exactly how much you belong to me?"

He slides one hand from my waist to my thigh, whispering it across my leg until it dips between and he teases the material covering me. "I always knew you wanted it like this. You wanted them to see."

"Lex," I breathe, tensing as he begins to circle his finger, gently teasing the sensitive bundle of nerves through the material.

Twisted City   RIA WILDE

"Say it," he takes the lobe of my ear between his teeth, nipping gently.

"I'm yours."

He presses his fingers in harder, groaning softly. Through the glass everyone mingles, drinking and talking while Lex works me up on his lap. Hot, throbbing need pulses in my very veins, my breath sawing from my chest.

"Fuck, little bird, you're so wet for me, you always are."

I press harder down into his cock, wanting it to fill me, to fuck me right here at this table.

The table obscures us but if anyone were to truly look, they'd see it all, see my legs parted, his hand between my thighs and I think part of that is building me higher, making me hotter, the risk of someone seeing.

"Lift a little," Lex commands softly. I push up onto my tiptoes, levitating over his lap. There's no mistaking the sound of his belt and zipper coming undone and then his hands pushing my dress higher, yanking my panties to the side and guiding the head of his hard cock into my pussy, lowering me as he does. He fills me completely and I have to bite down on my lip to stop from crying out loudly.

"God damn," he growls, "Fuck little bird, always so fucking good for me."

I roll my hips, bringing him out of me and back in slowly, but it's not enough. I wanted more.

It was controlled, his movements deliberate so we don't get caught but I was past the point of giving a fuck. I wanted him.

I grip the edge of the table and lift, slamming down onto him, keeping my eyes on the crowd through the window. I had no doubt it was obvious what we were doing but no one is looking. Not yet at least.

"Fuck yes," he praises, "just like that."

His hand comes between my legs and I snap, crying out and grinding down. It's at that moment a man beyond the window looks over, meets my eyes, shock and confusion filling his as my mouth drops open, Lex pumping into me.

"Shit," he hisses before abruptly pulling out of me and slamming his hand against a switch on the wall. The glass turns opaque, and the next moment Lex drags me up and wraps his hand around the back of my neck, forcing me down until my breasts press into the table. He yanks the dress up, the panties down and slams into me so hard my hips bite into the table edge. I moan. Loudly.

He fucks me hard, relentless, fingers pulling me back by the hips as he thrusts forward at the same, filling me, stretching me. His grunts are loud, his hold tight enough to bruise.

"Look at your tight cunt stretching for me," he rasps, slowing his hips. I feel him lean back as if looking, "You're full of me, little bird, so fucking wet you're soaking my cock."

"Lex, please," I push back, wanting the hard pounding he was just giving me.

"My perfect wife," He reaches around, pinching my clit between his fingers. I buck against him, "I like watching me fill you, I love how your pussy takes me. There is no better music than your moans, my love."

"Please," I beg again.

"Always such a good girl for me," he praises, slamming into me. I cry out. "That's it."

He increases his pace once more while simultaneously circling my clit, applying just the right amount of pressure to start tightening my muscles, my pussy pulsing around his cock.

My fingers curl, nails digging into the unforgiving surface of the table.

"Don't stop," I plead, feeling myself climbing, climbing.

"Come for me," he growls.

"God yes," I moan and that tether snaps and I shatter. My orgasm barrels through me, my muscles contracting which earns a long curse from Lex as his hips turn more erratic, less rhythmic and he follows me over the edge, bellowing his release as he fills me, pumps me full of him.

He collapses down onto my back, breathing hard where he then presses a tender kiss between my shoulder blades and pulls out slowly.

I stay there for just a minute but it's long enough for Lex to sit back down, his hands at the back of my thighs, widening me to see the evidence of what we've just done. I can feel his warm come slipping down my legs.

"Mm," he appreciates, "Full of me. Always mine."

I let out a shaky breath and flinch at the touch of his finger, pushing his come back up my leg and sliding his fingers inside, pushing himself into me more.

Twisted City — RIA WILDE

"You'll stay like this for the rest of the evening, little bird," He orders, "I want your panties soaked with me and you. I want them to smell me on you. Mine. Always fucking mine."

He puts my underwear back into place and gently helps me from the table, settling me at his side with his arm around me, tucking me against him. He kisses my forehead, "I told you it was better than the balcony."

I laugh, "Why, so you can fuck me anytime you want when we're here?"

"Obviously," he smirks, plucking his glass from the table to take drink before straightening himself back out, tucking his shirt and fastening his belt.

He kisses me once more before he leans across and presses the switch, clearing the glass once more.

Everyone had gone on like nothing was happening right here but if they could hear they'd know. Across the club I see the security guys stepping to the side to let in a few final guests.

The familiar face of Kingston Heart comes into view, at his side, his wife Eleanor, both dressed impeccably in designer clothes, his suit tailored to fit him perfectly and her dress, a stunning off white colour that glitters in the light. He meets my eyes and grins before he steps to the side, gently tugging Eleanor with him and my breath gets lodged in my throat.

"Wren?" Lex questions, concern filling his tone, "What's wrong?"

"She died," I stutter unable to fathom what I'm seeing,

"They both died."

"Who!?" He demands.

"Look."

He turns to see what I am, and goes deathly still at my side, "What the fuck!?"

Isobel Heart looks as gorgeous as ever, in her sapphire blue cocktail dress that accentuates every curve and line of her, her deep black hair dead straight and lips painted a blood red, and at her side, Hunter, his cold, heartless eyes finding ours. He grins wickedly and pulls Isobel to him, tucking her in close.

The four of them begin their advance on us and Lex stands, "These Heart's are fucking indestructible," He grumbles as he opens the door and lets them inside.

Silence falls around us as they stand before me, Lex closing the door and coming to my side.

"Smells like sex in here," Kingston comments with a grin.

But it's Isobel who keeps her eyes on me and smiles, showing teeth, "What's wrong Wren? You look like you've seen a ghost."

Twisted City   RIA WILDE

I'm not completely ready to give up this universe yet…

These characters have my whole heart and while it is not completely set in stone, you might see more of these characters in 2023!

For now, this chapter is closed and I will be bringing you all new characters soon!

Preorder No Saint, a dark mafia romance now!

Coming Fall 2022

ACKNOWLEDGEMENTS

When I decided to release this book as a set, I hadn't given myself nearly enough to time to get it prepared. That's, of course, my fault, however if it wasn't for my girls, I would not have had this done in time!

Thank you to all of you who have helped, encouraged, and pushed me in the last few months. It's been a hard one with too much going on and stress making me doubt myself. I'm glad to say you have helped me in more ways than you can imagine. A thank you doesn't seem sufficient enough but thank you.

I'll start of by shouting out my husband – because let's be honest, he's a real MVP right now. Thank you my love, thank you for believing in me, supporting me and reminding me why I started this. Thank you for being my rock and my anchor and keeping me grounded.

Claudia – GIRL. I love you. You have not left my side since I started this entire journey and I will forever be grateful for you.

Amanda, AKA, Batman – You ground me and remind me why I love doing this. From your running commentaries while reading my books to the jokes and conversations we have that serve as a well received break from the chaos. Don't ever change.

Charly – Girl! Just girl. You came into my life at the exactly the right time. The support, the questions, your availability to help, I don't think I have the words to thank you! And now my proof reader. You're never getting rid of me! Also shout out for managing this book in like no time at all!

Abbie. ABBIE! You're never allowed to leave me now. Just saying. Without your words of encouragement and tough love, I may have given up by now!

To my street team, you girls are incredible.

To the advanced readers of this book – thank you for taking time to read Lex and Wren's story. I miss these chracters and it warms me that so many of you love them as much as I do.

Lastly, to my readers. You are an amazing bunch of people, I never expected any of this and I'm still wonderfully baffled that there are so many of you!
Thank you for taking a chance on me and thank you for supporting, commenting and leaving reviews. These books wouldn't be where they are without you guys.
There are thousands of books out there and for some crazy reason you picked this one so THANK YOU!

Happy reading everyone!
Ria, x

Also by Ria Wilde

The Twisted City Duet – Complete Set

Book 1 – Little Bird

Book 2 – Twisted King

Wreck & Ruin Series (Standalone Spin offs)

Wicked Heart

Savage Heart

Coming Soon

A standalone Dark Mafia Romance

No Saint (Fall 2022)

ABOUT THE AUTHOR!

Ria Wilde is an author of dirty, dark and dangerous romance. A lover of filthy talking anti-heroes and sassy AF queens! She's always had a love of reading and decided to pursue her passion of words in late 2021 and hasn't looked back since! Little Bird and Twisted King, Ria's debut dark romance was the start of something amazing and she now has plans for several new series and spin-offs with some of your favorite characters as the main stars!

She currently resides in the UK with her husband, daughter and 2 dogs. You can often find her daydreaming or procrastinating with her head buried in a book!

www.riawilde.com

Join the newsletter!

www.riawilde.com/newsletter

Printed in Great Britain
by Amazon